"What do those gems do?" he asked, waving at a large section.

Evar shrugged. "I don't know exactly. I suspect that's an experiment. Some sort of weapon."

"Weapon?"

"For the city's defence, if we're ever invaded."

Lorkin nodded and said nothing more. Questions about weapons would be suspicious even to his new friend.

"Weapon stones have to do things that a magician can't already do," Evar told him. "For someone with little skill or training, or a magician who has run out of strength. I'm hoping they make one's strikes more accurate. I wasn't much good at battle training, so if we are ever attacked I'll need all the help I can get."

"Would you even be fighting?" Lorkin asked. "From what I understand, in battles with black magicians, lowly people like me and you are only useful as a source of extra magic. We'd probably give our power to a black magician then be sent somewhere out of the way."

Evar nodded and gave Lorkin a sideways look. "I still think it's strange that you call higher magic 'black.'"

"Black is a colour of danger and power in Kyralia," Lorkin explained.

"So you've said." Evar looked away, his attention moving around the room as if searching for something else to show Lorkin.

Then his eyes widened and he made a low noise. "Uh, oh."

By Trudi Canavan

The Black Magician Trilogy
The Magicians' Guild
The Novice
The High Lord

Age of the Five
Priestess of the White
Last of the Wilds
Voice of the Gods

The Magician's Apprentice

The Traitor Spy Trilogy
The Ambassador's Mission
The Rogue
The Traitor Queen

TRUDI CANAVAN

The ROGUE

Book Two of the
TRAITOR SPY TRILOGY

www.orbitbooks.net

Copyright © 2011 by Trudi Canavan

Excerpt from *The Magician's Apprentice* copyright © 2009 by Trudi Canavan

Orbit
Hachette Book Group
1290 Avenue of the Americas
New York, NY 10104
www.orbitbooks.net

Orbit is an imprint of Hachette Book Group. The Orbit name and logo are trademarks of Little, Brown Book Group Limited.

The Hachette Speakers Bureau provides a wide range of authors for speaking events. To find out more, go to www.hachettespeakersbureau.com or call (866) 376-6591.

The publisher is not responsible for websites (or their content) that are not owned by the publisher.

Printed in the United States of America

Originally published in hardcover by Hachette Book Group
First United States mass market edition: April 2012

10   9   8   7   6   5   4

OPM

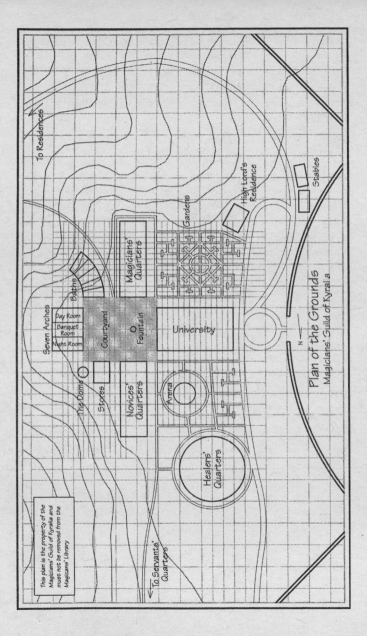

To Residences

Baths

Seven Arches

Day Room

Banquet Room

Night Room

Courtyard

Fountain

The Dome

Stores

Novices' Quarters

Arena

Healers' Quarters

To Servants' Quarters

Magicians' Quarters

Gardens

University

High Lord's Residence

Stables

N

Plan of the Grounds
Magicians' Guild of Kyralia

This plan is the property of the Magicians' Guild of Kyralia and must not be removed from the Magicians' Library.

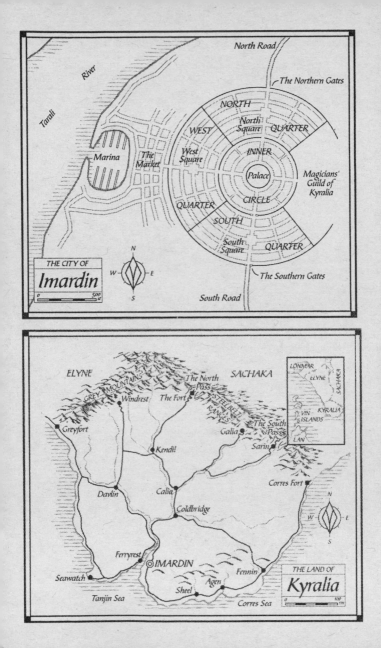

THE CITY OF
Imardin

North Road

The Northern Gates

NORTH QUARTER

River

Tarali

Marina

The Market

WEST

West Square

North Square

INNER

Palace

CIRCLE

Magicians'
Guild of
Kyralia

QUARTER

SOUTH

South Square

QUARTER

The Southern Gates

South Road

N
W—E
S

0   500 st

THE LAND OF
Kyralia

ELYNE

GREY MOUNTAINS

Windrest

The North Pass

The Fort

SACHAKA

STEEL BELT RANGES

Greyfort

Kendil

Galia

The South Pass

Sarin

Davlin

Calia

Coldbridge

Corres Fort

LONMAR

ELYNE

SACHAKA

KYRALIA

VIN ISLANDS

LAN

N
W—E
S

Ferryrest

IMARDIN

Fennin

Seawatch

Sheel

Agen

Tanjin Sea

Corres Sea

0   100 m

PART ONE

CHAPTER 1

THE STONE-MAKERS' CAVES

According to a Sachakan tradition so old that nobody remembered where it had begun, summer had a male aspect and winter a female one. Over the centuries since their founding, Traitor leaders and visionaries had declared the superstitions relating to men and women—especially women—to be ridiculous, but many of their people still felt that the season that exerted the most control over their lives had many feminine characteristics. Winter was relentless, powerful and brought people together in order to best survive.

In contrast, to occupants of the lowlands and deserts of Sachaka, winter was a blessing, bringing the rains that crops and livestock needed. Summer was harsh, dry and unproductive.

As Lorkin hurried back from the Herbery, all he could think was that it was colder than he'd expected in the valley. The chill in the air held a threat of snow and ice. He didn't feel like he'd been in Sanctuary long enough for winter to be this far advanced. Only a few short months had passed since he'd entered the secret home of the Sachakan rebels. Before then he'd been down on the warm, dry lowlands, fleeing in the company of a woman who'd saved his life.

Tyvara. Something in his chest tightened in an uncomfortable, yet strangely pleasant way. Lorkin drew in a deep breath and quickened his stride. He was determined to ignore the feeling as resolutely as Tyvara was ignoring him.

I didn't come here only because I fell in love with her, he told himself. He'd felt bound by honour to speak in Tyvara's defence to her people, because she'd saved his life. She'd killed the assassin who had tried to seduce and murder him—but the assassin had been a Traitor, too. Riva had been acting on behalf of a faction that believed he should be punished for the failure of his father, the former High Lord Akkarin, to uphold a deal he'd made with the Traitors many years ago. Nobody within the faction had admitted to giving Riva an order to kill him. To have done so would mean they had acted against the wishes of the queen, so they claimed it had been all Riva's idea.

There are rebels within the rebels, Lorkin mused.

His defence of Tyvara may have saved her from execution, but she had not evaded punishment. Perhaps it was the tasks that Riva's family had set for her that kept her away from him. Whatever the reason, he'd endured the loneliness of a stranger in a foreign place.

He had nearly reached the foot of the cliff wall that surrounded the valley. Glancing up at the multitude of windows and doors carved into this side of the valley, Lorkin knew there would be times he'd feel trapped within this place. Not because of the savage winter, which would make staying indoors necessary, but because, as a foreigner who now knew the general whereabouts of the Traitors' home, he would never be allowed to leave.

Beyond the windows and doors were enough rooms to house a small city's populace. They ranged from small cupboard-sized hollows to halls the size of the Guildhall. Most were not cut far into the rock wall, since there had been tremors and collapses in the past and people felt more comfortable living close enough to the outside that they could run outdoors quickly.

Some passages ventured a lot deeper. These were the domain of the Traitor magicians—the women who, despite their claims that this was an equal society, ruled this place. Perhaps they didn't mind living further underground because they could use magic to prevent being crushed in a collapse. *Or perhaps they like to stay close to the caves where the magical crystals and stones are made.*

At that thought, Lorkin felt a tingle of excitement. He shifted the box he was carrying to the other shoulder and strode through the arched entrance to the city. *Perhaps tonight I will find out.*

The city passages were busy as workers returned to their families. At one point Lorkin's path was blocked by the children of two Traitors who had stopped to talk to one another.

"Excuse me," he said automatically as he squeezed past.

The adults and children looked amused. Kyralian manners puzzled all Sachakans. The Ashaki and their families, the powerful free people of the lowlands, had too great a sense of entitlement to feel the need to express gratitude for the services of others—and thought thanking

slaves for doing what they had no choice in doing was
ridiculous. Though Traitors did not keep slaves and their
society was supposed to be equal, they hadn't developed a
sense of good manners. At first Lorkin had tried to do as
they did, but he did not want to lose his habit of being
polite to the extent that his own people would find him
rude, should he ever return to Kyralia.

*Let the Traitors think of me as strange. That's better
than ungrateful or aloof.*

Not that Traitors were unfriendly or without warmth.
Both men and women had been surprisingly welcoming.
Some of the women had even tried to lure him into their
beds, but he had declined politely. *Perhaps I'm a fool, but
I haven't yet given up on Tyvara.*

Close to the Care Room, the city's version of a hospice,
where he worked most days, he slowed down to catch his
breath. It was run by Speaker Kalia, the unofficial leader
of the faction that had ordered his execution. He did not
want her to think he had hurried back for any reason, or
needed to finish his shift on time. If she thought him
anxious to leave, she'd find a task to delay him. Likewise,
if there wasn't much to keep him occupied, he knew better than to sit down and rest or Kalia would find him
something to do, and often something unpleasant and
unnecessary.

Still, if he sauntered in as if he had all the time in the
world, she might punish him for that, too. So he adopted
his usual calm, stoic demeanour. Kalia saw him, rolled
her eyes and took the box from him with magic.

"Why do you never think to use your powers?" she
said, sighing and turning away to take the box to the
storeroom.

He ignored her question. She wouldn't want to hear about how Lord Rothen, his old teacher at the Guild, believed that a magician shouldn't substitute all physical exertion for magic to avoid becoming weak and unhealthy.

"Would you like me to help you with that?" he asked. The box was full of herbs that would be turned into cures—some that he'd like to learn the recipe for.

She glanced back at him and scowled. "No. Keep an eye on the patients."

He shrugged to hide his frustration and turned to survey the large main room. Not much had changed since the early morning, when he'd begun working for the day. Beds were arranged in rows. Not many were occupied. A few children were recovering from typical childhood illnesses or injuries and an old woman was nursing a broken arm. All were asleep.

It had been Kalia's idea to put him to work in the Care Room, and he was sure she'd done it to test his resolve to not teach the Traitors how to Heal with magic. So far there had been no patients likely to die from sicknesses or injuries he could only cure with magic, but it was bound to happen eventually. When it did, he expected Kalia to stir up animosity toward him. He had a plan to counter Kalia's, but behind her motherly appearance and demeanour was a shrewd mind. She may have guessed his intentions already. He could only wait and see.

Right now he couldn't wait. He needed to be somewhere else. He was late, and getting later every moment that passed, so he followed Kalia into the storeroom.

"Looks like you have a lot of work to do," he observed. She didn't look up at him. "Yes. I'll be up all night."

"You didn't get any sleep last night," he reminded her. "It's not good for you."

"Don't be stupid," she snapped, glaring at him. "I'm more than capable of doing without sleep. This has to be done *now*. By someone who knows what they're doing." She turned away. "Go. Take the night off."

Lorkin did not give her a chance to change her mind. He smiled wryly to himself as he slipped out of the Care Room. Guild Healers knew how damaging lack of sleep could be to the body because they could sense the effects. Not knowing how to Heal with magic, Traitors had never sensed their error and believed a good night's sleep was an unnecessary indulgence.

He hadn't tried to convince them otherwise, since reminding them of what they didn't know wasn't tactful. Many years ago, his father had promised to teach the Traitors to Heal in exchange for the knowledge of black magic, despite not having the approval of the Guild to pass on such knowledge and, more importantly, black magic being forbidden to Guild magicians.

At the time, many Traitor children had caught a deadly disease and knowledge of Healing magic might have saved them. Black magic had allowed Akkarin to escape the Ichani who had enslaved him and return to Kyralia, but he never came back to Sachaka to fulfil his side of the deal. Since learning of his father's broken promise, Lorkin had considered many possible reasons. His father had known that the brother of the Ichani who had enslaved Akkarin planned to invade Kyralia. He may have felt obliged to deal with that threat first. Perhaps he could not explain the threat to the Guild without revealing that he had learned forbidden black magic. He might have considered it too dangerous to return to Sachaka alone, risking recapture by the Ichani or the vengeance of his former master's brother.

Perhaps he never intended to uphold the deal. After all, the Traitors had known of his terrible situation for some time before they offered their help, whereas they helped others—mainly women of Sachaka—all the time without asking a price. That they hadn't helped Akkarin regain his freedom until it was an advantage to them certainly demonstrated how ruthless they could be.

The passages were quieter now, so Lorkin was able to travel faster, breaking into a jog when there was nobody around to observe. If someone from Kalia's faction noticed he was in a hurry, it might be reported to her.

Life here didn't quite live up to Tyvara's claims of a peaceful society—or even a fair one, despite the Traitors' principles of equality. *Still, they are doing better than many other countries, and especially the rest of Sachaka. They have no slavery, and the work people are given is mostly decided by ability rather than an inherited class system. They may treat men and women unequally, but so do all other cultures—the other way around. Most cultures treat women far worse than the Traitors treat their men.*

He thought of his newest and closest friend in Sanctuary, a man named Evar, who he was meeting tonight. The young Traitor magician had been drawn to Lorkin out of curiosity because he was the only other male magician in Sanctuary who had not yet paired with a woman. Lorkin had discovered that his first impression of the status of male magicians had been wrong: he'd assumed that if there were male magicians then the Traitors must offer them the same opportunities to learn magic as they offered women. The truth was, all male magicians here were naturals—magicians whose magic had developed naturally, forcing Traitor magicians to teach them or abandon them to die when they lost control of their powers. Magical knowledge was not otherwise offered to Traitor men.

The few fortunate male naturals were still not equal to the women, however. Men were not taught black magic. This ensured that even weak female magicians were stronger than the male ones, because they could boost their strength by storing magic taken from others.

I wonder... would I have been allowed into Sanctuary if I'd known black magic?

He did not ponder that, as he had finally reached his destination: the "men's room." It was a large room that accommodated Traitor males who were too old to live with their parents but had not yet been selected by a woman to be her companion.

Evar was talking to two other men, but left them as he saw Lorkin enter. Like most Traitor men, he was thin and small-boned, in contrast to the typical free Sachakan male from the lowlands, who tended to be tall and broad-shouldered. Not for the first time, Lorkin wondered if Traitor men had somehow grown smaller over time to fit their social status.

"Evar," Lorkin said. "Sorry I'm late."

Evar shrugged. "Let's eat."

Lorkin hesitated, then followed the other man to the food preparation area, where a steaming pot of soup had been cooked up by one of the men for them all to eat. This wasn't part of the plan. Had he returned too late? Had Evar's plans changed?

"Are we still going for that walk you suggested?" Lorkin ventured as casually as he could manage.

Evar nodded. "If you haven't changed your mind." He leaned closer. "A few of the stone-makers are working late," the young magician murmured. "Got to give them time to finish up and leave."

Lorkin felt his stomach knot. "Are you sure you want to do this?" he asked as they moved to one of the long dining tables, taking places at the end a little distance from the men already eating.

Evar chewed, swallowed, then gave Lorkin a reassuring smile. "Nothing I'm going to show you is secret. Anyone who wants to have a look is welcome to, so long as they have a guide, keep quiet and stay out of the way."

"But I'm not just anyone."

"You're supposed to be one of us. The only difference is you've been *told* you can't leave. If I tried to leave, well, I doubt I'd get far without permission, and that permission isn't likely to be granted. They don't like having lots of Traitors outside the city. Every spy is a risk, even with the mind-read-blocking stones. What if the stone was in your hand and your hand was chopped off?"

Lorkin grimaced. "Even so, I doubt anybody is going to be happy about me being there," he said, returning to the subject. "Or you taking me."

Evar swallowed the last bite of his meal. "Probably not. But dear Aunt Kalia loves me." Though Lorkin had never seen Kalia chatting sociably to Evar, she did appear to approve of her nephew. "You going to finish that?"

Shaking his head, Lorkin pushed the remains of his meal aside. He was too nervous to eat much. Evar frowned at the unemptied bowl, but said nothing, took it and simply finished off the leftovers. Since land for crops or livestock was limited, the Traitors didn't approve of waste, and Evar was always hungry. They rose, cleaned and packed away the utensils they'd used and then left the men's room. Lorkin felt his stomach twist and flutter with anxiety, yet at the same time he was full of impatience and anticipation.

"We'll go through one of the back ways," Evar murmured. "Less chance you'll be noticed going in."

As they travelled through the city, Lorkin considered what he hoped to find out. The Guild had maintained for centuries that there were no true magical objects, just ordinary things given structural integrity or enhanced properties—like magically strengthened buildings, or the walls that glowed in the University—because they were made from material in which magic acted slowly and so continued to have an effect long after a magician stopped working on it. Even glass "blood gems" didn't qualify. They channelled mental communications between the wearer and the creator in a way that prevented other magicians from hearing, but they didn't contain magic.

He suspected that some of the gemstones in Sanctuary did. Most were like blood gems in that magic was sent to them and was converted by the stone to a purpose. Others appeared to hold magic ready to be used in some way. All Traitors who ventured outside their secret home carried a tiny stone inserted beneath their skin that not only allowed them to protect their mind if a Sachakan magician read it, but also let them project innocent, safe thoughts instead. The corridors and rooms within the city were illuminated by gems that gave off light. The Care Room where Lorkin attended the sick contained several stones with useful properties, from producing a warm glow or a gentle vibration to soothe sore muscles, to stones that could cauterise wounds.

If the historical records Lorkin and Dannyl had encountered were correct, then it was possible for a gemstone to store a vast amount of magic. There had been one such storestone in Arvice, the Sachakan capital, many hundreds of years ago. According to Chari, a woman who had helped him and Tyvara get to Sanctuary safely, the Traitors knew of storestones but did not know how to make them. She might have been telling the truth, or lying to protect her own people.

If knowledge of making such storestones existed, it could free the Guild of the necessity of allowing some magicians to learn black magic in case Sachakan magicians invaded again. Magic could be stored within the stones instead, to be used in the country's defence.

Which was why he was risking this visit to the stonemakers' caves. He did not want to learn how to make stones, he wanted to confirm that they held the potential he hoped. Then perhaps he could negotiate a trade between the Guild and the Traitors: stone-making for Healing. It would be an exchange that would benefit both peoples.

He knew he would have to work hard to convince the Traitors to consider such a trade. Having hidden from the Ashaki for centuries, they were rigorously protective of their secret home and way of life. They didn't allow any mental communication in case it drew attention to the city. The only Traitors allowed in and out of the valley were spies, with few exceptions.

But as he followed Evar deeper into the underground network of passages, Lorkin worried that it was too soon to be visiting the caves. He did not want to give the Traitors reason to distrust him.

But as a foreigner, they might never trust him fully anyway. He only needed them to trust him enough that he could persuade them to trade with the Guild and Allied Lands. *Eventually they may realise I haven't been officially forbidden to visit the caves, and do something about it. I must take this opportunity now.*

Evar had another view: "*Traitors make their own decisions—or rather, they don't like letting others make decisions for them. If you want us to do something, you've got to let us think the idea was ours. Should someone discover us visiting the caves, you will have, at least, reminded everyone that we have something the Guild might want in exchange for Healing.*"

"Here we are," Evar said, glancing back at Lorkin.

They had been walking down a passage so narrow they couldn't walk side by side. Evar had stopped by a side opening. Over Evar's shoulder Lorkin saw a brightly lit room. He felt his heart skip a beat.

We're here!

Evar beckoned and stepped into the room. As Lorkin followed he looked around the huge space. It was empty of other people, as far as he could see. He turned his attention to the walls and drew in a quick breath.

They were covered in masses of glittering, colourful gemstones. At first he thought the distribution was random, but as he gazed at the swathes of colour he realised there were bands, swirls and patches of similar hues. He turned to regard the wall behind them and saw that the stones varied in size from tiny specks to crystals the size of his thumbnail.

It was beautiful.

"Over here we make the lightstones," Evar told him, beckoning and heading toward a dazzling section of wall. "They're the easiest to make, and it's obvious when you get them right. You don't even need a duplication stone."

"Duplication stone?" Lorkin repeated. Evar had mentioned them before, but Lorkin had never quite grasped their purpose.

"One of these." Evar changed direction abruptly and led Lorkin over to one of the many tables around the room. He opened a wooden box to reveal a single gemstone sitting in a bed of fine downy fibre. "With the lightstones you just have to imprint the growing gems with the same thought that you use to create a magical light. But for stones with more complicated uses, it's easier to take one that's already been successfully made and project the pattern within it. It reduces the rate of mistakes and flawed stones, and you can also raise several stones at the same time."

Lorkin nodded. He pointed to another section. "What do these stones do?"

"Create and hold a barrier. They're used for temporarily damming water or holding back rock falls. Look over here..." They moved across to a wall of tiny black crystals. "These are going to be mind blockers. They take a long time to make because they're so complicated. It would be easier if they only had to shield a wearer's thoughts, but they also need to allow the wearer to project the thoughts a mind-reader expects to read, to fool them into not realising there's anything going on." Evar gazed at the tiny stones in admiration. "We didn't come up with them—we used to buy them from the Duna tribes."

Dannyl's warning that the Traitors had stolen the stone-making knowledge from the Duna people flashed into Lorkin's mind. Perhaps that was only how the Duna people saw it. Perhaps it had been another deal gone wrong, like that between his father and the Traitors.

"Do you still trade with them?" he asked.

Evar shook his head. "We surpassed their knowledge and skills centuries ago." He looked to the right. "Here are some we developed ourselves." They approached a patch of large gemstones, their surface reflecting light with an iridescence that reminded Lorkin of the inside of exotic polished shells. "These are call stones. They're like blood gems. They allow us to communicate with each other at a distance, but only with the gems they were raised next to. It can be hard to keep track of which ones are linked, so we can't yet stop making blood gems."

"Why stop making blood gems?"

Evar looked at him in surprise. "You must know of their weaknesses?"

"Well…let me guess: the maker of these doesn't constantly see the thoughts of the wearer?"

"Yes, and only the message that the user sends is picked up by the gem receiving it, not all their thoughts and feelings."

"I can see how that would be an improvement." Lorkin turned to regard the room. There were so many patches of gems, and tables laden with objects faced the walls everywhere. "What do those gems do?" he asked, waving at a large section.

Evar shrugged. "I don't know exactly. I suspect that's an experiment. Some sort of weapon."

"Weapon?"

"For the city's defence, if we're ever invaded."

Lorkin nodded and said nothing more. Questions about weapons would be suspicious even to his new friend.

"Weapon stones have to do things that a magician can't already do," Evar told him. "For someone with little skill or training, or a magician who has run out of strength. I'm hoping they make one's strikes more accurate. I wasn't much good at battle training, so if we are ever attacked I'll need all the help I can get."

"Would you even be fighting?" Lorkin asked. "From what I understand, in battles with black magicians, lowly people like me and you are only useful as a source of extra magic. We'd probably give our power to a black magician then be sent somewhere out of the way."

Evar nodded and gave Lorkin a sideways look. "I still think it's strange that you call higher magic 'black.'"

"Black is a colour of danger and power in Kyralia," Lorkin explained.

"So you've said." Evar looked away, his attention moving around the room as if searching for something else to show Lorkin. Then his eyes widened and he made a low noise. "Uh, oh."

Turning to look in the direction toward which his friend was staring, Lorkin saw that a young woman had stepped into the room, entering from the larger main archway. He resisted casting about for the smaller back entrance; it must be several steps away and the woman was bound to see them before they got there.

Looks like we're going to get into that trouble Kalia wanted us to avoid.

A moment later, the woman looked up and saw them. She smiled at Evar, then her gaze slid to Lorkin and her smile faded. She stopped, looked at him thoughtfully, then turned and walked out of the room.

"Have you seen enough? Because I think it might be a good time to go," Evar said quietly.

"Yes," Lorkin replied.

Evar took a step toward the back entrance and then stopped. "No, let's go through the main way. We don't want to look guilty now that we've been seen."

They exchanged a grim smile, took deep breaths, and started toward the archway the woman had disappeared through. They had almost reached it when another woman appeared, scowling angrily. She saw them and strode over.

"What are you doing here?" she demanded of Lorkin.

"Hello Chava," Evar said. "Lorkin's here with me."

She looked at Evar. "I can see that. What is he *doing* here?"

"I'm taking him on a tour," Evar replied. He shrugged. "No rule against it."

The woman frowned and looked from Evar to Lorkin and back again. She opened her mouth, closed it again, and a look of annoyance crossed her face. "There may be no rule," she told Evar, "but there are...other considerations. You know the danger in interrupting and distracting stone-makers."

"Of course I do." Evar's face and tone were serious now. "That is why I waited until these makers had gone home for the night, and didn't take Lorkin to the inner caves."

Her eyebrows rose. "It is not up to you to decide when it is appropriate. Did you seek permission for this tour?"

Evar shook his head. "Never had to before."

A flicker of triumph in Chava's gaze set Lorkin's heart sinking. "You should have," she told them. "This must be reported, and I don't want either of you out of my sight until the right people have heard about this, and decide what to do with you."

As she turned on her heel and strode toward the archway, Lorkin glanced at Evar. The young man smiled and winked. *I hope he's right about not needing permission*, Lorkin thought as they both hurried after Chava. *I hope there isn't some law or rule that nobody told me about, too.* The Speakers had instructed him to learn the laws of Sanctuary and follow them, and he'd been very careful to do so thoroughly.

But he couldn't be as unconcerned as Evar was. Even if they were both right, Chava's reaction had confirmed Lorkin's fears: that he had tested the Traitors' trust in him by visiting the caves. He only hoped he hadn't gone too far, and ruined his hopes of them ever trading with the Guild—or letting him go home.

CHAPTER 2

AN UNEXPECTED ARRIVAL

D annyl put down his pen, leaned against the back of his chair and sighed.

I never thought that taking on the role of Guild Ambassador again, in a country like Sachaka, would have me sitting around doing nothing, bored and alone.

Since Sachaka wasn't part of the Allied Lands, he had no local youngsters hoping to join the Guild to test for magical ability, no matters concerning local Guild magicians to deal with, and no visiting Guild magicians to arrange accommodation and meetings for. Only the occasional communication between the Guild and the Sachakan king or elite came into his hands, or matters of trade to settle or pass on. That meant there was very little for him to do.

It hadn't been like this when he'd first arrived. Or rather, the nature of the work had been the same, but he'd also spent a lot of time—usually evenings—visiting important and powerful Sachakans. Since he'd returned from chasing Lorkin and his abductor all the way to the

mountains, the invitations to dine and converse with
Ashaki, the powerful elite of Sachaka, had all but stopped.

Dannyl stood up, then hesitated. The slaves didn't like
it when he paced the Guild House. They flitted out of his
way or peered around corners at him. He'd hear their
whispered warnings preceding him, which was distracting. He paced in order to think, and didn't need whisper-
ing interrupting his thoughts.

Eventually they'll learn to stay out of sight, he told
himself, stepping out from behind the desk. *Either that or
I'll have to get used to walking in circles around my room.*

As he emerged from his office into the main room of
his apartment, a slave standing against the wall threw
himself on the floor. Dannyl waved a hand dismissively.
The slave gave him a cautious, measuring look, then
scrambled to his feet and vanished into the corridor.

Walking slowly, Dannyl crossed the room and entered
the corridor. It was strange and a little ironic that the way
Sachakan homes were designed made them appealing
buildings for pacing. The walls were rarely straight, and
the corridors of the larger private part of the house mean-
dered in gentle curves that eventually linked together.

The next cluster of rooms had been Lorkin's. Dannyl
paused at the main entrance, then moved inside. Any day
now, a replacement assistant would arrive and take up
residence here. Dannyl moved to the bedroom door and
stared at the bed.

*I don't think I should mention that a dead slave woman
once lay there*, he mused. *I would find that knowledge
disturbing, and probably lie awake at night trying not to
imagine a corpse lying next to me.*

The body had been a nasty discovery, but worse had

been finding that Lorkin had disappeared, along with another slave. At first he had wondered if Sonea had been right to fear that the families of the Sachakan invaders she and Akkarin had killed over twenty years before would take their revenge on her son.

After questioning the slaves and following the clues he'd gathered, with the help of the Sachakan king's representative, Ashaki Achati, he'd discovered that this wasn't the case. The people who had abducted Lorkin were rebels, known as the Traitors. Achati had arranged for four Sachakan Ashaki magicians to join them, and they had chased Lorkin and his abductor into the mountains. Into Traitor territory.

A mere five Sachakan magicians and one Guild magician could never have stood up to a Traitor attack, however. Dannyl had eventually realised that the only reason the Traitors hadn't attacked was that it might have led to more incursions into their territory. If Dannyl and his helpers had come close to discovering the Traitor base, however, they'd have been killed. Fortunately, Lorkin had met with Dannyl and assured him that he wanted to go with the Traitors and find out more about them.

Dannyl turned from Lorkin's former bedroom and slowly paced out of the apartment, feeling a gloom settle over him. He'd been relieved to know Lorkin was safe. He'd even been excited at Lorkin's hopes of learning about magic the Guild had no knowledge of. What he hadn't grasped was how awkward the situation had been for his Ashaki helpers.

They had been obliged to continue searching until Lorkin was found. Giving up out of fear of attack would have been a slight to their pride. Dannyl had saved them that humiliation by making the decision himself. It had seemed only fair, after they had put themselves in danger for him and Lorkin. But he hadn't understood the harm it would do to his status within the Sachakan elite.

The corridor curved to the left. Dannyl ran his fingertips over the rendered white wall, then stopped at the opening to another apartment of rooms. These were for guests, and had rarely been occupied in the many years the Guild had used the building.

I've fallen out of favour, Dannyl mused. *For giving up the hunt. For fleeing from the Traitors like a coward. And probably also for letting a Guild magician I was responsible for and outranked join an enemy of the Sachakan people.*

He would have made the same choice, if faced with it again. If the Traitors did have knowledge of a new kind of magic, and Lorkin could persuade them to teach it to him and let him return home, it would be the first time in centuries that the Guild's store of magical knowledge had been added to. He did not count black magic as new; it was more of a rediscovery, and it was still considered dangerous and undesirable.

Ashaki Achati had assured him that some regarded Dannyl's "sacrifice" of his pride as admirably noble. Dannyl could have avoided it by asking his Ashaki helpers to help him come to a decision, thereby spreading the damage among them. But that would have risked a group decision to continue the hunt, and that wouldn't have done anyone much good.

Dannyl did not enter the guest apartment, instead moving on down the corridor. Soon he reached the Master's Room, the main public room of the building. Here was where the owner or person of greatest status within a typical Sachakan house greeted and entertained guests. Visitors entered the property from the main courtyard, were greeted by a door slave and led through a surprisingly humble door, down a short corridor, and into this room.

He sat down on one of the handful of stools arranged in a half-circle, thinking of the many delicious meals he'd been served while sitting on similar furniture in similar rooms. Achati, the king's representative, had been given the role of introducing Dannyl to important people, and instructing him on protocol and manners. It was both interesting and a little worrying that this man was the only one who was still able to visit Dannyl without any disfavour rubbing off on him. Was Achati immune to such social rules, or was it something else?

Is he visiting because his interest in me is more than political?

Dannyl remembered the moment Achati had indicated he would like to have a closer relationship than friendship. As always, he felt a mix of emotions: flattery, trepidation, caution, and guilt. The guilt was not surprising, he reasoned. Though he'd left Kyralia feeling frustrated with and detached from his lover, Tayend, they hadn't made any clear decision to part.

I'm still not sure I want to. Perhaps I'm being sentimental, not wanting to let go of something that only exists in the past. Yet when I ask myself if I'm interested in Achati, I can't answer either way. I admire the man. I feel we have a lot in common—magic, interests, our age ...

A slave entered the room and threw himself on the floor. Dannyl sighed at the distraction.

"Speak," he ordered.

"Guild carriage here. Two passengers."

Dannyl stood up quickly, his heart leaping with sudden excitement and hope. His new assistant had arrived at last. Though he had no work to hand over, at least he'd have some company.

"Send them in." Dannyl rubbed his hands together, took a few steps toward the main entrance, then stopped himself. "And get someone to bring some food and drink."

The slave scrambled to his feet and hurried away. Dannyl heard a door close and footsteps in the entry passage. The door slave stepped into the room and threw himself at Dannyl's feet.

The young Healer woman that followed regarded the slave with dismay, then looked up at Dannyl and nodded respectfully. He opened his mouth to bid her welcome, but the words never came out, because his eyes had been drawn to a gaudily dressed man stepping into view from behind her and taking in the room with avidly curious eyes.

Eyes that snapped to Dannyl's, and twinkled as a familiar mouth stretched into a smile.

"Greetings, Administrator Dannyl," Tayend said. "My king has assured me the Guild will supply accommodation for Elyne's foreign Ambassador in Sachaka, but if that is inconvenient I am sure I can find appropriate lodgings in the city."

"Ambassador . . . ?" Dannyl repeated.

"Yes." Tayend's smile widened. "I am the new Elyne Ambassador to Sachaka."

Despite the fact that associating with criminals was no longer against any Guild rule, and that it was logical for

Sonea to consult Cery when hunting down rogue magicians after he'd helped her capture one before, Sonea still met with him in secret. Sometimes he appeared mysteriously in her rooms in the Guild, sometimes she dressed in a disguise and met him in a secluded area of the city. One of the most secure places to meet had turned out to be the Northside hospice storeroom, reached by a hidden door to a neighbouring house Cery had bought.

It was safer to meet in secret because the most powerful Thief in the city, the rogue magician she was hunting for, did not look fondly on Cery for helping the Guild catch and lock up his mother, Lorandra. Skellin still had a lot of influence in Imardin's underworld and would do anything—including murdering the searchers—to prevent himself being captured as well.

Not that we've seen any sign of Skellin in the last few months. Though Sonea had finally been given permission to roam the city freely, none of her investigations had produced any clue to the rogue's location. Cery's people were more likely to hear of sightings of the rogue magician, but they'd heard nothing. A man as exotic in appearance as Skellin ought to catch someone's eye, but no reports of a reddish-dark-skinned, slim man with strange eyes had reached them.

"His rot sellers are all over my territory," Cery told her. "As soon as I shut one brazier house down, another opens. I deal with one seller and ten more turn up. No matter how I deal with them, nothing puts them off."

Sonea didn't want to ask what "deal with" involved. She doubted it meant asking them nicely to leave. "Sounds like they're more scared of Skellin than they are of you. Surely this means he is still in the city."

Cery shook his head. "He could have someone else spooking sellers into it in his name. You got enough people working for you, and allies, you can run business from a distance. Only downside is how long it takes to get orders to your people."

"Can we test that? We could do something that Skellin has to deal with personally. Something his allies and workers can't decide for him. We'll find out how long it takes to get a reaction, and that might tell us if he is in Imardin or not."

Cery frowned. "Might work. We'd have to think of something big enough to get his attention, but which won't put anyone in danger."

"Something convincing. I doubt he's the kind to fall into a trap."

"No," Cery agreed. "Trouble is, I can't—"

Sonea frowned. His eyes had fixed on something over her shoulder and he had tensed all over. A soft scraping sound came from the door behind her. She turned to see the handle of the door slowly turning, first one way then the other.

She was keeping the door closed with magic, so whoever was testing it had no hope of getting inside the room. But whoever was, was trying to do so surreptitiously.

"I had better go," Cery said quietly.

She nodded in agreement and they both stood up. "Let's both consider it." *How long has the person turning the handle been standing on the other side of the door? Did they hear anything we've said?* Nobody here but the Healers and helpers should be in this part of the hospice, and they would consider anyone lurking near the storeroom suspicious. *Unless it is a Healer.* A handful knew

about her meetings with Cery and supported her, there
were others who did not and who might find it objection-
able that she used hospice rooms for the purpose.

She approached the door, waiting until Cery had
silently slipped through the secret exit before she straightened and removed her magical lock.

The latch clicked and the door swung inward. A short,
thin man took a step forward, grinning maniacally. As he
saw her, and his eyes dropped to her black robes, his
expression turned to one of horror. He went pale and took
a few steps backwards.

But something stopped him. Something made him halt
and brought a crazed hope to his face. Something made
him put aside all fear of who and what she was.

"Please," he whined. "I got to have some. Let me have
some."

A wave of pity, anger and sadness swept over her. She
sighed, stepped out of the room, then closed the door and
snibbed the mechanical lock with magic.

"We don't keep it here," she told the man. He stared at
her, then his face darkened with anger.

"Liar!" he shrieked. "I know you have it. You keep
some to wean people off it. Give it to me!" His hands
became claws and he hurled himself at her.

She caught his wrists and halted his charge with a gentle
pressure of magic against his chest. He was already agitated
enough without her adding to his desperation by wrapping
him in magical force. She could see the flash of green cloth
in the corner of her eye as Healers further down the corridor, having heard his outcry, hurried to deal with him.

Before long the man's arms had been seized by two
Healers and they began half dragging, half guiding him

back down the corridor. A third Healer remained, and as she looked up at the man she felt her heart lift in surprised recognition.

"Dorrien!"

The man who smiled back at her was a few years older and tanned from plenty of hours spent in the sun. Rothen's son was the local Healer for a small town at the edge of the southern mountains, where he lived with his wife and children. A long time ago, when she was still a novice, he had come to the Guild for a visit and a friendship had started between them—a friendship that could have become a romance. But he'd had to return to his village and her to her studies. *Then I fell in love with Akkarin, and after he died I could not contemplate being with anyone else.* Dorrien had stayed in Imardin to help with the recovery after the Ichani Invasion, but his village had never stopped being his true home, and he eventually returned to it. He'd married a local woman and had two daughters.

"Yes, I'm back," Dorrien said. "A short visit this time." He glanced at the drug-crazed man. "Am I right in guessing the cause of his problem is something called roet?"

Sonea sighed. "You are."

"It's the reason I'm here. A couple of young men in my village returned from market a few months back with it. By the time they'd used what they'd bought, they'd grown reliant on it. I'd like advice on how to treat them."

She looked at him closely. Unlike Healers in the city, he was under no obligation to avoid "wasting" his magic on treating the drug users. Had he tried to use Healing magic to rid the young men of their habit and failed, as she had with most of the patients she'd secretly treated?

"Come with me," she said, then turned and unlocked the storeroom. As he stepped inside she followed, shutting the door behind her. He glanced around the room, eyebrows raised, but took the seat Cery had been sitting in without comment. She settled on the chair she had just vacated.

"Did you try to Heal them?" she asked.

"Yes." Dorrien described how the young men had come to him for help, realising belatedly that they couldn't afford a roet habit, and embarrassed to find they'd been caught up in a vice of the city. He'd searched with his Healing senses for the source of the problem in their bodies, and Healed it, as Sonea had done with the patients she had worked with. And, as she had, he'd had varying success. One of the brothers had been cured, the other still craved the drug.

"I've had the same result," she told him. "I've been trying to figure out why it's possible to Heal some people and not others."

He nodded. "So what do you advise for those that aren't?"

"They shouldn't use the drug again, in case the effect gets stronger. Some of my patients say keeping busy helps them ignore the cravings. Some drink. But not in small quantities—they say too little weakens their resolve to avoid rot."

"Rot?"

"It's the drug's nickname on the streets."

Dorrien grimaced. "I gather it's an appropriate one." He frowned and looked at her thoughtfully. "If we can't Heal away other people's addiction, can we Heal away our own? Not that I have a roet addiction," he added, smiling faintly.

Sonea answered his smile with a grim one of her own. "That's a question I've also been seeking the answer to, but with far less success. So far I haven't found one roet-using magician willing to be examined. I've questioned a few, but that's not going to produce the evidence I need."

"You need for what?"

"To convince the Guild this is a serious problem. Skellin's plan to enslave magicians with roet could have been successful—could still be successful."

Leaning back in his chair, Dorrien considered that. He shook his head. "Magicians have been blackmailed and bought by other means before. Why is this any different?"

"Perhaps only in the scale of the problem. That's why it needs more investigation. What percentage of magicians could be affected by roet? Are the ones not affected going to become addicts if they continue using the drug? Just how much does it alter thought patterns and behaviour?"

Dorrien nodded. "What is your guess? How big do you think the problem to be?"

Sonea hesitated as Black Magician Kallen came to mind. If Cery was right, and Anyi had seen the magician buying roet, the problem could be *very* big indeed. But she did not want to reveal what she knew until she was certain Kallen *was* using roet and she had proof that roet was as big a problem as she suspected. He might have been buying it for someone else. If she claimed he was an addict incorrectly she'd look a fool, and if she revealed it before she had proven that roet was dangerous to magicians then it would look like she was making a petty fuss about nothing.

Oh, but I wish I could tell someone. She had not told

Rothen. He would want to do something immediately. He did not like it that Kallen treated her as if she couldn't be trusted. Rothen was always urging her to put Kallen under as much scrutiny as he put her under. So would Dorrien.

"I don't know," she replied, sighing.

Ironically, the one person she thought she could probably tell and trust to remain silent was Regin, the magician who had helped her find Lorandra. *Ironic that the novice I once hated for making my life a torture is now a magician I'd trust.* He understood the importance of timing. Though she had met with Regin to discuss the search for Skellin, so far she hadn't been able to bring herself to mention Kallen.

Perhaps I'm even more afraid that Regin won't believe me, and I'll make a complete fool of myself. She smiled wryly. *No matter how much I tell myself we are not novices and deadly enemies any more, I can't shake the suspicion that he'll use any weakness against me. It's ridiculous. He's proven that he can keep a secret. He's been nothing but supportive.*

But he often did not make it to their meetings, or arrived late and was distracted. She suspected he had lost interest in the search for Skellin. Perhaps he felt that tracking down the rogue magician Thief was an impossible task. It had certainly begun to feel that way.

With Cery forced into hiding, and his people unable to find any sign of Skellin, she was not sure how they could find the rogue—aside from pulling the city apart brick by brick, and the king would never agree to that.

The Foodhall was, as always, noisy with the clatter of cutlery on crockery and the voices of novices. Lilia let out an unheard sigh and stopped trying to hear what her companions were discussing. Instead she let her gaze move slowly across the room.

The interior was a strange mix of sophistication and simplicity, the decorative and the practical. The windows and walls were as finely crafted and decorated as most other large rooms in the University, but the furniture was solid, simple and robust. It was as if someone had removed the polished, carved chairs and table in the grand dining room of the house she had grown up in, and replaced them with the solid wooden table and bench seats from the kitchens.

The occupants of the Foodhall were as varied a mix. Novices from the most powerful Houses to those born of beggars on the dirtiest streets of the city ate here. When Lilia had first started magic lessons, she had wondered why the snooties had continued to eat their meals in the Foodhall when they were rich enough to have their own cooks. The answer was that they didn't have time to leave the grounds each day to dine with their families—and they weren't supposed to leave without permission anyway.

She suspected there was a feeling of territorial pride at work as well. The snooties had been eating in the Foodhall for centuries. The lowies were the newcomers. The Foodhall had been the scene of many a prank between the lowies and snooties. Lilia had never been a part of either. Though she had never said it aloud, she was from the upper end of the lowie group. Her family were servants for a family belonging to a House of reasonable political power and influence—neither at the top of the political hierarchy nor in decline. She could trace her line back for several generations, naming which of her ancestors had worked for which families within the House.

Whereas some of the lowies were from very shabby origins. Sons of whores. Daughters of beggars. Plenty were related to criminals, she suspected. A strange sort of competition had begun between these lowies to lay claim to the most impressively low origin. If sewer ravi could be claimed as parents, some of them would boast of it as if it was a title of honour. Lowies from a servant family didn't boast or make anything of it, or they invited a lot of trouble.

The hatred some lowies had for snooties did not seem fair to her. Her parents' employers had treated their servants fairly. Lilia had played with their children when she was growing up. They had ensured that all of their servants' children were given a basic education. Since the Ichani Invasion, they had brought a magician in every few years to test all children for magical ability. Though none of their own had enough latent power to be accepted into the Guild, they had been overjoyed when Lilia, and servant children before her, had been chosen.

The two girls and boys she spent her social time with were lowies, and they were nice enough. She, Froje and Madie had been friends since starting at the University. Last year Froje had paired up with Damend and Madie with Ellon, making Lilia the odd one out. The girls' attention was mostly taken up by the boys now, and they rarely sought Lilia's opinion, advice or suggestions for things to do. Lilia told herself it had been inevitable and that she didn't mind too much, since she had always been more comfortable listening in than joining their conversations anyway.

Her gaze fell upon a novice she had been watching for a long time now. Naki was a year ahead of Lilia in University studies. She had long black hair and eyes so dark it was hard to find the edge of her pupils. Every movement she made was graceful. Boys were both attracted and intimidated by her. As far as Lilia could tell, Naki had shown no interest in any of them—not even some of the boys Lilia's friends thought were irresistible. Perhaps she thought herself too good for them. Perhaps she was simply choosy about her friends.

Today Naki was sitting with another girl. She wasn't talking, although the other girl's mouth was moving constantly. As Lilia watched, the talker laughed and rolled her eyes. Naki's mouth widened and thinned in a polite smile.

Then, without any little movement to warn that she was about to, Naki looked directly at Lilia.

Uh, oh, Lilia thought, feeling the heat of embarrassment and guilt beginning to rise. *Caught out*. Just as she was about to look away, Naki smiled.

Surprise froze Lilia. She wondered briefly what to do, then smiled in return. It would have been rude otherwise. She forced herself to look away. *She didn't seem to mind me watching her but...how embarrassing to be caught staring*.

A movement in Naki's direction tugged at Lilia's attention. She resisted the temptation to glance back, trying instead to decipher what she was seeing in the corner of her eye. A dark-haired person was standing near where Naki was sitting. That person was walking now. That person was coming in this direction.

Surely not...

She could not stop her head from turning and her eyes

from looking up. Naki, she saw, was walking toward her. She was looking right at her, and smiling.

Naki put her plate down next to Lilia's and then slid onto the empty space on the bench beside her.

"Hello," she said.

"Hello," Lilia replied uncertainly. *What does she want? Does she want to know why I was looking at her? Does she want to chat? What on earth will I talk about if she does?*

"I was bored. I thought I'd come over and see what you were doing," Naki explained.

Lilia could not help looking over at Naki's former companion. The talker was staring at them, looking confused and a little peeved. Lilia glanced at her companions. The girls were surprised, and the boys had that fearful and wistful expression they usually wore when Naki was close.

She said "...what you *were doing." It didn't sound like it included all of us.*

She turned back to Naki. "Not much," Lilia said honestly, wincing at the lameness of her reply. "Just eating."

"What were you talking about?" Naki prompted, glancing at the others.

"Whether we chose the right discipline," one of the others said. Lilia shrugged and nodded.

"Ah," Naki said. "I was tempted to choose Warrior, but for all that it's fun I can't see myself spending my life doing it. I'll keep up my skills, of course, in case we're ever invaded again, but I decided Alchemy would be more useful."

"That's what I thought about Healing," Lilia told her. "More useful."

"True, but I've never been much good at Healing." Naki smiled wryly.

As Naki continued chatting, Lilia's surprise slowly began to melt away. Somehow, by smiling at someone across the room, or perhaps because the talker at the other table had been boring, a beautiful and admired novice was chatting to her like they were new friends.

For whatever reason it had occurred, she resolved to enjoy the moment. Because she certainly didn't think it would happen again.

CHAPTER 3

ACCUSATIONS AND PROPOSALS

The three days since Lorkin and Evar had been ordered to remain in the men's room and stay there until the Speakers were all available to meet and deal with them had been surprisingly enjoyable.

"For doing what?" Evar had delighted in asking anyone who suggested that accusations or punishments would be directed at them. Nobody could say exactly what he or Lorkin were going to be accused of. Which gave Lorkin some confidence. *Everyone knows there isn't a rule or law or even an order that Evar or I have broken. If there was, I'm sure they'd have locked me away in a room on my own.*

The occupants of the men's room thought it was all very funny. Since the governance of Sanctuary was out of their reach, they delighted in any errors their leaders made—so long as those mistakes didn't affect everyone badly, of course. They were so pleased that Lorkin and Evar had showed the Speakers up for fools that they had brought them gifts and spent time making sure their new heroes never grew bored.

Three of them were teaching Lorkin a game involving gemstones that had failed to take on any magical properties and a painted board. The game was called "Stones," and they'd chosen it because gemstones were what he had got into trouble over.

A growing audience was hovering nearby. A few men were talking to Evar, and several more were scattered about the room, doing their usual chores or relaxing. So when the room began to quieten all of a sudden, everyone paused and looked up to see what the cause was. The men standing between Lorkin and the room's entrance shuffled aside. Lorkin looked beyond them, saw who was standing there, and felt his heart stop beating and stomach start to flutter.

"Tyvara," he said.

A smile fleetingly touched her lips, then she was serious again. She walked gracefully toward him, ignoring the men staring at her. Being the focus of those beautiful, exotic eyes sent a shiver of pleasure down Lorkin's spine. *Oh, I definitely haven't got over her*, he thought. *If anything, the time she's been away has made seeing her again even more exciting.*

"I want to talk to you in private," she said, stopping a few steps away and crossing her arms.

"Love to," he said. "But I'm not supposed to leave the room. On Kalia's orders."

She frowned, then shrugged and looked around the room. "Then the rest of you leave."

She watched as the men, muttering good naturedly, made their way out, and noted that Evar hadn't moved. She narrowed her eyes at him.

"Under the same orders—but don't worry," he said,

standing up and moving away. "I'll stay over there and try not to listen."

Tyvara watched, one eyebrow raised in amusement as he moved away to the food preparation area, before looking down at Lorkin.

He smiled. It was too easy to smile at her. He was at risk of grinning like an idiot. Her long dark hair was clean and the dark hollows under her eyes were gone. He'd found her alluring before; now she was even more beautiful than imagination had painted his memory of her.

I wasn't like this when we were travelling, he thought. *Maybe I was too tired...*

"I guess this will have to do," she said quietly, uncrossing her arms.

"What do you want to talk about?" he managed to ask.

She sighed, then sat down and fixed him with a direct stare that set his heart racing. "What are you up to Lorkin?"

He felt a vague disappointment. *What did I expect? That she'd invite me to her rooms for a night of...* He quickly pushed the thought aside.

"If I was up to something, why would I tell you?" he countered.

Her eyes flashed with anger. She glared at him, then stood up and started toward the door. His heart leapt in alarm. He couldn't let her leave so soon!

"Is that all you're going to ask me?" he called after her.

"Yes," she replied, without turning.

"Can I ask *you* a few questions?"

She slowed, then stopped and looked back at him. He beckoned. Sighing, she walked back to the seat and dropped into it, her arms crossed again.

"What then?" she asked.

He leaned forward and lowered his voice. "How are you? I haven't seen you in months. What has Riva's family got you doing?"

She regarded him thoughtfully, then uncrossed her arms. "I'm fine. I'd rather be out there doing some good, of course, but..." She shrugged. "Riva's family have me working the sewer tunnels.

He grimaced. "That can't be pleasant, or interesting."

"They think it's as nasty a task as they could come up with, but I don't mind it. This city needs its waste removed as much as it needs defending, and being a slave can involve much more unpleasant duties than that. But it is boring. I may end up hating it for that, alone."

"You should come by and visit. I'll try to entertain you, though I can't promise it won't be anything more than the silly mistakes a foreigner makes in an unfamiliar place."

She smiled. "Has it been difficult?"

He spread his hands. "At times, but everyone has been friendly, and while I never wanted to be a Healer, at least I'm being useful."

Her smile disappeared and she shook her head. "I never thought they'd put you in Kalia's hands, knowing that she wanted you dead."

"They know she'll keep an eye on me better than anyone else."

"And now you've made a fool of her," she pointed out.

"Poor Kalia," he said, without a trace of sympathy.

"She'll make your life hard for this."

"She does anyway." Lorkin raised his eyes to hers. "You didn't expect me to try to befriend her, did you?"

"I thought you smart enough to avoid giving her excuses to stir people up against you."

He shook his head. "Lying low and keeping out of trouble will not get me that."

She stared at him, her eyes narrowing. "One foolish Kyralian boy cannot change the Traitors, Lorkin."

"Probably not, if they don't want to," he agreed. "But it seems to me the Traitors do want to. It seems to me some major changes are definitely part of their future plans. I am no foolish boy, Tyvara."

Her eyebrows rose, then she stood up. "I have to go." She slowly turned and walked away. He watched her hungrily, hoping the sight of her would imprint in his memory clearly.

"Come visit some time," he called after her. She looked back and smiled, but said nothing. Then she was gone.

Moments later, the men began returning to the room. Lorkin sighed, then looked around to find Evar making his way across to the table. The young magician sat down, his eyes bright.

"Oh, what wouldn't I do to get under the rug with that one," he said quietly.

Lorkin resisted the urge to glare at his friend. "You're not the only one," he replied, hoping the young man would take the hint.

"No. Most men here would do anything for a night with her," Evar agreed, not picking up Lorkin's meaning—or pretending not to. "But she's picky. Doesn't want to get attached. She's not ready."

"Not ready for what?"

"Pairing. She doesn't want to stop doing the dangerous work. Spying. Assassination."

"Does having a man prevent that? I can't imagine men could prevent the women doing anything here."

Evar shrugged. "No, but when the women are away for long stretches, and might be killed, they know it's hard on a man. It's certainly hard for their children." His eyebrows rose. "Actually, Tyvara's caution is probably because of her mother, who died on a mission when she was young. Her father was devastated, and Tyvara had to look after him. She was...oh. I think it's time."

Lorkin followed the young magician's gaze to the room entrance. A young female magician was standing there, beckoning to him. He exchanged a sympathetic look with Evar.

"I think you're right," he said. "Good luck."

"You, too."

They stood up and headed for the doorway, Lorkin reached it first. The woman looked him up and down and smirked. Lorkin figured she was considering his ability to cause her trouble, but couldn't quite shake off the impression she was considering his potential for much more recreational physical activity.

"The Table is assembled and they want to talk to you both. You're to go first." She nodded at Lorkin. "Follow me."

They walked in silence. The people they passed barely glanced at them, adding to the impression that nobody was taking his tour of the stone-makers' caves all that seriously. Finally, they reached the entrance to the Speaker's Chamber and stopped. Seven women sat around the curved stone table at the low end, but the tiers of seats fanning out from it for an audience were empty. Lorkin noted that the gem-encrusted chair for the Traitors' queen was empty, as he expected. The old monarch only joined in the more important ceremonies, and he doubted she'd be at all interested in attending this one.

Director Riaya, a thin, tired-looking woman who guided proceedings, saw him and beckoned. He left Evar and the escort and walked toward the Speakers. Stopping before the table, he turned to face Riaya.

"Lorkin," Riaya said. "You've been summoned before us to explain your presence in the stone-makers' cave three nights ago. What purpose did you have there?"

"To view the stones in their stages of development," he replied.

"That is all?"

He nodded. "Yes."

"Why did you want to view the stones?" one of the Speakers asked.

He turned to regard her. Yvali was her name, and she tended to side with Kalia and the Traitor faction that had wanted him killed for his father's misdeeds. But she did not always support them, he'd noted.

"Curiosity," he replied. "I'd been told so much about them, their beauty and the skill involved in creating them, that I wanted to see them for myself. I have seen nothing like them before."

"Did you learn all you wanted to learn?"

He shrugged. "I would like to learn how to make them, of course, but I did not expect to learn that by looking at them. Evar assured me it was not possible, and if he had not I would not have gone there. Just as you respect my right to keep secure the valuable knowledge I am entrusted with, I respect yours."

There. That should remind them of the potential for a trade between the Guild and Traitors.

Kalia's eyes narrowed and her lips thinned, but the others looked more thoughtful than sceptical. As he let his gaze move along the line of women, he noted the faint-est smile curling Savara's lips, but it vanished as he met her gaze.

Speaker Savara had been Tyvara's mentor and was the unofficial leader of the faction that opposed Kalia's. She had been charged with making sure he was "obedient and useful" as well.

"Why didn't you inform anyone other than Evar of your intention to visit the caves?" she asked.

"I was not aware that I needed to."

Her eyebrows rose. "Someone who acknowledges that the secret of making the stones is ours to keep should be smart enough to work out that we want to be con-sulted before any tours of the stone-makers' cave are undertaken."

He hung his head a little. "I apologise. I still find the more subtle manners of Sanctuary a little confusing. I will try harder to learn and adapt."

She gave the faintest snort, but said nothing more, instead looking at the Director and shaking her head. The other Speakers also shook their heads, and whatever this indicated made the Director sigh faintly.

"Since you have not broken a law or rule, or disobeyed an order, you are not to be punished," Riaya said. "We are partly to blame for not anticipating this situation, but we can prevent it occurring again. Lorkin," she paused and fixed him with an unwavering stare, "you are ordered to keep away from the stone-making caves, unless taken there by a Speaker or her representative. Is that clear?"

He gave her a typical shallow Kyralian bow. "Perfectly."

She nodded. "You may go."

He walked away, fighting the urge to smile, knowing

that anyone who saw it might interpret it as proof he had been up to something—or at least did not take this little slap on the wrist seriously. Then Evar entered the room, his thin face taut with worry, and the urge to smile vanished.

As they passed, Lorkin nodded in what he hoped was a reassuring way. The young magician grimaced, but his eyes seemed to warm a little at Lorkin's gesture. Stepping into the corridor, Lorkin felt a pang of guilt at getting his friend into trouble.

Evar knew what he was getting into, he reminded himself. *It was mostly his idea, and I did try to talk him out of it. We both knew that if we were discovered, though we would break no laws, Kalia would find a way to punish us anyway.*

He suspected the young magician had his own reasons for arranging something that would irk the leaders of Sanctuary. There had definitely been some sort of vengeance or spite involved. Whenever Lorkin had tried to find out what it was, Evar had muttered things about the Traitors not being as fair as they claimed to be.

Whatever the reason, Lorkin hoped the young man had gained whatever satisfaction he'd been seeking, and that he wouldn't come to regret it.

As the carriage pulled to a gentle stop before the Sachakan king's palace, Dannyl drew in a deep breath and let it out slowly. A slave opened the door of the vehicle and stepped aside. Climbing out, Dannyl paused to smooth his robes and look up at the building.

A wide central archway lay ahead of him. From either side, white walls rippled outwards in wide curves. Above them, only narrow bands of gold were visible of the shallow domes that topped the building.

Dannyl straightened his back, fixed his eyes on the shadowed corridor within the archway, and strode inside. He passed immobile guards, one of the few classes of free servants in Sachaka. It was better to have willing, loyal men protecting you than resentful, easily cowed slaves, Dannyl mused. Guards who were obliged to throw themselves to the ground every time a free man or woman walked by weren't going to be much good at stopping invaders.

As in the typical Sachakan home, the entry corridor was straight and took visitors to a large room designed for greeting guests. Only this corridor was wide enough for six men to walk abreast. According to Ashaki Achati, the walls were hollow and contained concealed holes, so that attackers could shoot arrows and darts at unwelcome visitors. Dannyl could see no obvious holes and hatches, but he suspected the alcoves that were spaced along the corridor, each containing a beautifully crafted pot, could be reached from within, their inner surface broken if needed. Picturing such a scenario, he wondered if the warriors within the walls would carefully put the precious vessels aside, or knock them out of the way.

The other difference between a humble Sachakan mansion and the palace was that the corridor ended at a *very* large room. Dannyl entered the great hall, feeling his skin prickle in the cold air. Walls, floor and the many columns that supported the ceiling were polished white stone, as was the throne.

Which was empty.

Dannyl slowed as he approached the stone chair, trying

not to look dismayed or worried by the absence of the monarch who had summoned him. As always, there were a few Sachakan men in the room: a group of three to the left and a lone man to the right. All wore elaborately decorated short jackets over plain shirts and trousers, the traditional formal garb of Sachakan men. All were watching Dannyl.

Into the silence and stillness came slow, firm footsteps. All attention shifted to a doorway to the right. The four Sachakans bowed deeply as King Amakira strode past them. Dannyl dropped to one knee—the Kyralian obeisance appropriate to a king.

"Rise, Guild Ambassador Dannyl," he said.

Dannyl stood. "Greetings, King Amakira. It is an honour to be summoned to the palace again."

The old king's gaze was sharp, his expression thoughtful and amused as if he were considering something.

"Come with me, Ambassador Dannyl. There is something I wish to discuss with you and it would be better explored in more comfortable surrounds."

The king turned and strode back toward the side entrance. Dannyl followed, keeping a few steps back and to the side of the monarch, since he had not been invited to walk beside him. They moved into a corridor, crossed it and went through a door held open by a guard into a smaller room. The furniture and decorations were, once again, more elaborate versions of typical Sachakan ones. Stools were larger and highly decorated. Cupboards were so big they could only have been assembled in the room, since the doors, though large enough for two people to pass through side by side, were too small to allow them through. Cushions on the floor were encrusted with so many gemstones that Dannyl doubted they were comfortable, suspecting that sitting on them might even cause injury to clothing or skin.

"This is the audience room," Amakira told him. He sat down on a stool and indicated another. "Sit."

"It is magnificent, your majesty." Dannyl complied, glancing around at the hangings and precious objects in wall alcoves and cupboards. "Such fine examples of Sachakan skill and artistry."

"So your friend, the Elyne Ambassador, said. He was particularly taken with the glassware."

Surprise was followed by annoyance. How had Tayend managed to gain an audience with the king within a few days of arriving? *I suppose he is the first non-Guild Ambassador to take residence in Sachaka, whereas I was just another Guild Ambassador.* Dannyl made himself nod and hoped his efforts at hiding his jealousy were effective. "Ambassador Tayend has a great liking for brightly coloured, elaborate things."

"How is he? Settling in well?"

Dannyl shrugged. "It is too early to tell, and we have been too busy to exchange much more than greetings."

The king nodded. "Of course. I found him witty and insightful. I'm sure a man of his charm and enthusiasm will be popular among the Ashaki."

"I'm sure he will," Dannyl replied smoothly. He found himself remembering a conversation with Achati during their return from hunting for Lorkin: *"We make sure we know everything we can about the Ambassadors the Guild sends our way. And your choice of companions isn't exactly a secret in Imardin."* The king must know Tayend was Dannyl's former lover and companion. So did

Achati. But who else here knew? Did all the powerful
men of Sachaka know about them? If they did, they
couldn't be too bothered about Tayend's preference for
male lovers—since he was being as swamped with invitations to dinner as Dannyl had been when he'd first arrived.

Though Achati was acting as adviser and introducer
for Tayend, as he had for Dannyl, he always arrived early
to the Guild House so that he and Dannyl could spend
some time talking. Even when Tayend joined in these
conversations, Achati still directed most of his attention
toward Dannyl.

*For which I'm grateful. He may have other reasons
than to make me feel better about being upstaged by
Tayend, though. Perhaps he wants to demonstrate that
his interest hasn't shifted to Tayend. To remind me of his
proposal.*

Achati hadn't yet asked if Tayend's arrival had meant
the resumption of his former relationship with Dannyl.
*I'm not sure what to say if he asks. I hadn't considered us
officially parted. Now that he's here…it feels like we
have. Tayend hasn't behaved as if we're together.* He had
taken that as a cue. Or had Tayend taken Dannyl's manner
as a cue first?

The first emotion he'd felt at Tayend's arrival was
annoyance. To cover it, Dannyl had made sure to be as
polite and formal as an Ambassador should be to another.
Tayend had followed suit, which then made Dannyl start
to miss their old, teasing familiarity. *Even if it had been
laced with resentment in recent years.*

"I have my people looking for suitable accommodation
for the Elyne Ambassador," the king said. "It may take
some months. Are there any reasons of a political nature

that require the Ambassador to stay somewhere other than the Guild House in the meantime?"

Dannyl considered, then shook his head. "No." *Though I suspect I will wish there were sometimes...*

"If anything comes up, don't hesitate to inform Ashaki Achati. He will make alternative arrangements."

"Thank you."

"Now, to the matter I wish to discuss, Ambassador Dannyl." The king's expression became serious. "Have you heard from Lord Lorkin?"

"No, your majesty."

"Could you establish communications with him?"

"I doubt it." Dannyl paused to consider. "Perhaps with the Traitors' cooperation. I could see if the slaves would pass on—"

"No, I would not trust communications passed on by the Traitors. I mean communication with Lorkin directly."

Dannyl shook his head. "Not secretly. The only way I can contact Lorkin without the Traitors' help would be open mental communication—and all magicians would hear that."

The king nodded. "I want you to find a way. If you need Sachakan assistance—non-Traitor assistance, that is—Achati will arrange it."

"I appreciate your concern for Lord Lorkin," Dannyl said. "He did convince me that he joined them of his own choosing."

"Nevertheless, I wish this connection established," the king said firmly. His eyes were unblinking as he looked at Dannyl. "I expect any information about the Traitors to be passed on, in return for my people's efforts in helping you attempt to retrieve your former assistant. Cooperation between our nations can only be of mutual benefit."

A shiver ran down Dannyl's spine. *He wants Lorkin to be his spy.* Dannyl kept his expression neutral, and nodded. "It is, indeed." *Keep him happy, but don't make any promises*, he told himself. "Lorkin knew that joining the Traitors might prove to be a problem for the Guild, politically, and suggested that we officially expel him. The Guild would do so reluctantly, of course. It has not been a decision we wished to hurry, nor did we wish to do so unless it was absolutely necessary. The reason I mention this is ... *we* may not have any means to compel him to cooperate with *us*."

"The Traitors indicated that they would never allow him to leave their base," the king said. "That sounds like imprisonment to me. He could have been coerced into saying he was happy to join them. I'm surprised that the Guild is going to leave the matter as it is."

"Lorkin contacted his mother via a blood ring right before he met with me, to assure her that he was joining them of his own free will. She sensed no lie or distress. He then gave the blood ring to me," Dannyl added. "So that I could return it to her."

"I'm surprised his mother accepts this arrangement."

"She is understandably upset—but not about to march into Sachaka to fetch him home, I assure you."

The king smiled. "A pity he did not keep the ring."

"I expect he did not want to risk that the Traitors would search him and find it."

The king shifted in his seat. "I want you to endeavour to establish a safe form of communication with him, Ambassador Dannyl."

Dannyl nodded. "I'll do what I can."

"I know you will. I will delay you no longer." The king rose and, as Dannyl stood up, indicated Dannyl should walk beside him as they headed toward the door. "I regret that this situation occurred at all. We should have anticipated that the Traitors might turn their attention to the Guild at some point. But I am glad your assistant is alive and in no immediate danger."

"Thank you, your majesty. I am, too."

They reached the door and stepped into the corridor.

"How is your new assistant, Lady Merria, settling in?"

Dannyl smiled grimly. "Well, and adapting quickly." *She's already bored with the lack of work to do*, Dannyl wanted to add. *Perhaps...perhaps I can ask her to consider how we might contact Lorkin.*

The king shook his head. "I'd have advised strongly against a woman as your assistant, since she will have difficulty interacting with Sachakan men, but I would once have also reasoned that a woman would be a more likely target for the Traitors, and I have been proven wrong in that. I may be wrong about Lady Merria's success here, too."

"Your majesty is undoubtedly right in all other matters and I will always trust his wisdom, especially on Sachakan matters. That is why I am giving her work that does not require her to deal with Sachakan men."

The king chuckled. "You are a smart man." He stopped at the door to the throne room, gesturing for Dannyl to continue inside alone. "Goodbye, Ambassador."

"As always, an honour and pleasure to meet you, your majesty." Dannyl bowed. As the king walked away he turned and re-entered the great hall.

Well, at least I now have something to give Merria to do. Though giving her an impossible task like finding a way to contact Lorkin without using the Traitors seems a bit cruel. But it's not as if she is interested in my research, and I can't ask her to venture out alone into an Ashaki's personal library to examine books for me anyway.

It wasn't as if he'd had any invitations to any libraries himself lately, either. As far as his research was concerned, he was getting nowhere at all.

Sonea shifted the basket of bed sheets to her other hip, then tugged the hood of her cloak further down over her face. Though it was raining, and there was a chill to the air that warned of harsher days ahead, she was thoroughly enjoying herself. Maybe roaming the city in disguise would grow tiresome eventually, but for now she relished the freedom it gave her.

Not far from the hospice was a cleaner's shop that tackled most of the washing for the hospice. It had been a long time since she'd made that arrangement with the owner, and the shop had changed hands a few times since then. The hospice helpers always delivered the laundry, so there was little chance anyone at the cleaner's shop would recognise her—unless, of course, she had treated them or their family.

She ducked in through the open door and dropped off the basket quickly. There was no need to talk to anyone, and the staff were used to hospice workers being in a hurry. Next door was a sweet shop, and Sonea slipped through the door. She bought a bag of pachi fruit drops and spoke a code word. The middle-aged woman behind the counter waved her toward a door into a narrow passage.

Within a few steps she was knocking at another door. The number of taps had been agreed to weeks ago. A voice called out a code word and she pushed through into a small room bisected by a narrow desk.

"Greetings." A barrel-chested man rose and bowed to her as best he could in the small space. "They are waiting for you."

Sonea nodded and moved to a side door—she had to sidestep around the desk to reach it. Unlocking it with magic, she moved into a stairwell and locked the door behind her, adding a magical barrier stretched across the frame as an extra precaution.

The man in the small room was an employee of Cery's. As far as Sonea could tell, he was the husband of the sweet shop woman, and arranged debt collection. Descending the short staircase, Sonea entered a room not much bigger than the one above, furnished with only two chairs. Cery was sitting in one, but neither Gol nor Anyi had taken the other.

Pushing back her hood, Sonea smiled at her old friend and his bodyguards.

"Cery. Gol. Anyi. How are you all? What are you grinning at, Cery?"

Cery chuckled. "It's always nice to see you in something other than those black robes."

She ignored him and looked at Anyi and Gol. Both shrugged. They looked a little cold. The room was definitely chilly. She drew some magic and channelled it out as heat. Both bodyguards frowned, looked around, then turned to regard Sonea thoughtfully. Sonea smiled and sat down.

"I hope you've had some ideas on how to lure Skellin

into revealing how far from Imardin he is," she said, looking at Cery. "Because I haven't."

He shook his head. "None that don't rely on people I can't trust, or that will risk too many lives. I've lost too many allies. Even those that still deal with me are taking advantage of my problems. Gol has had several offers of employment."

"Me, too," Anyi said. "Just this afternoon. In fact, it gave me an idea."

All turned to regard her. Cery's daughter looked too young to be a bodyguard. But then, these days Sonea felt most graduating novices looked too young to be considered responsible adults.

"Go on," Cery said.

"What if I took up one of the offers?" Anyi said, her eyes gleaming. "What if I pretended to be fed up with working for you, and decided I was never going to get anywhere working for the least powerful Thief in the city? I could take a job and spy for you."

Cery stared at his daughter. His face did not appear to move, but Sonea saw subtle shifts in his expression: horror, fear, caution, speculation, guilt.

"They'd never trust you enough to put you anywhere you'd learn something useful," he told Anyi.

Why doesn't he just say "no," Sonea wondered. But as Gol glanced at Cery his expression was full of warning. *He knows Cery has to tread carefully. Perhaps if Cery blocks Anyi outright she'll be more likely to defy him.* Like Lorkin had been inclined to do to Sonea, from time to time.

Anyi smiled. "They will if I betray you," she said. "I could tell someone where to find you, perhaps. Of course, you'll know and can arrange an escape plan."

Cery nodded. "I'll consider it." He looked at Sonea. "Anything from Lorandra?"

Thinking of Skellin's mother, locked away in the Dome, Sonea winced. "Some of the Higher Magicians don't like me talking to her, and I suspect Administrator Osen only agrees to it because he thinks it would be cruel if nobody ever spoke to her. Kallen told us that she doesn't know where Skellin is so they can't see why I bother questioning her. They don't see that mind-reading has limits, and that she may be able to guess where her son is if prompted. I doubt I'll ever get permission to read her mind myself." She shook her head. "And talking *to* her is all I do. She never says a word."

"Keep at it," Cery advised. "Even if you feel ridiculous asking the same questions over and over again. It has a way of wearing a person down."

Sonea sighed and nodded. "If it doesn't wear me down first."

He smiled grimly. "Nobody said interrogation was easy. You're not the one locked up, though. She's got to be fed up with being shut away in a stone room for so long."

"We have little other choice. There's been talk of building a prison somewhere on the Grounds, but that could take several months."

"Why don't they just block her powers?"

"Same reason they were reluctant to read her mind. It could offend her people."

Cery's eyebrows rose. "She broke the laws of our country and plotted, with her son, to take over the city's underworld and enslave magicians. The Guild is worried about offending her people?"

"Yes, it's ridiculous. But I expect she'll be even less cooperative if we block her powers."

"She might be more cooperative, if you suggested you might remove the block later."

Sonea looked at Cery reproachfully. "Lie to her?"

He nodded.

"You Guild types are far too squeamish," Anyi said. "Things would be a lot easier if you weren't always worried about rules and lying to enemies or offending people."

"As if the life of a Thief is any different," Sonea pointed out.

Anyi paused. "I guess that's true, but your rules force you to be so darn nice all the time. Nobody expects a Thief to be nice."

"No." Sonea smiled. "But how different do you think the Allied Lands would be if magicians weren't forced to be nice."

Anyi frowned, opened her mouth, then closed it again.

"The word 'Sachaka' just popped into my mind," Gol muttered.

The young woman nodded. "I see what you mean. But perhaps there are times for being a little less nice to avoid something really nasty happening. Like Skellin getting control of the city."

Anyi looked at Sonea expectantly. Sonea suppressed a sigh. *She has a point.* She looked at Cery.

"I'll talk to her again," she promised. "But I won't deceive her unless there isn't any alternative. Even little betrayals tend to have nasty consequences later."

CHAPTER 4

VISITING

L ilia picked up her bag and paused to look around her room. Like most University entrants from the lower classes, she had been astounded to find she would have an entire room to herself in the Novices' Quarters. The rooms weren't big by snootie standards, of course. They contained a bed, a cupboard, a desk and a chair. Bedclothes and robes were washed and the room cleaned by the servants.

She knew that several years ago, with the number of magicians diminished due to the war and that of novices growing rapidly after lowies had been allowed to join the Guild, accommodation in the Novices' Quarters had been quickly filled and novices from the Houses had been allowed to share empty rooms in the Magicians' Quarters.

Not now. The Magicians' Quarters were full again. Graduating lowies were given priority whenever rooms became available, since magicians from the Houses were more likely to have respectable homes in the city to live in. Some lowie magicians used their income from the king to buy or rent houses in the city, too.

The Novices' Quarters were still too small, and the Guild had been forced to allow some of the snootie novices to live at home. They'd done so reluctantly, Lilia knew, because magicians weren't supposed to involve themselves in politics and the Houses were *always* involved in politics. Removing snootie novices from their families helped to distance them from that world.

Naki was one of the snooties living at home. She said she hated it. Lilia didn't quite believe her new friend, and it certainly didn't put her off accepting an invitation to stay the night.

Do I have everything? She looked at her bag and considered the contents: some toiletries, nightclothes and a spare set of robes. *We magicians don't need much.*

Turning to the door, she opened it and stepped out into the corridor. To her dismay, her friends from her class were walking past. Though they hardly paid much attention to her these days, now that they had paired up with the boys, they would notice anything unusual in Lilia's behaviour. Lilia's heart sank as they saw her and, noticing her bag, immediately looked curious.

Madie walked over, Froje following.

"Hai, Lilia! Where are you off to?"

"Naki's place," she replied, hoping she didn't sound too smug.

"Ooh-er. Friends in high places." Madie's tone was light-hearted and teasing, to Lilia's relief.

Froje frowned and stepped closer. "You know they say things about her, don't you?" she asked in a low voice.

Lilia stared at the girl. Froje wasn't one for gossip and

spite normally. The girl looked more concerned than mean, however.

"They say things about everyone," Lilia said lightly, then cursed herself. *I should have played along to find out what people are saying. Not that I'd believe it, but still... it might help Naki avoid trouble.*

Madie smiled. "Well, you can tell us if it's true or not, eh?" She looked at Froje and tilted her head toward the main entrance of the Novices' Quarters. "Have fun," she said. The pair continued on their way.

Gripping her bag, Lilia followed slowly, letting them gain a lead on her. As she emerged from the Novices' Quarters she saw Naki standing nearby and her mood immediately brightened. The late sun cast streaks of reflected gold in her friend's hair and made her pale skin glow. It was colouring all the novices' complexions too. *But none suit it so well as Naki. Half the boys out here are staring at her. I can't believe someone so beautiful and popular wants to be my friend.*

Naki saw her and smiled. Lilia's heart lifted, but at the same time her stomach fluttered uncomfortably as it had since Naki had first invited her to her home. *I had better not do anything to annoy her, because I don't have the good looks and charm that she has to ensure I'll always have people wanting to be my friend.*

"Father's carriage is waiting for us," Naki said as they met each other.

"Oh! Sorry. I must be late."

"No, not really." Naki shrugged and started toward the path through the gardens. "He often sends it early. It's annoying, as there are only so many carriages that can fit out the front of the University and they always get jammed. What do you want to do tonight? I thought we might put our hair up."

Lilia tried not to wince. Her mother had done fancy things to her hair when she was a child, and she'd hated the tugging and pinching, and how the clips made her scalp itch. Naki looked at Lilia and frowned.

"What's wrong?"

"Nothing." Lilia read disbelief on the other girl's face. "My mother used to do it to me for special occasions. There was always a hair pulling or a pin sticking into me."

"Don't worry. I promise there will be not one pulled hair. It'll be fun."

"I'll hold you to that."

Naki laughed—a throaty, deep laugh that made heads turn. They chatted more as they walked through the gardens. When they rounded the end of the University they found a mass of carriages waiting. Naki took Lilia's arm and guided her through them. She stopped at one and the driver leapt down to open the door for them.

The jam of carriages outside delayed them for some time, but Lilia barely noticed. She was too busy enjoying talking to Naki. They started by swapping amusing stories of encounters between servants and their masters, then an anecdote about a servant Naki had grown up with made her pause and look at Lilia thoughtfully.

"You know, you remind me a lot of her. I wish you could have met each other."

"She doesn't work for you anymore?"

"No." Naki's face darkened. "Father sent her away."

He seems to be the bad guy in all her stories, Lilia mused.

"You don't like him, do you?" she asked cautiously,

not sure how Naki would react to a personal and perhaps sensitive question.

Naki's face changed dramatically. Suddenly her gaze was darker and her face taut. "Not much. And he hates me." She sighed, then shook herself as if trying to throw off something bad. "I'm sorry. I didn't want to say anything, in case it made you afraid to meet him."

"I'm not that easily scared," Lilia assured her.

"He'll be perfectly polite to you. After all, you're a member of the Guild. He has to treat you as an equal. Well, as a novice anyway. He might turn all teacherly, though."

"I can handle that."

"And we don't have to tell him you're from a servant family for now," Naki said anxiously. "He's a bit...like that."

"That's fine. What matters is that *you're* not like that. I appreciate it."

Naki smiled. "And what I like about *you* is that you don't hate us, like the other...you know...do."

Lilia shrugged. "My family works for a nice, decent family. It's hard to agree with people who say—"

"Look! We're here."

Naki waved eagerly at the carriage window. Lilia peered out, looking where her friend pointed. They stopped outside a huge building. She'd known that Naki was from a rich and powerful House, but it hadn't quite sunk in until this moment. Nerves and excitement warred within her. She tried to quell them.

"Don't worry," Naki said, somehow picking up on Lilia's trepidation. "Relax and leave everything to me."

The next hour passed in a blur. Naki led her into the

house. First she introduced Lilia to her father, Lord Leiden, who welcomed her in a distant and distracted way. Then they went upstairs to a spacious collection of rooms that were all Naki's. Aside from the main bedroom, there was a room filled with clothing and shoes, and another with its own bath. Naki fulfilled her promise to put Lilia's hair up, combing through a special cream first, then using smooth silver pins that she somehow arranged so they didn't pull or irritate Lilia's scalp. Then they hurried downstairs for dinner.

Naki's father was at the table. Looking down at all the different types of cutlery, Lilia had a moment of panic. A messenger arrived and Lord Leiden stood up. He apologised at leaving them to eat alone and strode away.

As the door of the dining room closed behind him, Naki grinned at Lilia. Without saying a word, she slipped out of her chair and walked quietly to the door. Opening it carefully, she listened. A distant thunk reached Lilia's ears.

"He's gone," Naki announced. "Grab your glass." She picked up her own glass, freshly filled with wine, then moved to the door the servants had been entering through. As Naki reached it, the door opened and a servant woman carrying a tray of small bowls paused at the threshold.

"We're coming down," Naki told her. The woman nodded, then turned and disappeared the way she had come.

Lilia had managed to pick up her glass and slide out of her seat. Naki beckoned, then followed the servant, leading Lilia down a short corridor with a bench and cupboards to one side filled with vessels, cutlery and glasses. The servant woman was descending a stairway at the end. Naki hurried after her.

"I eat downstairs whenever Father isn't here," she explained. "Then there's no need for them to serve the food on the silverware and I have friends to chat to."

The stairway was long enough that Lilia suspected they were now two floors below the dining room. They entered a kitchen not unlike the one in her childhood home. Three women and a boy were working, their sleeves rolled up and their hair covered with caps that had flaps to tie around behind the ears. Lilia had worn these herself, as a child.

Naki greeted them with an affection that they did not seem surprised at. After introducing them, she moved to a well-worn old table and sat down on one of the stools beside it. Lilia took the stool beside her. She listened to the banter between Naki and her servants and felt at home for the first time in three years.

What a pair we make, she thought. *A snootie who's friendly and kind to servants and a lowie who doesn't hate the rich.* And the Guild—and magic—had brought them together. *That's an interesting idea. I'd have thought it would be having a similar background, from different sides of the situation. But it's really due to magic. And magic doesn't discriminate between rich and poor any more than it does between good and bad.*

Dannyl looked around, still struggling to believe Tayend had managed it. The Master's Room of the Guild House was filled with powerful and influential Sachakans. There were Ashaki here who were deadly enemies. They weren't exactly talking to each other, but they were in the same room, which apparently was a rare thing.

He didn't manage to get the king here, though. Tayend had said he'd sent an invite, but Achati had warned him that Amakira would not be able to attend. It was probably for the better. When the monarch was among a gathering of so many Ashaki, the inevitable political scheming spoiled the party. Or so Dannyl had heard. He'd never been in a gathering this big, nor any that included the king. The largest had been the greeting party Achati had arranged for Dannyl and Lorkin's arrival in Arvice.

Dannyl had to admit, he was impressed. Tayend had managed to organise the event within a few days of coming up with the idea of holding a "Kyralian" party. He'd even taught the kitchen slaves to make a few Kyralian dishes to be served in small bowls or plates. He had given up on the idea of having the slaves walk about with food on platters, since they could not put aside their habit of throwing themselves on the floor for him and Dannyl, let alone important Sachakans.

Tayend had even managed to find more sober Kyralian clothing to wear rather than his usual bright and flamboyant garb.

"Next time I'll have an Elyne party," Dannyl heard Tayend say. "Or maybe a Lonmar party. At least then the absence of women will suit the theme. You can't have an Elyne party without a little witty female conversation to liven things up." Tayend paused to listen to a response Dannyl could not hear, and then smiled. "Then perhaps I'll train a slave, or import some Elyne women for the day—or mimic one myself! Nothing spared for my Sachakan guests."

Laughter followed. Dannyl sighed and turned away. He saw Achati talking to Lady Merria and felt a wave of gratitude. She had looked uncomfortable earlier, with the other guests ignoring her. Watching to see what the

Sachakans would do when they saw her, Dannyl had noticed less displeasure and more uncertainty in their faces than he'd expected. Not used to women being among their social circle, since talking to someone else's woman was taboo, they didn't know what to do about her, so they pretended she wasn't there.

Achati looked up and beckoned to Dannyl.

"I was just telling Lady Merria of a group of three Sachakan women I know who meet socially."

"I thought that was frowned upon here."

"They get away with it because they are widows and a cripple, and because they hate the Traitors. One of the group believes they killed her husband." Achati smiled. "I thought Lady Merria might like to join them sometimes. She could become very lonely here otherwise."

Dannyl looked at Merria. "What do you think?"

She nodded. "It would be good to meet some local women."

Achati smiled and looked at Dannyl. "Should I enquire with them if your assistant would be welcome?"

Belatedly, Dannyl realised Achati was asking his permission, as if Merria's social life was his responsibility. Amused, he looked at the Healer. She looked a little distant, as if she hadn't heard the question, but perhaps her lack of expression came from her effort to show nothing of her true feelings.

"Yes, please do," Dannyl replied.

Achati looked pleased. "Perhaps I can find you something to do, as well," he murmured. Looking at Dannyl pointedly, he beckoned and headed toward an Ashaki whose partner in conversation had just moved away. Dannyl followed.

"Ashaki Ritova. I was just telling Ambassador Dannyl about your impressive library."

The Sachakan turned to face Achati. He wore a haughty expression that softened very slightly into respect toward Achati, but returned when he looked at Dannyl.

"Ashaki Achati. You need not boast on my behalf."

"Yet I always feel inclined to. Surely it is the best collection in Sachaka, aside from the palace library."

"It is a meagre pile of books in comparison."

"Even so, I am sure Ambassador Dannyl would be astounded at how old some of your records are."

The man glanced at Dannyl again. "I doubt you would find anything of interest, Ambassador." He sighed. "I do not have the time to look in there myself. Too busy discussing treaties with the eastern lands."

He shook his head and began a long and boring criticism of the peoples the Sachakans traded with over the Aduna Sea. It would have been interesting to learn more about these lands, but Dannyl quickly realised that the Ashaki's assessment was tainted with dislike and prejudice, and unlikely to be a true description. When Achati finally managed to extract them without insulting Ritova, he apologised.

"I hoped to get something out of that for you," he murmured. "But he is as stubborn as ..."

The Master of War, Kirota, drew near. Seeing Dannyl, he sidled over.

"Ashaki Achati. Ambassador Dannyl. A pleasure to see you again, Ambassador. I hear you and Ambassador Tayend are closely connected. Is this true?"

Dannyl nodded. "We have long been friends. Over twenty years."

Kirota frowned. "Ambassador Tayend said he lived in Elyne when you first met."

"Yes, as did I," Dannyl explained. "I was Guild Ambassador to Elyne. I met Tayend at the Great Library. He assisted me in some research for the Guild."

"Ah, yes! Tayend mentioned your research. How is it going?"

Dannyl shrugged. "I've made little progress recently."

Kirota nodded sympathetically. "Such is the life of a researcher. A big discovery one moment, long gaps between. I wish you more success soon."

"Thank you," Dannyl replied. "You expressed an interest in filling gaps in your own records last time we met," he added. "My offer to assist still stands."

The Master of War's face brightened. "I will be sure to take it up." His gaze flickered past Dannyl's shoulder. "Ah. More of those delicious rassook legs. This time I'm determined to get more than one before they all go. I like this Kyralian food." He grinned and hurried away.

Hearing a chuckle beside him, Dannyl turned to look at Achati. The man smiled.

"You did well there," he murmured. "It could be that, now that you're no longer the newest thing to examine, the best way to gain what you need is to trade for it."

Dannyl nodded and felt his heart lighten a little.

"Though I doubt Kirota can do much for you in return," Achati warned in a low voice. "Still...consider it an investment."

As the small flare of hope faded, Dannyl suppressed a sigh. He saw Tayend watching him from the other side of the room, a thoughtful look on his former lover's face, and suddenly all Dannyl wanted to do was leave the party.

But he had no choice but to stay, so he stiffened his back and followed Achati to the next group of Sachakans.

Lorkin had been expecting luxury and expensive decoration. He had expected the Traitor equivalent of servants hovering about, ready to do their monarch's bidding, and guards at every door.

But the rooms of the Traitor queen were not much larger or finer than those of the women he had visited while assisting Speaker Kalia in her visits to the sick or pregnant. The only obvious guard was a single magician sitting in the corridor outside, near the door. Maybe the young woman who had answered his knock on the door was a magician, too, though she seemed too young for the role of royal protector. She had greeted him with a cheerful, welcoming smile, introduced herself as Pelaya, then ushered him inside.

Now he stood within a circle of plain wooden chairs. An old woman was standing before one of them as if she had just stood up. She was not dressed in finery, but then she hadn't been the day of Tyvara's trial either. If he hadn't recognised her face, he might have mistaken her for another visitor waiting for the queen.

But her bright eyes were sharp and her stare very direct, and there was something about her composure and focus that spoke of confidence and command. He put a hand to his chest and waited for a response, as he'd been instructed to do when he had first entered the presence of the queen.

She waved a hand dismissively. "I don't bother with formality in my own home, Lord Lorkin. I am too old and tired for it. Please sit down." She reached backwards and, with obvious difficulty, began to lower herself onto a chair. He automatically took a step forward to help her, then stopped, not sure if touching her would be inappropriate.

"Wait for me, Zarala," Pelaya said, her voice gently scolding, as she hurried forward to assist the old queen.

"I'm fine," Zarala replied. "Just slow."

Once she was settled, the queen indicated the chair next to hers. Lorkin sat down. The young woman disappeared into another room. The queen regarded him thoughtfully.

"How are you finding living in Sanctuary?"

"It is a wonderful place, your majesty," he began. "I—"

"No formality," the queen interrupted, waving a finger at him. "Call me Zarala."

He nodded. "Zarala. It is a beautiful name."

She grinned. "I like flattery. It will gain you nothing, though. I am too old for that sort of thing to influence me. Not that you should stop, if you happen to enjoy it."

"I do," Lorkin replied. "And should you happen to enjoy it, you are welcome to send some my way, too," he added quickly.

To his relief, she laughed. "Go on. Tell me how you are doing."

"I am amazed at Traitor generosity and friendliness. Your people have welcomed me, given me food and shelter, and duties that make me feel useful."

"Why would you be surprised at that?"

Lorkin shrugged. "For a people so secretive, I would have expected it to take a long time to be so accepted among you."

She considered him closely. "You know that you haven't

been, don't you? Fully accepted, that is. A lot of people like you, and a lot appreciate what you did for Tyvara, but nobody is fool enough to trust you yet."

He nodded and met her gaze. "Yes, I do sense that. It's understandable. I suppose I am amazed that it isn't more obvious."

"I've heard only a few reports of people taking a dislike to you personally, but mostly they don't like you on principle."

He looked at her. "Because of my father."

"Yes—and Riva's death." All sign of her lighter mood was gone now. The wrinkles across her brows deepened. "I want you to know that I don't blame you for what your father did. It is ridiculous to think a child is responsible for what their parent does."

"I... I am glad you feel that way."

She leaned forward and patted him on the knee. "I'm sure you are. You'd probably be dead, otherwise." Humour had re-entered her voice and eyes, and he smiled.

"I don't resent your father any more either," she told him, looking away and growing serious again. Serious and sad. "Despite losing a daughter to a sickness that could have been cured. We went about things the wrong way. Something about your father had convinced me he was an honourable man. I thought I'd been wrong, but came to see that perhaps I wasn't, that I'd failed to see that there would be something he felt a stronger loyalty to."

"The Guild? Kyralia?" Lorkin suggested.

She looked at him. "You didn't know about the deal he made, did you?" she said quietly.

He shook his head. "I was appalled to find he made such a bargain and dishonoured it."

"He died before you were born. I suppose he never got the chance to tell you."

"And Mother never mentioned it. She couldn't have known."

"Why are you so certain?"

"She was determined to stop me going to Sachaka. If she'd had proof I would be in danger from the Traitors, she would have used it."

"Do you miss her?"

Her stare was very direct. He nodded. "And yet a part of me wants to be . . . to be . . ."

"Living your own life? Making your own decisions?"

He nodded.

She waved a hand at the room, or beyond. "And here you are, stuck in Sanctuary."

"It is a pleasant place to be stuck."

She smiled approvingly. "I hope you continue to think so." Her smile faded again. "Because life might not always be so comfortable here for you. I am old. I can't be certain who will succeed me. All know that Savara is the Speaker I favour to be the next queen, and she likes you, but that does not mean the people will vote for her. They certainly won't if they come to question my decisions." She pointed at him. "Like allowing a Kyralian magician into Sanctuary who turned out to be too nosy."

Her eyes were hard and ever so slightly accusing. His face began to warm and he looked away, not sure what to say.

"But they may be satisfied now that I have brought you in here for a good chiding. Savara has decided that it would be better if she forbids Tyvara from being seen with you, so it is clear that she disapproves of your exploration of the caves."

Lorkin's heart made a small lurch. *But it wasn't like we were seeing each other anyway*, he reminded himself. Zarala smiled and patted him on the knee again. "I have some friendly and free advice for you, young Lorkin. Be careful how much trouble you stir up. It might bring you, and others, a whole lot more than you realise."

He nodded. "Thank you. I will take your advice. No trouble."

She looked pleased. "You're a smart young man. There—I have flattered you in return. Would you like something to eat?" She did not wait for him to reply, but turned in the other direction, toward the inner door.

"Pelaya? Is there anything for our visitor to eat?"

"Of course there is," the young woman replied. She appeared in the doorway holding a simple wooden tray topped with glasses, water and a bowl of cakes, obviously having been waiting for the queen to call.

"Ah, my favourite," the queen said, rubbing her hands together. She smirked at Lorkin. "Pelaya is a fabulous cook. Does it all with magic." As the young woman carried the tray into the room, Zarala turned to stare at a nearby small table. It rose in the air and floated toward them, settling before Lorkin.

She may be old and too tired for formality, Lorkin mused, *but I can see why she is queen. And I'd wager she's still as powerful and smart as the day she became one.*

As Pelaya set the tray down and offered him a cake, he wondered how much the queen had guessed of his plans, because he doubted she believed he was content to settle into his place among the Traitors forever.

Perhaps she was telling him to hold off on them because he'd have a better chance of success after she died, if Savara succeeded her.

But having met her now, I really like her, and I hope that doesn't happen very soon.

CHAPTER 5

QUESTIONS, QUESTIONS

As the lamps were lit around the courtyard, Sonea started toward the strangest of the Guild buildings. The Dome wasn't really a dome, but a full sphere—a hollow ball of solid rock. Since half of it was buried in the ground it had a dome-like appearance.

It was as old as the Guild itself. Before the Guild had built the Arena—a shield of magic supported by huge curved struts—the more dangerous fighting lessons had been held inside the Dome. There had been many disadvantages to using the structure for this purpose. Unlike with the Arena, spectators could not watch the lesson inside. The thick walls would never have survived a strong attack, so all practice strikes had to be restrained. The strikes that did hit the walls could heat the stone up, making the interior intolerably hot. And the only way to get fresh air inside was to open the plug-like door.

According to the old records that Akkarin had found, the plug had been knocked out during lessons many times over the years, and once even killed a passing servant.

Now it was being held in place by magic. Twice a day it was removed and new air sent into the interior to replace the old. At the same time, food and water was taken in and the bucket that served as a toilet removed and emptied.

Sonea could not help thinking of her experience as a captive rogue. Rothen had kept her in his rooms, slowly gaining her trust with kindness and patience while teaching her about the Guild. But Lorandra was no ignorant young woman, come to magic by accident and of greater danger to herself than the Guild. She had her powers well in check and, with her son, had plotted against the Guild.

Yet I know what it's like to be locked in the Dome. When the Higher Magicians had discovered that Sonea had learned black magic, they had imprisoned her here for a night, and Akkarin in the Arena, while they roused the Higher Magicians in preparation for their trial. It was stuffy and oppressive. *I was in there for only a handful of hours. I can't imagine what it's been like to be stuck in there for months.*

Sonea took a deep breath and resisted the urge to turn and walk in another direction. While she felt some sympathy toward Lorandra, she was always reluctant to visit the woman. Skellin's mother had never spoken a word, and hate and fear had radiated from her. The woman's hate she could live with. It was the uncompromising hate of a mother toward those who would harm her son, and having experienced that emotion herself Sonea figured that it was fair.

No, it was the fear that bothered Sonea. She was used to people being a little afraid of her because of what she had done in her youth and was capable of doing with black magic, but Lorandra's fear was simple blind terror, and that made irrelevant all Sonea had done in her life to prove that she was an honourable and trustworthy person.

And Cery would have me lie to her.

The two guards standing on either side of the door looked bored and annoyed, but as they saw her approaching they straightened and nodded to her respectfully. Both were male and from the Houses, she noted. So far she hadn't seen any magicians from the lower classes standing guard. Did Administrator Osen not trust that they would keep a Thief's mother imprisoned? Surely he wasn't naïve enough to think that magicians from the higher class were immune from being blackmailed or bribed by the underworld. She stopped and nodded at the door.

"How long since it was last opened?"

"Three hours, Black Magician Sonea," the taller of the magicians replied.

"Did you get Administrator Osen's instructions?"

He nodded.

"Good. Let me in."

The two magicians stared at the door in silent concentration. Instead of swivelling open, it slowly slid forwards, then rolled sideways to lean against the Dome wall. The interior was dark. Lorandra had plenty of power with which to keep her prison lit, but if she used it she always extinguished her light when she heard the door opening. Sonea took a deep breath, created a globe light and sent it before her as she entered.

As always, the woman was sitting on the narrow bed in the centre of the room. Sonea walked down the curved slope of the "floor" and stopped a few steps away. The woman stared back at her, her face expressionless but her eyes dark and unfriendly.

Sonea considered what to say. In the past she'd tried indirectly approaching the questions she most wanted to ask by mingling them with others. Where did roet come from? Was it a drug from their home country? How was it made? Why had Lorandra been buying books on magic? Had she managed to find many? Where were they now? Why did Skellin think the Guild would be fooled into believing Forlie, the hapless woman he had set up as a fake rogue to prevent the Guild capturing his mother, was a magician? Where was Forlie's family?

Some of the questions were ones to which Sonea already knew the answers, some Sonea already knew Loranda *didn't* know the answer to. Cery had recommended this, because it was important to avoid revealing how much the Guild didn't know.

But Lorandra had said nothing.

So Sonea tried being more direct. Where was Skellin? How long had he lived in Imardin? Which Thieves were his allies? Which Houses were linked to him? Were any Guild magicians under his sway? Did he have allies in Elyne? Lonmar? Sachaka? How many Thieves had she killed? Had she tried to kill Cery? Had she tried to kill Cery's family?

No shift of expression had betrayed Lorandra's reaction to that last question. It was the one Sonea most wanted an answer to, aside from the whereabouts of Skellin.

If only Osen had chosen me to read Lorandra's mind at the Hearing, not Kallen. I could have sought the answer there and nobody would have known I had done so but Lorandra. But that would have meant Forlie's mind would have been read by Kallen, and Sonea would not have wished that on the poor, frightened woman.

Sonea remembered Lorandra's dismay and surprise that she could not stop Kallen reading her mind. Hopefully that meant the magicians of Lorandra's homeland did not know black magic—possibly did not even know *of* it. From what Kallen had described, Lorandra's people forbade all magic, though those who imposed the ban were magicians themselves. Lorandra had broken the law and learned magic in secret. It was likely she did not know how powerful the law keepers were.

The Guild is so worried about offending the people of her land if they block her powers, but if what Kallen says is true, the Guild's very existence would offend them. Lorandra is a criminal there as well as here. They would want not just her, but all of us, executed.

Igra was far away, with a reassuringly big desert between it and the Allied Lands. Chances were nobody there remembered Lorandra, since she had left many years ago, and if they did they probably thought she was dead. It was a pity she hadn't approached the Guild from the start. They might have taken her in, or allowed her to live in Imardin with some sort of arrangement that allowed her restricted use of magic. Instead she'd adopted the life of an assassin and, with her son, made herself rich by selling roet.

Sonea thought of all the people who had suffered and died because of this woman. This time she didn't push away the anger that rose or try to retain some compassion. This time she let it harden her resolve.

"I'm not here to question you," Sonea told the woman quietly. "I'm here to inform you that the Guild will block your powers soon. You won't be able to use magic. The good news is that you won't be stuck in here any more. I can't tell you what they'll do with you after that, but they won't be setting you free within the Allied Lands."

Lorandra's expression shifted slightly, from hatred to worry, and Sonea felt a surge of triumph far stronger than the change deserved. She turned away and stepped toward the door. A raspy croak sounded behind her and she paused, then forced herself on.

"Wait."

Sonea stopped and turned. Lorandra's dark eyes caught the light as she lifted her head.

"Will it hurt?" she asked in a whispery voice.

Sonea stared back at her. "Why should I answer your questions when you've answered none of mine?"

Lorandra's mouth pressed into a thin line. Sonea turned away, then stopped and looked back.

"Not if you don't fight it," she told the woman quietly, so the guards couldn't hear. Lorandra's eyes swivelled to meet hers. "And ... and it is reversible," Sonea added in an even quieter voice.

She made herself turn away and step out of the door, wondering if what she had seen in the woman's eyes was hope or suspicion.

"The first thing you need to remember is that pregnancy is not an illness or an injury," Lady Indria told the class. "But there are many problems that can arise from pregnancy and childbirth. Unlike the majority of conditions that hamper or prevent pregnancy, which we have covered so far this year, the problems of pregnancy and childbirth can cause death, to either mother or child, or both."

Lilia glanced at her friends. Both Froje and Madie were sitting with straight backs, listening to Lady Indria intently. *They're almost as captivated as they were during the lessons on preventing pregnancy*, Lilia mused. She looked around the room. Most of the novices looked interested in the lesson. Even the boys were, which surprised her even though all Healers were expected to learn how to advise a mother and deliver a baby.

A few of the girls had been missing from class until now. All were snooties. The Houses had never objected to their daughters learning how to prevent conception until it had become an official part of the University's Healing lessons. No parents of lowies had raised the slightest fuss. They couldn't afford to raise grandchildren while their daughters finished their education in the Guild.

I should find this more interesting than I do, Lilia thought. *I suppose I would, if I was in love with someone or likely to get married soon. That would give me reason to think about the future, and of having children. Right now that all seems so unlikely. Madie may be right when she says you can't tell when you'll find someone special, but even if that someone came along next week I doubt I'll want to have children for many years yet.*

She still needed to pay attention, though, because if she was to become a Healer she'd have to be able to help pregnant women. Forcing herself to listen, she started taking notes. When Lady Indria finally stopped lecturing and began answering questions, Lilia felt Madie's breath on her cheek as the girl leaned toward her.

"You meeting Naki tonight?" Madie murmured.

Lilia smiled. "Yeah. She's going to help me practise curved strikes."

Madie drew in a breath to say something more, then made a small noise of frustration.

"What?" Lilia asked, looking up.

Her friend's face was taut with indecision and worry.

"What?" Lilia repeated.

Madie sighed and glanced around the class. She leaned even closer.

"People are starting to notice you hanging out with her. You must know what they're saying."

Lilia's stomach swooped lower, a sensation that left her nauseated.

"What are they saying?" she forced herself to ask.

"That you and her..." Madie straightened suddenly as Indria spoke her name. Lilia listened as her friend answered the Healer's question. The teacher gave Lilia a stern look, then turned away and resumed her lecture.

Lilia leaned closer to Madie.

"What are they saying?"

"Sh. I'll tell you later."

For the rest of the class Lilia found it twice as hard to concentrate as before. What could people possibly find to gossip about concerning her friendship with Naki? Was it the lowie/snootie thing? Did it have anything to do with Naki's father? Naki had said he disapproved of lowies. Maybe he was threatening to stop Naki seeing Lilia.

By the time the University gong rang out, Lilia's notes were a fragmented mess and her thoughts not much better. She followed Madie and Froje out of the classroom.

"Well?" she prompted.

The two girls exchanged looks. Madie's expression was almost pleading. Froje's was expectant. Madie turned to smile thinly at Lilia.

"We'd better do this before we join the boys." She glanced around the hallway, then led Lilia and Froje into an empty classroom, checking to make sure there was nobody there. She turned to Lilia.

"It's said...people say..." She paused and shook her head. "Naki doesn't like boys."

"Well, she likes them, but not in the way that girls are *supposed* to like them," Froje injected.

"She likes girls." Madie looked at Lilia, then away. "In a way that girls are *not* supposed to."

A strained silence followed. Lilia found that she was not surprised. She was certainly not as shocked as they expected her to be. As a servant, she had seen and heard many things that novices who had grown up in more sheltered homes didn't know about. Her father had told her not to judge people too quickly.

Though they weren't looking at her, expectation flowed from Lilia's friends. As the silence lengthened, Lilia felt a rising panic. She should react, or they'd think she already knew.

And approved.

"Um," she began.

"You know what we mean, don't you. Girls who like girls in the way that boys—" Madie began.

"I know what you mean," Lilia interrupted. She bit her lip. "Is it true? I mean, people make these things up all the time—especially about people who they resent for something. Like being beautiful and rich. Or for not being interested in them. Naki's turned away a lot of boys—or so I've heard. That might make her just seem to like girls more."

The two girls frowned and exchanged another look.

"I think so," Madie said, though her tone held a hint of doubt.

"There's a story that she and one of her servants were . . . you know," Froje said, her voice hard with dislike. "But the servant wanted to end it. Naki found out. She set things up so her father would discover them together. He threw the servant and her entire family onto the street. My cousin knows the family. He swears it's true."

The pair looked at Lilia. She stared back at them. Her heart was quietly racing in her chest. She felt her friendship with Naki slipping away, and she didn't like the feeling. The story about the servant was disturbing. Could Naki have been so malicious and vengeful? *Maybe it's an exaggeration, made up by servants angry at being thrown out--probably for a more deserving reason.* She hated herself for thinking that, but she knew that not all servants were honest and loyal.

Maybe her friends were jealous of Lilia finding a prettier, richer friend than they were. *Well, they shouldn't have started completely ignoring me once they got their boys.* But she couldn't say that. It would make her liking Naki seem even more suspicious. Perhaps she could say something to help Naki. To help dispel the rumour.

"It doesn't make sense," she told them. "Naki doesn't like her father. Why would she trust him to know that about her? More likely the servant was thrown out for another reason; made up a story to make Naki look bad."

Froje and Madie looked thoughtful. They exchanged another look, this time doubtful. Then Madie smiled and turned to Lilia.

"Well, you're probably right. You know her personally; we only know the stories." She frowned. "But even if it's not true, we are still worried about you. People are going to talk."

Lilia shrugged. "Let them. They'll get tired of it eventually. Why should Naki have no friends because of nasty rumour?"

She turned and started toward the door. The two girls hesitated, then Lilia heard them following. She also heard a fainter sound. A quick whisper.

"Why are you bothering? We're not good enough for her now."

Lilia continued out into the corridor, pretending she hadn't heard, but she felt a bitter triumph. *I'm right. They're jealous.* Yet she also had to hide a pang of guilt as the girls joined her. It was true. Naki was a more interesting and exciting friend than they had ever been, even when they weren't distracted by the boys.

Especially if what they say about her is true.

She didn't want to think about that now. Not because she feared the stories might be true, but because she feared that her friends would somehow sense the simmering excitement that their warning had stirred deep within her. And because of the inevitable questions the feeling led to.

What if it is true of me, as well?

All she knew for certain was that she did not feel the distaste she ought to, and that was something she would never be able to tell her friends—or anybody else. Perhaps not even Naki.

As the Guild's carriage rolled through the streets of Arvice, Dannyl noted that Lady Merria was drinking in the sights with hungry eyes. Though she had only arrived ten days ago, she was already feeling the boredom of being stuck in the Guild House most of the time.

Or perhaps she is merely fascinated by a new place, Dannyl mused. *It could be that I'm the only one feeling stuck.*

Either way, she had been thrilled at the idea of visiting the market. Tayend had suggested it the previous night, before he'd headed off for another evening of fine food and company with one Ashaki or another. Dannyl hadn't yet seen the market, since anything he required was always quickly brought to the Guild House by slaves, so the visit was merely for entertainment—and perhaps education, too. Maybe he'd learn something about Sachaka, and of the lands it traded with in the east.

"How did your visit with the women Achati recommended go?" Dannyl asked.

Merria glanced at him and smiled. "Good, I think. They all believe that the husband of one of the widows was killed by the Traitors, and yet only the widow displays any convincing hatred. I suspect that there's more to it than they're saying. One of the others hinted to me that she whined so much about him that the Traitors thought she was serious about wanting to be free of him."

"So either the Traitors made a mistake, or she tricked them, or something else has forced her to claim to hate them to protect herself."

Merria gave him a thoughtful look. "I really need to train myself to see all the complicated twisted possibilities in these situations, don't I?"

He shrugged. "It never hurts. It's also wise to not get too attached to anyone."

She nodded and looked back out of the window,

thankfully missing Dannyl's wince as he realised the truth of his own words.

I shouldn't get attached to Achati for the same reason. But who else is there to talk to? I do like him a great deal—and not just because he's continued to associate with me even though I've become a social embarrassment here.

"Is that the market?" Merria asked.

Dannyl moved closer to the window on his side and peered at the road ahead. It ended where it met a cross-road. On the opposite side was a high white wall, broken by a plain archway through which a steady stream of people were passing. Those coming out were followed by slaves carrying boxes, baskets, sacks and rolled-up rugs. Both roads were lined with waiting carriages.

"I'd wager it is."

Sure enough, the carriage swung in a wide turn at the meeting of roads so that it stopped before the archway. It was now the subject of much staring and pointing. Merria reached out to the carriage door, then paused and withdrew her hand.

"You had better go first, Ambassador," she said.

He smiled grimly and waited for one of the slaves to clamber down and open the door. The man threw himself to the ground as Dannyl stepped out. A small crowd had gathered to watch, and a low murmur came from them as he appeared. But as Merria appeared, the sound rose to a louder hum of interest. She paused on the top step, frowning.

"Ignore them," Dannyl advised, offering a hand. "Don't meet anyone's eyes."

She lowered her gaze and took his offered hand for

support, but stepped down with dignity. Dannyl resisted a smile. Merria had told him she was a ship captain's daughter, which meant that while she hadn't been raised in squalor or poverty she also hadn't had the upbringing of a woman from the Houses. Yet she had studied the mannerisms and manners of those from the upper class when she joined the Guild, and learned to mimic them. Such a knack for adaptation would be very useful to her, both here and back in Imardin.

Dannyl released her hand, instructed the slave to move the carriage to an appropriate place out of the way of traffic to wait for them, then started toward the market entrance. The other slave leapt off the carriage to follow them.

Two guards watched the entrance, both eyeing Dannyl and Merria without expression.

They must be free servants, Dannyl thought. *Like those at the palace.*

Once through the archway he and Merria entered a market laid out in straight rows. The stalls on the outside, built against the walls, were permanent structures. The centre space was filled with neat lines of temporary carts and tables, most covered with a roof of cloth. He started along the first row.

Merria continued to be more interesting to the locals than Dannyl. Most likely they had never seen a Kyralian woman before, whereas Kyralian males were merely rare. He found that he was in the opposite position to Merria. He'd rarely seen Sachakan women before this. No women worked in the stalls, but plenty roamed the market, each with a male chaperone. They wore highly decorated capes that fell from their shoulders to their ankles.

He did not want to raise the ire of the locals by staring at their women, so he turned his attention to the wares on offer. Perfume, elaborate glassware, artistic pottery and fine cloth surrounded them. They had obviously entered at the luxury end of the market. Thinking back, he realised he hadn't seen anyone carrying vegetables or herding animals out of the archway. When they reached the end of one aisle, he squinted down the rows ahead. Sure enough, there were more practical goods on sale at the far end. Perhaps there was another entrance catering for that sort of produce.

They started down another aisle, stopping to look at goods from lands across the Aduna Sea. Merria was particularly impressed with the glassware. In the third aisle they were both instantly drawn to a stall covered in a glittering array of gemstones in all colours. But while Merria gazed at the stones, what had caught Dannyl's eye were the stallholders, as he instantly recognised the dusty grey skin and long limbs of Duna tribesmen.

At once he remembered the Duna tracker, Unh, who had helped him, Achati and the Ashaki helpers to search for Lorkin. He also recalled the cave he and Unh had discovered in the mountains, its walls covered in crystals. Dannyl had learned that the tribesmen knew how to turn such crystals into magical gemstones. He eyed the glittering stones before him thoughtfully.

Surely they wouldn't sell the magical ones here. He looked closer. The abundance on display and the roughness of their cutting suggested that these weren't of much value beyond ordinary trinkets.

"You like?" a tribesman said, leaning toward Merria and smiling broadly.

She nodded. "They're pretty. How much are—?"

"Do you have any finer gems?" Dannyl interrupted. "Or ones set into jewellery, or other objects?"

The man gave Dannyl a piercingly direct look, then shook his head. "People here not like our way of setting."

Dannyl smiled. "We are not from here."

The man grinned. "No, you are not." He looked from Merria to Dannyl, then beckoned. "Come inside."

They moved around the table and entered the shade under the roof covering. Watched by his frowning companion, the tribesman opened a dusty old bag and drew out two large bands. He lifted them up so Dannyl and Merria could see. They were made of some sort of unpolished, darkened metal, lined with leather. Gemstones glittered within crude settings. Small metal tags hung from holes around one edge of each band.

"They go here." The man pointed to a place just above the knee. "And more here and one here." He touched his skin above the elbow and then the cloth wrapped about his hips. "For ceremony we rub," he mimicked a circular motion, "so they shine. But let go dark other times so not so..." He waved at his face, widening his eyes. *Dazzling*, Dannyl translated.

"That must look wonderful," Merria said.

The man grinned and nodded at her. "We dance. If we dance well women choose us."

"Wouldn't be the first time a woman married a man for jewellery," Merria remarked, glancing at Dannyl. "What do women wear?" she asked the man.

The tribesman shook his head. "Just belt. Very plain. Over cloth..." He gestured in a sweeping motion from neck to knee.

Merria looked disappointed. "No jewellery? No gems?"

"Gems on belt."

"I'd love to see one of these ceremonies." Merria sighed wistfully. "Is this expensive?" She nodded to the leg bands.

"This one not for sale. But we bring one that is next time? Maybe belt, too."

"I'd like that." She glanced back at the table of gems. "So... how much are they?"

They returned to the table and a bit of haggling followed. Dannyl suspected that the tribesman let her beat him down to a lower price than he would usually accept. As the transaction finished, Dannyl decided that he could not leave without asking after the tracker.

"Do you know Unh?" he asked. "He works as a tracker."

The man's grin vanished, then returned looking unconvincing and forced.

"No." He glanced back at the other tribesman, who was now scowling. The man shook his head. "No."

Dannyl nodded and shrugged, then thanked them for showing Merria the bands. The pair replied with fixed smiles. Dannyl led Merria away.

"Who is Unh?" she asked, when they were out of earshot.

"The tracker who helped us search for Lorkin."

"Ah." She glanced back. "Is it only me that got the impression they do know him, but don't like him very much."

"Not just you."

"How interesting," she murmured. "I hope this doesn't mean they won't bring some of those bands for me."

They turned a corner and started down the next row. Dannyl looked up and came to a halt as he saw what lay before them.

Stalls filled with books, scrolls and writing implements lined each side of the aisle. He looked from side to side, his eyes drawn to piles of promising old tomes. Suddenly he knew why there had been a slight hint of smugness in Tayend's tone when suggesting a market visit.

It wasn't just that he'd suggested something I hadn't thought of. He knew I'd find this. He's probably been here already, what with his fondness for silly or exotic trinkets, and he probably guessed that I hadn't. He felt a pang of fondness for his former lover, but it was followed by a mix of guilt and annoyance that was growing familiar since Tayend had arrived in Arvice. *I'm going to have to thank him for this. I wish the prospect didn't fill me with doubt and dread.*

"I may take some time here," he told Merria apologetically.

She smiled. "I thought you might. It's fine. Anything you want me to look for?"

CHAPTER 6

A WARNING

As Lorkin paused in his work, he noted that more than half of the beds in the Care Room were occupied, though most of the patients would probably leave once they'd seen Kalia. Nearly every person had the same or similar illness. Even in isolated, remote Sanctuary, people came down with sniffles and coughs each winter. They called it "chill fever."

The treatment was so trusted and familiar that few questions were asked. Kalia's examination of those claiming to have the illness was perfunctory, and she rarely needed to explain the cures she handed out.

This was Kalia's area of expertise. Lorkin was given the task of looking after anyone who came in with other injuries or illness. No sufferer of chill fever ever approached him. If Kalia was occupied, they settled onto a bed and watched her patiently, only occasionally glancing at him in curiosity.

The main cures were a chest rub and a bitter-tasting tea. Children were given sweets to suck if they wouldn't drink the tea. The sweets were still quite strong and unpleasant, so that only those who truly had the sickness—and whose sense of taste was dulled—could tolerate them. Enough tea and sweets were handed out to last patients a few days. They had to return to be examined again, if they needed more.

It was the first time he'd seen the Traitors so strictly rationing their supplies. He knew that food stores would have to be monitored and controlled in order for the valley's produce to sustain the people through the winter, but so far he hadn't seen any tough restrictions coming into effect. They were talked about, however, and anyone seen to be eating more than was considered reasonable was treated with a teasing disapproval, but also an underlying tone of warning.

No magicians had come to the Care Room with chill fever, since they were naturally resistant to illnesses, so Lorkin was surprised to see one of them entering the room, her nose and eyelids a tell-tale shade of red. He turned back to the task of re-bandaging the ulcerated leg of an old man. The man chuckled.

"Thought she was a magician, didn't you?" he croaked.

Lorkin smiled. "Yes," he admitted.

"No. Her mother is. Sister is. Grandmother was. She isn't, but she likes to pretend she is."

"In the Allied Lands, all magicians have to wear a uniform so everyone knows what they are. It's illegal to dress as a magician if you are not one."

The old man smiled thinly. "Oh, they wouldn't like that here."

"Because it would make it obvious that not everyone is equal?"

The man snorted. "No, because they don't like being told what to do."

Lorkin laughed quietly. He secured the bandage and slipped the old man an extra dose of pain cure. *What will I do if we run out of it, and other cures?*

He could start to Heal patients, but the timing would not be good. *If I'm forced to use my Healing powers it should be for a better reason than because I let us run out of cures.*

"Have you ever been to the old viewing rooms high above the city?" the old man asked.

"The ones that were made long before the Traitors discovered the valley?"

"Yes. A friend of yours told me she was going there. Said to tell you."

Lorkin stared at the old man, then smiled and looked away.

"She did, did she?"

"And I need help getting back to my room."

Kalia didn't look suspicious when Lorkin told her the man wanted his help, but she did tell him to return as quickly as possible. Once they had walked a few hundred paces, the old man told Lorkin he was fine to continue on his own, but Lorkin insisted on accompanying him all the way to his room. Only then did Lorkin hurry away to the viewing rooms. He had to climb several stairs to get there, and by the time he arrived at the door to the first room he was breathing heavily.

Once he had passed through the heavy door his exhalations became billowing clouds of mist. The air was very cold, and he quickly created a magical barrier around himself and warmed the air within it. The room was long and narrow, the only furniture some rough wooden benches stacked up against the back wall. Glassless windows were spaced along the length.

A woman leaned against the window edge, and this time his heart flipped over at the sight of her. Tyvara smiled faintly. He managed to restrain the urge to grin in return.

"Why don't they fill them in with glass?" Lorkin asked, waving to the openings. "It would be a lot easier to heat the space."

"We don't have the materials to make that much glass," she told him, walking forward to meet him.

"You could bring some up here from the lowlands."

She shook her head. "It's not important enough to risk discovery over."

"Surely you've brought materials up here before?"

"A few times. We prefer to find out how to make things ourselves, or do without. We don't do without much, really." She beckoned him over to a window. The valley below was now covered in snow, the cliff walls rising stark and grey above the spread of white. "Did Evar tell you that we grow plants in caves lit and heated by stones?"

"No." He felt his curiosity spark. "Is that also how you protect the animals during winter—keeping them in caves?"

"Yes, though they are mostly fed grain and we will cull some and freeze the meat once it's cold enough to make ice caves."

"Ice caves. I would like to see them," he said wistfully. "But I don't expect anybody is going to take me on any tours of the caves of Sanctuary for a while."

She shook her head. "No." A frown creased her forehead and she looked away. "I'm not supposed to be talking to you."

"I know. Yet here we are."

She smiled faintly, then grew serious again.

"Have you seen Evar recently?"

He shook his head. "Have you?"

"Yes. But I am worried about him."

Lorkin felt a stab of concern. "Why?"

She looked at him, her expression doubtful. But it wasn't self-doubt, or indecision. She seemed to be weighing up whether to tell him something.

"I have a warning to give you, but I have to be indirect, and I don't want you interpreting it in other ways." She glanced around the room, then leaned toward him and lowered her voice despite there being nobody else in the room. "Women may try to lure you into their bed in the next few weeks. Don't accept any invites—unless you're absolutely sure they're not magicians."

He stared back at her, fighting the urge to grin.

"Some already have. I didn't—"

"That's different," she said, waving a hand dismissively. "This is...they won't be doing it because they like you. More the opposite." She looked at him closely, her expression serious. "Will you heed my warning?"

"Of course," he said, smiling and hoping it looked like one of gratitude rather than glee. *She's jealous. She wants me all for herself.*

"You're taking it the wrong way," she told him, her eyes narrowing. "There truly is a risk. What they could be planning can be dangerous. It can kill."

At that he felt his smug jubilation melt away and his stomach plummeted as he suddenly understood what she was alluding to: Lover's Death.

"They're planning to assassinate me?"

She shook her head. "No. That is against the law. But if you accidentally died, particularly in that way..." She let the sentence hang, merely spreading her hands in a helpless gesture. "The punishment is a lot milder."

He nodded and met her gaze, now able to keep his face straight with no effort. "I will not bed any Traitors until you say I can."

She rolled her eyes and stepped away toward the door. "It's only the magicians you have to be wary of, Lorkin. What you do with the rest is not my business. Though it would be appreciated if you did what's necessary to prevent siring a whole lot of children, because we already have a lot of mouths to feed." She looked back at him. "I have to go now."

"And I must get back to the Care Room, too." He sighed. "Not for love of Kalia's company, but I suspect this chill fever is going to get much worse."

She nodded, her eyes warm with approval, but then her expression became sad. "It happens every year. Always kills a few. Usually the old, young, or those who are already weakened by sickness. You had better be ready for that."

He nodded to show he understood. "Thanks for the warning." He smiled. "Both of them."

She smiled in return. Together they headed for the door and the warmth of the stairs beyond. She told him to go first, so that they wouldn't be seen re-entering the city together. He glanced back once to see her staring far beyond the walls surrounding her, looking both worried and determined. He felt his heart lift again. She had come to see him, defying orders to avoid him. He hoped her defiance wouldn't be noticed, and that she would search him out again.

• • •

"So when is Lord Dorrien setting out for home?" Jonna asked as she gave the wineglasses a last rub with her polishing cloth.

"Tomorrow morning," Sonea replied. She looked up at her aunt and servant, and caught a strange look on the older woman's face. "What?"

Jonna shook her head, set the wineglass down and scanned Sonea's guest room. She moved to the low table where the evening's meal would be served and began polishing the cutlery. Again. "Nothing important. Just thinking about ways things could have been."

Sonea sighed and crossed her arms. "Are you still lamenting that I didn't marry Dorrien?"

Jonna spread her hands in protest. "He is a very nice man."

Oh, no. Not this again. "He is," Sonea agreed. "But if I had married him I'd have moved to the country and you'd have never seen me."

"Nonsense," Jonna replied, her eyes flashing with triumph. "The Guild would never have let you out of their sight."

"Which would have forced Dorrien to stay here, and that would have been a cruel thing to do to him. He doesn't like the city."

Jonna shrugged. "He might change his mind when he gets old."

"That's a long—"

A knock at the door interrupted Sonea. She abandoned the old argument with relief and sent a little magic to the door latch. It clicked open and the door swung inward to reveal Regin standing outside.

"Black Magician Sonea," he said. "May I speak with you privately?"

"Lord Regin!" Sonea said, perhaps a little too enthusiastically. "Come in!"

He stepped into the guest room and glanced at Jonna as the woman slipped into Sonea's bedroom to give them privacy. Then the items on the table caught his eye.

"You're expecting guests," he observed. "I had best not linger." He straightened and met her gaze. "I'm here to tell you that a family matter has arisen that is going to take up much of my time and attention, and since I will not be able to reliably offer you my help in hunting and—more importantly—capturing the Thief Skellin then I feel you will be better served by another assistant."

Sonea stared at him in dismay. "Oh," she said. "That's..." She felt briefly disorientated. What was she going to do without Regin to help her catch Skellin? *I thought our search couldn't be going any worse.* She shook her head. *I can't believe this, but I'm going to sorely regret losing Regin's help.* "That's a great shame," she said. "I've appreciated your help and wish you were able to continue assisting me. But your family should have first claim on your attention," she added quickly.

His smile was rather grimace-like. He almost seemed to wince. "They always do."

"I hope this matter resolves itself quickly and painlessly."

"I dou—..." Regin's voice faded to silence as another knock came from the door. He glanced at it, then turned back to her and inclined his head. "It was a pleasure working with you, Black Magician Sonea. I had best be leaving you to your guests."

Sonea opened the door again. In the corridor outside, Rothen and Dorrien waited. They saw Regin and curiosity sparked in their gazes as they nodded to him politely.

"Lord Regin," they murmured.

"Lord Rothen, Lord Dorrien. I am just leaving. Enjoy your meal." As they stepped back, Regin moved past them. Sonea heard his footsteps in the corridor as he walked away, then her guests came inside and closed the door.

"Any news?" Rothen asked.

Sonea shook her head. "Not of the kind we want. On the contrary, Regin can't help us any more. A family matter, he says."

"Oh." Rothen frowned in dismay.

"That's what I said. Though in a more formal and verbose manner that included my gratitude and regret, of course."

"Of course." Rothen chuckled, but his frown quickly returned. "What will we do without him?"

Dorrien looked from his father to Sonea. "You needed his help that badly?"

"Not so much for the searching," Rothen replied. "Cery is in a better position to do that. For the actual capture of Skellin."

Sonea waved them to their seats. Jonna reappeared from the bedroom and raised an eyebrow at Sonea. At Sonea's nod she left to get the meal that was being prepared for them.

"So it doesn't have to be Regin. Could *I* take his place?" Dorrien asked, looking from Rothen to Sonea.

Sonea frowned. "You have to get back to your village."

"Yes, but I could make arrangements and return." He

smiled at her. "There's a Healer living in another village about half a day's ride away. We have an agreement that we'll look after the other's patients whenever we go to the city."

"But this could take a lot longer than a few weeks," Sonea warned.

"You should not leave Alina and the girls for too long either," Rothen agreed. He turned to Sonea. "I can help when the time comes."

"No—" Sonea began.

"You don't know how powerful Skellin is," Dorrien interrupted, frowning at his father in disapproval. "What if he is stronger than you? You're not as powerful as Lord Regin. You said so yourself."

"I'll be with Sonea."

"What if you're not? What if you two are separated?" Dorrien shook his head. "It's too risky for you, Father."

Sonea nodded. She didn't agree with Dorrien's reasoning, since Rothen wasn't any less powerful than the average magician, but Rothen was getting old and physically slower, which might be a problem if they had to chase someone.

"You're not much stronger than me," Rothen pointed out.

"But I *am* stronger," Dorrien said. He looked at Sonea, his gaze bright. "Alina and I have been thinking we should move to the city for a while so that Tylia can get used to life here before she joins the University. We intended to at least stay here for the first few months after Tylia starts lessons." He turned to his father. "I've already told Lady Vinara of my plans, though no specific dates as yet. It would not be difficult to move here earlier."

Rothen regarded his son without speaking, obviously caught up in conflicting emotions. *He would love to see more of his grandchildren*, Sonea guessed, *but doesn't want to agree to something that could put his son's life at risk.*

Her own heart had lifted at the thought. It would be nice to have Dorrien around for longer than his usual visits to the Guild. She could do with his help, too. Though she, too, would rather not put him at risk, she'd also rather not put *anybody* at risk. At least he was willing to work with her and sensible enough to know when to keep secrets.

The tense silence was broken by yet another knock at the door. As it opened, three servants, led by Jonna, filed in carrying platters of food. Jonna's eyebrows rose when none of them spoke. She gave Sonea a look that said *"I'll be back to find out what all this is about,"* before she left, taking her assistants with her.

When the door had closed, Sonea leaned forward and began serving.

"I wonder what family matters we have to blame for taking Regin away from us," she said.

Rothen looked thoughtful. "Sometimes I wish I hadn't stopped going to the Night Room to listen to the gossip."

"I'll see what I can find out," Dorrien said, shrugging.

"In one night?" Sonea scoffed.

Dorrien's eyes twinkled with mischief. "When you only visit the Guild for a few weeks a year, everyone falls over themselves to fill you in on the latest scandals. I'll have to leave you both a little earlier tonight to be there at the right time, but if there's an answer to be had I'll have it for you tomorrow morning."

• • •

Soft, slippery cloth cascaded over Lilia's head and tumbled toward the floor, but at the last moment it was pulled tight at her waist and swung into artful folds. Naki stepped back.

"It fits perfectly." There was amusement and annoyance in her voice, and she crossed her arms and affected a pout. "It's not fair. I've grown out of everything, and there's no point giving it to you because we'll never get to wear gowns again." Then she smiled. "You look great. Go take a peek in the mirror."

Lilia approached the mirror hesitantly and stared at herself. She didn't quite fill out the chest of the dress, but that could be fixed with some padding. Though she had often seen her former employer's wife and daughters dressed so fancily, she would have never dared try on their clothing.

"You look beautiful," Naki said, coming up behind Lilia. She placed her hands on Lilia's shoulders. Her fingers were cold, and sent a shiver down Lilia's spine. She remembered what Madie and Froje had said about her new friend, then quickly pushed the thought away.

Naki frowned. "You're all tense. What's wrong? Is it uncomfortable?"

Lilia shook her head. "I feel...well...we're doing something forbidden. Magicians are supposed to always wear robes."

Naki's lips curled into a mischievous grin. "I know. It's kind of fun, isn't it?"

Looking at her friend's grin, Lilia could not help smiling. "Yes, but that's only because nobody else can see us."

"It's our naughty secret," Naki said, turning away. She

stooped to grab the hem of her dress and hauled it up and over her head in one movement. Underneath she was wearing only an undershift, and Lilia quickly averted her eyes.

"In fact, you should do something *really* naughty," Naki continued as she shrugged into her novice overrobe. "Then you'll be able to do mildly naughty things like this and not get all uptight about it." She paused to think, then grinned. "I know just the thing. Stay there. I'll be right back."

Naki disappeared through the main door to her bedroom. Taking the opportunity to change while her friend wasn't watching, Lilia slipped off the dress and hurriedly changed into her robes. As she was tying the sash, Naki returned carrying a small black object. She held it up with a triumphant flourish.

It was like a metal bird cage, only smaller and chunkier. Lilia stared at it in bemusement. Naki laughed. She gave the cage a direct look, and smoke began curling out of the openings. Understanding came to Lilia in a rush of realisation, dismay and curiosity.

"It's a roet brazier!"

"Of course." Naki rolled her eyes. "You're so innocent, Lilia. It's hard to believe you are a daughter of a servant family."

"My family's employer didn't approve of roet."

Naki shrugged. "Lots of people don't. They don't trust new things. Eventually they'll see that roet isn't any worse than wine—and in some ways is better. You don't get hangovers." She began scooping the air toward herself and breathing deeply. After a few breaths she closed her eyes and sighed with appreciation. Her gaze was dark and seductive as she looked at Lilia, and beckoned. "Come closer. Try it."

Lilia obeyed. She leaned toward the brazier and breathed deeply. A fragrant smoke filled her lungs. She coughed, and Naki covered her mouth and giggled. Instead of feeling hurt that her friend had laughed at her, Lilia found she didn't mind. More smoke filled her chest. Her head began to spin.

"I found a great place for this last time," Naki said, moving to her bed. She hung the brazier on a clothes hanger, pushing the dresses to the other end of the rail. Then she flopped on the bed.

Lilia laughed again. Turning to smile at her, Naki patted the bedcovers. "Come lie down. It's very relaxing."

To Lilia's relief, the prospect of lying on a bed next to Naki roused only a mild, distant echo of the nervousness she would have once felt. She sank onto the mattress beside her friend.

"Still worried about getting into trouble?" Naki asked.

"No. Suddenly I don't care about anything."

"That's what roet does. It stops you caring. Stops you worrying." She turned her head to regard Lilia. "You seem worried a lot lately."

"Yes."

"What about?"

"The girls in my class. The ones that were my friends. They said things about you."

Naki laughed. "I bet they did. What did they say?"

Why did I say that? Curse it. I can't tell her...or can I? It would be good to know the truth... "That...that you like women. Instead of men. I mean..." Lilia took a deep breath and coughed again as the smoke filled her lungs. "I mean you prefer women lovers the way some men prefer male lovers." She covered her mouth with a hand. *Why did I do that? Why did I just blurt it out? Naki is going to hate me!*

But Naki only laughed again. A carefree, mischievous laugh. "I bet that gave them interesting dreams for months."

Lilia chuckled. She tried to imagine Froje and Madie daydreaming about... *no, don't think about it.*

"You want to know if it's true."

Lilia blinked in surprise, then turned her head to look at Naki.

Her friend met her eyes and smiled. "It is. And it is for you, isn't it? Or... you're not sure."

Face burning with sudden heat, Lilia looked away. "I..."

"Go on. You can tell me."

"Well... I think so... um... any advice about that?"

Naki turned over and pushed herself up into a sitting position. "My advice is to not worry about it." She reached up and unhooked the brazier. It had stopped smoking. "Women have fallen in love with women for centuries. Men always assumed they were just close friends. Which is the opposite to men, who can't be close friends for fear others will think they're really in love." She giggled, then got off the bed and beckoned. "Girls like us can keep secrets easily because nobody pays us the attention they should. Let's go to the library."

Lilia sat up, then paused and closed her eyes as her head began to spin. "The library? Why the library? Why now?"

"Because there's something I want to show you before Father gets home. I want some more roet."

"You keep roet in the library?"

"Father does."

"Your *father* uses roet?"

Naki gave a humourless laugh. "Of course he does."

She led the way out of her rooms and through corridors and down staircases. Lilia wondered what time it was. Late enough that there were no servants about, it seemed.

"My father's family have lots of sordid habits," Naki said. "For my uncle it was girls. I don't mean he likes women a lot. I mean he likes *little* girls. The servants knew and kept me out of his way whenever he came visiting. Father never believed me when I told him."

Lilia shuddered. "That's horrible."

Naki glanced back and smiled, but her eyes were hard. "Oh, he paid for it in the end." She turned away and stopped at a door. "Here we are."

She pushed through the door into an enormous room. Lilia could not restrain a gasp as she took in all the shelves stuffed with books and rolls of paper. She had learned quickly that Naki thought that appearing to be too interested in study was boring, but she couldn't contain her awe and delight now.

"I thought you'd like it."

Lilia looked at Naki, who was grinning widely, and pretended to look embarrassed.

Naki laughed. "You're a terrible actor. Come see something."

She headed for a glass-topped side table. Lilia saw that the glass covered a drawer-like cavity filled with very old books, scrolls, a few sculptures and some jewellery. Naki ran her hand down the narrow side. There was a soft click.

"Father has the top locked with both key and magic,

but he's not so powerful a magician that he'd waste magic protecting the whole case," Naki murmured. She reached inside and drew out a small book, then handed it to Lilia.

The cover was soft skin, slightly powdery with age, and the title had worn off. Opening it, Lilia was disturbed by the brittle stiffness of the pages. They felt as if they would shatter if she attempted to bend them. The writing was faded but still readable, and in an old formal style that was not easy to read.

"What is it?"

"A book on how to use magic," Naki said. "Most of it we know already. Magicians have learned a lot in the last seven hundred years."

"Seven hundred," Lilia breathed. "It's amazing this is still intact."

"It's not that old. This is a copy of the original, and has been rebound several times." Naki looked at Lilia closely. "There is one kind of magic in there that we don't know. Can you guess what it is?"

Lilia considered. "Seven hundred years? Before the Sachakan War...oh!" She turned to stare at her friend. "You're not serious!"

"Yes." A single glint of light lit Naki's dark eyes. "Black magic." She took the book from Lilia and put it back in the case. "I told you my father's family had some dark secrets."

"They don't...they don't *know* black magic, do they?"

"No. Well, I don't think they do. It wouldn't be hard to hide, you know. Black Magician Sonea knew it for ages before the Guild found out, and they only found out about her because High Lord Akkarin got caught. And he was only caught because the Sachakans set him up." She looked at the case. "I reckon you could keep it secret for all your life, and nobody would know. Now this *is* old."

She reached inside and brought out a ring. It was made of gold and a pale stone was set into it.

"My grandmother on my mother's side used to wear this. It was passed down to her by her grandmother, down the line of women for centuries. Mother told me that the stone is magical and she would teach me how to use it one day. Of course, she died before she had a chance to, and Father said I couldn't have it."

"What is it supposed to do?"

"She said it helped a woman to keep secrets."

"Not much point unless you have a secret to hide."

"Or someone to hide it from."

"Have you tried to discover how it works?"

"Of course. It's why I found a way to get to it. But I haven't been able to find a way to test if it works, and the one secret I'm sure it won't hide is whether it's been stolen or not, so I have to put it back each time."

"How could something like that work?"

"Who knows? I think it's just a silly story my mother told me to keep me entertained." Smiling wryly, Naki put back the ring and replaced the side of the case.

"Maybe your father doesn't know black magic. After all, surely he'd wear the ring if it helps hide secrets—if it really does."

Naki's nose wrinkled as she thought about it. Then she shook her head. "I don't think even he would try learning it. He's not one for taking big risks."

Lilia nodded in agreement, surprised at how relieved she was to hear Naki say so.

Her friend suddenly looked up and grinned. "Let's steal more of Father's roet!" Without waiting for an answer, she skipped away to the other side of the room, and Lilia followed.

CHAPTER 7

DECISIONS AND DISCOVERIES

Whenever the Higher Magicians met in the Guild-hall without the rest of the Guild present, their voices echoed in a way that Sonea always found disturbing. She looked out at the two sets of tiered seating that lined the longer walls of the hall. Between was a long, empty space that was only occupied on the few occasions each year when novices were included in ceremonies. At the far end were two large doors. They were the original doors of the building, still sturdy despite being over six hundred years old and having spent a few hundred exposed to the elements before the University was built around the old hall.

The other end of the hall, known as the Front, was where Sonea and the Higher Magicians were seated. The steeply tiered chairs were reached by narrow staircases. Not only did this arrangement allow a good view of the hall for them all, but it made clear the hierarchy of power among the magicians. The topmost seats were for the king and his advisers. The next row down was for the

Guild's leader, the High Lord, and the two newest Higher Magicians—the black magicians.

I've never felt comfortable with the decision to put us up here, Sonea mused. While she and Kallen had the potential to become stronger than any other magician in the Guild, they had no greater power or influence than any other Higher Magician. They were forbidden to use black magic unless ordered to and, unlike most ordinary magicians, were restricted in where they could go.

Perhaps putting us up here was intended as compensation for that. But I suspect the main reason was to avoid having to do some major carpentry to the Front. There's simply no room to add two more magicians below us.

Her attention snapped back to the meeting as Administrator Osen's voice rose to address them all.

"Those in favour of blocking Lorandra's powers, raise your hands."

Sonea lifted hers. She counted the raised hands around her and was relieved to see that most of the Higher Magicians supported the action.

"The vote is cast; Lorandra's powers will be blocked." Osen looked up at Kallen. "Black Magician Kallen will establish the block."

A few magicians glanced at Sonea and she resisted a grim smile. There was no reason a black magician had to put the block in place, but it had become one of the duties that she and Kallen were expected to perform. *I think everyone assumes it's easier for us, since we can get around a mind's natural tendency to push out an unwelcome visitor. Perhaps it is; I never had to do it before I learned black magic, so I have no way to compare.*

Forcing a block onto an unwilling person was never a

pleasant task, but she would have made herself do it if it
had given her the opportunity to read Lorandra's mind.
When Administrator Osen had asked if she would do it,
however, she'd had to refuse. If she was to bribe Lorandra
with the promise of unblocking her power, the intention
of dishonesty might be faintly detectable, and warn the
woman to not trust Sonea. She hadn't been so specific
when explaining the reason for her refusal to Osen. She'd
simply said she didn't want to give Lorandra even more
reason to refuse to cooperate with her in the search for
Skellin.

Sonea did not want to have to deceive Lorandra, but
the search for the rogue magician was going nowhere.
They'd lost Regin's help. Cery was expending as much
effort keeping out of the reach of Skellin's people and
allies as in trying to find where Skellin was. To send Anyi
off to spy for Cery, or to drag Dorrien's family to Imardin
so he could risk his life helping her, seemed far worse
than lying to a woman who had defied the Guild's laws,
murdered Thieves and imported roet in the hope of setting her son up as king of the underworld.

*I admit that, for all that I was impatient for the Guild
to stop dithering and make the obvious decision, I was in
no hurry to start the deception. Until Lorandra's powers
were blocked there was nothing to bribe her with. But
now . . . she sighed . . . now there will be no putting it off for
much longer.*

Osen announced the meeting was over, and the hall
began to echo with the sounds of boots on wooden steps,
voices and the rustle of robes. Rothen waited for Sonea to
descend to the level of the Heads of Studies, then followed
close behind her.

"It turns out Dorrien is as good as he claims to be at attracting gossips," he murmured.

Reaching the floor, she moved a little apart from the rest of the magicians.

"What did he say?"

"That Lord Regin and his wife are at odds."

"That's illuminating," Sonea said dryly. "Did he find out what they were at odds over?"

Rothen opened his mouth, then, as he saw Lady Vinara coming toward them, closed it again and shook his head.

"Lady Vinara," Sonea said as the woman reached them, Rothen echoing the greeting.

"Black Magician Sonea, Lord Rothen," the elderly Healer said, nodding at each of them in turn. "You must be looking forward to having Lord Dorrien and his family living in Imardin sooner than first planned."

Sonea looked at Rothen, who returned her questioning look with one of his own.

"So he's made definite arrangements now?" Rothen asked, his tone full of resigned amusement.

Vinara smiled sympathetically. "Yes. He set a date so I can schedule him in to work at the Healers' Quarters." She turned to Sonea. "He wants to work at the hospices, but I felt it would be wise to have him for a short time where I can evaluate his grasp of recent Healing advances before I set him loose on the city."

Sonea nodded. "I agree. Thank you," she said, with heartfelt gratitude. She had never needed to order Dorrien around, and suspected he would be more challenging to direct than any other Healer. As a more senior Healer, who had once been his teacher, rather than a younger woman he had first met as a novice, Vinara would have no trouble correcting any bad habits Dorrien might have picked up.

Vinara nodded and moved away. Turning to Rothen, Sonea gave him a speculative look. He spread his hands and opened his eyes wide.

"Don't look at me like that! I didn't know!" He shook his head in exasperation. "He realised we'd both work together to make him promise not to come back to the Guild if he told us before he left."

Sonea shrugged. "Do you mind if he joins me? Just because he's moving back to Imardin earlier than planned doesn't mean he has to be involved in the search."

Rothen's eyebrows rose. "I doubt you'd be able to stop him."

She smiled wryly. "No, not once he starts working at the hospices. I'm sorry Rothen. I'll do what I can to ensure he stays safe."

"Why are you apologising to me?"

"For getting your son involved in a dangerous search for a rogue magician."

"You haven't done anything to encourage him," he pointed out. "Instead, I should apologise for raising my son to be such a stubborn, persistent man."

Sonea laughed bitterly. "I don't think either of us can be blamed for how our sons turned out, Rothen. Some things are out of a parent's hands."

The record books that Dannyl had bought in the market had cost him a small fortune. The seller wouldn't tell him at first where they'd come from, but when Dannyl had hinted he'd be keen to buy more the man had admitted they came from an estate at the edge of the wasteland which, like many, was failing due to the advance of the dust and sands.

The seller might have meant it as a reproach, but Dannyl had felt a guilty excitement in response. If other estates were selling their property to survive, there might be more records to buy. The drying effect of the wastes had kept the books and scrolls in good condition, too.

Not surprisingly, the records Dannyl had purchased often referred to the wasteland.

> *Visited Ashaki Tachika. He took me to see the dam-age to his estate. All within the area was burned. Not even bones of animals to remind us of the deaths here. The exact edge is hard to find, as wind has blown ash into the unburned land, and in the weeks since the blast plants have begun to sprout within the burned parts. The air smelled of smoke and unanswered questions. Agreed to twenty gold for five reber, including a young male.*

The record Dannyl was reading was written in an eco-nomical style, but from time to time the Ashaki author slipped from strict record-keeping into evocative descrip-tion. Dannyl was intrigued by the reference to plants growing within the wasteland so soon after its creation. It made him wonder afresh why the land had not recovered. Had these plants struggled for a time, then failed?

Reading on, Dannyl spent hours skimming the record before he found anything interesting again. When he did, he checked dates and was surprised. Nearly twenty years had passed before the author mentioned the wasteland again.

Ashaki Tachika has sold his estate and moved to Arvice. He says he will be dead before the damaged land recovers and worries that the land will never support crops again. It is a pity. He had such success at first, but recently many estates have suffered the same reversal. It is a mystery why this is so.

Mentions of the wasteland grew in frequency after that. Picking up the last of the record books in the set, he soon encountered what he had begun to anticipate.

The wastes have passed the boundary. The slaves reported it to Kova, and when he told me I rode out to see it for myself. It has taken more than thirty years for it to touch my estate, though the dusts have preceded it since the day after the great blast.

Ashaki Tachika's land is gone. Will mine and Valicha's die in the next thirty years? Will my son inherit a doomed estate and future? Despite all the Ashaki say to deny it, their rejection of my son's proposals of marriage to their daughters reveals their lie. Maybe it will be better if there is no grandson to inherit our troubles.

Not long after the entry, the handwriting changed. The son reported his father's death and continued in the old man's habit of brief entries mainly recording trade agreements. Dannyl's heart was heavy with sympathy for the family, even after reminding himself that they were black magicians and slave owners. In the world that they knew and understood, they were sliding toward poverty and extinction.

Dannyl looked at his notes, leafing back to where he'd started. The record had begun a few years after occupation by Kyralia. The original author had been young, perhaps having inherited from an Ashaki who had died in the war. He wrote little about his Kyralian rulers. On the day the wasteland was created he described a bright light coming in his window, and later mentioned that it had taken three days for the slaves blinded by it to recover enough to work.

He did not speculate in the record on the cause of the light or destruction. *Perhaps he was wary of putting any accusations or discontent toward Kyralians down on paper.*

One last book remained of the pile he'd bought. It was a small and tattered thing, and grains of sand had worked their way into every fold and crack, suggesting it had once been buried. When he opened it he saw that the writing was so faded it was almost impossible to read.

He was well prepared for that. Librarians at the Great Library in Elyne had developed methods for reviving old texts. Some of these ultimately destroyed the book, while others were gentler and could revive the ink for a short time. How effective they were depended on the type of paper and ink. In either case, if pages were treated one at a time a copy could be made before they disintegrated or faded.

Taking out jars of solutions and powders from a box on his desk, he set to work testing them on the corners of a few pages. To his relief, one of the less destructive methods enhanced the ink enough to make the writing just readable for a while. He began to apply it to the first page, and as the words became clear he felt his heart beat a little faster.

The book, written in very tiny handwriting, had belonged to the wife of an Ashaki. Though she began each page with a heading suggesting that the text was about some domestic or cosmetic matter, the writing that followed quickly changed to matters of politics. "Salve for Dry Hair and Scalp," for example, turned into a scathing assessment of the emperor's cousin.

"Emperor"? Dannyl frowned. *If there is an emperor, then this was written before the Sachakan War.*

He read on, carefully treating each page with the solution and impatiently watching the words appear. Soon he realised he was wrong. The woman only referred to the defeated emperor by his title because she did not have an alternative, and the Sachakans hadn't yet adopted the term "king" for their ruler.

Which means this diary was written some time after the war but within twenty years of it.

The writer had included no dates, so he had no way to know how much time had passed between entries. She never used names, instead referring to people by physical appearance.

Useful Cures for Womanly Times
Once a month a cycle of events brings many ills. Leading up to it there is often much anxiety, bad temper and bloating, and when the time comes it may be a relief, though it is always draining. The challenge is containment. The careless will experience leaks—often not noticing until it is too late. How else do I find out what the pale ones are planning? They trust the slaves, thinking them grateful for freedom. It is not hard to make the slaves talk.

The crazy emperor knows. That is why he claimed the betrayer's slave for himself. Better to keep an eye on it always. Take the hero's property and you replace the hero in the slaves' eyes. The crazy emperor wanted the pale ones to take our children and have their own people raise them. Make our little ones hate us. But the kind one argued against the plan and the others supported him. I bet they regret making the mad one their leader.

As Dannyl waited for another page to respond to the treatment, he considered the last passage he'd read. The woman had referred to the "crazy emperor" many times. He didn't think the man was an actual emperor, just a leader. If the "pale ones" were Kyralians then this was the magician who had led them, Lord Narvelan. Dannyl was intrigued by the suggestion that Narvelan had adopted a slave as his own. The slave of the "betrayer," who was also a hero. He squinted at the slowly darkening text.

Proper Manners Toward Visitors

Respect is given first to the Ashaki, then to the magician, then to the free man. Men before women. Older before younger. Theft is a great offence, and today our pale visitors were robbed by one of their own. By their own crazy emperor. He took the weapon from our throats and ran. Many of the pale ones have given chase. It is a great opportunity. I am angry and sad. My people are too cowed, even to take the advantage they have. They say the crazy emperor may return with the knife, and punish us. They are cowards.

From the way the writing changed from neat letters to a scrawl, he guessed that a jump in time had occurred in the middle of the entry and the latter part was added hastily or in anger. The reference to a weapon was not new—the diary's author had referred to it already as a reason the Sachakans feared to rise up against the Kyralians. But now Narvelan had stolen it. Why?

> *How to Respond to News of a Rival's Death*
> *Our freedom is inevitable and comes at the hands of a fool! A great blast of magic has scoured the land to the north-west. Such power could only have come from the storestone. No other artefact or magician is that powerful. It is clear the crazy emperor tried to use it when his people confronted him, but lost control of it. We are rid of both of them! Many of the pale ones died, so there are still far fewer here to control us. There is fear that they have another weapon. But if they do not bring it here, my people will rise out of their cowardice and take back their own land. The land burned by the storestone will recover. We will be strong again.*

Dannyl felt a chill run down his spine. In her excitement, the diary writer had referred to the weapon by its real name: the storestone. So if she was right, Narvelan had taken the stone. He had attempted to use it, lost control and created the wasteland.

It all makes sense when put together like that. Except that there is no obvious reason why Narvelan would steal the storestone. Perhaps he didn't need a good reason if he was truly as mad as the records paint him.

Suddenly the binding cracked and several pages fell out. Looking back at the first page, Dannyl saw that the writing was already fading again. He drew out several sheafs of paper and topped up the ink in the well. Then he called for a slave to bring sumi and some food.

I am copying out this book now, he decided. *Even if it takes me all night.*

Lilia hesitated, eyeing the large, stern man inside the doorway. Though he had bowed, it had been a token gesture. Something about him made her uneasy. The man scowled when she didn't slip in after Naki. His eyes flickered to the street behind her, checking for something. Then he opened his mouth.

"Coming in or not?"

The voice was surprisingly high and girlish, and for a second Lilia fought the urge to giggle. Her nervousness disappeared and she moved past him into the dingy hallway.

It wasn't much of a hallway. There was just enough room for the guard to stand and people to pass him and reach the staircase. Naki began to climb to the next floor. Odd, muffled sounds were coming from behind the walls and the air smelled of a mixture of the strange and familiar. Lilia felt anxiety begin to pluck at her again.

She had guessed what sort of place this was. She'd known from Naki's mysterious behaviour—refusing to say where they were going—that it was unlikely they were headed for more conventional evening entertainment. While novices weren't forbidden to enter such places, they weren't supposed to frequent them.

They were called brazier houses. Or pleasure houses. As the two girls reached the landing at the top of the stairs, a woman in an expensive but rather tacky dress bowed and asked them what they desired.

"A brazier room," Naki replied. "And some wine."

The woman gestured that they should follow her and started down the corridor.

"Haven't seen you here in a while, novice Naki," a male voice said from behind Lilia.

Naki stopped. Lilia noted there was no eagerness in Naki's face as she turned to look back. The smile her friend wore was forced.

"Kelin," she said. "It has been too long. How's business?"

Lilia turned to see a short, stocky man with squinty eyes standing half in, half out of a doorway. His lips parted and crooked teeth flashed. If it was a smile, there was no friendliness about it.

"*Very* good," he replied. "I'd invite you in," his eyes flickered to Lilia, "but I see you have better company to distract you."

"I do, indeed." Naki stepped forward and hooked an arm in Lilia's. "But thank you for considering it," she called back over her shoulder, taking a step forward and guiding Lilia after the serving woman.

They were led upstairs and to a small room with a roomy two-seater chair and a tiny fireplace with a brazier sitting on the tiles before it. A narrow window allowed a mix of moonlight and lamplight in, which was barely challenged by the small shaded lamps hanging either side of the fireplace. The air smelled of fragrant smoke and something faintly sour.

"Tiny, but cosy and private," Naki said, gesturing at the room.

"Who was that man?" Lilia asked as they settled on the chair.

Naki's nose wrinkled. "A friend of the family. He did my father a favour once, and now acts like he's a relation." She shrugged. "He's all right though, once you understand what he values." She turned to Lilia. "That's the secret to people: knowing what they value."

"What do you value?" Lilia asked.

Her friend tilted her head to the side as she considered. The lamplight set her profile glowing softly. *She looks best at night*, Lilia found herself thinking. *It's her natural time of day.*

"Friendship," Naki said. "Trust. Loyalty." She leaned closer, her smile widening. "Love." Lilia's breath caught in her throat, but her friend leaned away again. "You?"

Lilia breathed in, then out, but her head was spinning. *And we haven't even started on the roet.* "The same," she said, afraid she was taking too long to answer. *Love? Is it possible? Do I love Naki? I definitely have more fun when I'm with her, and there's something about her that's both exciting and a bit scary.*

Naki was staring at her intently. She said nothing; she just stared. Then a knock came from the door. Naki looked away and opened it with magic. Lilia felt a warring relief and disappointment as the serving woman brought in a tray carrying a bottle of wine, goblets and an ornate box.

"Ah!" Naki said eagerly, ignoring the serving woman's bow and retreat. She picked up the box and dumped a handful of the contents into the brazier. A flame flared among the coals, no doubt fired by Naki's magic, and smoke began to curl into the air.

Lilia busied herself opening and pouring the wine. She handed a goblet to Naki as the girl returned to the seat. Naki lifted the glass.

"What should we dedicate the wine to?" she asked.

"Well, of course: trust, loyalty and love."

"Trust, loyalty and love," Lilia repeated. They both sipped the wine.

A comfortable silence fell between them. The smoke from the brazier wafted across the room. Naki leaned forward and breathed deeply. Chuckling, Lilia did the same, feeling as if her thoughts were knotted muscles slowly loosening and unravelling. She leaned back in the chair and sighed.

"Thank you," she found herself saying.

Naki turned to smile at her. "You like it here? I thought you might."

Lilia looked around and shrugged. "It's all right. I was thanking you for...for...for making me less wound up, and showing me how to have fun, and...just being good company."

Naki's smile faded and was replaced by a thoughtful look. Then a familiar glint of mischief entered her eyes, and Lilia could not help bracing herself. Whenever her friend got that look, what followed was likely to be surprising, and not a little confronting.

This time Naki leaned in and quickly but firmly kissed Lilia.

Lips warm and tingling, Lilia stared at her friend in astonishment and, she was all too aware, hope. Her heart was racing. Her mind spun. *That was certainly surprising*, she thought. *But, like everything Naki does, not as confronting as it seemed it might be.*

Slowly, deliberately, Naki did it again, only this time she did not move away. A rush of sensations and thoughts went through Lilia, all of them pleasant and none that could be explained away by the roet smoke or the wine. *The wine*... She was still holding the goblet and wanted not to be. *I think*... Naki's arm had snaked around her waist and she wanted to reach out to her friend—*should I still call Naki "friend" after tonight?* Leaning to one side, she tried to set the goblet on the floor. *I think I am in love*.

But she must have set the glass on an uneven surface, for she heard a clunk and slosh as it fell over.

Uh, oh, she thought. But though she did not make a sound, she heard a faint voice utter it for her. A voice coming from the direction of the fireplace.

That's strange.

She could not help herself. Tilting her head, she looked at the fireplace. Somewhere within the cavity something flickered. Looking closer, she got the strangest impression that something blinked at her.

Someone is watching us.

A shiver of horror ran down her spine and she pushed Naki back a little.

"What is it?" Naki said, her voice even more deep and throaty than usual.

"I saw..." Lilia shook her head, tore her eyes away from the fireplace, which looked dark and ordinary now, and looked at Naki. "I...I don't think I like this place after all. It doesn't seem very...private."

Naki searched her gaze, then smiled. "Fair enough. Let's finish the wine and get out of here."

"I spilled mine..."

"Don't worry." Naki leaned down and picked up the goblet. "They're used to little accidents happening here, though usually when the customers are a bit more inebriated than we are." She refilled the goblet, then held it out to Lilia and smiled. "To love."

Lilia smiled back, feeling the buoyant, exhilarating mood return and her earlier discomfort fade.

"To love."

CHAPTER 8

CONSEQUENCES

The small girl sitting on the edge of the bed was coughing hard, pausing only to take a gasping breath. As Lorkin gave cure-laced sweets and Kalia's instructions to her mother—a magician who, he knew, was aligned with Kalia's faction—the girl looked up at him. He saw in her eyes a pity quite different to the sympathy he felt for her. *She pities me? Why would she pity* me*?*

The mother nodded, took her daughter's hand and moved away. He watched as she walked over to Kalia. Though it had happened before, with other patients, he still felt his stomach sink.

Kalia was busy and he didn't care to watch as the woman checked what he'd told her. He moved on to the next patient, an old woman with dark circles under her eyes and a more concerning, wrenching cough. Now that the chill fever had spread through the city, the Care Room was busy night and day, and Kalia had been forced to involve him in the treating of it. Most Traitors accepted this without question, but now and then someone could not bring themself to trust him—or pretended not to, in order to needle him.

"How many times do I have to tell you?" Kalia said loudly. The old woman's eyes flickered away and then back to Lorkin.

"She means you," she muttered.

Lorkin nodded. "Thanks." He straightened and turned to find Kalia striding toward him. One hand was clasped around something, and she brandished it at him. The mother and daughter trailed behind.

"I told you no more than four a day!" she declared. "Do you want to poison this child?"

Lorkin looked down at the girl, who was grinning widely, excited by the scene she was a part of.

"Of course not," he replied. "Who could ever harm such a pretty child?" The girl's smile faltered. She liked to be flattered, he guessed, but knew her mother would not like her to respond in a friendly way. Not knowing what to do, she looked up at her mother, then frowned and regarded him suspiciously. "I did wonder why you told me to give her more sweets than the other children," he added, unable to resist hinting that Kalia might be favouring her friends with more of the limited supply of cures.

"I did *not* tell you to give her six!" Kalia's voice rose to a higher note.

"Actually, you did," a huskier voice replied.

Startled by the new voice, Lorkin turned to look at the old woman, who gazed back at Kalia unflinchingly. He felt a small surge of hope. However, if Kalia was dismayed she was hiding it well. She looked as if she was humbly thinking back on her instructions, but her eyes were dark and calculating.

Whoever the old woman was, she was influential enough that Kalia hadn't dared to claim she was hard of hearing, or mistaken. Lorkin decided he had to learn the identity of this unexpected ally, as soon as he was free to.

"Perhaps you are right," Kalia said, smiling. "We have been so busy here. We are all tired. I am sorry," she said to the old woman, then she whirled around to face the mother and daughter. "I apologise. Here..." She gave them the sweets and prattled away as she herded the pair toward the door.

"She *must* be tired," the old woman muttered, "if she thought anybody would believe that little charade."

"Not everyone is as smart or observant as you are," Lorkin replied.

The old woman's eyes brightened as she smiled. "No. If they were, she would never have been elected."

Lorkin concentrated on checking the old woman's pulse and temperature, listened to her lungs and examined her throat. He also surreptitiously listened with his magical senses to confirm his assessment. Which was that the old woman was surprisingly healthy apart from the chill fever symptoms. Finally, after giving advice and cures, Lorkin quietly thanked the old woman.

Not long after he'd moved to the next patient, he heard a hum of interest in the room and looked around. All eyes were on the entrance, where a stretcher was floating into the room followed by a magician. The woman was unsuccessfully trying to smother a smile. Looking at the stretcher, Lorkin felt his heart skip.

Evar!

He hadn't seen his friend in some days. The rumour in

the men's room was that Evar had found himself a lover. They'd laid bets on whether Evar would eventually swagger back into the men's room and collect his things, or limp in with a broken heart. None of them had wagered that he would reappear unconscious on a stretcher.

Kalia had noticed and hurried over to examine him. Flipping aside the blanket carelessly, she revealed a completely naked Evar to the room. Smothered giggles and gasps came from all around. Lorkin felt a stab of anger as Kalia didn't bother to re-cover the young man.

"Nothing's broken," the smiling magician told Kalia.

"Let me be the judge of that," Kalia replied. She squeezed and poked, then placed a hand on Evar's forehead. "Over-drained," she pronounced. She looked up at the magician. "You?"

The woman rolled her eyes. "Not likely. It was Leota."

"She ought to be more careful." Kalia sniffed disdainfully, then looked around the room. "He's not sick, and should not take up a bed. Put him over there, on the floor. He'll recover in his own time."

The magician and stretcher moved over to the back of the room where, to Lorkin's relief, Evar would be hidden behind the rows of beds. The woman was grinning as she strode out, not bothering to pull the blanket back over Evar. Kalia ignored the new patient, and scowled at Lorkin when he started toward his friend.

"Leave him be," she ordered.

Lorkin bided his time. Eventually Kalia disappeared into the storeroom for more cures. He slipped over to Evar and was surprised to find the young man's eyes open. Evar smiled ruefully at Lorkin.

"I'm okay," he said. "Not as bad as it looks."

Lorkin pulled the blanket up to cover his friend. "What happened?"

"Leota."

"She used black magic on you?"

"She took me to bed."

"And?"

"Same thing. Except more fun." There was a shrug in Evar's voice. His eyes focused somewhere beyond Lorkin and the ceiling. "It was worth it."

"To have all your energy drained out?" Lorkin could not hide the disbelief and anger from his voice.

Evar looked at him. "How else am I going to get into a woman's bed, eh? Look at me. I'm scrawny and a magician. Hardly good breeding material, and nobody trusts male magicians."

Lorkin sighed and shook his head. "You're not scrawny—and where I come from, being a magician—and a natural—would make you *very* desirable breeding material."

"Yet you left," Evar pointed out. "And chose to stay here for the rest of your life."

"Times like these I wonder if I was sold a lie. Equal society indeed. Will this Leota be punished?"

Evar shook his head. Then his eyes lit up. "I moved. I haven't done that in hours."

Sighing again, Lorkin stood up. "I have to get back to work."

Evar nodded. "Don't worry about me. A bit of sleep and I'll be fine." As Lorkin walked away, he called out. "I still think it was worth it. You doubt me, go have a look at her. Without her clothes."

The incident with the cures had been irritating, but

Lorkin was used to it. What had been done to Evar filled him with a simmering rage. Since Tyvara had warned him not to accept any invitations to a magician's bed he had turned down more propositions than usual. At least he now had a better idea which magicians were in Kalia's faction.

How stupid do they think I am? That's how Riva tried to kill me. He felt a stab of guilt. *I should have warned Evar. But I didn't think they'd harm Kalia's nephew.* Well, they hadn't harmed him: they—Leota—had drained Evar to the point of helplessness, then humiliated him by making his mistake public.

Even so, Evar should have known better. He had known they'd find a way to punish him for taking Lorkin to the stone-makers' caves. Surely it had been obvious what Leota intended when she'd invited him to her bed?

Lorkin shook his head. Perhaps Evar was simply too trusting of his own people. That this was how they repaid his trust disgusted Lorkin, and for the rest of the day he switched back and forth between wondering if he had been wise to come to Sanctuary, and questioning whether the Traitors could ever be made to see how unequal their society really was.

Winter was slowly tightening its grip on Imardin. Standing water froze overnight. The crunch of ice underfoot was strangely satisfying, and brought back childhood memories. *You had to avoid the deeper puddles,* Sonea thought, *as they usually only had a skin of ice, and if the water underneath got into your shoes your feet would hurt from the cold all day.*

Getting water in her shoes hadn't been a concern for

many years. The boots made for magicians were the best in the city and as soon as they showed the slightest sign of wear, servants would fetch replacements. *Which is annoying when you've just worn them in.* Unfortunately, the shoes she was wearing now were neither weatherproof nor worn in to suit her feet. They were cast-offs—part of the disguise she wore when venturing out to meet Cery.

The basket of laundry in her arms was fuller and heavier than usual. She'd had to stop and pick up sheets once already, when they'd tumbled off the top of the pile to the ground. Of course, she couldn't use magic to hold or catch them. That would have revealed that she was more than a delivery woman.

She slowed and ducked into an alleyway. It was a short-cut that the locals often used. Today it was empty but for one other woman hurrying toward her, carrying a small child. As Sonea drew closer, the woman looked up at her. Sonea resisted the urge to pull the hood further over her face. The woman's gaze flickered to something behind Sonea and she frowned, then looked quickly back at Sonea as she passed.

Was that a look of warning?

Resisting the temptation to look back, Sonea slowed her pace and listened carefully. Sure enough, she picked up the soft scrape and pad of footfalls several paces behind her.

Am I being followed? The alley was well used, so someone walking behind her was not so strange. Something else must have alarmed the woman. Perhaps she was naturally suspicious. Perhaps not. Sonea could not afford to ignore the possibility that the woman had reason to be. She quickened her pace.

Reaching the end of the alley, she turned in the opposite direction to the one she had intended to take, crossed the road and entered another alley. This one was wider and filled with workers from the industries housed on either side. Wood for furnaces had been piled up against walls. Barrels of oils and noxious liquids, huge tightly bound bundles of rags, and wooden crates waited to be carried inside. The people and obstructions forced her to take a winding, dodging path until she reached a tower of crates filled with some kind of wilted plant that smelled like the sea.

She slipped behind it and put down the basket. Workers further along the alley eyed her, but as she began rubbing her back, they politely looked away. She looked back down the alley. Sure enough, a short, thin man with a mean expression was making his way toward her. He looked like he belonged here as much as she did. The workers paused when they saw him and gave him a wide berth. They, like her, knew the look of a Thief's man when they saw one.

Looking at the obstructions between herself and her pursuer, Sonea found what she was looking for. She sent out a little magic and held it in place. Then she turned and continued down the alley, keeping to her former hurried pace.

She counted down in her head and gave a push with the magic. A crash came from behind her, then yells and curses. She paused to look back, feigning surprise. Her pursuer's path was now blocked by a woodpile that had collapsed under its own weight. She turned and hurried on.

A few streets and another alley later, and several stops

to check, she decided that she was no longer being followed and made her way to the laundry, sweet shop and the room beneath. Cery and Gol looked relieved as she entered the room.

"Sorry I'm late," she said as she sat down. "Had to deal with a tag."

Cery's eyebrows rose, then he smiled thinly. "Nobody talks like that any more."

Gol made a smothered choking sound. She looked from one to the other.

"Like what? You mean slum slang?"

"Yes." Cery rose. "Or so my daughter tells me."

"Where is she?"

He grimaced. "Off playing spy for me."

She felt her heart skip a beat. "You let her...?"

"Not really a matter of *letting* with Anyi." He sighed. "She rightly pointed out that we've had no other ideas for months." He paced a few steps to the right. "Her intention is to convince whoever employs her that she's truly turned on me by betraying my location." He stopped and paced to the left. "Of course, Gol and I will make a narrow escape." He turned to face her. "That's where you will come in."

"I will?"

"Yes." He shook his head, not bothering to hide his worry and doubts. "You'll be the factor she couldn't plan for."

"I see."

Cery resumed his pacing. "I was hoping to have you and Regin lined up for this, so that if one of you couldn't make it the other could step in—"

"Wait a few days and I'll have a replacement for Regin."

"Really?" Cery stopped. "Who is it?"

"Dorrien. Rothen's son."

"I thought he lived in the country."

"He did, but he's decided to move to the city to get his daughter settled here before she starts at the University."

Cery chuckled. "I bet Rothen doesn't know whether to be pleased or horrified."

She smiled and nodded. "I wish we didn't have to bring him into this. I wish *you* didn't need to involve Anyi."

"It's our children's purpose in life to make us worry," Cery replied wryly. He looked up. "Have you heard from Lorkin?"

Sonea felt a stab of pain, but it was more a dull ache than the sharp terror she'd felt when he'd first disappeared. "No. I guess I should be glad *he* isn't being dragged into this."

He nodded. "Perhaps I should have sent Anyi off to Sachaka." His expression suddenly became distant and thoughtful. He shook his head and looked at Sonea. "Anything else?"

"No. You?"

"Nothing. I'll send a message to the hospice when I know what Anyi is planning. Could you stay here a while, just in case you were followed?"

"Sure. I did lose the t . . . whatever you call them now."

"Of course you did," he said in a consolatory tone.

"You doubt my ability to lose a tag?" She crossed her arms.

"Not at all."

She narrowed her eyes at him. He feigned innocence. Behind him, Gol slid a panel in the wall open.

"Coming?" he asked.

Cery smiled and turned away. Shaking her head, Sonea watched as they slipped through into darkness and the panel slid shut again. Then she sat down and waited until they'd put some distance between themselves and the shop before she headed back to the hospice.

Stomach full, and with a mouth burning pleasantly from the spices he'd consumed, Dannyl sipped his wine contentedly. It was good to get away from the Guild House. These days the only Sachakan home Dannyl saw the inside of was Achati's. It followed the typical format, but the interior walls were painted a softer colour than the traditional stark white. The carpets and decorations were simple and elegant. He preferred the soft light of lamps to magical globe lights.

Dannyl had seen no glimpse of Achati's source slave and lover, Varn, since their journey in search of Lorkin. Achati had not mentioned his interest in Dannyl beyond friendship since then either—at least not directly. Dannyl was not sure if the Ashaki had given up on such a liaison happening, content to enjoy their friendship, or whether he was giving Dannyl time to contemplate the idea.

I must admit, I hope he hasn't given up, but at the same time, the fact that Achati is such a powerful man is as sobering as it is interesting. Not to forget the fact that he is Sachakan and I'm Kyralian, and some still feel we are enemies. Having a Sachakan friend would be seen to be beneficial, encouraging respect and understanding between our people. Having a Sachakan lover would raise suspicions of divided loyalties.

"So the treasure that was stolen from the palace was a magic-storing object," Achati said, his expression thoughtful.

Dannyl looked up and nodded. "The king told me something had been taken long ago. I thought you'd be interested to know what its purpose was."

"Yes." Achati's eyes wrinkled with amusement. "We did not remember what it was, only that it was stolen. If only we'd remembered that it was an object used to control us—an object powerful enough to create the wasteland—we might not have nursed such resentment. Or resented it as much," he added. "Since your people did use it to create the wasteland."

"A resentment that is deserved." Dannyl shuddered as he thought of the lifeless land he'd travelled across to get to Arvice. "I've often wondered how the Kyralians maintained control here. As far as I can tell, there weren't as many Kyralian magicians here as there were Sachakan magicians. Perhaps the threat of the storestone is the answer."

"It wasn't long after the object was stolen that the Kyralians relinquished control of my country," Achati told him.

Dannyl nodded. "We always assumed it was because the wasteland was considered protection and deterrent enough."

Achati grimaced. "It certainly weakened Sachaka. Our most fertile lands were gone, and we were already a country bursting with more people than we could feed, despite losing so many Ashaki in the war." He sucked in a breath, then let it out slowly. "The king will be interested in what you said earlier: that there was initial success in reclaiming the wastes. Restoring the land is a hope of his."

"It would be a great achievement."

"Yes." Achati frowned. "It is a peculiar thing that Kyralians have no memory of this storestone."

"I can only assume that all reference to it was lost when Imardin was destroyed, which I now believe happened centuries later." Dannyl sighed. "All good discoveries raise more questions. Why did Narvelan steal it? Why did he use it? I doubt we'll ever know, since he and those that might have confronted him did not live to tell the tale."

Achati nodded. "I'd like to know where the storestone came from. Did it originate in Kyralia? Was it made or natural?" He shook his head. "I'm sure you would like to know as much for Kyralia's sake as for your book. All would face as great a threat of disaster as Sachaka suffered, if such a weapon fell into the hands of an enemy."

"Thankfully, storestones don't appear to be very common. They may not even exist any more."

The two men were quiet for a while, thinking about this, then the Ashaki smiled again. "I must admit, I am finding myself drawn into this research of yours. I've been considering how else I might help you."

"The book merchants at the market are going to inform me when they buy more old records," Dannyl told him. Achati had done enough already by persuading various Ashaki to open their libraries to the Guild Ambassador, and Dannyl didn't want his new friend and ally losing respect for continuing to promote the cause of an unpopular foreigner.

"You can't rely on them," Achati told him. "They'll sell to the highest buyer. And there is no need for you to wait until an estate's owner is desperate enough to sell their old records. There is no need to buy them at all. We can go to them."

Dannyl blinked at the man in surprise. "Go to them? Visit them?"

"Yes. As you know, estates are obliged to provide food and beds for travelling Ashaki, and as the king's friend and representative I warrant extra attention and favours. If we show an interest in their old records there is a good chance they'll show them to us. That way there is no need for you to buy anything, which may be seen by some as benefiting from the downfall of victims of the wasteland your people created."

"But . . . what of your duties as the king's representative and adviser? What of mine as Guild Ambassador?"

Achati chuckled. "The king has more than one friend and adviser, and you are hardly being swamped with work. If any matter does arise, I'm sure Ambassador Tayend and your assistant can take care of it." Then he sobered. "I want you to find out as much as possible about the storestone. If one should still exist, or was created, it could be terrible for all countries."

Dannyl caught his breath. Achati was right: if a store-stone existed or could be made it would be a great danger to both Sachaka and the Allied Lands. What would the Traitors do if they got hold of one? They would rise up against the Ashaki. Once they had conquered Sachaka, would they be content to remain there? Would they seek to expand their borders further?

Then he felt a pang of guilt and anxiety. He hadn't told Achati everything, of course. In particular, nothing about the gemstones that Unh said the Traitors made. The only people Dannyl had given that information to were Lorkin and Administrator Osen. Osen had agreed that it was best to keep it a secret, as it might endanger Lorkin if Dannyl gave information about the Traitors to the Sachakans.

He shivered. *Can I warn the Sachakans about the*

Traitors' gem-making ability somehow, without it seeming like I already knew? He didn't think he could.

Should I accept Achati's help in finding out more about the storestone? If knowledge of such a weapon did exist, it would exist in Sachaka. The Sachakans would find it eventually, if Dannyl didn't find it first. He should take advantage of the fact that Achati was willing for a Kyralian to do the searching.

Where would I start looking first?

He almost smiled as the obvious answer came to him.

"Could this tour take us anywhere near the Duna lands?" he asked.

"Duna?" Achati looked surprised.

"Yes. They are, after all, traders in gemstones. Perhaps they can tell us something about storestones."

Achati frowned. "They aren't much inclined to talk to us."

"From what I remember of our last journey, Sachakans aren't much inclined to listen to them."

His friend shrugged, then his eyes narrowed. "That's right. You and Unh got quite chatty. What did he say that makes you think his people might tell us what they know of storestones?"

Dannyl considered his next words carefully. "We found a cave with a patch of gemstones growing from the wall. He told me they were safe. I knew what he meant, because I have encountered gemstones with magical properties before, in Elyne. Nothing like the storestone, of course."

Achati's eyebrows rose. "You *have*?" When Dannyl didn't reply, he looked amused. "So... Unh knew they could be unsafe. You think his people have storestones?"

"No, but I think they might know something about

them. Perhaps only stories and legends, but old tales can contain truths and history."

The Ashaki considered Dannyl, then began to nod. "Duna, then. We will go to visit the ash desert, and hope that your powers of charm and persuasion work as well on them as they did on Unh." He turned to the slave waiting nearby. "Bring raka. We have some planning to do."

A thrill of excitement ran over Dannyl's skin. *Another research trip! Like when Tayend and I...* A stab of guilt muted his enthusiasm. *What will Tayend think of me going off on an adventure with Achati just as he and I did back when we'd first met? Will he be jealous? At the least, it will be a reminder of what we don't share any more. It seems an unkind way to repay him for drawing my attention to the booksellers at the market.*

"What is it?" Achati asked.

Dannyl realised he'd been frowning. "I...I would have to gain the permission of the Higher Magicians."

"Do you think them likely to refuse?"

"Not if I put it the way you just did."

Achati laughed. "Then be sure to be a good mimic. Though not too good. If you sound like you're becoming a Sachakan Ashaki, they might call you home instead."

CHAPTER 9

ANTICIPATION AND BETRAYAL

As Damend's strikes broke through Pepea's defensive shield, Lilia felt the inner shield she was holding weaken under the attack and quickly sent it more power.

"Well done," Lady Rol-Ley said, nodding to Damend. "Third round goes to Damend. Froje and Madie will fight next."

The two girls grimaced, rose and made their way over to the teacher reluctantly. Lilia let the inner shield around Pepea disappear and waited for instructions from the teacher. Ley was of the Lans people, who were a race that prided themselves on their warrior skills—in both men and women. Yet they produced few magicians, and not very strong ones, so while Ley was fit and good at strategy, she needed help to run classes safely.

Ley glanced at Lilia. "Protect Madie. I'll shield Froje."

Reaching out to lay a hand on Madie's shoulder, Lilia sought a sense of the other girl's power so that she could create an inner shield attuned to it. If it wasn't in tune, it would prevent Madie striking.

She sensed nothing. Madie was rigid and tense. Looking up, she saw her old friend abruptly look away, avoiding her eyes. The girl's power was suddenly there, clear to her senses. Annoyed, Lilia created the inner shield.

"I don't see the point of this," Froje complained. "I know all magicians are supposed to keep their fighting skills up, in case we're invaded again, but we're both terrible at it. We'd be more of a liability in battle than a benefit."

Ley chuckled. "You might surprise yourself."

"I doubt it. Surely we'd have no power to fight with anyway. We'd have all given it to Black Magicians Sonea and Kallen."

"You could have hours—even half a day—to recover some strength before a battle began, so you wouldn't be completely powerless. Even if Sonea and Kallen were defeated, our enemy would be weakened by the fight. It would be a pity if we could not finish them off and save ourselves, just because some of us were too lazy to keep up our warrior skills. Now go take your positions."

The two girls shuffled away to the entrance of the Arena. Ley shook her head and sighed.

"They wouldn't be so bad at it if they practised," she said.

Lilia shrugged. "They'd practise if they liked it. And they'd like it if they were good at it."

Ley glanced at Lilia and smiled. "Do you like Warrior Skills?"

"I'm not good at them. I never have worked out what sort of strike to use, or when."

The teacher nodded. "You don't have the mind of an attacker. You're strong, though, and you pay attention. It makes you a good defender."

A warm feeling of gratitude filled Lilia. *So I'm*

*not terrible at this, but neither am I going to be a great
Warrior.* There was a kind of relief at knowing that her
decision to not choose that discipline was the right one.
Now I just have to decide between Healing and Alchemy.

At least she had a whole year and a half to make up her
mind. Naki had only half a year, and she was torn between
Warrior Skills and Alchemy. She was worried she would
come to regret choosing the former, though it was her
favourite and best discipline, because the only useful
thing she could do with it during peaceful times was
teach, and she didn't think she'd be a good teacher.

*Whereas I find Alchemy more interesting, but it seems
so indulgent when I could be more useful to others as a
Healer.*

If they both chose Alchemy, it would be something
they had in common during the year Lilia would continue
at the University. Naki would be a graduated magician
free to do whatever she chose.

A stab of worry went through Lilia's gut. She couldn't
help fearing that Naki, once she had graduated, would
grow sick of Lilia always being tied down to lessons, and
find someone else to befriend. *But I'm getting ahead of
myself*, she thought. *I'm not even sure Naki wants to
spend that much time with me anyway. I don't know if she
loves me in return.*

As if to argue with that thought, a memory flashed
through her mind of Naki pressing a finger to her lips,
then leaning across the carriage seat and pressing it to
Lilia's in turn. She'd dropped Lilia off at the Guild after
they'd left the brazier house. Lilia had been unable to hide
her disappointment. She'd hoped Naki was taking her
back to her house.

"I'll see you tomorrow," Naki had said. "Remember, we must not show a hint that we might be anything more than friends. Do you understand? Not a hint. Not even when you think you're alone. It's the watcher you don't see who catches you out."

"More than friends." Surely that means Naki loves me, too.

A sudden impact on her shield snapped her attention back to the Arena and she instinctively drew and sent more magic to it.

"First round goes to Froje," Lady Rol-Ley announced. "Begin round two."

The day after their visit to the brazier house, Naki had said Lilia could stay over at her house at the end of the week. Lilia tried not to think about that. Instead she took a deep breath and forced herself to concentrate on the two girls fighting in the Arena, and on keeping her shield strong.

But inside, her stomach fluttered with anticipation.

Once he opened the door Lorkin understood straightaway why Evar's instructions had referred to the passage as a tunnel. The walls were roughly cut. For one long stretch it looked as if he was walking along a natural fissure, the floor filled in with slabs of stone and the roof gradually narrowing to a dark crack far above him. His guess was proven right when the floor abruptly ended. He peered over the edge and sent his globe light floating downward. The crack descended below the floor, which was, indeed, slabs of stone wedged between the walls. The distance of the drop below was impossible to guess at. The glow of his globe light did not penetrate far enough into the darkness.

Shuddering, he turned to a large hole carved into the rock to one side and stepped through into another roughly cut passage. This continued in a straight line for quite a distance, and he realised he must be far from the occupied caves of the city now.

I hope I'm not technically leaving the city, he thought. *Then I'll be breaking a rule. I could argue that I didn't know the sewers were outside the city, but I don't think as many Traitors would be so willing to believe in my innocence as last time if I'm found to be sneaking about again.*

If only Tyvara was allowed to see him. He could have simply visited her then at her rooms. He would have liked to see what her rooms were like. What would they tell him about her?

Sometimes it feels as if I know too little about her, he thought. *I only know what people tell me, and what I learned of her on the journey from Arvice to Sanctuary. People aren't going to describe her rooms to me. I'm sure it would not make me love her less if she had terrible taste in furnishings or kept her rooms a mess.*

The passage began to curve gently. After several hundred more steps he saw a light ahead. He shrank his globe light until it was just bright enough that he wouldn't trip in the dark, and quietened his footsteps.

As he neared the end of the tunnel a rushing sound reached him. He peered out, but could see nobody close by. Emerging from the tunnel, he found himself on a ledge carved into the side of a huge, natural underground tunnel. The rushing sound abruptly grew louder and gained a rhythmic beat. He leaned forward to look down and saw a narrow but swiftly running river below; the ledge was several times the height of a house above it. A large water wheel pushed water out of a side tunnel to join the larger flow. This water was a darker colour.

That's the sewer, he realised.

The air was not as fragrant as he'd feared, perhaps because of how far away the dark water and water wheel was. *If you can operate such a mechanism from a distance, why wouldn't you? And I suppose you could create a magical shield to keep the bad air away, too.*

"Lorkin."

He jumped at the voice and looked around, but could not see anybody.

"Up here."

Looking up, he saw that two women were peering down at him from a ledge above, both sitting on a stone bench carved out of the rock. One was Tyvara and the other...

He blinked in surprise and dismay as he realised the other was the queen.

Recovering, he hastily performed the hand-on-heart genuflection. The queen smiled and beckoned to him. He looked to either side. There were no stairs or ladder.

"You can levitate, can't you?" Tyvara asked.

He nodded. Creating a disc of force beneath his feet, he lifted himself upwards until he was level with the ledge, then remained floating.

"Am I breaking any rule doing this?" he asked of the queen. "I know Tyvara isn't supposed to talk to me."

"Never mind that," Zarala replied, waving a hand. "Nobody is here to see. Actually, we were just talking about you."

He looked from her to Tyvara and back, noting the

glint of humour in their gaze as he stepped onto the ledge. "All praise and admiration, I hope."

"Wouldn't you love to know?" Zarala laughed, the wrinkles deepening around her eyes.

Once again he found himself liking her automatically. He wondered where her helper was. How had she got here all on her own?

"So, why are you here?" the queen asked. She patted the seat beside her.

He looked at Tyvara as he sat down. "To thank Tyvara for a favour she did me."

"Oh? What favour?"

"Some advice of a personal nature."

Zarala's eyebrows rose and she looked at Tyvara. The younger woman stared back at her with a challenge in her eyes. The queen's smile widened and she turned back to Lorkin.

"It wouldn't have had something to do with the state your friend Evar was in a few days ago, would it?"

He scowled. "I must say, my opinion of the Traitors was lowered when I learned there would be no punishment for it."

The queen's expression became serious. "He was not forced into it."

"But surely to be left so exhausted is dangerous."

"Yes, it was careless."

"And deliberate?"

She gave him a stern look. "Be careful what you accuse others of, Lord Lorkin. If you make such claims you had best be able to prove them."

"I'm sure Evar was the only witness, and is hardly going to cooperate. He seems to think being humiliated and harmed is the natural cost of bedding a woman." He looked at Zarala, deliberately meeting her eyes.

She nodded. "Our ways are not without flaws. We may not be fair and equal in all things, but we are much closer to that ideal than any other society."

"At least we *have* an ideal of equality," Tyvara added. "A lot of the resistance to change comes out of the knowledge that we are the only people ruled by women. If we do not isolate ourselves we may end up like everyone else."

"But we can't stay this way forever," Zarala continued, her expression sad. "We have only so much room. Only so much workable land." She looked down at the sewer. "Even this has limits. Our predecessors carved out tunnels and changed the courses of rivers to carry away our detritus to the other side of the mountains. If we let it flow into Sachakan waterways the Ashaki might notice and follow it back to its source. But if we grow in numbers even the Elyne rivers may not be large enough to hide our waste, and they might start to wonder where it is coming from."

"Some of us want to restrict the number of children we have," Tyvara said. She looked at him. "Some even want to stop non-magicians having any children at all."

The queen sighed. "They don't see that such measures would still change who we are. Change is inevitable. Rather than let the ill consequences of neglect decide our future, we should choose to change ourselves." She looked at him and smiled. "As your people have done."

He stared back at her, wondering what changes she was referring to. The intake of novices from outside the Houses? Or—he felt a stab of alarm—the limited acceptance of black magic?

I didn't think they knew about that . . .

"What changes would you choose to make?" he asked, to divert the subject.

She grinned. "Oh, you'll just have to wait to find out that." Slapping her knees, she looked from Lorkin to Tyvara. "Well, it is time I got on with my rounds and left you two together."

As she began to rise, Tyvara slipped her arm under the old woman's. Lorkin quickly did the same. Once standing, Zarala paused, then took a step forward. At once she began to float away from them. Lorkin looked at the shimmering air under her feet and smiled.

So that's how she got up here.

"Don't get too distracted, Tyvara," she called over her shoulder. Then she disappeared into the tunnel, the faint glow of a globe light flaring into existence illuminating the walls for a moment.

Tyvara sat down. Lorkin followed suit.

"So . . . did Kalia let you out or did you sneak away?" she asked.

He shrugged. "Things got quieter, so I started pestering her with questions about the cures she was making."

She smiled. "That'd do it. Why'd you come here?"

"To thank you. Thank you, by the way."

"For the warning? I thought you said you had no intention of getting into anyone's bed?"

"That's correct."

She regarded him thoughtfully, opened her mouth to speak but then closed it again.

"Unless you told me to," he added.

Her eyebrows rose and a faint smile curled her lips, but then she looked away, down at the sewer. It was hardly a romantic distraction, so he decided to change the subject.

"So . . . you're turning that wheel with magic?"

"That's right."

"It must get boring after a while."

"I find it relaxing." She looked up and sighed. "Sometimes too relaxing."

"Shall I stay and keep you entertained?"

She smiled. "If you have the time. I don't want to keep you away from the Care Room."

He shook his head. "Kalia said to stay away for a few hours."

Tyvara made a rude noise. "She's not the only one who knows the recipes for cures. It would be stupid to have only one person know that sort of thing."

"It would." Lorkin shrugged. "But I suppose if I'm not willing to share Guild healing secrets then why should she share hers? Besides, it does give me some free time to come and see you. Even if I'm not supposed to."

She smiled. "If we're discovered, we claim you did all the talking, and I never said a word."

"We can. Or that if you said anything, I never heard it. Are you sure anybody will understand what we mean, rather than assume I was just being a typical male?"

She laughed. "I can't promise that, but I'm sure we'll get our real meaning across eventually."

"We might get snow tonight," Rothen said.

Sonea glanced at him, then grimaced. "First snow of the year. When I see it, I can't help remember the Purge. Even after all these years."

He nodded. "I do, too."

"You know, there are *adults* who never experienced it."

"Who will never appreciate how horrible it was—and that's a good thing."

"Yes. You want your children to take it for granted that they have a better life than you, but at the same time you hope they don't take it for granted in case they let bad things return out of ignorance."

"Such worries turn us into boring old men and women," Rothen said, then sighed.

Sonea narrowed her eyes at him. "Who is calling who 'old'?"

He chuckled and said nothing. She smiled and looked back at the University building. How long had it been since she'd noticed the elaborate façade that had once awed her? *I'm taking wonderful things for granted, too.*

"Here they come," Rothen murmured.

Turning back, Sonea saw that the Guild Gates were opening. A carriage waited behind them. Soon the entrance was clear and the horses stirred into motion, hauling the vehicle through and along the road to the University steps.

The driver drew the horses to a stop. The carriage swayed and settled, then the door opened and a familiar robed figure leaned out and grinned at them.

"Nice of you to wait up for me," Dorrien said. He clambered down, then turned and reached out, taking a gloved hand that emerged from the doorway. A sleeve appeared and a woman's head. She peered out, blinking first at Sonea, then at Rothen.

A look of recognition came into Alina's eyes as she saw her husband's father, and she smiled faintly. She looked at Sonea again and a line between her eyebrows deepened. Her gaze dropped to Sonea's robes and she schooled her expression into a serious one.

Dorrien helped her to the ground, then offered the same assistance to his two daughters. The eldest, Tylia, emerged first. She favoured her mother in looks, Sonea noted. Yilara, the younger, ignored her father's offered hand and jumped down the steps nimbly. *And that one favours Dorrien*, Sonea mused.

Introductions and welcomes followed. Sonea was amused to find that Alina said nothing in response to her greeting, then busied herself checking that her daughters were presentable. Once satisfied, she took Dorrien's arm and looked at Sonea with an expression that was almost defiant.

I wonder what I'm doing wrong, Sonea thought. *Or if there's something about me that she finds off-putting.* She resisted the urge to laugh bitterly at her thoughts. *Well, there are these black robes and the magic they represent.*

Or it could be that Dorrien had told Alina that he and Sonea had nearly formed a romance of sorts. That they had once kissed.

Surely he hasn't. He might have told her about our very brief connection, but nothing more than that. He's smart enough to know you don't torment the woman you love with the details of the encounters you had before her. She remembered her own jealousy, when Akkarin had told her of the slave girl he had loved. Despite knowing that the girl was long dead, she had not been able to help feeling a twinge of resentment.

"Black Magician Sonea!" a new voice called.

She turned toward it, and saw a messenger hurrying in her direction.

"Yes?" she replied.

"A message...arrived...Northside hospice," the man said, between deep breaths. "I came straight...on foot, no delays." Reaching her, he handed her a folded piece of paper.

"Thank you," she said. She unfolded the paper. "*Meet the Traitor at the Pachi Tree in One Hour.*" Cery certainly had a fondness for capitalising words, she mused. "And could you arrange a carriage for me, as quickly as possible."

The messenger bowed and hurried away.

"What is it?" Dorrien asked.

She looked up at him, his family and Rothen. "I'm sorry, but I won't be able to join you for dinner."

Dorrien took a few steps toward her, forcing Alina to let go of his arm. The woman scowled.

"Is this to do with the search? Can I help?"

Sonea smiled crookedly. "There'll be plenty of opportunities for you to help, Dorrien. Tonight I'm just helping out a friend. You go have something to eat and settle in."

"Is it Cery?" Dorrien's eyes were afire with interest. Alina's were smouldering with anger and worry. The girls' eyes were wide with curiosity.

Sonea shook her head in exasperation. "As if I'd tell you right here, in front of the University. You had better learn to be a bit more subtle than that, if you're going to be of any use to me."

He smiled at her teasing tone. "Very well, I'll let you have all the fun tonight. But you'd better not leave me out next time."

The crunch of hooves and carriage wheels sounded in the direction of the stables. Sonea started toward the sound. "I'll see you all tomorrow," she tossed over her shoulder.

The driver of the carriage, seeing her haste, urged the horses to a greater speed, then drew them to a halt as he reached her. She told him the destination and hauled herself inside the cabin.

During the journey, she considered Alina's badly concealed hostility toward her. *Was I imagining it?* She shook her head. *I don't think so. Was I doing something to cause it? Not unless smiling and welcoming someone is considered rude in Dorrien's village, which I doubt. And Dorrien would tell us if it was.*

Alina had visited the Guild a few times before. The first time she had been a shy young woman whose attention was so fixed on Dorrien that she possibly hadn't even noticed Sonea. The next time she had been so occupied with a tiny baby and a young child that Sonea had not seen her once. Another time, Sonea had been too caught up in treating a seasonal bout of fevers at the hospices to see Dorrien or his wife.

Well, Dorrien is determined to stay until Tylia is in the University, so I have six months and more to find out what Alina is so bothered by—be it past romances or black magic—and to assure her she has no reason to worry.

The carriage slowed, then turned into the hospice entrance. Sonea hurried out of the carriage and into the building, greeting Healers and hospice helpers. Healer Nikea, the leader of the Healers who had helped Sonea catch Lorandra, led Sonea into the storeroom.

"Staying here or going out?" Nikea asked.

"Out," Sonea replied. "But no disguise," she added as the young woman headed toward the box containing

Sonea's hospice worker garb. "Just something plain to put on top."

Nikea nodded and disappeared down the dim back of the room. She came back carrying a garment with sleeves.

"Here," she said. "Cloaks are regarded as being a bit old-fashioned on the streets. These are more popular."

It was a coat of surprisingly light material. Sonea shrugged into it. Though tailored like an ordinary coat to just below the bust, it flared out from there. The hem brushed the floor. "It's a bit long for me."

"That's how they wear them. It only buttons to the thigh, so the fronts open up when you step. People will see your robes, but they'll assume it's a skirt."

Sonea shrugged. "I don't want them to recognise me until I'm right in front of them."

"Then this will do just fine." Nikea smiled, then checked that the corridor was clear of anyone but Healers before waving Sonea through the door.

Soon Sonea was walking through Northside. She slowed her pace. The Pachi Tree was not far away and she did not want to arrive too early. A block away from the bolhouse, one of Cery's trusted workers stepped out of a doorway and shoved a basket in front of her.

"Signal is for the screen in the top right window to slide open," the man said, drawing out a brilliant-yellow glass bottle and holding it up to her nose. A sickly sweet smell assaulted her senses.

"And then?" she asked, waving the perfume away.

"Go in. Straight up the left-hand stairs to the third floor. Last door on the right." He stoppered the bottle and quickly lifted another one, this time a pale purple. The scent was overpoweringly musky. She winced.

"Left stairs. Third floor. Last on right," she repeated.

"Good. My wife sells these. Some she makes herself; some she buys at the markets."

The third bottle was black. The contents smelled of bark and earth, which was surprisingly pleasant.

"You like that one," he said, his eyebrows rising.

"Yes, but I can't imagine wearing it."

"You wear perfume often?"

"Actually...not at all."

"Well, try this one—it's new."

The next bottle was squat and a deep blue. The scent was a crisp, light one that reminded her of a sea breeze— but not in a fishy or rotten weed way—or the fresh smell of the air after a storm.

"That's...interesting."

"You don't have to wear it," he told her. "You can just put a few drops on a cloth and let it scent a room."

She found herself reaching for her money bag. "How much?"

He named a price. She didn't bother to haggle, as a movement in the corner of her eye drew her attention to the window he'd pointed out, and the screen was sliding open.

He handed her the bottle, smiling and bobbing in a display of gratitude as he backed away. She nodded to him once, then strode on to the bolhouse, slipping the stoppered bottle into one of the inside pockets of the voluminous coat.

Several patrons looked around as she entered, and it was obvious that they'd noted she wasn't the usual sort of visitor. She headed for a narrow wooden stair built against the left wall of the room. It was steep, and soon she had reached the third floor. Two men stood in the corridor. They eyed her suspiciously. The door to the last room on the right was open, and she could hear voices. One was Cery's. Raised in anger.

Whatever confrontation Cery and Anyi had arranged, it was taking place now.

The two men stepped forward to block her path. She pushed them away with magic. As soon as they comprehended that the force they'd encountered was magical, they backed away from her hastily. One shouted out a warning.

A man peered out of the doorway of the last room and saw her. A heartbeat later, three people ran out of the room and bolted down the stairs at the end of the corridor. One was Anyi, she saw. Realising she had arrived too late to prevent the attack on Cery, she hurried to the doorway and looked inside the room.

Cery and Gol stood at the far side of the small room, knives in hands, but smiling and unharmed. She sighed with relief.

"Looks like I arrived just in time," she said, stepping inside and closing the door.

Cery smiled. "It was perfect timing," he said. "Thanks."

"The least I could do," she replied. "So, do you want to stay here or make yourself scarce?"

He glanced at Gol, who was looking a little pale and very relieved. "I think we had better move on. Would you like to come with us?"

"Would I?" she asked in reply.

Cery grinned. "Don't worry. I won't take you any place you won't want anyone to see you in." He tapped a foot and a trapdoor sprang up from the floor beside him.

*Of course he'd have an escape route handy, though
I doubt he'd have had a chance to use it if I hadn't
turned up.*

Cery took a step toward the trapdoor, then paused and
looked back at her appraisingly. "By the way," he said.
"Nice coat."

CHAPTER 10

SECRETS SHARED

S omething was gripping Lorkin's shoulder and shaking him. His eyes flew open and he found himself staring at a grinning Evar.

"What?" he asked, pushing away a heavy, cloying tiredness. "What's happened?"

"Nothing," Evar assured him. "But if you don't get up soon you'll be late."

Lorkin sat up and blinked at the empty beds around him. If most of the men were up and gone, he was already late. He groaned and rubbed his face, then got up.

"I wish you Traitors had time pieces," he complained. "How am I supposed to wake up on time when you don't have alarm gongs?"

"Some of the women have them. But here...what would we set them to?" Evar said, shrugging. "We all sleep and get up at different times."

Lorkin sighed and started changing out of his bed-clothes and into the simple trousers and shirt he liked best of all the Traitor styles of garb. Evar brought over a plate of bread covered with a layer of sweet fruit paste so thick that it must have broken the rules of winter rationing. Lorkin ate quickly, telling himself it was only so he could get to the Care Room faster, not to hide the evidence of Evar's excess.

"Leota spoke to me last night," Evar said between bites.

Lorkin paused and regarded his friend. The man's expression was wistful.

"She said she enjoyed our evening together," Evar continued, smiling faintly.

Chewing and then swallowing quickly, Lorkin fixed his friend with a stern stare.

"I'm sure she did."

Evar looked at Lorkin and shrugged, his smile gone. "Oh, I know it's more likely she means she enjoyed reaping the magical and political rewards, but there is a chance she wasn't faking the other kind of enjoyment."

"Are you tempted to find out?" Lorkin asked.

Evar shook his head. "Well, at least not until I feel like the cost is worth it again," he added, then took another bite.

"You'd trust her again?" Lorkin was unable to keep the disbelief from his voice.

"I never trusted her the first time," Evar said, between chews. He paused to finish the mouthful. "I knew what might happen. There were going to be people who thought I should be punished for taking you to the caves. If they didn't do it that way, they'd find another." He grinned. "This way I got a bit of fun out of it. And while Leota may be opportunistic, she's also got a great body."

Lorkin stared at his friend, unable to decide what to

say to this. *I can hardly say "Evar, you're not as stupid as I thought you were." Nor would he like it if I told him he was as ruthless as the women. But he's not been as powerless or clueless as he appeared to be. In fact, he may have been planning this since before our tour of the stone-makers' caves.*

"And if she did happen to enjoy more than gaining some magic and the satisfaction of punishing me, then maybe she will come back for more," Evar added, his gaze turning misty again.

Or maybe he's just making it up as he goes along, Lorkin amended. *I still have to admire him for it. He seems to be able to find an upside to any situation.*

"Better you than me," Lorkin said. He dusted the crumbs off himself, then stretched. "Not that I'd have time. I'm off to the washrooms, then back to work."

Evar grimaced. "I've heard things are getting bad there."

Lorkin nodded. "It looked like the number of fever patients was easing off for a while, but then we got twice as many sick people arriving, and some of them are much sicker than before."

"That happens every year."

"So Kalia tells me. But I don't believe everything Kalia says, in case she tries to trick me again."

"Good idea," Evar said, popping the last piece of bread in his mouth. He uttered a muffled farewell as Lorkin headed for the door.

The city seemed quieter than usual as Lorkin made his way to the washrooms, then on to the Care Room. Coughing echoed down the corridors and from behind closed doors. Only when he neared the Care Room did he realise that there was something he *wasn't* hearing: the constant hum of voices throughout the city. When he finally heard the sound it was coming from the Care Room—from a queue of waiting patients extending into the corridor beyond the room's entrance.

People saw him and scowled. Some glared. Others looked at him in a measuring way.

Kalia has no doubt been making it known that I'm late. He wasn't *that* late, however. He'd made up time by bathing very quickly, which he hoped wasn't going to make him unpleasant to be around. *If only a good bath was all it took to make Kalia pleasant to be near.*

Entering the room, his heart sank as he took in the sight and smell of so many sick people. Kalia saw him and immediately stalked across the room toward him. He braced himself for a scolding, but instead she grabbed his elbow and led him over to a couple hovering over a girl of about six years.

"Examine her," she said. "Come and tell me your assessment."

He looked at the parents and felt his heart sink even further. Both stared back at him with dark, desperate eyes and said nothing. Turning to the girl, he saw that she was pale, her breathing was laboured and when she coughed it was weakly, her lungs rattling with congestion.

He knew even before he touched her and sent his senses within that she was sicker than she ought to be. The chill fever always claimed a few Traitors each year. The old and the young were the most likely victims, and those already weakened from some other illness.

He also knew that he would have to face this at some point. Kalia had known it too. He had already decided what he would do. But he would not do it now. Not while all these people were watching him so closely.

And not, he realised, until he'd had a chance to ask Tyvara if he'd guessed correctly what the consequences would be.

As the Guild House slaves began serving dinner, Dannyl was surprised to hear Tayend's voice in the corridor.

"Then I'll join him," Tayend said. A moment later he stepped into the main doorway of Dannyl's rooms. "Would you like some company for dinner?"

Dannyl nodded and gestured to a nearby stool. He had feared that he and Tayend would have an argument or some sort of confrontation, but nothing of the sort had happened and so far they had settled into their new roles without any conflict. And perhaps, since Tayend was so often out visiting Sachakans, it made sense to take advantage of the chance to catch up on ambassadorial business.

"No Ashaki to visit tonight?"

Tayend sat down and shook his head. "I asked Achati for a night off. I'm surprised he didn't invite you out instead."

Dannyl shook his head. "I'm sure he has other people to see than us Ambassadors. You've been getting along with the Sachakans very well."

A slave hurried into the room with a plate and knife for Tayend, so that he could begin serving himself from the platters of food the others were offering.

"I have, haven't I? It certainly appears so. Or am I wrong in assuming that? From what Ashaki Achati tells me, *you* were popular when you first arrived. Perhaps I, too, will fall out of favour."

"You don't have an assistant for anybody to abduct."

"No. Though I could do with one—preferably of the kind that nobody would want to kidnap." Tayend grimaced. "I want to work out what the situation is here, before I get anybody else involved. Whether it was safe. How things worked." He moved some of the spicier meat onto his plate, then some stuffed vegetables, before indicating that the slaves could leave.

"I suspect finding out how things *really* work would take quite a few years."

Tayend smiled crookedly. "Even so, I think I've worked out some things," he said. "How about I tell you what I've guessed and you tell me if I'm right." Popping food into his mouth, Tayend chewed and regarded Dannyl expectantly.

Dannyl shrugged. "Go ahead."

Tayend swallowed, drank a mouthful of water, then cleared his throat. "I've worked out that you and I are no longer a couple."

Surprise was followed by a flush of guilt. Dannyl forced himself to meet Tayend's eyes. Tayend's gaze was steady.

"I guess not," Dannyl replied. *Rather lamely*, he added silently.

"I worked that out when you put me in the guest rooms," Tayend added. "And don't tell me it would have caused a scandal if I'd slept in your bed. The Sachakans knew all about us before you got here." He speared another portion off his plate.

Dannyl coughed in protest. "They might still have disapproved—enough to demand we be replaced, or to refuse to deal with us."

"There's nothing to make deals over. We have no work to do. They don't need to trade with our countries. Having us here is a gesture of goodwill, nothing more. Other than that, our value to the Sachakans is merely as a novelty or entertainment. I suppose it has taken you longer to work this out." Tayend waved a hand dismissively. "I've also worked out that Achati is a lad, and rather fancies you." His eyes narrowed. "I haven't quite worked out if you fancy him in return."

Once again, Dannyl felt his face warming, but this time not out of guilt.

"Achati is a friend," he said.

"Your *only* friend among the Sachakans," Tayend continued, pointing his knife at Dannyl for emphasis. "You won't be able to string him along forever. What are you going to do when he gets sick of waiting? He doesn't seem the sort of man I'd want to make angry."

Dannyl opened his mouth to protest, then shut it again. "You once would have said that about me," he managed.

Tayend smiled. "Then I got to know you, and you're not at all scary. Sometimes you're even a little pathetic, always worried about what people think, burying yourself in your research to make yourself feel worthy."

"It's important research!" Dannyl objected.

"Oh. Yes. Very important. More important than me."

"You were interested in it too, once. As soon as it stopped being about roaming around having adventures and started being about hard work, you didn't care for it any more."

Tayend's gaze flashed with anger, but then he hesitated, and looked away. "I suppose it must look that way. To me it felt like I had nothing more to contribute. The writing part was always yours. Once I was out of the Grand Library, I was a poor excuse for a scholar."

Indignation faded at Tayend's assessment of himself. "You were never a poor excuse for a scholar," Dannyl told him. "If I had known you were still interested in the research, I would have found something, some way, for you to stay involved."

Tayend looked up and frowned. "I thought you were keeping me out. Going to Sachaka without me confirmed it."

"It was ... I believed it was dangerous here for you."

"You certainly had me worried. When my king approved of my proposal to be the first Elyne Ambassador in Sachaka I was sure I had taken on something much more dangerous than this has turned out to be, so far."

"How did you convince him?"

"I didn't. Others did." Tayend shrugged. "It seems everyone thought it was a great idea to send someone here now that Kyralia had done so, but nobody was stupid enough to suggest it in case they were given the job."

"Who supported you?" Dannyl asked, mainly out of curiosity.

Tayend smiled. "That would be telling." He looked down at his plate. "We should eat or the food will go cold."

Dannyl snorted softly. "Elynes and their convoluted politics."

"We are good at it—and it has been of benefit here. I might even be able to keep *you* out of trouble."

Returning to his half-eaten meal, Dannyl considered what his former lover had said. "So did you come all this way only to see what I was up to?"

Tayend's eyes narrowed again. He didn't answer immediately, instead chewing thoughtfully. "No," he said eventually. "When you left, you made me see that I was bored. Turns out you are right: having a purpose does make life more interesting."

"And that purpose is?"

Tayend was chewing again.

Being the first Elyne Ambassador in Sachaka, Dannyl answered. He had to admit, he was impressed at Tayend's daring, and the flamboyant man was well suited to the job. He did have a good grasp of politics—even if he did often choose to ignore social taboos and traditions—and he was very perceptive about people.

But I hope not too perceptive, when it comes to Achati.

Dinner with Naki and her father was always filled with long silences. Lord Leiden always asked how their studies were going, and Naki's answers were usually polite but short. He also enquired after Lilia's family, but she did not see them often so there was not much to tell him, and he did not seem that interested in her answers anyway.

This time, Lilia felt as if the dinner had stretched on for hours longer than usual, and the pretence of interest for the sake of manners had started to irritate her. Even the excellent food did not make up for the boredom. She wasn't sure if it was the long days of anticipation that had made her impatient to be alone with Naki, or if she was picking up on Naki's mood.

Her friend was definitely in an odd frame of mind. Naki's answers to her father's questions had been shorter than usual—verging on snarly. At one point she'd asked him about someone and he'd winced, frowned at her disapprovingly, and changed the subject. To Lilia, however, she was overtly friendly, leaning over and patting her on the leg, winking at her or pulling faces. Lilia was relieved when the meal had finally ended.

Naki led her upstairs to her bedroom as usual. As soon as the door closed, Naki began pacing and broke out into a tirade of curses unlike anything Lilia had heard since one of her visits to the wharves in her childhood.

"What's wrong?" Lilia asked.

Naki sighed and turned to her. "I can't tell you the details. All I can say is that *he* found out about a little project I've had going on the side, and to punish me he took something—no, he *stole* something—from me." She clenched her fists and stalked to the bed, sitting down on the edge of it. Looking up at Lilia, her expression changed to a forlorn one. "You know, he only gives me enough money to pay for what I need at the University. If I want to have any fun I have to find some other way to pay for it. And now I don't have such a way."

The brazier house. The wine she sneaks into the Guild. She's always paid for it. I haven't paid for anything. Lilia felt a pang of guilt. She moved over to the bed and sat down beside her friend.

"What about the allowance we get?"

Naki grimaced. "*You* get it; *I* don't. Because I'm from one of the Houses I don't get anything. My family is supposed to pay me an allowance instead."

"You've always paid for things," Lilia began. "I should—"

"No!" Naki headed her off. "Don't go offering to pay for my little indulgences."

"*Our* indulgences," Lilia corrected. "At least let me pay for them until you . . . find another way to earn some money. It would be nice to be able to spoil *you* for a while."

Naki gazed at Lilia in surprise, then her lips curled in a wide smile. "Oh, Lilia. You are so good." She wrapped her arms around Lilia and hugged her.

Lilia hugged her friend back. The simple warmth of the embrace filled her with happiness. As Naki began to pull away, she let go, but the other girl only leaned back a little. Lilia looked up to find Naki staring at her intently, her expression thoughtful.

Then Naki leaned in and kissed her.

Once again, all the sorts of hopes and ideas that the other novices disapproved of came rushing into Lilia's mind, and her heart began beating very fast. She kissed back, not daring to think what might happen next, and not wanting to risk spoiling the moment.

Inevitably, Naki broke the kiss. Her eyes were dark and her expression impossible to read. Lilia wanted to tell her she loved her, but she hesitated, afraid that she was wrong and Naki would be repelled.

Suddenly Naki grinned and leapt off the bed.

"Let's go to the library," she said. "I have some roet stowed there."

Can't we do anything without roet? Lilia pushed the sullen thought aside and stood up. "All right . . ."

Naki grew even more fey and restless as they crept quietly to the library, her movements all agitation and excitement. Once she had a brazier burning, she urged Lilia to breath in the smoke deeply. They settled into two large chairs.

"Your father won't come in here?" Lilia asked, before the drug stopped her caring enough to worry about it.

"He'll be asleep," Naki replied. "He was complaining, before you arrived, about how it had been a long day and he was *so* tired."

They relaxed for a while, enjoying the roet, then Naki got up and moved over to the glass-topped table. She leaned on it, gazing down at the contents, then straightened as if coming to a decision and opened the side. Reaching inside, she took something out, and as she started back toward the chairs Lilia saw that it was the book Naki had shown her previously. The one that contained instructions on using black magic.

A faint unease stirred within Lilia, but she was feeling too lazy to even frown.

Naki dropped back into her chair with a sigh. She lifted the book and regarded it thoughtfully. Opening it, she gently turned the pages.

"I could probably quote whole sections of this."

"How often have you looked at it?" Lilia asked.

"More times than I can remember." Naki shrugged. "My father should know that if he says I'm not to do something I'll take it as a challenge."

"Have you read the whole thing?"

Naki looked up at Lilia and smiled. "Of course. It's not a big book."

"So you've read the bit...the part..."

Naki's smile widened. "The part about black magic. Yes. I have." She looked down. "It's amazingly straightforward. I've often wondered if I could do it, using these instructions."

"But you can't learn black magic from a book," Lilia reminded her. "It has to be taught mind to mind."

"That's true. I wonder why they bothered writing it

down, then." Naki flicked through the pages, then held the open book out to Lilia. "What do you think?"

Despite the roet, Lilia hesitated. Even to read about black magic was forbidden.

"Go on," Naki said. "I've always wanted to show someone and get their opinion, but I never trusted anybody enough."

Lilia's heart lifted and she smiled at Naki as she reached out to take the book. *She trusts me. She thinks my opinion is worth something.* Looking down at the open page, she started to read.

... means by which the body achieves this are not so much understood as sensed. So it is, too, with the higher magics. In early training, an apprentice is taught to imagine his magic as a vessel—perhaps a box or a bottle. As he learns more he comes to understand what his senses tell him: that his body is the vessel, and that the natural barrier of magic at the skin contains his power within. And so it is that if he should happen to encounter a breach of another person's barrier (as in the ritual of higher magic) he can extend his senses into the other's body in a quite different way to Healing, detecting the power within, not the physical body. He can also influence this power, removing or adding to it. While it is possible to sense how much power a person contains, it is not possible to judge how strong he is. You may sense the physical exhaustion of a man who has been stripped of his magic, which suggests that once the magical energy is removed the physical energy is tapped, but if not depleted to

*the point of physical impact you cannot sense if
magic has been removed at all. It is also difficult to
sense and manipulate magic simultaneously with
sensing and manipulating the physical body
through Healing . . .*

The author rambled on about Healing from that point.
His writing is terrible, Lilia mused. *It just goes on and on
and never comes to the point. There are no paragraph
breaks.* She flicked through the pages. *None in the entire
book.*

"Well? What do you think?" Naki asked, slipping
some more roet into the burner.

Lilia turned back to the page on black magic and made
herself read it again. "There's not much."

"More than anyone's told us before," Naki pointed out.
"I've tried sensing my magic the way it describes."

Lilia looked up. "And?"

Naki smiled. "I think I've got the knack of it." She
leaned forward. "Try it."

"Now?" Lilia protested weakly. She felt too lazy to be
attempting any mind tricks.

"Yes. It's easy once you have the right idea. And it's a
real head-spinner when you've got a bit of smoke in you."
Naki's eyes sparkled.

Shrugging, Lilia closed her eyes. She struggled against
lethargy, then brought up an image in her mind of the
door she had been taught to see as the entry point to her
magic. She opened it and felt her senses tingle and the
effect of roet subside a little.

As always, she imagined a room inside herself, small
and sparsely furnished, which reminded her both of the

tiny bedroom she had shared with her siblings and of her room in the Novices' Quarters. It was filled with a warm light.

But the book says this is just a way to visualise my power. The real walls are the barrier at my skin. So I should be able to...

She let the walls go, and they faded into darkness. The warmth and glow of the light slowly faded from her sense of touch or sight, leaving only an awareness of another kind. She reached out and felt the boundaries of it. They weren't leg and arm shaped, she found, and yet...she had a sense of her physical form as if a faint outline of *herself* was imposed over the magic within her.

For a measure of time she pondered this, then she remembered Naki and drew her awareness back out of herself.

"That's...amazing," she breathed.

Naki smiled. "You got it? I knew you would. You're too clever." She got up and came closer, leaning on the arm of the chair, reaching out and turning Lilia's hands so she could read the book. "Let's try something else. Let's see if you can sense my magic."

"But...you'd have to cut yourself for me to be able to do that."

Naki leaned close. Her breath smelled of roet. Her lips curled in an inviting way. "I'll do that for you. I'd do anything for you."

Lilia stared at her friend, feeling her heart warm and expand. "I'd do anything for *you*," she replied with feeling.

Naki's smile widened with delight. "Let's do it," she said. She cast about, then danced over to the glass-covered table and reached inside again. Whatever she'd taken was small and hidden in her palm. "It's old, so I don't know if it's sharp enough...ow! Yes, that worked."

Perching on the chair arm again, Naki held out her hand. A tiny knife lay there, and a small red line seeping little beads of blood marred her skin. Lilia felt a chill that threatened to clear her head.

"Go on. Before it heals up again."

I'd do anything for you. Reluctantly, Lilia took the knife in one hand and clasped Naki's hand in the other. She closed her eyes.

It was not hard to return to her new awareness of her magic. Somehow she knew where to send her mind to find her hand. And then she sensed it. The presence of another was faint...except *there*. The cut felt like a slash of light in her mind. It attracted her like the promise of sunlight at the end of a tunnel. When she reached it...*Naki*.

The other girl radiated a familiar restless excitement and curiosity, with an undertone of anger—old and directed elsewhere, so most likely her lingering anger over her father.

—*Have some of my power*, Naki's voice said at the edge of Lilia's mind.

A flash of magic leapt from the break in Naki's barrier into Lilia's. At once she understood how easy it would be to reach through and draw that energy within herself. But she didn't want or need to do it. Drawing back from Naki's presence, she opened her eyes.

"I think it worked. Except...it's too easy." She frowned. "I can't be doing it right."

A finger was tracing a lazy pattern along her arm and hand. She looked down, then up at Naki. The girl's eyes were burning with eagerness. "Let me try." She gave Lilia a meaningful look. "We do this together."

Lilia felt a surge of affection. Picking up the little knife, she clenched her teeth then ran it across the back of her arm. Naki beamed at her, then gently touched the cut. As she closed her eyes, Lilia did the same, wondering how it would feel to be the one whose barrier was damaged.

This time her awareness instantly took the new form. The breach in her defences was easy to locate; it roused a sense of urgency that made her feel edgy. Suddenly she felt Naki's presence again, but this time there was no sense of her emotions.

A strange weakness, like the disconnection from will that roet brought, came over her and she sensed energy flowing out.

But as quickly as it began, it stopped. She felt Naki let go of her arm, and drew her consciousness back to the physical world. Her friend was frowning and shaking her head.

"I don't think it worked."

"No?" Lilia said in surprise. "I'm sure I felt you taking power."

Naki shook her head again. Her lips formed a small pout and she walked over and flopped into her chair. "I couldn't sense anything. Not the breach in your barrier. Not you." She sighed. "All the years I've wanted to try it... and now that I have someone I trust to try it with it doesn't work..."

"Well, if it was that easy it *would* be possible to learn it from a book. We can try again, if you like," Lilia offered.

Naki shook her head. She looked at the brazier

sullenly, then used a little magic to open it and stamp out the burning contents. Getting up, she stowed it away.

"Let's go to bed."

Relieved, since she was starting to get the dizziness and headaches that meant she'd had a little too much roet, Lilia got up and followed her friend out of the library. Naki passed her bedroom and entered the guest room where Lilia slept when she stayed over. She went straight to an elaborately carved chest, dug beneath some bundles and produced a bottle of wine.

"Thirsty?"

Lilia hesitated, then nodded. Though her head was still spinning a little from roet, she was very thirsty. Naki opened the bottle and raised it to her lips. After drinking a mouthful, she grinned and handed it to Lilia, the contents sloshing as she did. "No glasses in here. Father has forbidden wine and roet, but I have friends among the servants."

Lilia gulped awkwardly from the bottle. With a sigh, Naki flopped down onto the bed. She waved the bottle away as Lilia offered it back.

"He's not my real father," she murmured. "Mother married him after my real father died. When she died, Leiden got everything she had, including me. We never liked each other. He'll marry me off as soon as I graduate, to the first person who asks, just to get rid of me." She sighed again.

Setting the bottle aside, Lilia lay down beside her friend. "That's awful." The thought of Naki being married off to a man, who she clearly would never desire, made Lilia's heart ache. *If he does it after she graduates... that's half a year away!* Would they still be able to see each other? Could they keep their love secret?

"I wish he was dead," Naki murmured. She turned her head to look at Lilia. "You said you'd do anything for me. Would you kill him, if I asked?"

Lilia smiled and shrugged. The wine was going to her head and she had no energy to form a reply. *There must be another way to solve Naki's problems. Murder is a bit extreme.* But what if there wasn't? *Could I use black magic and hide it? Make it look like an accident?* Naki was murmuring something, but the words were distant and took too much concentration to understand.

Mind full of dark thoughts, Lilia slipped into strange and vivid dreams where she ridded Naki of all her problems, and they lived a life of love and secrets in a house full of staircases and hidden doors and cabinets filled with frustratingly cryptic books.

CHAPTER 11

A MISUNDERSTANDING

As the carriage pulled up in front of the tower, Sonea smiled wryly.

Finding a suitable prison for Lorandra had proven difficult. The city Guard had objected to keeping a magician—even one whose powers were blocked—in their prison. No prison existed in the Guild grounds and there was no room in the Magicians' Quarters for her—even if there had been Sonea doubted the magicians living there would have been happy about having Lorandra as a neighbour. The Servants' Quarters were considered briefly, but they were even more crowded—something that ought to be dealt with soon, Osen had commented. Keeping Lorandra in the Dome permanently was only suggested in jest.

The temporary solution was to use the Lookout as a prison. The rebuilding of the tower had begun before the Ichani Invasion, at Akkarin's suggestion. Afterwards, it was completed and for a few short years used by Alchemists to study the weather. Eventually it was loaned out to the Guard for training purposes, with the condition that it was maintained and always occupied.

Though the Guard had made it clear they didn't want Lorandra in their prison, they readily agreed to guarding her at the Lookout, so clearly the knowledge that Lorandra was a magician didn't bother them. In retrospect, Sonea could see that guarding the tower against a rescue mission from Skellin would be easier here than in the city prison. Corruption among the prison guards had led to escapes before. There was less chance of one of them releasing Lorandra if her guards were a smaller group, carefully chosen for their loyalty and trustworthiness.

Or perhaps they know it's more likely the Guild will continue to post a magician to help guard Lorandra here. How long would magicians agree to watch over her, if they had to do it at the dirty, unpleasant city prison?

Stepping down from the carriage, Sonea looked up at the building and felt a small pang of sadness. *Would you have been pleased that we finished it, Akkarin?* she thought. *Or did you mean for it to be a distraction to keep the Guild's attention away from you, as some believe?*

It was a plain building, just a round tower twice as tall as the trees surrounding it. The surface was smooth and the windows small, reminding her of the Fort with its magically bonded stone face and tiny windows. Guards were posted around the exterior. One of them, standing beside the heavy wooden door, bowed as she approached, then opened the door for her.

She stepped into a large room lit by several small lamps. Two more guards and their captain rose and bowed. They had been sitting at a table with a young Warrior, who nodded respectfully to Sonea.

The captain stepped forward and bowed again.

"Black Magician Sonea. I am Captain Sotin," he said.

"I'm here to see the prisoner," she told him.

"Follow me."

He led her up a winding staircase and stopped at a wooden door into which a small hatch had been recently cut. Opening the hatch, he gestured for her to look inside. She saw a bed and a desk, and a familiar reddish-skinned old woman sitting in a chair. Lorandra's attention was on something in her hands.

"Black Magician Sonea is here to see you," the captain announced, his voice loud in Sonea's ear.

The woman looked up and stared at the hatch without expression. Her gaze dropped back to her still-moving hands.

"She doesn't say much," the captain said apologetically.

"She never has," Sonea replied. "Unlock the door."

He obeyed, taking a ring of keys from his belt and releasing the locks. *Two locks,* Sonea noted. *She must really make them nervous.* Sonea stepped into the room and heard the door close behind her. Lorandra looked up again, giving Sonea a hard stare before turning her attention back to the object in her hands. Looking closer, Sonea saw that it was some sort of fabric, which the woman was creating with thick thread and a short, bent piece of thick wire. The speed with which the makeshift hook moved through the edge of the fabric and formed looping knots suggested many years of practice.

"What are you doing?" Sonea asked.

Lorandra regarded Sonea with narrowed eyes. "It is called 'binda' and most of the women of my homeland know it."

The fabric shifted in her hands, revealing that it was forming a tube. Surprised and encouraged by Lorandra's willingness to speak, she considered how she could encourage the woman to continue.

"And what are you making?"

Lorandra looked down. "Something to keep me warm."

Sonea nodded. *Of course. We are not far-off mid-winter so it's only going to get colder. She can't use magic to warm the air any more. There is no fireplace and the guards won't trust her with a brazier.* Yet the room wasn't particularly cold. The warmth from the rooms below must go some way toward easing the chill.

"We usually use a stick with a hook carved into the end, but they think I'll use it to kill myself," Lorandra added.

Sonea couldn't help smiling a little. "Would you?"

The woman shrugged and did not answer. *She would not expect me to believe it, so why bother.*

"Are they treating you well?" Sonea asked.

Lorandra shrugged again.

"Anything I can bring you?"

A disbelieving twitch of the mouth. And no answer again.

"Your son, perhaps?" Sonea asked, allowing a little scepticism into her voice. She was not surprised when Lorandra didn't answer. Suppressing a sigh, she moved to the low bed, sat down and returned to the subject the woman seemed willing to talk about. If she could foster a habit of conversation, who knew where it would lead? "So what do the women of your homeland make with binda?"

Lorandra worked on in silence but something about the

set of her mouth told Sonea she was considering answering.

"Hats. Gloves. Garments. Blankets. Baskets. Depends
on the thread. Softer and finer for gloves. Strong and resil-
ient for baskets."

"Does it take long?"

"Depends what you're making and how thick the
thread is. Binda stretches, which is good for some things
and not for others. If we want a firm cloth we weave."

"What do you make the thread out of?"

Lorandra's gaze became distant. "Reber wool mostly.
There is a type of grass that can be softened and spun for
baskets, but I haven't seen it south of the desert, and a
fine, soft thread spun from the nests of bird moths that
only the rich can afford."

"Moths? Here moths eat clothing, not make thread to
weave clothing from." Sonea smiled. "What is the cloth
like?"

"Soft but strong. It's usually polished to a shine, and
more thread is used to stitch patterns and pictures onto it."
Lorandra frowned. "I've heard of women wearing skirts
that took years to stitch."

"You've not seen them yourself?"

Lorandra scowled. "Only bird cloth I've seen was worn
by the *kagar*."

Catching a hint of contempt and fear in the woman's
eyes and voice, Sonea considered who these "kagar"
might be.

"Are they the people who kill anyone possessing
magic? Who are magicians themselves?"

Lorandra shot her an unfriendly look. "Yes."

"Why do they kill magicians?"

"Magic is evil."

"But they use it themselves?"

"Their great sacrifice, in order to cleanse our society." There was bitterness in her voice.

"Do you think magic is evil?"

Lorandra shrugged.

"Do you think, with your powers blocked, they'd let you live if you went back?"

The woman turned to regard Sonea.

"Planning to send me back?"

Sonea decided not to answer.

Lorandra sighed. "No. They aim to purge magic from our bloodlines. It wouldn't matter that I'm too old to bear children. I might teach the evil to others."

"It is incredible. They must have no enemies to defend themselves against. What of neighbouring lands? Do they forbid magic, too?"

The woman shook her head. "We have no neighbouring lands. The kagar defeated them all a hundred years ago."

"*All* of them? How many were there?"

"Hundreds. Most of them small, but together they make your Allied Lands look tiny." Lorandra smiled grimly. "You had best hope they never look across the desert, or Sachaka will be the least of your worries."

Sonea felt her stomach clench, but then she remembered how Lorandra had not known that Kallen would be able to read her mind. *Lorandra's people don't have black magic, and they are actively trying to purge the magic from their bloodlines.* And yet they had conquered all their neighbours.

"If they did, and truly are a threat, you and Skellin

would be in as much trouble as us," Sonea pointed out. "It is a pity you didn't join us when you arrived. We would have learned about a new land, and you would have had our protection. If Skellin—"

"Black Magician Sonea," came a voice from the door.

Sonea turned to see the captain peering in.

"Yes?"

"Someone here to see you. It's . . . important."

Rising, Sonea walked to the door. As the captain unlocked it she looked back at Lorandra. The woman stared at her for a moment, then looked back down at her work. The tube had grown considerably during their conversation, Sonea noted.

She found one of Black Magician Kallen's associates waiting. One of the magicians who had once tracked her movements, she noted. She tried not to radiate instant dislike, not the least because he looked alarmed and upset.

"Forgive the intrusion, Black Magician Sonea," he said. "But there has been a murder. A magician. In the city. Black Magician Kallen is already there. You are to meet him."

She drew in a sharp breath. The murder of a magician was alarming enough, but Kallen's involvement and her summoning meant only one thing.

The victim must have been killed with black magic.

Dannyl sighed, leaned back in his chair and looked around his office. Being able to rest against the supportive back of a chair was a simple comfort that reminded him of home. The desk before him was also an object of Kyralian practicality and functionality that he hadn't seen in

Sachakan homes. If it weren't for the curved walls, he could have imagined himself back in Imardin.

Perhaps chairs and desks existed in Sachakan homes, in the personal rooms he hadn't seen. Maybe Sachakans had even better furniture for work and study. *If they have, they haven't bothered to supply the Guild House with them. This will do me just fine.*

Before him were his notes and the books he'd bought at the market. He'd just written a list of what he'd learned since arriving in Sachaka, and he was feeling quite pleased with himself.

The first item was "*Proof that Imardin wasn't destroyed in the Sachakan War*," which he'd found in records in an Ashaki's library not long after arriving in Arvice. Below that he'd written "*The existence of the storestone*," which Lorkin had found in the same collection of records.

Between this and the next set of items he'd squeezed in "*That the Duna tribesmen knew (and perhaps still do) how to make magical gemstones. That these gemstones are made (not natural). That the Traitors stole the knowledge from them.*" All this he'd learned from Unh, the tribesman who had tracked Lorkin and his Traitor abductors.

Next was a longer set of observations from the records he'd bought.

That Narvelan, the leader of the Kyralians ruling Sachaka, had owned a slave, was considered crazy, stole the storestone, and used it to create the wasteland either deliberately or in a confrontation between himself and his Kyralian pursuers.

That the threat of using the storestone most likely kept the stronger force of surviving Sachakan magicians under control, and once it was removed Kyralia was forced to return the country to Sachakan rule.

That the wasteland appeared, at first, to begin recovering, then failed as the area began to grow instead.

It was a good list, Dannyl decided. It was only frustration at making no progress recently that made it seem like he hadn't achieved anything here. However, there were still questions to be answered.

Leaning forward, Dannyl began to write a list of what he still wanted to find.

"Proof I can take home with me that Imardin wasn't destroyed in the Sachakan War." Achati seemed to prefer that Dannyl didn't buy Sachakan records, but maybe he wouldn't mind the occasional purchase. If Dannyl was to convince anyone of his theory that Imardin had been destroyed later, he would need to have a document to show them.

"Proof that the mad apprentice destroyed Imardin." Dannyl didn't think he'd find this in Sachaka, however.

"Where did the storestone come from? How was it made? Was it made, or natural? Do any still exist? Does anybody know how to make them?"

Dannyl could not help wondering if Lorkin knew the answers to these questions. The Traitors had stolen the secret of making magical gemstones from the Duna. If anyone other than the Duna knew the answers, the Traitors did.

Dannyl winced as he remembered the Sachakan king's

request that he establish communications with Lorkin. He'd asked Merria, his assistant, to investigate if she stumbled upon any information. *But who are we supposed to enquire of? The Ashaki no longer invite me to dinner and I never took her with me anyway. I doubt the slaves have any way of reaching Lorkin other than through the Traitors.*

He considered his lists again. The idea behind writing them was to give him a clear idea of what he was looking for while visiting the Duna tribes or Sachakan country estates. While he had answered some questions he'd had about history, it was always better to have several sources to quote from when claiming that an event happened or went a certain way, so he would still have to look for references to Imardin surviving the Sachakan War and Narvelan stealing the storestone. As for information about storestones, he had only one source to draw upon: the Duna. He couldn't ask the Traitors, so he had to rely on Lorkin recording what they knew and eventually getting the information to him.

The only worry he had about the coming journey was how the Duna would react to him and his questions. Unh had been friendly, but the tribesmen in the market had reacted badly to his mention of Unh. *But they were friendly before then. Maybe if I* don't *mention him...*

"Ambassador Dannyl?"

He looked up. The voice was Merria's and came from the main room.

"Come in, Lady Merria," he called. Footsteps drew closer and she stepped into the doorway of his office. He beckoned, gesturing for her to sit on the chair for visitors. "How are you doing?" he asked.

She shrugged. "Fine. I imagined there'd be a lot more

paperwork and not very much interaction with the people, due to their customs in regard to women. It's been very much the opposite."

"You've been seeing a lot of the women Ashaki Achati introduced you to?"

"Yes, and their friends. They have quite a network. They never meet all at once, of course. The men would think they were forming a secret rebel society." Her smile told him how much this amused her. "You'd think having all these women passing on messages to each other would make them suspicious, but..." She shrugged. "Maybe they don't notice."

Dannyl nodded. "I haven't heard anything about it. Do you think they're organising anything?"

"I wouldn't have thought so, except that a few days after I commented that Lorkin's mother would like to hear from him I got a message saying he is in the Traitor city and is fine. I was also invited to send him a message in return."

Dannyl's heart skipped. "Where is this message they gave you?"

Merria shook her head. "It was verbal. The women never write anything down."

He considered what she had told him. "Do you think this came through the Traitors?"

She nodded. "I can't see how else such messages would get to him, if he's in the Traitor city and only Traitors ever go there. Unless there are spies among the spies."

"It's possible."

She shook her head. "I think it's more likely the women only say they hate the Traitors so that the men let them see each other."

Dannyl nodded in agreement. "Don't say that to any-one else," he advised.

Any sort of communication with Lorkin was better than none. Though King Amakira had told him to contact Lorkin some other way than through the Traitors, Dannyl did not want to lose this opportunity. He had plenty of questions for Lorkin, though what he could ask was limited by the fact that others would hear or see the message.

He should also contact Administrator Osen through his blood ring and find out if Sonea wanted to send Lorkin a message, too. That would make Sonea very happy. And the more Higher Magicians who considered what message to send, the less chance they'd send one that would have political ramifications.

"Stay there," he said to Merria. "I'll see what the Guild has to say."

Lilia woke to the sensation of pounding in her head. She groaned. Roet had left her feeling dull, low and tired before, but not this sick. Maybe the wine had been stron-ger than usual. She hadn't drunk that much of it.

Then a different pounding started *outside* her head. Someone was knocking on the door. She forced open an eye, but naturally she couldn't see through doors. It was probably the servants.

"Go away," she said weakly, closing her eye again.

The knocking stopped. She frowned. Maybe the ser-vants could give her something for the headache. She opened her mouth to call out.

The door opened. Both of her eyes sprang open as if by their own volition. She saw magicians entering the room instead of servants, and it took a moment for her mind to catch up and comprehend this.

She pushed herself up onto her elbows. At once she was aware that she was no longer dressed in her robes. When had she changed into bedclothes? She grabbed the sheets to pull them up and cover herself, and felt something dry and powdery on the skin of her palms. She turned over her hands. Something dark had dried onto them.

Wine? I don't remember getting it on my hands. And it would be sticky...

The magicians surrounded the bed. She looked up at them, recognising one of Lord Leiden's Healer friends and...her heart stopped...Black Magician Kallen.

"Lady Lilia?" Kallen asked.

"Y-yes?" Lilia's heart began beating again, much too fast. "What's going on?"

"Lord Leiden is dead," the Healer said.

She stared at him in horror. "How?" Even as she asked, a shiver of guilt ran down her spine. *We tried to teach ourselves black magic last night? What were we thinking?* "Where's Naki?"

"*HOW COULD YOU DO IT?*" The voice was a shriek, but it was still recognisably Naki's. Lilia winced. Her friend might have wished her father dead but she hadn't... Someone pushed past the magicians and was grabbed by the Healer. Naki struggled to throw them off, while glaring at Lilia.

"You!" Naki growled.

"Me?" Lilia stared at her friend.

"You *killed* him!" Naki shouted. "My *father*!"

"I didn't." Lilia shook her head. "I fell asleep. Didn't wake up."

Naki shook her head in disbelief. "Who else *could* have? I shouldn't have let you read that book. I just wanted to impress you."

A chill ran down Lilia's spine. Suddenly she was too conscious of Kallen's gaze boring into her. "How did he die?" she asked weakly.

"Black magic," Naki spat. Her gaze dropped. "What's that? What's on your hands?"

Lilia looked down at the dark stains. "I don't know."

"It's blood, isn't it?" Naki's eyes widened in horror. "My father's..." Then her eyes filled with tears, she spun about and ran from the room.

Lilia stared after her. *She thinks I killed her father. She hates me. I've lost her. But...I didn't kill her father. Or did I?* Her memories of the night before were vague in places. That always happened when she drank too much wine or had too much roet. Her dreams—had they been dreams?—had included a fantasy where she'd got rid of Naki's father, though they hadn't dwelled on how.

"Did you kill Lord Leiden?" Black Magician Kallen asked.

She forced herself to look up at him. "No. I don't think so."

"Have you learned or attempted to learn black magic?"

How to answer that? She found she could not find the words. Her head was pounding so hard she thought it would split open at any moment.

"Lady Naki has confessed to an attempt to learn black magic from a book," the Healer said. "She says that Lilia did as well."

Lilia felt a traitorous relief. She nodded. "She has a book. Well, it is—was—her father's. He keeps it in the library in a glass-topped table. She took it out and we read it—but it's not supposed to be possible to learn black magic from a book."

Kallen's gaze was unwavering. "Yet it is still forbidden to try."

She looked down. "I didn't kill her father." Again, doubt stirred and wound itself into her thoughts.

"Is this the accused?" a new voice said.

The magicians turned to look toward the door, allowing Lilia to see past them. She felt her stomach sink as she saw Black Magician Sonea approaching. Not that another black magician arriving made her situation any worse. She had always admired Sonea, though the thought of what she had done in her life made her very intimidating in person.

"Yes," Kallen said, moving away from the bed. "I am going to the library to look for a book containing instructions on using black magic. They have both confessed to reading it. Could you read their minds?"

Sonea's eyebrows rose, but she nodded. As Kallen left the room she turned to the other magicians.

"We should at least allow her to get dressed," she said. "I'll stay."

"Find out what's on her hands before she washes it off," the Healer advised.

Lilia watched them go, then when the door was closed she slipped out of the bed.

"Let me see your hands," Sonea said. She took them in her own hands, which seemed strangely small for a magician so powerful. *Not that magic makes your hands get bigger*, Lilia thought. *Now* that *would be unpleasant*. Lifting one of Lilia's hands, Sonea sniffed, then drew Lilia over to the wash basin and poured some water in.

"Wash," she ordered.

Lilia obeyed with some relief. The stain took some rubbing to come off, and coloured the water in swirls.

"We need more light," Sonea muttered. She looked over to the screens covering the windows, which began to slide open. The room filled with morning light. Looking down, Lilia caught her breath.

The swirls of colour were red.

"But how...? I don't remember..." she gasped.

Sonea was watching her thoughtfully. She stepped back. "Get changed," she said, her tone somewhere between an order and a suggestion. "Then we'll see what you remember."

Lilia obeyed, changing into her novice's robes as quickly as she could manage. When she'd finished tying the sash, she walked over to Sonea. The black magician reached out to touch the sides of Lilia's head.

Lilia had never had her mind read by a black magician before. She'd never had it read by an ordinary magician either. Her lessons in the University had occasionally required a teacher to enter her mind, but novices were always taught to hide their thoughts behind imagined doors. In a cooperative mind-read, the subject was supposed to bring out the memories hidden behind the doors for the reader to see.

This was very different. At once Lilia was aware of the older woman's presence in her mind. It was a distant thing, like hearing voices through a wall. Then she felt something influencing her thoughts. She could not sense the will behind it, so her instinctive effort to resist had no impact. Forcing herself to yield, she watched as memories of the night began to return.

Embarrassment and fear rose as she recalled Naki's kiss, but she could detect no disapproval from Sonea. Her memories were a little less vague now that someone else was examining them, but with stretches of time that were indistinct.

One of those stretches was the time after Lilia had lain down next to Naki, after drinking the wine. Her thoughts *had* been murderous, she recalled with shame. But she did not remember actually *murdering* anybody. Except in her dreams. *But were they dreams?*

What if she had murdered Naki's father while caught up in a wine- and roet-induced walking dream?

What if their experiment had worked, and she had learned black magic from a book?

—*Oh, you most certainly did*, Sonea's voice spoke into her mind. *It's not supposed to be possible. Not even Akkarin believed it was. But there has been at least one other novice in history who learned it without the help of another magician, and the magicians of that time must have had reason to be so determined to destroy anything written about it. Unfortunately, being the one to prove we were wrong is not an achievement anybody is going to look favourably on. Why did you attempt it when you knew it was forbidden?*

—*I don't know. I just went along with Naki. She told me...*

She'd told Lilia she trusted her. Would she ever again? *I love her and she hates me!*

Suddenly the loss and shock welled up and she burst into tears. Sonea's touch disappeared from her head and moved to her shoulders, rubbing them gently but firmly as Lilia struggled to regain control of herself.

"I won't tell you everything will be fine," Sonea said, sighing. "But I think I can persuade them that it wasn't exactly deliberate, and to choose a more lenient punishment. That will depend on what Naki remembers, though."

A more lenient punishment? Lilia shivered as she remembered what she had been taught in history classes. *Akkarin was exiled only because the Guild didn't know if it could defeat him. They would have executed him otherwise. But then, he had killed people with black magic. I haven't... I hope.*

If she hadn't, Sonea would find no evidence in Naki's mind. Suddenly Lilia badly wanted Sonea to go and find that out. The last urge to cry vanished.

"Are you all right now?" Sonea asked.

Lilia nodded.

"Stay here."

The wait was torture. When Sonea finally returned, with Black Magician Kallen and the two other magicians following, her expression was grim.

"She did not witness the death of her father," Sonea told her. "Nor is there any proof in her mind that you killed him, other than the manner of death and the blood on your hands. Either could be coincidence."

Lilia sighed with relief. *I didn't do it*, she told herself.

"Her memories of last night are very different to yours," Sonea continued. "But not in ways that a misunderstanding would not explain." She shook her head. "Despite what you recall sensing, she has not learned black magic."

A bittersweet relief rose at that. At least Naki had not committed as great a crime as Lilia had, though she *had* tried to learn black magic, so Lilia doubted she would escape punishment completely.

Perhaps, now she knows I didn't kill her father, we can face this together.

But when the magicians escorted Lilia out of the room, Naki was there, glaring at Lilia with an intensity that set her hopes withering.

CHAPTER 12

DELIBERATIONS

T he sound of the underground river surrounded Lorkin as he stepped out of the tunnel. Tyvara was sitting on the bench seat, as before, gazing thoughtfully at
the sewer waterwheel. He was tempted to call out to
her mentally, but even if it would not reveal that they were
meeting, the Traitors had even stricter rules forbidding
mental communication than the Guild, since they could
not risk that even the shortest call would be picked up by
other magicians, and lead searchers to Sanctuary.

So he waited until she noticed him and beckoned.

"Lorkin," she said as he stepped onto the ledge. "I
wasn't expecting you to have time to visit for a while. Isn't
the chill fever in the second stage?"

He nodded and sat down beside her. "It is. It's why I'm
here. But first, how are you?"

Her eyebrows rose in amusement. "You Kyralians.
Always so formal. I'm fine."

"Bored?"

She laughed. "Of course. But I get visitors. And..."

She pulled a ring from one of her fingers and held it up for a moment before stowing it into a pocket. "People keep me informed on what's happening in the city. I've just been told that Kalia is furious at you leaving, by the way."

He shrugged. "I don't have time to wait for things to quieten down."

Tyvara frowned. "You're not neglecting my people because of me, are you?"

"Yes and no." He grimaced. Even with magician volunteers helping out in the Care Room, there was a lot of work to do. He couldn't stay long. It was time to get to the point. "I need your advice."

Her gaze became wary. "Oh?"

"It was inevitable that someone would get sick or be injured so badly that the only way they'd survive is if I Healed them," he said. "I've always planned to help them. I've always known there would be consequences. I want to know what you think they'll be, and if I can avoid or reduce them."

She regarded him in silence, her expression serious, then nodded. "We have discussed this," she said, and somehow, by a subtle change in her tone, he knew that she did not mean her and him, but her faction within the Traitors.

"And?"

"Savara thought you would refuse to Heal them. Zarala said you wouldn't, but you'd wait to be asked."

"*Should* I wait? Is Kalia ruthless enough to let the girl die?"

"She might be." Tyvara scowled. "Her excuse will be that you made it clear Healing wasn't something you were willing to give, and she was respecting your decision by not pestering you. People will have to decide if it was worse that she did not ask you, or that you did not offer, and they will probably favour her. You haven't used your Healing powers before, and have not indicated that you would do anything but refuse if asked to."

"So I shouldn't wait. Will people regard my using Healing as flaunting what I refuse to teach them, and what my father failed to?"

"Perhaps. Not so much if you use it only in greatest need, when the patient would die otherwise."

"What about those in pain?"

"It would show you have compassion, if you helped them, too."

"A toothache hurts. As do many everyday ailments. At what point will people feel it is reasonable for me to refuse Healing? Will they expect I treat everything, once I start?"

She frowned, then suddenly grinned. "It might be worth the trouble, if it put Kalia out of a job." Then she grew serious again and shook her head. "But that would be foolish. Kalia has too many supporters." Her shoulders rose and fell in a sigh he couldn't hear over the rushing water. "There will be different opinions on when it is reasonable for you to refuse to Heal with magic, and a person's opinion may change if they happen to be the one with the toothache. I think most people will agree that there's a point where you are right to refuse, but it will be interesting to see if they allow you to be the one to decide that."

He nodded. "Anything else?"

"Make sure you get the patient's or parent's permission before you do anything," she added.

"Should I ask Kalia?"

She winced. "Zarala was most concerned about this. If you ask Kalia, she will forbid you to use magic to Heal anyone, insisting that you teach her how to instead. Then if the patient dies, it is still your fault for refusing. If you do not ask her, you will not have respected her as your superior, and as a man that is especially bad. But if you save someone's life, people will forgive that disrespect. As many people dislike Kalia as support her." She spread her hands. "In your defence, point out that nobody here has to seek permission from Kalia before treating a sick or injured Traitor. Patients *choose* to go to the Care Room."

Lorkin sighed. "I can't avoid annoying Kalia, but so long as I annoy as few other people as possible I'll have to live with that."

"And you'll be saving lives," she said.

He smiled in reply. "You Traitors have the easier decision," he told her. "Keeping stone-making knowledge to yourselves doesn't involve anybody dying."

"You enjoy the benefits of the stones even if you don't make them yourself," she pointed out. "So why shouldn't we get the benefits of magical Healing in return?"

He grinned. "Well, that makes it sound very fair and reasonable."

"It would be, if it weren't just one Kyralian benefiting from the stones and many, many Traitors potentially benefiting from your Healing magic."

Meeting her gaze, he saw something there that made his heart lighten. *She understands. And she's letting me know that she understands—and perhaps agrees—with my reason for being here.*

He suddenly had a strong urge to kiss her, but resisted it. After all, she hadn't shown any sign of agreeing with his other reason for being in Sanctuary: her.

"Thank you," he said, standing up.

"Good luck," she replied.

Reluctantly he turned away and headed back to the tunnel. Though he knew that the decision he'd already made was going to cause him a lot of trouble, talking to Tyvara had reassured him that he could make it without the consequences being any worse than they needed to be.

The only decision he needed to make now was *when*.

When Dannyl arrived at the Guild House, returning from Achati's home, he found Tayend and Merria enjoying a late-night drink and chat in the Master's Room. He paused to consider them. Achati's arrangements for the journey to Duna were coming together quickly, and Dannyl would have to tell his assistant and the Elyne Ambassador about them sooner than he expected.

No point putting it off, he told himself. Walking over to the stools, he nodded toward the bottle of wine.

"Any left?"

Tayend grinned and waved to a slave standing against one wall. "Fetch another glass," he ordered, then patted the larger stool in the centre of the seating meant for the house's master. "We saved it for you."

Dannyl snorted softly and sat down. Though he was the person of highest rank in the Guild House, he doubted Tayend would have avoided the seat for that reason.

"What have you both been doing?" he asked.

Tayend waved a hand dismissively. "More important

people to visit, more delicious meals to consume. That sort of thing."

"Enjoy it while it lasts," Dannyl told him. He looked at Merria.

She shrugged. "I went to see my new friends and gave them Black Magician Sonea's message. You?"

The slave returned, offering the wineglass with bowed head and lowered eyes. Tayend picked up the bottle and filled the glass. Dannyl took a sip, then sighed with appreciation. "Ashaki Achati and I have been planning a trip to Duna. Looks like we'll be leaving sooner than I expected: in a week—maybe even a few days."

Merria's eyes widened in surprise.

"Research or ambassadorial duties?" Tayend asked, a knowing look in his eyes.

"Mostly research," Dannyl admitted. "Though it won't hurt, politically."

"It was the books from the market, wasn't it?" Tayend looked smug.

"I guess in a way they did lead to Achati suggesting a research trip." To Dannyl's satisfaction, the smug look vanished.

"So when are we leaving?" Merria asked.

Dannyl lifted an eyebrow at her. "We?"

Her face fell. "You're not taking me with you?"

He shook his head. "I can't."

"It's a habit of his," Tayend murmured. "Always leaving people behind."

Dannyl gave Tayend a reproachful look. The scholar's eyes widened in mock innocence.

"Surely you'll need an assistant on this journey," Merria persisted. "More so than you do here, anyway."

"I—the Guild—needs you to stay here," Dannyl told her. "To take care of things, in the unlikely event that something comes up. We can't leave the Guild House unoccupied by Guild magicians."

"That's true," Tayend agreed, quietly. "They'd kick me out, since I'm supposed to be finding my own premises."

"But," Merria was beginning to sound panicky. "If anything important comes up, they won't want to deal with a woman."

"They'll have to, or else wait until I return. If it's urgent..." He pursed his lips and considered. He would have to leave Osen's blood ring behind, so that Merria could consult with the Administrator if anything important came up. So she could pass messages on to the Guild, and Sonea. *If only I could make my own blood ring. Or had someone else's...ah, of course! I have Sonea's ring. Perhaps she would agree to me leaving it here for Merria.* He would contact her tomorrow, he decided.

"If it's urgent, you will contact Osen or Sonea via one of their blood rings. I'll take one with me and leave one here." Dannyl straightened and placed a hand on her shoulder. "You'll be fine, Merria. You have found your way into the hidden world of Sachakan women and established links with the Traitors, all in a remarkably short time. I have no doubt that, if something comes up— which seems unlikely—you'll be able to hold things together."

"I have no doubt of it either," Tayend added.

Her strained smile was more like a grimace, but she did look calmer and less uncertain, though disappointed.

"How long will you be gone?" she asked.

"I don't know exactly," Dannyl told her. "A few weeks,

maybe more. It depends on seasonal winds or something and whether the tribesmen agree to see us at all."

Merria made a small huffing sound. "Now you're rubbing it in. I'd love to visit the tribes."

"Perhaps we'll go back there someday," he suggested. "Once I know if they are as restrictive in their regard for women as the Sachakans are."

Immediately her eyes brightened. "The men in the market were friendly."

"Yes, but we can't assume they are all like that. Traders have every reason to relax whatever customs they might normally follow in the pursuit of customers."

She frowned. "What if a message comes from Lorkin while you're gone?"

"You'll pass it on to the recipient via the blood ring," he told her.

She nodded. "Perhaps the Traitors could get one to you."

"I doubt they have connections in the tribes," he pointed out. "And it may be wise to not grow too reliant on the Traitors. They aren't our enemy, as far as we know. But they aren't allies, either."

The Administrator's office was full of Higher Magicians. As always, there were more magicians than chairs and Sonea was amused to note who was sitting down and who standing up. The Heads of Disciplines were traditionally the more vocal of the group. Lady Vinara, Lord Peakin and Lord Garrel were seated closest to Osen's desk. Though High Lord Balkan outranked them, he chose to stand against the wall to one side, arms crossed.

The Heads of Studies, Lords Rothen, Erayk and Telano,

and University Director Jerrik were also sitting down, but on the plainer dining chairs that had been brought over from the little table Osen had in the room. Sonea had often wondered if Osen ever had small dinner gatherings here and, if so, how often. She had never been invited to one.

The Healer and Alchemist who had been in Naki's guest room when Sonea arrived were also present, standing at the back. One of the king's advisers sat to one side, and Sonea, not for the first time, wondered if they received training in how to avoid attracting attention—remaining unobserved while observing all.

As always, she and Black Magician Kallen were standing. Kallen had been looming over the others when Sonea arrived, and though she told herself that it would be easier if they could all see her when she reported her findings, she had to admit there was a small, defiant part of her that didn't want to seem less authoritative than he, sitting down while he towered over everyone.

The door opened and all turned to see Novice Director Narren enter the room. The man was younger than his predecessor, Ahrind, had been when Sonea was a novice, but he was equally strict and humourless. As Osen welcomed him he looked around and nodded politely. When his gaze fell on her and Kallen he frowned.

"Who is guarding Lilia?" he asked, alarmed.

Sonea looked at Kallen and saw a flicker of the same amusement she felt. "Lilia is no stronger than her natural limit," she reminded him. "The two magicians guarding her will have no more trouble restraining her than myself and Black Magician Kallen would."

He blinked, then flushed a bright red. "Ah. Forgive me. I forgot."

"So Lilia hasn't taken power from anyone?" Vinara asked, looking at Sonea.

"I detected no unnatural level of power within her. She may have taken power, then used it, but she doesn't recall doing so, except—"

Osen cleared his throat and raised his hands to indicate they should stop talking. "Forgive me for interrupting, but we should begin at the beginning." He looked to the back of the room. "Lords Roah and Parrie, please tell us when you first learned of Lord Leiden's murder."

The Healer and Alchemist moved forward. All turned to observe them, but it was the latter who spoke.

"I was talking with Lord Roah when a message came from Lady Naki that her father had been murdered during the night. We went straight to her house, where she showed us Lord Leiden's body, and told us that Lilia must have killed him. Lord Roah examined Leiden and found he was drained of power, while I questioned Naki on why she thought her fellow novice was responsible." He paused and looked troubled.

"She confessed to spending the previous evening with Lilia studying a book on black magic. They had both experimented with the directions, thinking themselves safe from the dangers of success because they had been told it could not be learned from a book. She hadn't succeeded and Lilia claimed failure as well, but now that her father had been killed with black magic she could not think of anyone else who could be to blame." He glanced at Kallen. "Black Magician Kallen arrived and we proceeded to the guest room. Lilia was asleep, but woke on our arrival. She appeared surprised, and shocked at the news and Naki's accusations."

"But there appeared to be dried blood on her hands," the Healer added. He looked at Sonea. "Was it blood?"

Sonea nodded. "It was. Was there much blood on and around Lord Leiden?"

"A little. The cut had been wiped clean."

"That is odd," Lady Vinara said. "Why clean the corpse but not her hands?"

"Perhaps in the excitement and darkness she did not notice they were soiled," Garrel suggested.

"Lilia does not recall how it got on her hands," Sonea told them. All attention turned to her. She looked at Lord Parrie, who nodded to say he was finished. "Lilia was still in bed when I arrived," she explained. "Kallen left to find the book while I examined the blood and read Lilia's mind.

"She had a nasty headache resulting from a night of roet and wine, and I suspect much of her memory loss is due to those influences. She remembers Naki taking the initiative with the book. They went to the library, where Naki removed the book from its keeping place—as she had done before. Naki opened the page and urged Lilia to read. They then took it in turns to try the steps described. Lilia was first, then Naki."

Sonea paused and resisted the urge to grimace. "Lilia clearly recalls achieving the state of mind required, and even taking a little power from Naki." A collective soft intake of breath sounded around the room. "She also recalls Naki taking strength from her. Then they went back to the guest bedroom to drink some wine and talk, and during the conversation Naki expressed a wish for Lilia to get rid of her father, who had been restricting her access to wine, roet and money. Lilia remembers nothing after that until she was woken in the morning.

"However, Naki remembers the same events, but with a very different perspective. She recalls Lilia persuading her to get the book and encouraging her to try the lesson it contained, and Naki complied because she wanted to impress her—and didn't think she would succeed. She did not make sense of the instructions, however, and when I sought a memory of the sensations or knowledge of using black magic I found nothing. Naki did, however, express a wish for Lilia to get rid of her father, which she now regrets."

"How can they have such different recollections?" Peakin asked.

"They were making great assumptions about each other," Sonea told him. "They misunderstood each other's motives and desires. Each thought the other was pushing them to try black magic, and that if they refused they would be seen as weak and boring." Once again, Sonea hesitated to reveal the infatuation Lilia had for Naki. She had learned, as a youngster in the former slums, that bonds could naturally form between women as well as men. She did not see any more harm in it than a love match between a man and a woman. But she knew many didn't agree, and it was true that not all infatuations, regardless of gender, were good for those involved. Though Lilia's had been a one-sided thing, Naki had evidently encouraged it. It had clearly been a part of their reckless pleasure-seeking adventures.

Lady Vinara sighed. "Ah, the young can be such fools."

How true that is, Sonea thought. *But this is a private matter and it isn't yet relevant to the crimes committed. It would be cruel to expose it.*

"We told them that they couldn't learn black magic

from books," Director Jerrik reminded them. "Though we also forbade them to read about it. That always makes something more attractive, to a certain kind of person. And having told them that they couldn't learn black magic by reading of it, we suggested it was a safe way of defying rules."

"We were wrong," Garrel said, and even looked regretful about it, Sonea noted.

"Yes, we are partly to blame for this," Osen said. "Which is going to make deciding what to do with Naki and Lilia even harder."

Sonea saw many nods of agreement.

"I don't think anyone would think us neglectful if we chose a more lenient punishment than the old standard," Vinara said.

This time all nodded. *To execute two novices for fooling around with something we told them was safe would cause an outrage now*, Sonea mused. *How attitudes toward black magic have changed.*

"Naki has not learned black magic," Peakin said. "She cannot be guilty of her father's death. She should be given a more lenient punishment."

More nods of agreement followed. Sonea felt a twinge of discomfort. The two girls were equal in their guilt, as far as she was concerned. There was no proof that Lilia had killed Lord Leiden. The only provable crime was that they had tried to learn black magic. That Lilia had succeeded was an unfortunate result, but not a deliberate one on her part.

Was there some prejudice here? Naki was of the higher class; Lilia from a servant family. Naki was pretty and popular; Lilia was quiet and had few friends.

"The punishment must be strong enough to deter other novices attempting to learn black magic," Vinara added.

"I suggest we delay Naki's graduation," Director Jerrik said. "She has lost a father. That is painful enough. She must also cope with the sudden responsibility that comes with being the sole inheritor of her family fortune. She will likely fall behind in her studies anyway."

"She should make a public apology," Garrel added. "And her return to the University be dependent on her not committing any other crime."

"How long would we delay her graduation?" Osen asked.

"A year?" Jerrik suggested.

"Three," Vinara said decisively. "The punishment is supposed to be a deterrent, not a holiday."

"Any objections or suggestions?" Osen asked. None spoke. He nodded. "What of Lilia's punishment?"

"That depends on whether she killed Lord Leiden," Peakin pointed out. "What proof do we have?"

"None," Kallen said. "There were no witnesses. The servants heard and saw nothing. There is only Naki's conclusion that Lilia had learned black magic, and being the only person in the house with the knowledge, must be the culprit."

"Put that way, it seems obvious that it was Lilia," Vinara said. She looked at Sonea and the corner of her mouth curled upward. "If it weren't for the fact she can't remember anything of it. Does she seem the murdering sort?"

Sonea shook her head. "No. She is quite appalled, and afraid that she might have done it in her sleep, or under the influence of roet."

"Could she have acted in some drug-induced state, and not remembered it?" Peakin asked. "Naki had suggested it to her, after all."

Sonea shuddered. "I have learned not to be surprised when it comes to the many detrimental effects of roet, but I have not heard of this happening before. If something so extraordinary has happened, it still means Lilia did not consciously and deliberately murder Lord Leiden. It could only be considered an accident."

The room fell into a brief, thoughtful silence. High Lord Balkan moved forward.

"One thing is known: Lilia has learned black magic. The king and the people will expect us to ensure she is no danger to anyone if she is to remain alive."

"We have to block her powers," Vinara said.

"Can her powers be blocked?" Peakin asked, looking from Kallen to Sonea.

"Nobody has tried blocking a black magician's powers before," she told him. "We won't know if it's possible until we try."

"If we can, then what do we do with her?" Garrel asked. "She is no longer a magician and therefore not a member of the Guild, but we can't cast her out onto the street."

"She'll have to be watched constantly," Peakin said. "Who is going to do that?"

Glances were exchanged. Expressions became grim. Sonea felt a chill run down her spine.

"Surely we've got a better option than putting her in the Lookout," she found herself saying aloud.

"I don't see that we have any choice," Vinara said. The others nodded.

"Until the cause of Lord Leiden's death is discovered we don't know whether she can be trusted or not," Garrel added. "If she killed someone in her sleep...well, we don't want that happening again."

"The Guild hasn't held a prisoner in years," Lord Telano muttered. "Suddenly it has two."

Sonea suppressed a shiver. The last prisoners had been her and Akkarin, though they hadn't been held for long.

"Let's ensure she is as comfortable and well looked after as possible," Osen said. "It does seem right that her punishment be less strenuous than Lorandra's, who we know has broken laws and killed others. Are we in agreement?"

Murmurs of assent followed. Osen looked at Sonea. "You look troubled, Black Magician Sonea."

She nodded. "I agree that a harsher punishment is needed, but...she isn't a bad person and she is so young. It is a shame to lock her up for the rest of her life. Perhaps we could reconsider her case in a few years if she, too, has displayed good behaviour."

He pursed his lips as he considered. "How many years?"

"Ten?" someone suggested. Sonea winced as the others murmured agreement, but nodded as Osen looked to her. She doubted she'd be able to talk them into a shorter length of time.

"So, who will block her powers?" he asked, looking from her to Kallen.

"I will," she replied. "Unless you have any objections, I want to have another look at her memories."

He smiled and nodded. "No objections. If you can find

out anything that further explains what happened last night, it will be most welcome." He looked at the other magicians. "And now we have the matter of Lord Leiden's murder to consider. We know where Sonea and Kallen were at the time. If Lilia didn't kill him, who did?"

CHAPTER 13

DIFFICULT DECISIONS

A scraping sound drew Lilia out of her thoughts and she turned to see the door of the Dome recede. As it moved aside it was replaced by a circle of cold light against which a silhouette of a magician stood. The magician beckoned, so Lilia stood up and obediently walked up to and out of the entrance.

As her eyes adjusted to the light, she saw that it was late afternoon. *I was inside for less than a day*, she thought. *It felt like longer. Though it could be a day and a half. But then I'd be hungry.* Her stomach growled. *Well, hungrier than this.*

"It's time, Lilia."

Lilia realised the magician was Black Magician Sonea and sketched a hasty bow. Sonea regarded Lilia with a sympathetic expression. Two other magicians waited a few steps away. Lilia avoided their eyes, falling into step as Sonea started toward the University.

"I wish we could avoid this Hearing," Sonea said. "It's

unavoidable, I'm afraid. You and Naki must be judged before the Guild."

Lilia nodded. "I understand."

"You're not to talk to each other," Sonea added quietly. "Only speak when you are requested to, or to answer a question."

Lilia nodded. She could see in the corner of her eye that Sonea was watching her closely, and realised something more definite was expected to indicate she had really heard and understood her, and wasn't just responding automatically.

"Yes," Lilia managed, her voice husky from crying and lack of use. "No talking to...unless asked to." She could not say Naki's name, but Sonea looked away, apparently satisfied.

They walked down the length of the University to the front entrance. The numbness that had come over Lilia since arriving at the Guild and being locked away in the Dome began to slip away as they climbed the stairs, and was replaced by a growing dread. She was going to have to stand in front of all the magicians of the Guild and endure their stares and judgement. All would be wondering if she was a murderer. All would know she had learned black magic. Whether they thought she had done so due to foolishness or evil intent, they would despise her.

She thought of her family's disappointment, and quickly pushed the thought away. Best to dwell on only one confrontation full of shame and humiliation at a time.

They quickly passed through the spectacular entry hall of the University and down the corridor to the Great Hall. The space around the ancient building within the huge hall was empty, to her relief. She'd expected that some novices would find their way there, to watch what they could.

The doors to the Guildhall opened and her blood went cold.

The space between the tiered seating on either side of the room was filled with seats, and the seats were filled with brown-robed novices, twisting around so they could see her enter the building.

She fixed her eyes on the floor. Her heart thundered in her ears as she forced her shaky legs to carry her down the aisle. If any of the novices whispered anything—if any called out—she did not hear it. Blood was rushing in her ears, drowning out all noises. She concentrated on breathing, and on putting one trembling leg in front of the other.

They reached the Front of the hall and moved to the right-hand side, where Sonea stopped and placed a hand gently on Lilia's shoulder.

"Stay here," she murmured, then she strode forward and climbed the steep stairs to her seat among the Higher Magicians. Watching her, Lilia saw that some of the Higher Magicians were frowning. One said something, but Sonea waved a hand in a reassuring, dismissing gesture.

Then Lilia met the eyes of a Higher Magician who was staring at her, and quickly looked back down at the floor.

"You have heard the accounts of the few witnesses to these events," a male voice boomed. Lilia glanced up and saw that the blue-robed Administrator was standing in the centre of the Front. She had been staring at the floor so hard that she hadn't noticed him there. "You have heard what Black Magician Sonea discovered in the minds of the two young women standing before us. Now let us hear what they have to say. Lady Naki."

A shiver ran down Lilia's spine and she followed Osen's eyes to find that Naki was standing just ten or so strides from her, on the left-hand side of the room. Her heart began to lighten at the familiar, beautiful face, but the feeling faded and was replaced by a pain that made Lilia's breath catch in her throat.

"Yes, Administrator Osen," Naki replied calmly, and a little coldly. She was standing with her back straight and her head high. Dark circles shadowed her red eyes. *She looks strong, but also like she might crumble any moment*, Lilia thought. *What do I look like, all stooped and unable to look at anyone? I must look as guilty as she thinks I am.*

Naki told her story. At every word, Lilia felt a little colder, until she was chilled to the core. *But she was the one who wanted to read the book and try black magic! It was all her idea!* As Naki described finding her father's body, she turned and glared at Lilia.

"She killed him. Who else could it have been? She must have learned from the book. Maybe she already knew it." Naki's face crumpled and she covered her face with her hands. "Why? Why did you do it?"

Lilia's heart twisted in sympathy. "I didn't, Naki. I..." Lilia began, but Osen frowned at her and she choked back the words.

After a pause while Naki recovered her composure, the Higher Magicians questioned her, but it seemed to Lilia that they expected to learn nothing more than they had already been told. Osen turned to face Lilia, and she drew in a deep breath and hoped her voice would remain steady.

"Lady Lilia," he began. "Tell us what happened the night you stayed at Lady Naki's home."

She tried to explain, but every time she described something differently to Naki the girl made a small noise of disgust or protest, and she found herself hurrying. Only when she had moved on from the subject of the book did Lilia realise she should have mentioned that Naki had shown it to her before, but by then it didn't seem worth going back to add that detail. When Osen asked her about the blood on her hands, she suddenly remembered that she'd sensed Naki taking power, but when she tried to tell Osen he took it as an attempt to divert attention from questions about the blood. Finally, his questions became more direct.

"Did you attempt to learn black magic?"

"Yes," she replied, feeling her face heat.

"Did you succeed?"

"Yes," she forced out. "At least, Black Magician Sonea says I did."

"Did you kill Lord Leiden?"

"No."

He nodded and looked at the Higher Magicians, and Lilia braced herself for their questions. They had more for her than for Naki. When the torture was over, and Osen's attention finally moved from her to the rest of the hall, she felt an immense relief.

"There is not enough evidence to accuse anyone of Lord Leiden's murder," he said. "Though investigations are far from over. Two crimes have been confessed to, however: the attempt to learn, and the learning of black magic. The Higher Magicians have decided upon appropriate punishment for these crimes, taking into account the age of the accused, and the intent behind their actions."

He paused. "The punishment for Lady Naki, who admits that she attempted to learn black magic but did not succeed, is a three-year expulsion from the University, with her powers blocked, after which her conduct will be reviewed and, if deemed satisfactory, she may return."

A faint sigh rose from the watching magicians and novices, followed by a low rumble of discussion, but the sounds quietened as Osen spoke again.

"The punishment for Lady Lilia, who admits that she attempted to learn black magic and succeeded, is expulsion from the Guild. Her powers will be blocked and she will be required to abide within an appropriately secure place. We will review her punishment in ten years."

No sigh came from the watching magicians and novices. Instead the murmuring began immediately and rose in volume. Osen frowned, hearing the tone of dissatisfaction. Lilia felt her stomach sink.

They don't think it's tough enough. They think I should be executed. They—

"Favouritism!" someone behind her said loudly.

"Naki made her do it!" another voice declared.

"No! You lowies have always been a bad influence," came the retort.

"Please escort Lady Naki and Lady Lilia out of the Guildhall," Osen said, his magically amplified voice cutting across the arguments. The room quietened a little, then the two magicians who had accompanied Lilia and Sonea earlier stepped forward and gestured to indicate she should go toward a side door nearby.

"We're on your side, Lilia!" someone called out.

She felt the briefest lightening of her heart, then someone shouted "Murderer!" and it shrivelled again. *I'm
going to be locked away. For ten years. And more,
because no matter how well behaved I am, I'll still know
how to use black magic, and that means I'll still be a
criminal. Oh, how I wish they could block my memories
as well as my powers. Why did I let Naki talk me into trying to learn black magic?*

Because she loved Naki. Because neither of them had
thought it would work. But it had, which explained why
reading about black magic was banned. The Guild
wouldn't have wanted to admit that it was possible,
because then someone with bad intentions would get hold
of a book and try it. *I should have realised that.*

Then she realised what she and Naki had done. *Everyone knows you can learn black magic from books now.
We've uncovered a secret that should have remained hidden. And like black magic, it's a secret that can't be
unlearned.*

It had been a long day for Lorkin. Not only because Kalia
had taken out her anger at him for slipping away from the
Care Room, but because he had watched the sick child's
health diminishing, all the while wondering how he was
going to Heal her without Kalia seeing and stopping him.

His dilemma had resolved itself in a surprising way,
however. Some time in the late evening the girl's parents
had decided that they did not want their child dying in the
very public, often noisy Care Room, but at home with her
family. Kalia had tried to talk them out of it, but they had
made up their mind.

This had unsettled Kalia, and she had been

absent-minded for the rest of the day. *No doubt preoccupied with trying to figure out if she could gain anything from the situation without making herself look bad.*

Two more patients were suffering badly from the chill fever: an old woman and a teenage boy who already had other health troubles. Kalia did not leave the room to visit the sick girl, perhaps because she hadn't been asked to, perhaps because she was afraid Lorkin would Heal the other dangerously ill patients while she was gone. She kept Lorkin working until late in the night, then finally dismissed him when a high-ranking magician dropped by with her sick husband, and questioned the wisdom of Kalia working so late and exhausting herself, when magicians had volunteered to watch over the patients at night to avoid that.

As he left, Kalia called out his name. He turned.

"You may go," she said. "Don't visit Velyla without me."

He nodded to show he understood. As he headed toward the sick girl's room he wondered what his disobedience would cost him.

He did not reach it.

A woman stepped out of a side room and beckoned. He knew her as one of Savara's supporters, but even so he hesitated before following her into the room. When he saw the four people waiting there his doubts evaporated.

The room was a large, half-empty food store. On a makeshift bed lay Velyla, unconscious. Her parents hovered over her. Beside them stood Savara.

"Lorkin." Savara smiled. "I thought she'd never let you leave," she said.

He grimaced. "I think she was hoping..." He caught

himself and looked at the parents. *Hoping that the girl would die before I had the chance to Heal her. I can't say that in front of them.* He walked over to the makeshift bed, then looked up at the couple. "I will try to Heal her with magic, but I can't promise that I will be able to save her. Magical Healing does not always succeed, though I've never known it to do any harm. I will only try if you give me permission to do so."

"We do," the father said, his wife nodding.

"And I will stand as witness," Savara added softly.

Lorkin looked at her. Tyvara must have told Savara of his plans. Perhaps Savara had convinced the parents to remove their child from the Care Room so that Kalia could not prevent or intervene in her Healing. Perhaps she, too, had guessed that Kalia would forbid him to visit Velyla alone, so had arranged for the girl to be brought here instead.

Savara smiled, and there was a glint of both smugness and approval in her eyes.

Turning back to the child, Lorkin put a hand on her forehead and sent his senses within her body. What he saw sent a chill down his spine. The sickness was everywhere, attacking everything. Her lungs were full of it, and her heart was weak.

He began by simply sending her body energy. Often this was enough—the body automatically used it to heal itself. This sickness that had invaded her systems was too virulent for her defences. If he had looked inside the Traitors who were not badly affected by the chill fever, he knew he would have seen their bodies fighting back. But Velyla's body was losing that fight.

It could be that her body's defences were slow and

weak, and that all it needed was a boost of energy in order
to last long enough to win the battle. Or it could be that it
would never win it, no matter how much extra time he
gave her. *Kalia will say that I prolonged her pain, if I
don't succeed. But I have to try.*

Next he forced the liquid out of her lungs—which was
not pleasant for anyone but would allow the girl to breathe
properly for a time—and Healed as much of the damage as
he could. This last step drained much of his strength, but he
did not use a great deal of his power working in the Care
Room anyway, and a night's sleep should restore him.

"Keep using Kalia's cures," he told Velyla's parents.
"They will help to keep her lungs clear and soothe her
throat." He looked down to see the girl's eyelids flutter,
and quickly added, "I've done all that can be done with
magic, which is to give her body another chance to beat
chill fever. I can do it again if she worsens, but if her body
won't fight it..." He left the sentence hanging and shook
his head.

The parents nodded, their expressions grim. "Thank
you," the father said. *Interesting that he has been the one
to speak, when the woman is considered the head of the
family*, Lorkin mused.

He felt a hand on his shoulder, and turned to see Savara
standing beside him. "You'd best get some rest. I suspect
that takes more magic than it appears to."

He shrugged, though she was right. She looked to the
woman who had brought him into the room, who now
opened the door a little to check the corridor outside, then
turned back and nodded.

"You go first," Savara murmured. "We'll leave separately, to arouse less suspicion if we're seen."

Slipping out into the corridor, he started toward the men's room. It seemed as if Savara meant to keep his healing of the girl secret. If Velyla recovered, would it seem suspicious? The girl was still ill, however, and would not be surprising anybody by romping around in perfect health tomorrow. She would take some days yet to regain some energy—assuming she did at all. Most people would not question it, but would Kalia, who knew how ill she had been?

I guess I'll find out soon enough.

As Achati's slaves took away the last of the meal, Dannyl went to take another sip of wine, then thought better of it. It was a particularly strong vintage, and the food had been extra spicy. His head was spinning in an almost unpleasant way.

It was never wise, as a magician, to get too drunk. All magicians maintained a constant level of control over their power, and that could slip a little under the effects of alcohol. Generally it was more embarrassing than dangerous, though there had been more than a few magicians over the years who had burned down their house by accident after indulging a little too much.

Some drugs—better known as poisons—could remove all control, which could be spectacularly fatal. He had read of a few incidents in early Kyralian history, mostly from before the discovery of Healing. Fortunately the drugs had side-effects that alerted victims to the danger, giving them time to remove the poison from their body if they knew how to.

Dannyl looked at Achati, who was watching him thoughtfully. At once he felt a tingle of anxiety, but also a small quickening of his pulse. He remembered the day Achati had revealed his interest in them being more than fellow magicians and diplomats. More than friends.

Dannyl had been flattered, but also cautious. Seeing him hesitate, Achati had suggested Dannyl consider the idea for a while.

How long is a while?

Dannyl had to admit, he *had* been considering it. He liked Achati a lot. He was attracted to Achati in an entirely different way than he had been to Tayend. Achati was intelligent and interesting to talk to. Not that Tayend wasn't, but he was also inclined to be flippant, foolish and occasionally thoughtless. Achati was never any of these things.

But something was making Dannyl hesitate, and he had a fairly good idea what it was: Achati was a powerful man, both magically and politically. Dannyl found this attractive, until he remembered that Achati was a Sachakan and a black magician, and then he could not help remembering the Ichani Invasion, and how Kyralia had come so close to being conquered by mere outcasts of this powerful society.

He is no Ichani, Dannyl reminded himself. *Sachaka is not full of ambitious, murderous black magicians intent on conquest. Achati is the opposite of the Ichani— civilised and intent on peace between our countries.*

Even so, it's never wise to mix politics and pleasure... unless your pleasure is *politics.*

If the entanglements and tragic romances of the courtiers of the Allied Lands were anything to go by, things could get *really* messy, and ultimately bad for at least one of the party. But this was not like those inter-racial romances involving secret weddings or scandalous affairs. It was nothing that would bring his loyalty to Kyralia into question. He could not imagine Achati having unreasonable expectations and making unrealistic promises...

"What are you thinking about?" Achati asked.

Dannyl looked at his companion and shrugged. "Nothing."

The Sachakan smiled. "It is a strange habit of Kyralians, claiming to have a void of thoughts when they don't want to discuss them."

"Or if their thoughts are too mixed and disjointed—most likely from the wine—to explain—which is probably also because of the wine," Dannyl added.

Achati chuckled. "Yes, I can see how that might be." He looked at Dannyl and frowned. "There is something I have to tell you, and I'm not sure if you will be displeased or not."

Dannyl felt a small pang of disappointment. He had almost convinced himself to accept Achati's proposal, but now that Achati was being more serious, Dannyl's doubts were creeping back in.

How would such a connection, if it were discovered, affect our standing in Sachakan society? Then it occurred to him that they were about to leave Arvice. *Out of sight and out of minds. This trip could be the perfect opportunity...*

"I've agreed to take another person on our research trip," Achati said. "He was quite persuasive, and I can't fault his reasoning. I'd already promised that if things got a bit too intense here I'd help him escape the Ashakis' interest."

Dannyl felt his heart sink. Then his disappointment at Achati's words was followed by a rising suspicion.

"Who?"

Achati smiled. "I've agreed to take Ambassador Tayend with us."

Dannyl looked away to hide his dismay. "Ah," was all he trusted himself to say.

"You are displeased." Achati sounded worried. "I thought you two were getting along."

Dannyl forced himself to shrug. "We are." *I suppose I can't ask Achati to leave Tayend behind without causing all sorts of embarrassment and insult.* "There is one possible setback, though. I suspect he has neglected to tell you something very important."

Achati frowned. "What is that?"

Dannyl did not have to force a chuckle at the memory. "Tayend gets horribly, insufferably, near-mortally seasick."

CHAPTER 14

SCHEMES

L ilia stared at her surroundings, not sure if she was awake or still dreaming. She lay still for some time, then concluded that she must be awake because there was no sense of impending threat in the room, as there had been in her dreams.

Nothing moved, nothing changed, and nothing made a noise or spoke. *Ah. I was wrong. There is a kind of threat here, but it's more subtle and sinister. It's the complete lack of anything happening. It's the threat of endless, unchanging hours going on and on into the future.*

It was the threat of boredom and of wasted years. Of never being loved, or loving another. Of being forgotten.

But it could have been worse. Looking around the room, she took in the comfortable, well-made furniture and furnishings. Not many prisons looked like this. Perhaps none but this one did. The meal the night before had been as good, if not better, than those she'd eaten in the University Foodhall. The guards were polite and, if anything, seemed to feel sorry for her. Maybe she reminded them of their daughters.

I bet their daughters never get themselves in as much trouble as I have.

She winced then, as she remembered the brief meeting she'd had with her parents, who had come to the Guild to see her before she was sent off to the Lookout. She'd been too dazed to say much. She remembered saying "sorry" a lot. Her mother had asked simply "why?" and she couldn't answer. How could she tell her mother that she loved another girl?

There had been tears. The memory was more painful now than the meeting had been at the time. She got up and dressed just to have something else to think about, her breath misting in the chill air. Someone had decided she should wear the sort of simple trousers and tunic that most servants wore, but of a better-quality cloth. A warm undershift was included. Robes would have been too thin and light to ward off the cold, even if she had been allowed to wear them. She shivered and suddenly felt the loss of her magic keenly.

A brazier had been installed in the room, with a flue that sent the smoke out through the exterior wall of the building. Beside it was a pile of wood and kindling. She guessed that, since the Lookout had been built for magicians, no fireplaces or chimneys had been included. When the Guard had taken over they would have worked out that braziers were the easiest non-magical way to keep the rooms warm.

Spark sticks had been provided, so she set about lighting the brazier. She didn't try to use her powers, sure that the blockage Black Magician Sonea had placed on her mind was impenetrable, and that striving against it would be unpleasant. She could barely remember it being put in place. Her mind had been numb with shock.

Sonea asked me some questions, she recalled. *I wasn't of much use to her, but at least she was still trying to help. Or, at least, to find out who killed Naki's father.*

Would the Guild give up trying, now that she was imprisoned? She hoped not. Though Naki hadn't liked her stepfather, she had been obviously distressed by his death. She deserved to know what had really happened.

Especially since she might be in danger. Whoever killed her father might come after her.

Lilia's heart began to beat faster, but she took a few deep breaths and told herself that Naki could look after herself. She didn't entirely believe it though. Naki was too easily distracted by the latest indulgence. How well would she defend herself when caught up in the seduction of roet?

Well, that's something I won't have any problems with. No more roet for me, here in my prison.

The thought sent a shiver of anxiety through her. She shook her head. It wasn't as if she *needed* roet. Or even wanted it that much. But it would have helped her forget everything. To not care about the things she couldn't change or do. To stop feeling so stupid for trying out the book's instructions on black magic. To endure not knowing whether Naki was in danger or not. Perhaps even to smother the love she felt for Naki. Didn't the songmakers and poets say that love only brought pain?

Had she not loved Naki, she might have felt resentment towards the girl getting them into this mess in the first place. *Trouble is, her recklessness is part of what I love about her. Though maybe it isn't a part I like so much any more.*

The brazier was small, and her skin was prickling with cold. Getting up, she drew a blanket from the bed around her shoulders and paced the room. For a while she stood at one of the slim windows, looking down on the forest outside. It was the same forest that backed onto the Guild buildings. She had never explored it. Having grown up in the city, the prospect of entering a wild, animal-filled mass of trees was strange and a little frightening. From her high vantage point—on the second floor of a tower built on a ridge overlooking the forest—she could see that the spaces between the trees were packed with an untidy tangle of dead trunks and vegetation. She tried to imagine how a person might walk through the forest without tripping over. *Probably very slowly.*

When she grew bored with staring at the forest, she occupied herself by looking closely at objects in the room. All were practical. There were no books, no paper or writing tools. Would the guards bring her some, if she asked?

The door to the corridor was of heavy, quality wood. A small square of glass had obviously been installed as an afterthought, so guards could check where their prisoner was before they opened the door. There was a door between her room and the next. She had tried the handle the previous night, thinking it might lead to a second room—perhaps a more private washroom—but it would not turn. Approaching it again, she wondered what was beyond. Out of curiosity she pressed her ear to the wood.

To her surprise, she could hear a voice. A woman's voice. She could not hear what the woman was saying, but the sound was quite musical. Perhaps the woman was singing.

A knock at the main door made her jump violently. Knowing that she would have been observed listening to her neighbour, Lilia stepped hurriedly away from the side door.

The main door opened and a smiling guard entered, carrying a tray. He was young—only a few years older than her. The tray held a typical Kyralian morning meal.

"A good morning, Lilia," he said, putting the tray on the small dining table. "Did you sleep well?"

She nodded.

"Warm enough? Need more blankets?"

She nodded, then shook her head.

"Would you like me to bring you anything?" His demeanour was strangely compliant for a man wearing a uniform usually associated with authority and force.

She considered. *Better take up the offer. I'm going to be here a long time.*

"Books?"

His smile widened. "I'll see what I can rustle up for you. Anything else?"

She shook her head.

"Well, you're easy to please. The one next door always wants thread made from reber wool, so she can make blankets and hats."

Lilia glanced at the side wall between herself and her singing neighbour. "Who...?" she began.

For the first time, the guard's smile fell away and he frowned. "Lorandra. The rogue magician that Black Magician Sonea found. Strange-looking woman, but polite and no trouble."

Lilia nodded. She'd heard about this rogue. The woman's son was also a magician, and he hadn't been caught yet. He worked for a Thief, or something like that.

"My name's Welor," the guard told her. "I'm to make sure you're comfortable while you stay with us at the Lookout. I'll get you some books. In the meantime," he nodded at the tray, "a bit of food will help warm you up."

"Thanks," she managed. He nodded and retreated to the door, smiling once more before he closed it.

For all the friendliness and obliging manner, the clunk of the lock turning was firm and unhesitating. With a sigh, Lilia sat down and started eating.

When Lorkin had arrived back at the Care Room that morning, Kalia was in an inexplicable mood. With a neutral tone and a blank expression, she told Lorkin that the old woman suffering from chill fever had died during the night.

She said nothing about Velyla, but he soon found the night's secret Healing fell to the back of his mind as he began to worry about how the Traitors might react to the old woman's death. He braced himself for accusations and censure.

None came. As the hours passed, all that was said by the patients and visitors to the Care Room was that the woman was very old already and, while it was sad that she had died, it had not been unexpected. Nobody cast any pointed looks in Lorkin's direction. If Kalia felt any temptation to hint that he could have saved the old woman, she resisted it.

The teenaged boy was not doing well, however, and as Lorkin began to feel weariness from a short night's sleep creeping in with the approaching evening, the boy's parents arrived and told Kalia they were taking him back to their rooms.

The narrowed-eyed look Kalia cast at Lorkin sent a warning chill down his spine. He endeavoured to look puzzled, or at least tired and uncomprehending. She said nothing, and insisted on escorting the family.

Will I be waylaid on the way back to the men's room tonight? he wondered. *How long will it be before Kalia works out what's going on? If she hasn't already.*

Drawing a little magic, he soothed away the tiredness in his body and turned back to the task he'd been engaged in before the family arrived. Not long after, he heard footsteps from the entrance and looked up to see if it was a new patient.

Evar smiled and nodded at Lorkin, glanced around the room, then came over. His nose was red and his eyes puffy.

"What great timing you have," Lorkin said.

"What do you mean?" Evar asked, blinking with false innocence. He coughed. "Urgh," he said. "I hate chill fever."

"*You* have chill fever?"

"I have a sore throat."

Lorkin chuckled, indicated that Evar should follow him, then headed for the cures Kalia had brought out of her storeroom for the day.

"Where's Kalia?" he asked.

Evar shrugged. "On her way to somewhere. I didn't see where exactly. I just saw she was out and about and came straight here."

Lorkin handed his friend a small measure of the tea. "You know the dosage?"

"Of course. Had it every year for as many years as I can remember."

"And yet you're a magician," Lorkin said. Not that Guild magicians never succumbed to illnesses. They tended to recover quickly though. Even if Evar did have chill fever, Lorkin would not have been surprised if he woke up tomorrow completely well again.

Evar looked around. "How is it going?"

"A little better. We'll start seeing fewer people soon, mainly because the fever is running out of people to infect."

"I was starting to think I'd evaded it this y—"

"*Lorkin.*"

They both looked up to see Kalia standing in the entry-way. She crossed her arms and strode toward him, her firm footsteps echoing in the room. Her eyes were narrowed and her lips were pressed into a thin line.

"Uh, oh," Evar breathed. He took a step back as Kalia approached. She stopped a little closer to Lorkin than might be considered normal or comfortable, and glared at him.

Glared *up* at him, Lorkin noted. It was petty, but there was something comical about her trying to physically intimidate him when she was at least a handspan shorter. He hoped his face was as expressionless as he was striving to make it.

"Did you heal Velyla with magic?" she asked, speaking slowly and in a voice that was low, but still loud enough for everyone in the room to hear.

A rustle of cloth filled the room as the patients and visitors shifted to watch the confrontation; then silence.

"Yes," Lorkin replied. "With her parents' permission," he added.

Kalia's eyes widened, then narrowed again. "So you went to their rooms without me, despite my orders—"

"No," he interrupted. "I didn't go to their room."

A crease between her eyebrows deepened. She opened her mouth to say something, then closed it without speaking a word. Her chin rose and she gave him an imperious glare, before turning on her heels and stalking out of the room again.

A murmur of voices arose once she was gone. Lorkin looked at Evar, who smiled in reply.

"She's mad. She's very, very mad. But you were expecting that, weren't you. Did the magical Healing work?"

Lorkin grimaced. "Judging from her reaction, it looks like it might have."

"You mean you don't know?" Evar sounded surprised.

"No. Magical Healing can't cure everything. A fever like this one could still be fatal, if the patient's body is incapable of fighting it. All magic can do is Heal the damage and restore some strength."

Evar shook his head. "If Kalia's allies had known that, they might not have been so keen to play this waiting game with you."

"Well, I hope they're enjoying this game, Evar," Lorkin replied curtly. "Because I don't like playing with people's lives."

Evar looked at Lorkin thoughtfully, then nodded. "If the girl lives, then at least you'll have that to feel good about."

Lorkin sighed. "Yes." He looked at his friend. "I don't suppose you could find out how she is for me?"

His friend straightened. "I can do that. If Kalia is back by then I'll wink if all is well, shrug if they can't tell, and cross my eyes if she's doing badly." He grinned. "Good luck."

Turning away, Evar headed for the corridor. Lorkin watched him go, then someone called his name and his attention returned to the patients.

"The Westside hospice sees fewer local patients," Sonea explained as she led Dorrien down the main corridor. "But that is more than made up for by the foreign patients, since we are closer to the Marina and the Market."

Dorrien chuckled. "I guess they don't have hospices in their homelands."

"Actually, some of the Allied Lands do," she told him. "Vin and Lonmar have a few each, and Lan is in the process of opening their own. They were set up either by Healers who were inspired to start hospices elsewhere, or Healers from those lands who wanted to help their own people in the same way as Kyralia does."

"Not Elyne?"

She shook her head. "Not for lack of trying. The Elyne king won't allow it. The Elynes still have their guild of non-magical healers, founded long before the Guild, who don't look fondly on magicians robbing them of their trade. Now, the treatment rooms here are set up much the same way..."

Sonea moved to a door bearing the number she had been told to look for. She knocked softly, and soon afterwards the door opened and the familiar face of one of the Healers from Northside grinned out at them.

"Go on in," Sylia said, slipping out, waving them inside, then closing the door behind them.

The room was similar to those at the Northside

hospice. A table divided it, with a couple of seats for patients and anyone they might have brought with them, and a seat for the Healer on the other side of the table.

Instead of a Healer, Cery was waiting for them. He smiled, but his posture was hunched and tense. His gaze moved from Sonea to Dorrien.

"So this is your new assistant and bodyguard?" he asked.

Sonea snorted softly. "Assistant, yes. As for whether Dorrien is my bodyguard or I his..." She looked at Dorrien, who smiled crookedly. "We'll have to see how things turn out. Cery, this is Dorrien. Dorrien, this Cery."

The two men nodded politely.

"Have you been waiting long?" Dorrien asked.

Cery shrugged. "A while. I got here early."

"Checking the place out?"

"Of course."

"How's business?" Sonea asked.

Cery's smile slipped away, leaving him looking gaunt and tired. "Not good. It is a good thing I've stowed plenty away in case of times like these."

"Will it last?"

He grimaced. "A year at most. I'd be tempted to leave you to it and get out of town earlier if it weren't for..." He spread his hands.

Anyi, she thought. *I hope she manages to slip away without raising suspicion.*

Cery had received a message saying that Anyi would be visiting a Healer here. They could only hope it had come from his daughter and wasn't part of a plot to ambush him. *Which is why Dorrien and I are here.*

They chatted for several more minutes. She had

warned Dorrien not to ask for details about Cery's business, and thankfully he was following her advice. If he didn't know about anything he was supposed to report to the Guard, he wasn't in danger of breaking any laws for the sake of catching Skellin.

A knock at the door brought all three around to face the entrance. Sonea stepped forward and opened the door a crack. She sighed in relief to see Anyi and Sylia waiting. Opening the door, she thanked Sylia and let Anyi in.

Cery rose to his feet, his eyes roving all over his daughter protectively.

"Are you . . . is everything . . . is that a bruise?"

"I'm fine," Anyi told him. "I told Rek that I thought I might have broken my wrist in practice and I'd better get it checked out. An injured guard isn't as good at her job as an uninjured one."

"What has he got you guarding?"

She smiled. "His mistress. She seems to think that 'guard' means 'servant,' and I'm having some fun convincing her otherwise."

Cery sat down again. "So. What news do you have for us?"

Anyi looked around the room, her mouth forming an unconvincing pout. "Isn't my fine company enough? Haven't you missed me?"

"You wouldn't have risked this meeting if you didn't have news."

She rolled her eyes and sighed. "You could at least pretend to have missed me." She crossed her arms. "Well, as it happens, I do have news. I know for sure that Rek has been given tasks to do by Jemmi that were favours for Skellin."

"Jemmi is a Thief," Sonea murmured to Dorrien.

"What animal is a Jemmi?" he murmured back.

"The Thieves don't always adopt animal names now."

"Ah."

"How often?" Cery asked his daughter.

"Often enough." Anyi's eyes gleamed. "There's a delivery of roet happening in a few weeks. I can try to find out where. I don't know if Skellin will be there, though."

"But Skellin's men will be?" Dorrien asked.

Anyi nodded.

Dorrien looked at Sonea, his eyes bright with excitement. "So we catch them and you can read their minds and find out where Skellin is." He frowned. "Wait... that would be breaking the rules for black magicians, wouldn't it?"

Sonea shook her head. "Osen has given Kallen and I permission to read minds if we need to. But the real problem is: what if Skellin's men don't know where Skellin is? We'll have revealed that Anyi is a spy for nothing."

"Hmm," Cery said. He looked at Anyi. "Though I'd rather have you back with me, we should wait until we learn of a meeting that Skellin will definitely go to."

Anyi shrugged. "I'll keep my ears open. Something better is bound to come along."

They discussed strategies and ways to communicate until there was a tap at the door. Sylia reported that it was being noted they were taking a little long for a Healing consultation. Anyi farewelled her father and left. Cery stared at the door after she had gone, then sighed and looked at Sonea.

"Heard anything from Lorkin?"

She winced at the pang of worry that went through her,

and shook her head. "But Dannyl sent word that the Traitors might be amenable to carrying messages between us, so I've sent him one in case they are."

"That's a start," he said, managing a smile.

She nodded. "I'd better get on with showing Dorrien around. Good to see you Cery. Take care of yourself."

"You too," he replied.

After she and Dorrien had left the room, Sylia slipped back in to arrange smuggling Cery out of the hospice. Sonea led Dorrien down the corridor to the storeroom.

"That is one very worried man," Dorrien said, when he'd checked to ensure they were alone.

"Yes," Sonea agreed.

"I think of my daughters, and I'm not sure I could send either of them into danger to spy for me."

"No, but he didn't exactly send her. She sent herself. She's quite a determined young woman."

Dorrien looked thoughtful. "She would have grown up in the harder part of the city, wouldn't she? And she'd have to grow up tough, being a Thief's daughter."

"She didn't grow up under Cery's protection. When her mother left him, she took Anyi with her. She was a proud woman, and wouldn't accept Cery's help even when they were desperately poor. Anyi grew up fast and tough, but for other reasons."

"Still, to have lost a wife and children and then watch your only daughter put herself in danger..." He shook his head.

"That's why we must be careful. We must be sure that when we find Skellin, there is no chance it will put Anyi or Cery in danger."

Dorrien nodded in agreement. *Good*, Sonea thought. *I*

was beginning to think he is getting a bit too eager to prove himself, and might seize the first opportunity that came along if I wasn't there to stop him. Now he'll think through the risks before he acts.

Hopefully, with Anyi playing spy, a better opportunity would come along soon—and not just because they needed to catch Skellin. Cery looked like he hadn't slept in a month.

CHAPTER 15

UNINVITED COMPANY

Sachaka traded mainly with lands to its north and east, across the Aduna Sea, and this was more apparent at the docks than anywhere else in the city. Dannyl was startled by the size of the exotic ships moored there, and the sheer number of them. Masts waved like a great leafless forest, stretching from the shore out into the broad bay of Arvice.

The Guild House slaves were unlashing travelling trunks from the back of the carriage and lifting them down with the help of Achati's two personal slaves. Dannyl noticed how Achati was following the procedure closely. A Kyralian magician would have moved the trunks with magic, but Sachakans did not lower themselves to such menial work. The slaves were using ropes and a winch built into the back of the vehicle for the purpose, but from the way the four thin men were having little trouble lifting the heavy trunks, Dannyl suspected they were getting magical help from their master anyway.

Achati's trunk required two men to carry it. Tayend's

was of about the same size. Dannyl's was considerably smaller. *Sometimes having to wear a uniform for most of your life has its advantages*, Dannyl thought. But he had also brought an additional trunk—more like a large box—containing writing implements, notebooks, and space for any records or objects he might acquire.

A sigh drew Dannyl's attention away. He glanced at Merria, whose scowl softened only slightly as she met his gaze. His assistant was still angry at being left behind. She had barely spoken to him since learning that Tayend was going on the research trip as well.

He resisted the urge to look at Tayend. The Elyne Ambassador was standing beside Dannyl, rocking gently in his elaborate, expensive shoes. Dannyl had barely spoken to Tayend after returning from Achati's house and asking his former lover why he wanted to travel with them.

"Oh, as Ambassador I really ought to learn as much as I can about this country," Tayend had replied. *"I've seen plenty of Arvice. Time to see something beyond the city walls."*

Dannyl hadn't heard Tayend and Merria conversing, either. With most of its occupants not talking to each other, the Guild House had been very quiet.

He considered Tayend's excuse. Was that all there was to it? *I doubt he's coming because he's interested in my research. Or is he? If he knows about the storestone he might be as concerned as Achati and I are about the possibility another may exist or be created. But how could he know about the storestone? I haven't told him. Surely Achati hasn't...*

Maybe there's another reason Tayend wanted to accompany them. He had already shown he was aware of Achati's personal interest in Dannyl. Was he trying to ensure Dannyl and Achati did not become lovers?

Dannyl frowned. *Why would he do that? Jealousy? No. Tayend was the one to point out that he and I are no longer a couple. He never said he wanted to change that.*

Beside him, Tayend cleared his throat. He paused, then drew in a breath to speak.

"Ambassador?"

Dannyl reluctantly turned to look at him.

"Are you sure you don't mind me coming along?"

"Of course not," Dannyl replied.

He returned to watching the slaves. Achati's pair were not the same two as those who had accompanied him on the search for Lorkin. Dannyl wondered what had happened to Varn. Then his thoughts slipped back to his companions as he sensed that Merria was staring at him. He turned to look at her, and she smiled. This struck him as odd. There was amusement in the smile, and he couldn't help feeling it was at his expense.

"Here is the captain," Achati announced. He waved at the ship the slaves were carrying the trunks toward. It was smaller than the exotic trading vessels surrounding it, intended to transport only passengers—important passengers. On its cabin had been carved the name *Inava*, inlaid with gold that sparkled in the sun. A Sachakan dressed in all the finery Dannyl would expect of an Ashaki was standing on the deck, waiting for them to come aboard along the narrow bridge strung between wharf and ship. The slaves carried the trunks toward a second bridge further down the vessel. "Time to say your goodbyes," Achati added.

Dannyl and Tayend turned to Merria. She smiled brightly.

"Have a good trip, Ambassadors, Ashaki," she said, nodding politely. Then a knowing, slightly smug look entered her eyes. "I hope you don't get on each other's nerves."

So that's what she's finding so amusing, Dannyl mused. "Goodbye, Lady Merria," he replied. "I know I am leaving the Guild House in capable hands."

Her smile faded to a resigned look. "Thanks." She backed toward the carriage and made a shooing motion. "Don't keep the captain waiting."

Turning away, Dannyl followed Achati to the bridge, and across it onto the ship's deck. Introductions were made, and the captain welcomed them to his vessel.

"Are you ready to set sail?" he asked of Achati.

"I am. Is there any need to delay?" Achati replied.

"Not at all," the captain assured him. He walked away, calling out orders to the slaves. Achati led Dannyl and Tayend to a safe position from which to watch proceedings.

"This will be a nice change from city life," Achati said as the ship moved away from the wharf.

Dannyl nodded. "It's been too long since I've travelled on a ship."

"Yes. An adventure for all of us," Tayend said, his voice a little strained. Dannyl noted that his former lover was already looking a little pale.

Achati smiled at the Elyne Ambassador. It was an indulgent smile. Almost a fond one. Suddenly the possibility that Achati *wanted* Tayend with them occurred to Dannyl. He had assumed the Ashaki had been politically and socially cornered by Tayend. He turned to the Elyne.

"Let me know if you need any assistance," he offered.

Tayend nodded in thanks. "I have the cures Achati recommended."

"As your guide, I am obliged to ensure your journey isn't too onerous," Achati told him. "But remember: they may have other effects."

Tayend inclined his head. "I haven't forgotten. I...I think I will sit down now."

He moved to a bench a few steps away. Dannyl resisted the urge to look at Achati and search for any signs of...he wasn't sure what.

Maybe he's interested in being more than friends with Tayend, too.

Maybe they already are. Maybe Tayend's warning about Achati was spurred by jealousy...

Oh, don't be ridiculous!

As the ship moved further from shore, Dannyl found himself wishing that Achati—or even Tayend—would strike up a conversation so that he had a distraction from the suspicions his mind was conjuring up. When neither spoke, he considered what subject he could raise himself.

He knew what he'd like to talk about, but with Tayend present he couldn't speak of what he hoped to learn on this journey in case the Elyne didn't know of the storestone.

Then Achati gestured toward the shore.

"See that building? That's one of the few mansions over two hundred years old not built in the Sachakan style. It was built by..."

Dannyl let out a silent sigh of relief. *Thank you, Achati,* he thought. *Though I think you've just condemned yourself to filling in silences with facts and history for the rest of the trip, at least it's a solution to days of awkward silence.*

Lilia had always assumed that imprisonment was meant to, among other things, give someone nothing to do but think about their crime.

I don't think it's working for me, she mused. *Oh, I've spent plenty of time regretting learning black magic and feeling a fool about it. But I've spent a lot more thinking about Naki, and that feels a lot worse.*

Even when she tried to think of something else, in particular whether Lord Leiden's murderer had been found yet, she knew she was really worrying about Naki.

Since the Guild had not found any proof that she had killed Leiden, she had decided that she couldn't have. She hoped, for Naki's sake, that someone discovered who had. *If Leiden's murderer is found, surely someone will come and tell me.* It wouldn't make any difference to her punishment, since that was for learning black magic, but at least Naki would stop hating her. *Black Magician Sonea would tell me*, she thought. *It would be even better if Naki did. Maybe she'll make regular visits…no, best not get my hopes up. Ten years is a long time. But if she loves me like I love her, surely she'll visit.*

She'd tried to turn her thoughts to happier ones, but something always turned them sour. It was like when they were at the brazier house and she'd imagined someone was looking at them. Her mind always managed to shift to gloomier matters.

At times she sought distraction, and walked around the room, putting her ear to the side door. Occasionally, she could hear the other woman, humming to herself.

Returning once more to the window, beside which she'd pulled up a chair, she leaned on the sill. At least the view outside changed occasionally, even if it was just a bird flying over the treetops, or the angle of the shadows as the hours slowly passed. She was growing increasingly sick of the sight of her room.

A knock interrupted her thoughts. She sat up straight and turned to stare at the main door. She could see part of a face in the window, then it vanished. The lock clattered. The door opened.

Welor entered carrying a tray. *But I'm not even hungry...*

"A good evening to you, Lady Lilia," he said, placing the tray on the dining table. "Your meal—and I have something else I promised."

He took two hard rectangular objects out from where they were wedged between his arm and his side. Her heart leapt as she recognised what they were. *Books!*

She was on her feet and hurrying forward before she realised it. He grinned as she took them from him.

"They're from the Guards' library," Welor told her. "Maybe not as interesting as books on magic, but there are some exciting stories in them."

She read the titles and felt her heart sink a little. *Battles of the Vin Fleet before the Alliance* was imprinted in tiny letters across one cover, and *Strategies for Effective Control of Crowds During Processions and Events* was surrounded by an elaborately decorated frame on the other. She looked up at Welor, saw that he was watching her expectantly, and hoped her disappointment didn't show.

"Thank you," she said.

"It's all I could get my hands on," he explained. "Until I have a day off."

"It's more than I should ever expect," she told him, looking down.

"Well...we are supposed to make sure you're comfortable." He shrugged. "If you like those, I can get more. Or maybe...my wife likes those romantic adventures. I don't know if they're to your taste, but I'm sure she'd let you borrow them."

Lilia smiled. "I could give them a try. If she thinks they're good."

He grinned. "She likes them a lot." He stood a little straighter. "Well, best eat before it gets cold."

He made a sketchy bow and left.

Since there was nobody to offend by reading at dinner, Lilia examined the first book as she ate. The introduction was long and dry, and the first chapter not much better. She wasn't sure whether to be impressed that Welor had read and enjoyed such a challenging book, or not. Not all men who joined the Guard could read, and those of the classes who could afford an education but resorted to a career in the Guard usually did so because they weren't smart enough for higher-paid jobs.

Perhaps Welor is an exception. Perhaps he likes being in the Guard. She pursed her lips in thought. *But how then did he end up with the lowly job of prison guard?*

It was a mystery she would have to unravel. Or maybe it wasn't much of a mystery; maybe being reduced to living in a smaller world only made it seem so.

Finishing the meal, she picked up the books and headed toward the window, but as she passed the side door she heard three sharp taps.

She froze, then turned to look at the door. Her heart beat four . . . five times, and then the taps came again.

This is crazy. The slightest sound from outside and I'm all jumpy. Moving toward the door, she bent and put her ear to it.

"Don't be fooled by what he says about the wife. He likes you."

Lilia leapt backwards and stared at the door. She felt a flash of anger and moved back again.

"You think he's lying? That he hasn't got a wife?"

A low noise, muffled by the door, came from the other room. Possibly a chuckle.

"Maybe not. Or maybe he's telling you about her to make you trust him."

"Surely he'd tell me about her to make sure I didn't get the wrong idea."

"Wrong idea about what?"

"About him doing favours for me. Being nice."

"Maybe. But you watch out. If he starts telling you how lonely he is, don't be surprised if he wants something in return for those favours."

Lilia pulled away from the door a little. Did this woman have something to gain from Lilia not trusting Welor?

"Why are you telling me this?"

"Just trying to help. You're young. You've never been a prisoner before. You want to feel safe, but you shouldn't let that desire blind you to the dangers of your situation."

Lilia considered that. Though it made her feel uneasy, what the woman had said made sense. *I've already got too comfortable in this place, and it's only been two days!*

"My name is Lorandra," the voice said.

Leaning forward, Lilia rested her head on the door. "Mine is Lilia."

"I'm here because foreign magicians have to join the Guild or not use magic," Lorandra said. "I didn't see why I should have to join if I didn't want to."

Though Lilia already knew why the woman was locked away, suddenly it seemed a little unfair. *Why should a foreign magician have to join the Guild?* Maybe if this woman hadn't been forced to choose between the Guild and hiding, she would not have got mixed up with Thieves.

"Why are *you* here?" Lorandra asked. "If you don't mind telling."

"I'm here because I learned black magic—but we were just being silly and I didn't expect what I was doing to work."

The woman didn't speak for a long moment.

"That is the magic the ones in black use?"

"Yes." Lilia found herself nodding, despite knowing Lorandra couldn't see her, and made herself stop. "Black Magicians Sonea and Kallen."

"They bound your powers, too?"

"Yes."

"And you say you didn't expect what you were doing to work. Do you mean trying to learn it?"

"Yes. They told us we couldn't learn unless a black magician taught us, so I thought what I was doing was safe."

"So they were wrong. That doesn't sound very fair."

"Trying to learn it is forbidden, too."

"Ah. So why did you try?"

Lilia regarded the door thoughtfully. She probably

shouldn't be talking to this woman. But who else was there to talk to? And so long as she didn't describe how she learned black magic—and she kept her desire for Naki to herself, too—she wouldn't be telling Lorandra anything she shouldn't. And it wasn't as if Lorandra was going to be able to use or pass on any information Lilia told her.

Taking a deep breath, she began to explain.

Lorkin wasn't sure why he hadn't simply walked out of the Care Room and gone to bed, or at least ignored Kalia's order to start early. Kalia had kept him back so late he'd had less than four hours' sleep on average over the last two nights.

She was, no doubt, punishing him for managing to Heal with magic without generating disapproval among the Traitors, instead generating some for her. It was very likely she was also trying to stop him visiting and Healing the young man sick with chill fever.

But she couldn't keep him working all night, and eventually she'd had to let him go. He hadn't been surprised when he was waylaid again on the way to the men's room, and taken to see the sick young man. Already struggling, due to lack of sleep, to recover properly from the first Healing session, he was left almost staggering with exhaustion after a second. He had no magic left to Heal away the tiredness.

Tomorrow I will ignore Kalia's early start. In fact, I may not have much choice. Once I'm asleep I suspect it'll take an advancing army to wake me.

He turned a corner and forced his legs to carry him onwards. It wasn't far to the men's room now. Just another hundred paces—or two . . .

Something settled against his cheek. He reached up to brush it away and realised, simultaneously, that he couldn't see any more, that there was a dry vegetable smell in the air, and that something was wrapping itself firmly around his shoulders.

A sack? Yes. It's a sack. He tried to push it back off his head but something smashed against his back and knocked him to the ground. He instinctively reached for magic. *Ah, but I have none.* Strong hands took hold of his arms and forced them behind his back, and he knew there was nothing he could do.

How did they know? Or was this deliberate? Kalia wasn't just keeping me back late to punish me, was she?

To his surprise, the sacking covering his face lifted, though not far enough that he could see anything beyond the floor and two pairs of legs. He took in a deep breath of clean air.

But that was a mistake. Something was pressed over his mouth and nose, and a familiar smell filled his nostrils. Though he caught and held his breath, enough of the drug had entered his body to set his senses reeling. He gasped and began to pass out.

The last thing he heard was a low, hoarse voice, laced with disgust and satisfaction.

"Too easy," it said. "Pick him up. Follow me."

PART TWO

CHAPTER 16

FEARS AND CONCERNS

As the carriage left the Guild, Sonea looked at Rothen and noted a thoughtful look on his face.

"What is it?" she asked.

"Only a few months ago, you would have had to gain permission to visit Dorrien and his family," the old magician said. "Now nobody questions it. How quickly things can change."

Sonea smiled grimly. "Yes. But they could change back just as quickly. It would take only one unfortunate incident and I'd be keeping Lilia company."

Rothen looked pained. "She did deliberately try to learn black magic."

"True. I wonder if she would have, if she hadn't been addled with roet."

"How do you mean?"

"They say it makes a person stop caring. Which is appealing if you have worries you would like to forget for a while, or need a little false courage, but roet also removes any concern for the consequences of your actions—and it seems to do so much more effectively than drink."

"Do you think others might make the same mistake as she?"

"Only if they happened to stumble on some books containing instructions on learning black magic while under the full effect of roet. That depends on there being any other books like that out there." Sonea sighed. "Lord Leiden was breaking a law by not surrendering his to the Guild."

"Should we start searching private libraries?"

"I doubt we'd find anything. Unless the owner doesn't know what he or she has stored in theirs, they'd remove and hide anything suspicious as soon as they heard a search was possible."

Rothen nodded in agreement. "It would take years to go through the bigger libraries thoroughly enough," he added. "Are we any closer to finding Leiden's killer?"

She shook her head. "Obviously someone else has learned black magic. Either that or it was Kallen, and the people who claim they saw him that night were lying. I'm surprised Osen hasn't asked us to read each other's minds, yet." The carriage came to a halt. She unlatched the door and climbed out, then turned and waited as Rothen followed.

"I heard that there were enough witnesses to confirm you were both elsewhere when the murder occurred that a mind read isn't needed."

She looked at him in surprise. "Nice of him to tell me that. Having my mind read, or reading Kallen's, isn't something I look forward to."

"I'm sure he would tell you, if you asked. Shall we go inside?"

She turned to face the door of the building. The Guild was renting it as a way to deal with the shortage of rooms in the grounds for magicians. When Dorrien came to the Guild on his own he stayed with his father, but there wasn't enough space in Rothen's room for an extra two adults and two older girls.

From the outside it looked like a single, though large, family home. Sonea walked up to the door and knocked. A man in a Guild servant uniform opened it. He greeted them, stepped aside and bowed as they passed through into the entry hall.

It was a lavishly decorated room, with staircases winding up to a second floor. Once, it would have been the home of a rich family from one of the Houses, but now it had been divided into four parts, which provided accommodation for four magicians and their families. At first, this idea of dividing up a large house had been rejected, because it was assumed that magicians would be too proud to share a building with others. But the concept proved popular among young magicians with families from the lower classes, who saw immediately that it provided much more space for their children than an apartment of rooms in the Magicians' Quarters.

The servant led them upstairs to a large door that filled what would have once been an opening to a corridor. He knocked, and when Dorrien answered the door the man bowed and introduced them formally.

"Thank you, Ropan," Dorrien said as he ushered Sonea and Rothen inside a large guest room. Tylia and Yilara were sitting in two of the chairs, and Sonea noted they were wearing dresses more in the city style. "Welcome to our new home. It's four times the size of our house. Alina is worried we'll get so used to it, it'll feel like a tight fit when we move back. Here she is."

His wife had appeared in a side doorway, her hands clasped together and an anxious expression on her face. Her eyes snapped to Sonea, dropped to the black robes; then her expression hardened and she looked away. She smiled nervously as Dorrien urged her to join them. The two girls reluctantly stood and bowed, hovering a pace or two away as the adults exchanged pleasantries.

"How are you finding it here?" Sonea asked Alina.

Alina glanced at Dorrien. "It will take a little getting used to," the woman said quietly. "I prefer to cook meals myself, but Dorrien says to leave it to the servants."

"Where do they do the cooking?"

"In the basement," Alina replied. "They cook for all the families staying here. It looks like there are more servants there tonight. I hope that's not our fault."

Dorrien smiled. "Lord Beagir is entertaining guests, too," he said. He looked at Rothen and Sonea. "Come into the dining room."

"Dining room, eh?" Rothen chuckled and opened his mouth to say more, but Dorrien frowned, shook his head and glanced at Alina, who had turned away. *Looks like Alina isn't comfortable with all the luxuries here*, Sonea mused. *Dorrien doesn't want Rothen teasing him about it, as it'll make her feel worse.*

They moved into a room featuring a large table and eight chairs. A gong the size of a dinner plate sat in an alcove at the end of the room. When all were settled in the chairs, Dorrien glanced at it and the striker moved, filling the room with a pleasant ringing. Alina's lips thinned and she shook her head.

It probably seemed like a fancy extravagance, but the sound let the servants know that the family was ready for their meal. Sure enough, a pair of male servants appeared carrying trays laden with bowls and plates of food. As they finished arranging the food on the table they tucked their empty trays under their arms and asked which drinks were required. Dorrien requested wine and water, and the men hurried away.

Foregoing the old-fashioned custom of serving guests himself, Dorrien simply invited them to start. They helped themselves to the dishes and began eating. Alina looked up at Sonea, her expression serious.

"How is your hunt for the rogue going?" she asked.

"Right now it has turned into an exercise in patience," Sonea told her. "We're waiting for information. Good information, because we don't want to endanger our sources by acting too quickly."

"You mean this spy working for the other Thief. The daughter of your friend?"

Sonea paused and resisted looking at Dorrien. He'd given his wife more information than Sonea would have liked. The fewer people who knew she was still friends with Cery the better, but if the fact became known it would not risk anybody's life. However, the information that Anyi was Cery's daughter could definitely put her life at risk, if it were discovered.

"Yes," she replied. "It is a dangerous task, and I know my friend is very worried about her."

"If it's dangerous for her..." Alina looked at Dorrien, then straightened a little and turned back to Sonea. "Is it dangerous for us?"

Sonea blinked in surprise. "No."

"But none of us are magicians." Alina gestured to her daughters and herself. "What if these people you're chasing find out that Dorrien is helping you, and that he has a family, and that we live here, not in the Guild grounds?" Alina's voice rose a little. "What's to stop them coming here when Dorrien is out, and threatening us—or worse?"

Sonea schooled her expression to hide the amusement she felt. Alina was genuinely worried. *Does she have reason to worry?* The scenario Alina imagined was not impossible, just unlikely. It would take a particularly bold and cunning assassin or abductor to enter a magician's home, especially this one which housed several magicians. *Someone as bold and cunning as the assassin who killed Cery's family?* Perhaps, but this was no hidden Thief's lair, where secrecy also ensured nobody would notice a break-in was occurring and come to help.

"The living arrangements you have here work to your advantage," Sonea told Alina. "Having other magicians living nearby means that, even when Dorrien isn't here, you have someone to call upon for help, or the servants can fetch help for you. One magician in a house is a big deterrent, but you have four. Which also makes it harder for an outsider to know if they're all at home or not.

"You should come up with rules to stick to," Sonea added as Alina opened her mouth to argue. "Who to let into your rooms and who not to. How to be safe when you're out in the city. What to do if you think someone is following you, or trying to get into the house." Sonea looked at Dorrien, who nodded resignedly. "I'm sure you can work it out between you."

As Sonea had hoped, Alina's attention now shifted to

Dorrien. "We will." She glanced at Sonea briefly. "And we appreciate the advice."

"The sooner we find Skellin, the sooner you can stop worrying about this," Dorrien said.

Rothen hummed in agreement. "And nobody will be safe if we don't."

"What will happen if you don't find him?" Yilara asked.

Sonea looked at the girl and smiled in approval at her interest. "He wants to gain control of..." A knocking from the guest room interrupted her.

"I'll see who it is," Dorrien said, rising and hurrying out of the room.

The rest of them continued eating, listening in silent curiosity to the sound of Dorrien opening the door and another male voice, then the door closing again.

Footsteps told them he was returning. He stepped into the dining room doorway and looked at Sonea.

"A message for you. Osen wants you to return to the Guild immediately. Lady Naki has disappeared."

A day's sailing had brought Achati, Dannyl and Tayend to a smaller port north of Arvice. Achati had arranged for them to spend the night on shore, at an estate owned by an Ashaki who grew crops of raka. Ashaki Chakori had sent a carriage to fetch them from the docks. The smell of the roasting beans was recognisable long before they reached the estate.

Unlike most Sachakan homes, the mansion and work buildings were not surrounded by walls. The main house stood to one side, and the work buildings were a few hundred paces away from them. From one of two circular

structures came a plume of smoke, forming a dark stain
against moonlit clouds.

"My dear cousin," Achati had said when formal introductions were over. "It is good to see you again."

It had surprised Dannyl that Achati hadn't told them of
his relationship to their host. Since his Sachakan friend
had taken on the responsibility of organising the journey
it had seemed rude to press for too many details.

Ashaki Chakori radiated a kind of strength mixed
with contentment. He was of an old and powerful
Sachakan family, which allowed him to live away from
the city and do what he most enjoyed—growing and producing raka—without risking losing any standing among
the Ashaki.

"Our fathers were brothers," Achati explained as he
noted Dannyl's curiosity. "The younger inherited a city
mansion, the older this estate." He turned to Chakori.
"How are your son and wife?"

"Kavori is in Elyne, exploring trade options. Inaki is
well."

Achati's eyebrows rose. "In Elyne? How is that going?"

"Not as well as we'd hoped." He looked at Tayend
thoughtfully. "There is a perception that raka is a commoner's drink. Is this so, Ambassador?"

Tayend nodded. "It is growing in popularity, however,
due to magicians returning from their time of learning
in the Guild with a new taste for it."

Chakori's attention shifted to Dannyl. "So it is not a
commoner's drink in Kyralia."

"It was," Dannyl said apologetically. "But the Guild
has, for the last twenty years, invited people from all
classes to seek entry. Those who came from the common

classes introduced raka to the rest, and it is popular with novices studying late into the night."

"It would be," Chakori chuckled. "There is another exotic product that Kyralians have embraced in recent years that begins with an 'r,' isn't there?"

"Roet." Dannyl shook his head. "It has become quite a problem."

The Ashaki nodded. "Slaves of one of the southern estates acquired some, recently, though I do not know how. Perhaps an enterprising trader from Kyralia brought it across the mountains. It had an alarming effect, causing slaves to rebel or refuse to work. Their owner has forbidden its use—and the possession of it, too—and recommended that others do the same."

"A good idea," Dannyl said. *And yet... if roet induced slaves to revolt, perhaps it could be the key to ending slavery in Sachaka. But afterwards the country would be in trouble, with most of its workforce rendered useless. It would take a ruthless or desperate enemy to do that, and if roet production took hold here what would that mean for Kyralia?*

"Would you like to eat, or wait until later?" Chakori asked. "I could take you around the estate, if you are not tired from your journey."

Achati looked at Dannyl and Tayend. Dannyl lifted his shoulders to show he was amenable to either choice. Tayend nodded.

"Both are inviting offers," Achati told his cousin. "Whatever is most convenient."

The Ashaki smiled. "Then I will give you a tour, since I have ordered a special dish prepared for you that is always best cooked for at least three hours."

Chakori led them through the mansion. Though the estate was unconventional in its lack of an outer wall, the mansion's interior layout and decoration were traditional. A main corridor wound from the Master Room where they had met Chakori past two clusters of rooms, but unlike in the Guild House the corridor branched and the passage Chakori led them down took them to a rear entrance.

They stepped out into a generous courtyard area and headed toward the work buildings. The two tall, circular structures made the mansion look small and meek. The smell of raka beans roasting was strong.

Chakori gestured at the buildings. "The one on the left is for storage and fermentation; the one on the right for roasting and packing." He headed toward the store, ushering them through a heavy wooden door into a lamp-lit room. A globe light fizzed into existence above his head and brightened to light the whole interior.

The room was divided into sections, with wooden walls radiating out from a central area. Slaves had removed one of these walls and were raking a great mound of beans into the neighbouring space. Another group were shovelling beans into barrows. As a slave moved from one group to another, clearly watching over the progress, Dannyl felt a shock of recognition.

It's Varn!

Chakori led his guests into the central area, the slaves throwing themselves onto the floor at their master's arrival, and as Varn turned, his eyes flicked from Chakori to Achati. He hesitated for the tiniest moment in surprise, before dropping in turn.

Dannyl looked at Achati. Varn's former master looked

surprised, and a little dismayed, but he quickly recovered his composure.

"I used to own your supervising slave," he told Chakori.

His cousin nodded. "Yes, the man I bought him from told me Varn was yours once. He has been a good worker."

"He is. A good source slave, too. Why did Voriki sell him, do you know?"

Chakori shrugged. "I don't know. I suspect he needed the money. Do you regret selling him? Do you wish to buy him back?"

Dannyl was glad he was standing behind the two Sachakans, and they couldn't see him wince at the way they so casually discussed buying and selling *people*.

Achati didn't answer straightaway. "It is tempting, and at times I do regret selling him, but no."

Nodding, Chakori gave the order for the slaves to resume work, and began explaining the storage and fermentation process. Dannyl resisted the urge to watch Varn to see if he cast any looks in Achati's direction, and whether they'd be reproachful or not. He could not help remembering catching sight of the two of them during the hunt for Lorkin, when they thought themselves unobserved and that nobody would see the obvious affection and desire between them. But what was it that Achati had said later?

"Only when you know the other could easily leave you, do you appreciate when he stays."

Was that why Achati had sold Varn? Had he come to suspect that Varn's adoration was faked? Or had he known it, from reading Varn's mind?

As Chakori finished explaining, he invited them to

look around the room. They moved around the storage segments, inspecting the glistening beans. A pile of discarded leaves that looked like large elongated bowls stood nearby. Dannyl turned to their host as they drew level with Varn and the slaves raking the fermenting beans.

"What do the raka plants look like?" he asked.

Chakori smiled, pleased at the question. "They are small trees about double the height of a man. The beans come in pods—like these." Dannyl followed as Chakori headed for the discarded leaves, but Achati hung back. Chakori picked two up and handed one each to Dannyl and Tayend. They were thick and as inflexible as gorin leather.

"Do you make anything from these?" Tayend asked.

"I give them to a neighbour, who chops them up and spreads them over his fields. He swears they repel insects and make the plants grow faster." Chakori shrugged.

"They look like little boat hulls," Tayend observed. "Or they could be used as bowls. Do they burn? Does the smoke smell like raka?"

Dannyl glanced back at Achati. His friend was talking to Varn. The slave's gaze was lowered, but he smiled faintly and nodded. Achati looked relieved. Dannyl turned back to find Tayend rubbing the inside of his pod.

"Shoes," he muttered. "I wonder if you could carve them into shoes."

Achati appeared at Dannyl's elbow. "I wouldn't want to walk for long in them."

"No. You're right," Tayend agreed. He gave the pod back to Chakori, who tossed it back on the pile.

"Now," Chakori said. "Let me show you the roasting process."

•   :   •

Lorkin had discovered something that nobody in the Guild, perhaps not even his own mother, knew.

Being drained of magic over and over gives a person a dreadful headache.

His captors had kept him from recovering magically by taking power at regular intervals. It left him unable to even remove the blindfold over his eyes. Even when he'd had the strength to move, the few attempts he had made to push the blindfold off by rubbing his head against the wall had resulted in a whack over his head that left his ears ringing.

Having no strength also left him unable to ease the strain and ache from having his arms tied behind his back and the sleepless hours lying on the cold, uneven stone floor. It should not have left him incapable of calling out with his mind, however. Something else was preventing that. He was not sure what. The idea that someone might have blocked his magic while he was unconscious had left him feeling very vulnerable and violated, until it occurred to him a little while later that they wouldn't be draining his power so often if he couldn't use it.

The hours that passed were long and miserable.

He could do nothing but think, and try to find a way out of his predicament. His captors were most probably members of Kalia's faction. It was very unlikely that outsiders were living in Sanctuary, though he couldn't dismiss the idea. Perhaps the Guild had arranged for his rescue, recruiting disgruntled Traitors or promising them something—like Healing knowledge—in return for rescuing him. Perhaps the Sachakan king already had spies here, and wanted Lorkin removed from Sanctuary before it was invaded.

Trouble was, in either case it didn't make sense for him to be abducted like this.

The most likely culprits are Kalia's people, he concluded once again.

He told himself that they wouldn't dare kill him, but he could not help worrying that he was wrong. Execution of a Traitor was punishable by death, but Kalia's faction would most likely reason he wasn't truly a Traitor. Perhaps one of them was willing to take the blame and sacrifice themselves in order for Sanctuary to be rid of him.

When he asked himself what else they might want with him, the answer made his heart beat faster with both fear and anger.

No matter what they intend to do with me, they are going to read my mind. When they do, they'll dig up all I know about Healing.

This had led him to wonder what he would do if they demanded that knowledge in exchange for his life. It was highly unlikely they would do so, since there was no need for them to gain his cooperation, but while you could pick up the basics of Healing from a mind-read, there was no substitute for experience and practice.

If they do...would I give it to them? Is keeping this knowledge from them more important than my life?

Sometimes he didn't think it was. He had never liked having to withhold knowledge that would help these people. He couldn't blame them for resorting to unscrupulous tactics to gain it.

But it wasn't his decision to make. The knowledge was the Guild's to give. Would the Guild expect him to die to protect that right?

Do I really have to bow to the Guild's authority? I told

Dannyl everyone should act as if I'd left the Guild. Did I really mean that? Do I still consider myself a Guild magician?

He didn't get the chance to consider that for long. The sound of a door opening and closing set his pulse racing again. He heard footsteps. Something about the rhythm of them made his heart sink and anger stir within him. He'd know that short, crisp gait anywhere.

Kalia.

"Where have you been? We've guarded him for hours," a woman complained. One of the guards who had been watching over and draining him, Lorkin guessed.

"I couldn't get away sooner. I was being watched," Kalia replied.

"Of course you were. Someone else should be doing this," the second guard pointed out.

"I am Sanctuary's healer," Kalia replied archly. "It is my responsibility to ensure our people get the best treatment."

The two women said nothing to that. Footsteps came closer. He heard the creak of joints. His skin itched under the blindfold. Something cool and alive touched his forehead.

He jerked reflexively, shaking off the hand. Then a pressure gripped his head, holding it firmly against the floor. The rough surface dug painfully into the back of his head. The cool touch returned.

He felt a presence at the edge of his mind. He felt it effortlessly slip *into* his mind. Though it made his head-ache increase, he tried to fight the will that took hold of his memories. But it was useless. Nothing stopped the greedy mind in its searching and examining.

—You won't get away with this, he thought at the invader. *If you use magic to Heal people they will know you stole the knowledge from me.*

—But you gave it to me willingly, Kalia replied. *Right before you left for home. I'll tell them I tried to talk you out of it, of course. Said you should wait so I could organise a guide for you or you would freeze to death. But, being the ignorant Kyralian that you are, you were too proud to accept the offer. It will be your own fault you died.*

—They won't believe it.

—Of course they won't. But they'll have to accept it, since there will be no other witnesses.

Lorkin felt despair threatening to overcome his self-control. He pushed it aside and, as Kalia delved into his memories again and called knowledge of magical Healing to the surface, he tried to distract her with other thoughts. She ignored them, too eager to learn what he knew. Only when her curiosity was satisfied did her attention stray. And when it did, she prompted his mind for memories and facts he would not want her to see.

The mind was a traitor, and did not need much prompting. Normally he would have been able to put those memories behind imagined doors in his mind, safely out of sight. Normally the magician who stepped inside his mind would politely ignore those doors. But not Kalia.

She chased after memories of his childhood in the Guild, amused as she saw how he had been mocked over his mother's low origins and unmarried state; gleeful at learning how he'd had his heart broken by his first love, Beriya; derisive of expectations that he would do something as heroic as his father; and contemptuous of his attraction to Tyvara...

A sound broke Kalia's concentration. Lorkin's ears told him it was loud, but with his attention locked within his mind he did not *feel* it. Then his awareness snapped back to the physical world. His senses reeled.

"What?" Kalia snapped.

"You were followed. We've distracted them, but we don't have long until they realise."

Silence followed. Lorkin could hear Kalia's breathing.

"Is it done?" one of the guards asked.

"Perhaps," Kalia replied, in a speculative tone that sent a chill down his spine. "Get him up. I know the perfect place to hide him."

Head still reeling, though now more from lack of food and water, Lorkin felt hands haul him to his feet, then push him forward into the close-sounding space of a passage.

CHAPTER 17

MIND GAMES

The snow that had fallen the night before lay in drifts on either side of the road. It lingered in the shade of the trees, where the sunlight had not yet touched. Sonea leaned closer to the window to look up at the Lookout, wondering if the building was colder than those of the city. Something drew her gaze to the third row of windows.

Is that someone looking out? She frowned and looked closer, making out the face of a young woman in one of the windows. *Lilia.*

The girl was watching the carriage. It seemed as if their gazes met, though Sonea was too far away to tell if it was her imagination or not. Then the carriage turned and they were no longer in sight of each other.

Ten years is a long time, Sonea found herself thinking. *But at least she's alive and safe.*

Her thoughts turned to Naki. The girl had been missing for a week. Her servants had not reported her absence until Naki had been gone longer than usual. Apparently she had occasionally disappeared for a few days without explanation. All of the household staff had been questioned by magicians and their guesses at her location followed up, but investigations had proven them wrong. Relatives had been contacted but none had heard from the girl.

Naki had received no visitors recently, but plenty of letters. One servant had told how Naki had not looked happy after receiving the letters, and had burned them with magic immediately.

But when Kallen pointed out that Naki's powers had been blocked, so she couldn't have used magic, the servant looked thoughtful. She said she had seen Naki throw a letter into the fire recently, but thought it was out of anger. It didn't occur to her that it was because Naki couldn't use magic any more.

Kallen had asked if the letters had stopped since Naki had left the house. The servant had thought about it, then nodded. *Clever Kallen*, Sonea thought. *I was thinking about asking when the letters started, not if they stopped coming.*

The carriage slowed to a halt at the base of the tower. Sonea climbed out and felt the chill air surround her. The guards standing around the tower were well rugged up. She resisted the habit of creating a shield about herself and heating the air within. The crisp air was refreshing and she had always loved to see her own breath mist. It had seemed magical to her as a child, even though it usually meant she was shivering with cold.

A memory flashed into her mind of being huddled in an old coat, her feet aching as the cold penetrated her thin-soled boots. Then the door of the Lookout opened and the memory faded. A guard was bowing and beckoning hastily at the same time, eager to avoid letting cold air into the building.

After the usual polite exchange with the captain and the magician on duty, Sonea followed another guard up the stairs. He opened the small hatch in the door of Lilia's room.

"You have a visitor, Lady Lilia," he called out. Closing the little hatch, he turned his attention to the lock. When the door was open, he stepped aside so that Sonea could enter.

Lilia was standing beside a chair, over by the window. Her eyes were wide and she stared at Sonea hopefully before seeming to recollect herself.

"Black Magician Sonea," she said, bowing.

"Lilia," Sonea replied. Looking around the room, Sonea noted that it was comfortably furnished and warm. Two books were sitting on a small table beside the chair. "I have some questions to ask you."

The girl's expression shifted from hope to disappointment and resignation. She nodded, then gestured to a small table and two wooden chairs. "Please sit."

Sonea accepted the invitation, waiting until Lilia had taken the other seat before she met Lilia's gaze.

"Naki hasn't been seen for over a week." Sonea saw alarm in Lilia's face. "There was no sign of violence or note of explanation at her house. We have searched all the places the servants know Naki liked to visit. Is there anywhere you know of that she might have gone, that they wouldn't know of?"

Lilia grimaced. "A few brazier houses." She listed some names.

Sonea nodded. "The servants mentioned these, too. Anywhere else?"

Lilia shook her head.

"No other friends—perhaps ones she was no longer friendly with?"

"No. Though...there were rumours in the Guild that she'd been friendly with a servant girl but her father threw the family out."

"Yes, we've contacted them and they haven't seen her either. Were there any boys who pursued her, even though she had no interest in them?"

Lilia's gaze dropped and her face reddened. "Not that I know of."

"Did she...did she have any connections to criminals—perhaps roet sellers?"

"I...I don't know. I guess she had to buy the roet from somebody. If she wasn't stealing her father's supply." Lilia looked up. "Have you found out anything about his murderer yet?"

Sonea paused, a little annoyed at the change of subject. *But she will be anxious to know, since her friend did blame her for it.*

"No," Sonea told her. "At least, if the magicians investigating it have learned anything, it hasn't been important enough to report to the Higher Magicians."

"So...you're not investigating it yourself?"

Sonea smiled wryly. "I wish I could, but I have a rogue magician to find. It is Black Magician Kallen's responsibility."

"But you're looking into where Naki is."

"I offered to question you, since we have talked—communicated—a little already."

Lilia nodded.

"According to the servants, Naki was receiving letters

that upset her. She was receiving them for some time before Lord Leiden's death until the day she was last seen at home. Do you know anything about these letters?"

Lilia shook her head, then sighed. "I'm not much use, am I?"

"What someone doesn't know can be as useful as what they do know," Sonea told her. "It is interesting, considering how Naki was willing to trust you to know about the book with black magic instructions in it, but never told you about the letters. It suggests a far greater secret."

"What could be worse than black magic?" Lilia asked in a small voice.

"I don't know." Sonea rose. "But we intend to find out. Thanks for your help, Lilia. If you think of anything, get the guards to send someone to me."

Lilia nodded. "I will."

Conscious of the girl's eyes on her, Sonea left the room. As the guard locked the door behind her, she considered the next door along. *Lorandra. Is there any point in me visiting her again? I guess, since I'm here already...*

What are you doing, Naki? Where are you? Did you go there deliberately, or did somebody take you?

Are you even alive?

Once again, Lilia's stomach clenched. All day the questions had repeated in her mind. At first she had encouraged them, hoping that the answers would somehow rise to the surface and she could call out to Welor and send him off to find Sonea. With her help, Naki would be rescued—or else just simply located. Her friend might realise that she would never harm her. Or else the Guild would be grateful for Lilia's help, and perhaps...

Let me out of here? I doubt that. Lilia sighed. *That will only happen if I somehow forget how to use black magic.*

Forcing herself to stop pacing, she sat down and picked up one of the books. Even though she had started to see why Welor liked it—the battle descriptions had obviously been written with relish—not even the most exciting tale could have held her attention for long. Not when the person she loved most in the world was missing. She put it down again.

A sound from the next room drew her eyes to the side door. She'd listened in as Sonea had talked to Lorandra. It had been an odd conversation, mostly one-sided since Lorandra wasn't inclined to answer Sonea's questions, and when she did speak she often changed the subject completely. Though both said nothing that could be considered impolite or threatening, the whole meeting gave Lilia an impression of antagonism. Lorandra did not want to cooperate. Lilia wasn't surprised when Sonea gave up and left.

With nothing to listen in on, she wandered the room. A tap from the door made Lilia jump.

"Finished pacing now?" a muffled voice asked.

Lilia smiled wryly. If she had made a habit of listening to the other woman, then it was no surprise Lorandra was doing the same to her.

"For now," she said, moving over to the door.

"You had some bad news?"

"Yes. My friend is missing." Though Lilia had told Lorandra of Naki, she had only described them as close friends.

"Do you know where she is?"

"No." *Lorandra would have heard me say that . . . but I*

suppose she'd have to allow that I could have been lying to Sonea.

"I bet you wish you could go into the city and find her."

"I do. Very much." Lilia sighed. "But even if I wasn't locked up here, I wouldn't know where to look."

"Do you think it's more likely she's been taken against her will, or gone into hiding?"

Lilia considered. "Why would she go into hiding? If she had learned black magic it would make sense, but Black Magician Sonea would have seen it in her mind. So it's more likely she's been taken against..." Lilia could not finish the sentence. She shuddered. And yet she felt a little bit better. This was, at least, an answer. Even if it wasn't a good one.

"Who would want to do that?"

"I don't know."

"What does she have that others might want?"

"Money. She inherited her father's fortune when he died." Lilia's heart skipped. "Maybe she found out who killed him!"

"If she did, she's probably dead."

Lilia felt her heart constrict. She didn't want to think about that.

"What if she isn't dead?" Lilia asked. "What if she's being held captive? What if she's being blackmailed?" *What if someone is trying to force her into telling them the instructions in the book on black magic?*

Lorandra was silent for several breaths. "I guess you won't know unless the Guild finds out and bothers to tell you. Do you think they will?"

Lilia's heart sank. "I don't know."

"It sounded like Sonea had her doubts."

"Did it?" Lilia thought back. She couldn't remember. Her mind had been caught up in shock and worry over Naki.

"Yes." Lorandra tapped quietly on the door, as if drumming her fingers in thought. "Once, I would have been able to find out for you. I have contacts in the city. Many, many contacts. Most aren't particularly respectable ones, but that's partly why I'm in here. If I was free, I would help you find your friend, or find out what happened to her."

Lilia smiled, though she knew the woman couldn't see it. "Thanks. It's nice to know you would, if you were able to." *How strange that this woman, who the Guild regards as a criminal, understands better than anyone else what I'm going through. Well, it's said that loyalty is important to Thieves and people in the underworld.*

"Your powers were blocked before they put you in here, weren't they?"

"Of course." Lilia frowned at the change of subject.

"Have you ever tried to break the block, or get past it?"

"No."

"Why not?"

"I . . . why bother? Black Magician Sonea put it there. I'm hardly going to break a block she made. I'd just give myself a headache trying."

"So . . . it makes a difference how strong the magician is who makes a block? Or if that magician is a black magician?"

Lilia shook her head. "I don't know. All I know is that it separates your will from your power, so it doesn't matter how strong you are."

"It can't separate all control, though. Otherwise we'd be dead."

"Of course."

"How do they do that?"

"I don't know." Lilia winced. She'd been saying "I don't know" a lot today.

"It seems to me that black magicians are not just stronger than normal magicians but have a different kind of magic. A different way of controlling it."

"They're not stronger unless they've taken power from other people," Lilia corrected. "Though Sonea and Kallen were both stronger than most magicians before they learned black magic, they're no stronger than that. They aren't allowed to take power without permission, and it would only be given if the lands were under attack, or faced some other threat."

"*Really*? Then I'm right. It's a different kind of magic."

Lorandra's tone was that of someone who had just learned something, and was very pleased about it. *If she didn't know that...should I have told her? She's right, though. I didn't learn black magic by taking power; I learned it by trying out a different way of sensing it.*

"So their powers are different," Lorandra pointed out. "They can do things other magicians can't. Like read minds. They can get around someone's defences, unlike ordinary magicians."

"Yes." That much was obvious.

Lorandra paused again, but not for as long.

"It seems to me that being able to do different things with your mind ought to mean any block in that mind would have to be different, too. Did Sonea put the usual kind of block in your mind? Don't answer that," she added. "I'm just thinking aloud. But answer this if you can: has anyone put a block on a black magician before?"

"Not that I know of. There's nothing in the history lessons that mentions it."

"I think you should try to get past the block. If nobody has put one on a black magician before, and black magic gets around normal restrictions, then how do they know they got it right?"

Lilia stared at the door. Her heart was beating a little faster. She wanted to point out that Sonea would simply replace the block. *If she found out it was gone. So long as I never used magic when anyone was here nobody would know.* But she was ignoring the obvious consequence of succeeding: Lorandra wouldn't be content with remaining in the Lookout. *She'll want me to get us out.*

Normally Lilia would have refused. She would have stayed put, knowing that Sonea and Kallen would chase her down, and the punishment for escaping would be worse than mere imprisonment.

They'd probably execute me.

But if she found Naki, perhaps it would be worth it. Reason told her that she did not know the city well enough to find Naki before the Guild caught her, but here was a woman who knew the city well. Who knew the underworld, where Naki was most likely imprisoned. Who wanted to help Lilia.

Lilia wanted more than anything to find Naki, but what did Lorandra want?

Well, she wants to exchange her help for me busting her out of this prison, Lilia thought. *I should get her to agree to some conditions.*

"How long will it take to find Naki, do you think?"

Lorandra chuckled. "You're a quick one, Lady Lilia. I can't tell you exactly. I'd have to locate my people, and if they don't already know they'd have to spend some time finding out."

"Do you think we could slip away each night, then return by morning, without the guards knowing?" *That would gain us more time than if we left and the Guild started hunting for us. We could spend weeks searching for Naki, if necessary. If they did find we'd been slipping out, they might forgive me given that we returned each time. We might even find Naki without the Guild knowing we'd ever left the Lookout.*

"Possibly." Lorandra's tone was hard to read. "It depends on whether we can get in and out of here without anyone noticing. If I had access to my powers I could levitate..."

"I can do that," Lilia said quickly. She did not want to be talked into unblocking Lorandra's powers. It was bad enough letting the woman loose, but releasing her on the city in full control of her powers was another matter entirely. "So...if I get us out of here, do you promise to help me find Naki?"

"Yes."

"And we'll try to slip away and back without anyone noticing?"

"Yes."

"Then I'll do it. If I can undo the block."

"If you learned black magic in the first attempt, I suspect it'll be the same for this. Either you'll be able to do it, or you won't."

"I hope so. While I'm trying, you think about how to get us out of here."

"I will. Good luck."

Lilia stepped away from the door. She cast about, then moved to the chair by the window and sat down. Closing her eyes, she started a breathing exercise to calm and focus her mind.

When she felt ready, she sent her attention within. At once she was aware of the block. All other times she had done this, she had found the ball of energy within herself straightaway. Now there was something in the way. It was like a magical shield or barrier, and yet it wasn't one.

She prodded it gently. It resisted. She pushed against it, but it was like a hard, cold wall. *I need to try harder. It's going to hurt. I need to be ready for that.* She tried to brace herself for pain, but she had no idea how to do that mentally. It wasn't as though she had muscles in her mind to tense.

Gathering her determination, she threw her will against the wall. At once a sharp pain exploded in her mind. She gasped, opened her eyes and grabbed at her head, which was now throbbing worse than any headache she'd suffered before.

Oh. That was bad. Rocking in the chair, she concentrated on her breathing and waited as the pain slowly faded away. Closing her eyes again, she considered the block. A powerful reluctance came over her to extend her senses anywhere near it again.

I love Naki. I have to help her. I have to find a way through this.

She pondered the block. *How strong is it?* It didn't have a sense of strength. It was just *there*.

She thought about what Lorandra had said about black magic being a different sort of magic. She remembered the instructions in the book.

"In early training, an apprentice is taught to imagine his magic as a vessel—perhaps a box or a bottle. As he learns more he comes to understand what his senses tell him: that his body is the vessel, and that the natural barrier of magic at the skin contains his power within."

My body is the vessel, she told herself, then she sought that expanding of awareness that she had experienced before. It came back to her instantly, and she felt a rush of excitement. She sought the block. It was still there.

But now it was irrelevant. The block protected the place she had been taught to reach for magic, but her *whole body* was full of magic. She could tap into it from anywhere...

Lilia opened her eyes. She reached for magic and felt it respond. She channelled it out and used it to lift Welor's books from the table. A rush of triumph went through her.

I did it!

She jumped out of the chair and hurried to the door.

"I did it!" she exclaimed. "You were right!"

"Well done. Now get away from the door and be quiet," Lorandra said in a low voice. "I can hear someone coming."

Lilia's heart skipped a beat. She backed away from the door and listened. Sure enough, the faint sound of a single set of footsteps could be heard.

"Dinner," she said. "I'll come talk to you afterwards."

"Good girl."

Turning away from the door, she moved toward the little table where she ate her meals and waited for Welor to enter, one moment exhilarated by her achievement, the next pushing away guilt over what she was intending to do.

I'm doing it for Naki, she told herself. *It doesn't matter what happens to me afterwards, so long as she's safe.*

It seemed like Lorkin had been waiting for someone to kill him for days now, never knowing if he had minutes or hours to live. Though he successfully fought the panic that constantly threatened to overwhelm him, nausea was relentless. Each time the prick of a blade on his skin heralded the draining of his recovering powers, he wondered if this time he would be dragged past exhaustion to oblivion. Each time the draining stopped, he felt a bitter relief.

I doubt the guards will be the ones to finish me off, he told himself. *Kalia will want to do it herself.*

Or would she? It was probably safer if some lesser magician dispatched him. Then she could argue that *she* hadn't been the one to kill him, if his death was found to be suspicious. If her mind was read, however, he could not see how she could hide the fact that she'd given the order to kill him.

A new sound sent his heart pounding: that of the door opening and closing. Then came the sound that sent shivers of terror down his spine: Kalia's voice.

"Is it time?" a guard asked.

"Not yet. I want to be sure I have everything I need."

Lorkin's stomach sank. He heard footsteps draw closer and wasn't surprised when a force pinned him to the floor. Hearing the grunt of effort as Kalia crouched gave him a small sense of satisfaction. Cold fingers touched his forehead and he shuddered as her vile presence filled his mind.

At once he sensed that she was in a hurry. She probed

his memories hastily, grasping those of Healing as soon
as they rose, then she seemed to force herself to take more
time, examining what she had learned the day before. He
knew that she could see that the application of the knowledge had to be shaped and refined according to the illness
or condition, but she didn't have time to draw the details
out of him. She would have to learn the rest by trial and
error. Right now she only wanted to know how best to
avoid doing harm.

"Speaker..."

The guard's voice sounded distant, as if spoken from
the other side of a wall or door. Kalia paused, then reluctantly released Lorkin's mind and vanished from his
senses.

He felt a tired, simmering anger. *If you ever find out
the truth, Tyvara*, he thought, *make sure she gets what
she deserves.*

"There's no other way ou—"

"Be quiet," Kalia snapped. She sounded close, as if she
was still leaning over him.

Then he heard what they were listening to. Footsteps.
Voices.

Kalia cursed.

The sound of the door opening reached him. Someone
drew in a breath in shock.

"Get OFF him!"

"No, Tyvara," another voice commanded.

Tyvara! Lorkin's heart leapt. The force holding him
down vanished. He struggled up into a sitting position and
tried to rub the blindfold off against the rough wall behind
him. Suddenly there were fingers roaming over his face
again, only this time they were warm.

"Wait. Let me get this off," Tyvara's voice murmured. The blindfold slid upwards, releasing him reluctantly. He blinked in the brightness, then grinned as he saw Tyvara crouching in front of him, her face full of concern.

"Are you hurt?" she asked.

He shook his head. "No. Not now you're here." He couldn't stop smiling. "Are you going to get into trouble for talking to me?"

"Don't be silly. Turn around."

He obeyed, and felt the bindings around his wrists fall away. At the same time he felt a little part of his mind freed from a constraint he'd been barely aware of. Looking down at the bindings, he saw a pale yellow gemstone among a pile of bandages.

They tied me up with bandages. That they'd used materials meant for healing as restraints made him despise them even more. *Did the stone stop me from calling out mentally? I suppose they'd need to create something like that, in case they had to stop a prisoner revealing their location.*

Tyvara rose and helped him get to his feet. He felt giddy. Relief at no longer having to worry what would happen swept over him. He resisted a sudden urge to kiss her. She had turned to face the room, and he reluctantly dragged his eyes away from her to look at the other Traitors in the room.

Two Speakers faced Kalia. One was Savara. The other was Halana. More Traitor magicians stood in the corridor behind them.

"Did you learn how to Heal with magic from him?" Savara asked.

Kalia shrugged. "I might have."

Savara looked at Lorkin. "Did she?"

He nodded, then shivered as he remembered the mind looking through his memories. The relief and elation at his rescue faded. *That's something I'm never going to forget*, he thought. It would come back to him in nightmares.

"You have broken our law," Savara told Kalia. "You will be judged."

"Of course," Kalia replied. "Let's get on with it, then." With chin held high, she walked out of the room. Halana followed.

Savara glanced back once, to look at the two guards. "Take them as well," she ordered. The waiting magicians entered the room and ushered the pair out.

Tyvara did not move to follow. Lorkin looked at her. She was staring at him with a strange expression on her face.

"What?"

She smiled. Then she took his head in both hands and kissed him.

Desire rushed through him, followed by dizziness. He took hold of her as much to pull her closer as to stop himself falling over. She chuckled and pulled away a little.

"You're not completely unhurt, are you?" she asked. "They'll have been keeping you drained. Did they even feed you?"

"Um," he replied, then forced himself to think about her questions. "Yes, yes and no."

"Drained is not what I'd call unhurt," she told him.

"I doubt your fellow Traitors would agree with you."

"Even Kalia would agree that to be drained against your will is to be harmed. Which is why we have laws against it. She'll—"

This quibbling was too much. He cut off her words with another kiss. It was long and lingering, and to his surprise it was he who broke it.

"The books have it all wrong," he said.

She frowned. "Books? What books?"

"The ones Kyralian women like so much. Women are always being rescued by men in them. They say the stories are never the other way around because that's not thrilling, and nobody would read the books."

"And you don't agree?"

"No." He grinned. "It's *very* thrilling."

She rolled her eyes and pulled out of his arms, ignoring his protests. "Come on. There's a very thrilling scandal about to stir up the whole of Sanctuary, and people are going to want to hear your side of the story."

"Can't it wait?"

"No."

He sighed. "Very well. I guess I'm afraid you'll not want to kiss me again if we leave this room. What made you change your mind about me?"

She smiled. "I haven't changed my mind about you. I changed my mind about what to do about you."

"Sounds like I ought to thank Kalia for that."

Tyvara pushed him out of the room. "Don't you dare."

CHAPTER 18

ON THE HUNT

It was very warm in Administrator Osen's office. Too warm, Sonea decided. She wondered if Osen had made it this way, or one of the other Higher Magicians was to blame. It was easy to produce heat with magic, but much harder to cool things down.

The Higher Magicians had settled into their usual places. As always, this meant she and Kallen were standing either side of Osen's desk. All waited quietly, expressions grim.

The door to the office opened and all turned to watch as Captain Sotin and a young guard entered the room, accompanied by the Warrior who had been on duty at the Lookout last night. All three went a little pale at the scrutiny of the Higher Magicians. The trio moved to Osen's desk, then stopped, clearly unsure if they ought to be facing the Administrator or the rest of the magicians.

The captain chose to bow toward Osen, and the guard hastily followed suit.

"Administrator," the captain said briskly.

"Captain Sotin," Osen said. "Thank you for coming here. This is?" Osen looked up at the guard.

"Guard Welor, Administrator. He was in charge of seeing to the Lady Lilia's needs. He was not on duty for all of last night, but is—was—the only guard to have regular contact with her."

Osen nodded and gestured to the rest of the magicians. "Tell us what you know, Captain."

The man turned to face the room. "The men on duty report that none noticed anything and all swear that none of them fell asleep, were drinking or were otherwise distracted from their duty. No sounds came from the prisoners or from outside the tower. But at some point, the door to Lady Lilia's room was opened, as was the inner door between Lady Lilia and Lorandra's rooms."

"How were they opened, do you think?" High Lord Balkan asked.

"I cannot say. There was no sign they were forced. The keys are not missing. So either they were picked or magic was used." The captain grimaced. "We had a second lock on Lorandra's door, out of reach so it could not be picked, but we did not have one on the inner door."

"And the main door to Lilia's room?"

The captain shrugged. "We used to keep it double locked as well. Once she was there ... well, we assumed she would not know how to pick locks."

"Since neither can use magic, we must assume Lorandra picked both the inner door and the main door to Lilia's room," Lady Vinara said. "Once they got out of their rooms, how did they get out of the tower?"

"They could not have escaped via the stairway to the ground floor, as it ends at the office and that is always occupied by my men," the captain said. "We think they went up to the roof. We did not keep guards up there, but the hatch to the roof was locked on the inside and blocked by magic—"

He looked at the Warrior who had been on duty.

"Both were intact," the young man murmured.

"—but we found that the old observatory dome had come loose and could be levered upwards enough to allow someone of a small build to crawl out," the captain finished.

"It is made of glass and very heavy," Lord Peakin pointed out, shaking his head. "I doubt Lady Lilia and the old woman would have been able to lift it, even together."

"They must have," Vinara said.

"Then how did they get off the roof?" Lord Garrel asked. "Is there any sign of the use of ropes or ladders?"

The captain shook his head.

"You are confident that your men are telling the truth," Lady Vinara asked of the captain.

The man straightened and nodded. "I trust them all. They are rare honest men." He paused. "And if they weren't, and had allowed the prisoners to escape, surely they would have made up a story about being drugged, or some other excuse. They are puzzled and ashamed, and I have had to talk some of them out of resigning."

The guard beside him bowed his head.

"Guard Welor," Osen said. "Did you notice anything in Lady Lilia's behaviour to suggest she may have been planning an escape?"

The young man shook his head. "I don't think she had time to think about it yet. She was still getting a grasp of what had happened to her. I found this note this morning."

He brought a piece of paper out of his chest pocket, unfolded it and handed it to Osen. "It was in a book I gave her, so I think she meant me to find it."

The Administrator read the note and his eyebrows rose. "*Must find Naki. Will return by morning*," he read.

"She hasn't," Vinara said. "Either she lied or she has been prevented from returning."

"Why lie?" Peakin asked.

"Perhaps she thought it would gain her more time," Garrel replied. "If we'd discovered her missing last night, we might wait to see if she returned."

"But how did they get off the roof?" Osen asked. "How far is it to the ground—or the nearest trees?"

"If they had climbed down they would have been noticed by the guards below. The trees are considerably further down the slope and therefore are lower than the tower," the captain said. "A rope would have to be strung very tight, and it would be more of a matter of sliding than climbing down it. Then there's the matter of getting one end up there in the first place without anyone noticing." He shook his head. "We have always expected that if Skellin attempted to rescue his mother via the roof he would levitate up there."

"I'd wager he did, and nobody noticed," Vinara said. "Why would he take Lilia...?" Her expression changed to one of horrified realisation. "Oh."

The room went very quiet. Sonea looked at Kallen, wondering if he had already considered what Vinara had just realised. His expression was one of forced patience. *Yes, he's well aware of the danger—and itching to do something about it.* She resisted the temptation to smile, knowing it would be taken the wrong way.

"Why were they put next to each other?" Garrel asked suddenly. "A cunning rogue and a bl—...an easily manipulated young woman. Surely this was a disaster waiting to happen. Lilia could have told Lorandra how to use black magic, without them even leaving their rooms."

Some of the Higher Magicians looked at the captain. Garrel, and a few others, were looking at Sonea or Kallen. Sonea looked at Rothen, who met her gaze with a knowing expression. He'd warned her that she could easily be blamed for Lilia's escape, since she had visited Lorandra and Lilia and hadn't noticed any flaws in their prison arrangement.

"We were told to ensure they were treated well," the captain replied. "We thought that, since both were women, they could keep each other company. I...I see that was a mistake, now."

Sonea's heart went out to the man. It wasn't entirely his fault that the pair had escaped either. She frowned. *Is he trying to shift the blame all onto himself, to save his men?*

"Now Lilia and Lorandra are keeping Skellin company," Osen said. "I..."

He paused at a knock at the door. Looking up, he narrowed his eyes at it and it swung open.

Dorrien stepped inside. "Forgive the interruption, Administrator," he said. "But I have information that may be of importance to this discussion."

The door closed behind him, and Osen beckoned. "What is it, Lord Dorrien?"

"A woman who services one of the Inner City houses facing the Guild wall came to the hospice this morning," he said. "It took some time for her to see a Healer, since she obviously wasn't ill," he added wryly. "She told us that she saw two women climb over the wall last night, a few hours after dark. One was old and had dark skin, the other was young and pale. When she heard about the prisoners who had escaped from the Guild, she remembered it and came to tell us."

"Nobody else was with them?" Osen asked.

"No."

Sonea frowned. *So if Skellin didn't rescue them then how did they…?* As a suspicion crept over her, the room didn't feel as warm. *Surely not…*

"Why did she come to the hospice?" Lord Peakin asked. "Why not come here?"

Dorrien smiled crookedly. "Her services aren't of the respectable kind."

"How do you know she is telling the truth? Did she ask for money?" Garrel asked.

"I don't and no, she didn't," Dorrien told him. "She was, as I expect the rest of the city to be, frightened by the thought of a rogue magician and a black magician free in the city."

"How did this news get out so quickly?" Vinara asked, looking around the room.

Osen sighed. "A slip of the tongue, I'm sure," he said. "It's out; let's concentrate on what this woman's information means. Lord Dorrien, thank you for bringing it to us."

Dorrien inclined his head and left. The Administrator turned to the captain and his guard and the Warrior from the Lookout, and thanked them for their assistance. The trio took the cue and departed, too. Once the room was occupied only by Higher Magicians, Osen moved to the front of his desk and crossed his arms.

"We have one small gleam of hope left to us. Unless

Skellin sent Lilia and Lorandra on alone after he freed them, they weren't in his company. Working out how they escaped the Lookout is not as important as finding them before they join Skellin." He looked at Kallen. "That is your task. Find them."

Kallen inclined his head, then headed for the door.

Osen turned to Sonea.

"As always, yours is Skellin. Find him."

This was not a time for raising doubts by protesting that if it was as simple as that, she'd have caught Skellin already—or for showing any resentment at Osen ordering her about like a mindless soldier. She turned and strode for the door.

I am a mindless soldier, as far as the Guild is concerned, she thought sourly, as she entered the corridor. *That is why they allowed me to stay. I am their black magician, to be sent out to fight on their behalf, and they'd much rather I did what I was told than suggest how things should be done. Well, they will have to accept that sometimes I will do things my way, if they want me to risk my life to save theirs.*

Dorrien was waiting for her on the University steps, a Guild carriage standing ready.

"I thought you might want a lift," he said.

She felt a sudden mad desire to hug him, but resisted, knowing how Alina would take it if someone saw and mentioned it to her.

"We need to arrange a meeting with Cery," she told him as she climbed aboard the carriage. "As soon as possible."

"I thought you might," Dorrien said. "I hope it was the right thing to do, but I've sent a message to him already."

She nodded. "Thanks. But as for whether it's the right thing to do...I certainly hope so. If Anyi dies because the Guild wants us to hurry things up, I don't think I'd forgive myself."

Dorrien's expression became serious. "Nor I."

Though small for a ship, and built for speed, the *Inava*'s interior was surprisingly roomy. The slave crew slept in the hull. Dannyl had once glimpsed it through the hatch: rows of hammocks swinging like the limp, empty husks of some sort of exotic tree nut. Above deck were only two neat rooms—one for the captain and one for guests.

In the guest room were two single fold-down beds and a table that converted into a larger bed. Only Tayend's bed had been used in the last three days, as he spent all the time they were at sea sleeping under the influence of the seasickness cure. They had all spent the nights on dry land, at estates along the coast.

The cure for seasickness that Achati had given Tayend made him groggy and sleepy, but the Elyne had accepted this with no complaint, spending most of each day's journey snoring softly on the bed. Dannyl and Achati occupied themselves on deck in good weather, or inside during squalls. The morning of the third day had brought rain and a chill wind from the south, so today they were keeping warm inside.

"Ashaki Nakaro gave me this last night," Achati said, his voice quiet so as not to disturb Tayend. He placed a book on the table. "He said we might find something useful in it about the Duna."

Dannyl picked up the book. It had no title, but the lack was explained when Dannyl opened it and saw the dates next to the entries. It was another record book. The pages had opened at a slim black plaited thread, similar to many place markers that Dannyl had found in Sachakan records.

We have arrived at the camp. My first impression is that it is too large to call it that any more, and many of the Ashaki are now adopting the slaves' habit, and calling it Camp City. I expect it will soon be named after somebody. Not the king, in case the enterprise is a failure. More likely Ashaki Haniva.

"Haniva," Dannyl said. "Isn't that where we're heading?"

Achati nodded. "It is the port town closest to the Duna lands. The camp was further inland, at the top of the escarpment, but Haniva was smart enough to avoid having it named after himself. He knew that attempts by Sachakans to rule the Duna and settle their land had been failures many times in the past, and wasn't about to risk that his own name would be remembered in connection to another one."

Dannyl looked down at the book, turning pages and skimming. "So this is a record of that attempt?"

"Yes. More a diary than a record."

"It is less than a hundred years old."

Achati nodded. "We have repeated this stupidity even in recent times. Someone decides there is glory to be had in conquest, and Duna appears to be the best way to gain it. Much easier than Kyralia or Elyne. In fact, more than one past king has sent an overly ambitious Ashaki off to Duna in order to keep him occupied."

"I'm sure the Duna thanked them for that."

"They've survived admirably well. As a land of

primitives, with little magic, you would think they surely could not put up much resistance. But that is how they defeat us: they don't fight. They retreat into the volcanic lands and wait while we attempt to occupy their land, which always leads to us starving, packing up and going south again." Achati gave a short, sour laugh. "That Kariko chose to invade Kyralia was unusually smart and bold."

"But still not regarded as a good idea, I hope," Dannyl said.

"No." Achati chuckled. "Though I suspect it has occurred to King Amakira that if he was faced with an overly ambitious upstart Ashaki too smart to be tricked into invading Duna, then Kyralia seems to be well capable of defending itself."

Dannyl felt a shiver of cold run down his spine. He looked at Achati, who smiled crookedly.

"Let's not test that idea," Dannyl suggested, choosing his words carefully. "Not the least because, if he's wrong, then he'll have an overly ambitious upstart Ashaki in a better position to cause him trouble than before, and also because, if we defeat him, we might not then be the quietly resentful neighbours that the Duna have been."

"I assure you, he isn't considering it a serious proposition."

"That is good to hear."

Achati gestured at the book. "Read," he invited.

Dannyl continued from where he had stopped. The diary keeper described, to his surprise, how tribesmen were being paid to bring food up from the valley below the escarpment. Were the Duna oblivious to the Sachakan's intentions?

*It became clear that these leaders did not have full
authority over their people and therefore could not
sign over ownership of the land. Authority appeared
to be shared with tribesmen known as the Keepers
of the Lore. Ashaki Haniva asked to meet with the
Keepers. This was, apparently, impossible. After
much confusion and mis-translation, it became
clear that nobody knew who the Keepers were. This
was very frustrating.*

As Dannyl read on he was heartened to see that
Haniva had attempted to negotiate a peaceful acquisi-
tion of the land. This was no brutal conquest... yet.
Haniva tried many times and different approaches, but
though the Duna appeared to be cooperative and amenable to the idea of selling, there was no clear owner of the
land.

*It appears that they regard the land as belonging to
everyone and nobody at the same time. When
Ashaki Haniva asked if that meant he, too, owned
it, they said yes. Perhaps this is why they have never
resisted us taking control of the land before.*

Dannyl considered this strange way to regard land. It
was as if they considered it to be "un-ownable." It was an
intriguing concept. *And not too different from the idea
that a person shouldn't be owned. No wonder the
Sachakans, with their acceptance of slavery, couldn't
grasp the Duna way of thinking.*

The Duna's way of thinking would not have been particularly practical, if their land had not been so difficult to

live on. As Dannyl worked his way through the diary, he learned that Haniva and his Ashaki partners eventually gave up on gaining any official document stating they'd bought the land, drove out the Duna and settled. By the end of the record, there were already signs that crops were not growing as hoped.

Achati had been writing in his own diary while Dannyl read, and as Dannyl put the book down he looked up and set his pen aside.

"What did you make of that?"

"The Duna are an interesting people. They clearly have a very different way of thinking."

Achati nodded. "It is a wonder they have survived this long."

"It is these Keepers of the Lore that we need to talk to—if they still exist." Dannyl frowned. "But that could be difficult to arrange, if nobody knows who they are."

"Difficult? It will be impossible."

"I assume the Keepers know who they are."

The Sachakan looked thoughtful, then smiled. "Of course. So perhaps we just keep asking and see if one admits to it."

"I imagine they won't want to unless they've given it some consideration, and judged that we are not a threat. We should make it known that we want to talk to one of the Keepers, and see if any come to us."

Achati frowned. "That could be slow. And all Duna consider Sachakans a threat."

"Yet they still work with you. Unh, for instance. And traders in the markets."

"Tracking doesn't involve giving away the secrets of your people. Nor does trading."

"No," Dannyl agreed. "That is why we have to let them come to us. This is not something we can force out of them. Otherwise, you'd have done it already."

Achati nodded. "That's true. We Sachakans aren't a patient people." He looked at Dannyl and smiled. "I have no doubt that you could charm them into talking to you. I hope that my presence doesn't prevent that."

Dannyl met his gaze. "Will you be offended if I do this alone?"

The man shook his head. Dannyl held the man's gaze.

"And if I don't share all that I learn with you?"

Achati's eyebrows rose and a hardness came into his gaze, yet he shook his head. "I will accept that it may be politically necessary that you don't. But it would be better if you simply didn't tell me if there is anything you must keep to yourself. I do hope you will divulge anything that is of importance to the safety of Sachaka—or rather, I would expect it of a nation that seeks to become our ally."

Dannyl nodded. "We are aware that anything that could endanger Sachaka would likely endanger Kyralia as well. And I owe you and King Amakira for getting me to Duna in the first place."

Achati smiled and waved a hand dismissively. "That is nothing. If you must consider it a favour you'd like to return, promise me you'll take me on a tour of Kyralia one day. I would love to see your Guild."

Dannyl inclined his head with deliberate Kyralian politeness. "Now *that* I can promise."

Lilia had no idea where she was.

She was worn out and scared, and filled with doubt that escaping with Lorandra had been a good idea. She had lost count of the number of times she'd told herself she was doing this to save Naki, and of all the places she and Lorandra had been. She had no idea where she was, only that it was somewhere in the city.

The first stop they had made had been the brazier house in the Inner City to which Naki had taken Lilia. Lorandra had been recognised immediately and was treated with respect. While she was talking to one man another had appeared, and stopped to stare and grin at Lilia. He said nothing, just stood there grinning at her until Lorandra returned, when he had turned pale and hurried away.

A carriage had taken Lilia and Lorandra to a place outside the old city walls. There had been a lot of laughing going on in rooms there, and the seemingly ominous groans coming from behind one door had worried Lilia until they'd passed an open door and she'd glimpsed the scantily dressed women inside.

She felt very naïve and foolish after that, but there was worse to come. A journey on foot took her through cold alleyways strewn with mud, garbage and the occasional shivering person huddled in a doorway, and ended with them hiding in the shadows, waiting for three thugs to finish beating another man senseless. Lilia was horrified when Lorandra then approached the men, but even more so when it turned out they knew the old woman.

The men had invited Lorandra inside a house, which turned out to be the home of several members of a gang who hired themselves out to do "strong work." Listening quietly, Lilia guessed that this officially involved lifting and carrying things, but was generally understood to also mean beating and killing people.

They were surprisingly nice to her, asking if she was hungry and offering her the least worn-out chair in the guest room. Though she followed Lorandra's lead and said she wasn't hungry, their leader sent one of the group out to buy hot bread from the local baker for her to eat, and when he pressed a mug of bol into her hands she decided it would not be prudent to decline.

It was sickly sweet and made her sleepy. The late hour didn't seem to bother Lorandra, who talked and strode about tirelessly. A longer journey followed, Lilia following her guide through a confusing series of rooms and corridors and tunnels, only occasionally emerging into the night air for a few steps. Finally, they stopped in a warm room and when Lorandra gestured to a chair Lilia collapsed into it.

The chair was surprisingly comfortable. It was a lot newer than the houses and buildings they had passed through. Lilia looked up, noting that the room's decoration and furniture were expensive. She heard her name and realised that the man sitting opposite her, watching her with narrowed eyes, was very well dressed indeed. He smiled, and she forced herself to smile in return.

"The friend of this missing girl," Lorandra told him.

He nodded, his expression becoming serious as he turned to her. "Then we must find Naki. The sun is well up. It is many hours since you escaped. I have rooms here you can sleep in, if you wish."

Lorandra hesitated.

The sun is up? Lilia sat bolt upright. The latter part of their journey had taken them along corridors and through tunnels, and she realised she hadn't seen the sky in hours. "But we have to get back!" she exclaimed.

"I'm sorry, Lilia," Lorandra said. "Dawn came and went some time ago. We have missed our chance to go back. I did not think it would take this long to find someone who could help us. Do you wish to return now?"

Lilia stared at the woman. *If we do return now, the Guild will make sure we never escape again. We won't be able to help Naki.*

She should have known this would happen. She'd expected that they'd make enquiries each night, returning to the Lookout before their absence was noticed, until they found and rescued Naki. Even when she'd levitated them both off the top of the Lookout, she'd known escaping would not be an easy thing to repeat. They had been lucky that one of the guards had been mostly asleep on his feet, glancing up at the tower far less often than into the forest. He hadn't looked up as they'd floated out and away into the tree tops. They might not be that lucky again.

"No," Lilia said.

Lorandra smiled and nodded approvingly. "Don't worry. We'll find Naki. They'll forgive you for running away when you bring her back to them."

Lilia managed a smile. "Thank you for helping us."

Lorandra turned back to the man. *He's probably a Thief,* Lilia thought. *But then, she is a rogue magician. What fine company I'm keeping. Naki would find it amusing.*

Entering Imardin's underworld in Lorandra's company had frightened Lilia more than it ever had in that of Naki. But then, brazier houses were probably the safest places to encounter criminals. The trade there was designed to attract, not put off, customers. She and Naki had only really entered the edge of that world. Lorandra had brought Lilia into the middle of it.

She doesn't have to help me. I've done my part: got her out of the Lookout. If she'd been untrustworthy she would have just left me somewhere and disappeared. But she's doing what she promised: helping me find Naki.

Knowing Lorandra was holding to her side of their deal was the only reassuring thing in this unfamiliar, dangerous world. It had been a risk to trust her, but she'd felt it was one worth taking.

How strange it is that the foolish thing Naki got me to try—to learn black magic—has been the thing that got me out of the Lookout and into the company of someone who can save her.

CHAPTER 19

ESCAPEE

Lorkin opened his eyes, saw that Tyvara was sitting beside the bed, and smiled.

"I thought you weren't allowed to see me?"

Her eyes widened and snapped to his, and she leaned forward.

"How are you feeling?" she asked.

"Good. Better. Have you been sitting there all the time I was asleep?"

She shrugged and looked around the room. "Not much else to do." Then she turned back and her lips twitched. "Better than watching a sewer."

"I'm glad you think so." He sat up and stretched, remembering just in time that he was naked under the bedcovers. Tyvara's gaze dropped to his chest and her eyebrows rose.

She stood up and gestured to a chair, where a fresh set of trousers and tunic were draped. "You had better wash and get into those. The judgement of Kalia is about to begin, and you smell as bad as a sewer."

She slipped out of the room, closing the door behind her. Getting out of bed, Lorkin found a large bowl of water and washing cloths in an alcove and made use of them. His abductors had provided him with a bucket, but had made no attempt to assist him in relieving himself, which had been difficult blindfolded and with hands bound behind his back. He wasn't surprised that he stank.

He'd had only energy enough after his rescue and some food to peel his clothes off and collapse into the bed before falling asleep. Now he looked around, wondering where he was. The room was small and two chairs were the only other furniture apart from the bed.

Once dressed, he opened the door to the room and blinked in surprise. It opened onto a corridor, which was filled with people. Tyvara was standing beside the door, and hooked a hand under his arm as he emerged.

"Good timing," she told him, guiding him to the right. People turned to watch him pass. Some looked friendly, others hostile. Kalia's kidnapping of him was more than a mere scandal and, in the middle of winter with everyone stuck indoors most of the time, it would be attracting attention in a way it might not at other times.

It has probably created more division among the Traitors, he thought. *I hope that doesn't lead to worse problems for them, which become yet another thing they'll blame me for.*

Before long he and Tyvara reached the entrance to the Speakers' Chamber. They passed through and were immediately pulled aside by a magician and asked to stand by the wall to one side of the lower section. Once in place, Lorkin looked around the room.

All of the Speakers were in their seats except for Kalia,

who was standing on the opposite side of the room to Tyvara and Lorkin, flanked by two magicians. The rest of the room was crowded with people, all standing up, their voices combining into an intense chatter.

A bell rang out. Heads turned and the sound of voices dropped. Lorkin saw that Director Riaya was holding a bell much smaller than would normally have been needed to produce the sound. Those of the audience standing in the tiered part of the room began to sit down, while the rest retreated to the walls. When nearly all were settled, another person entered the room. At once almost complete silence descended, the last of those standing among the tiers sat down hastily, and the Speakers rose from their seats to greet the queen as she walked stiffly to her chair.

Before sitting down, Zarala turned to face her people. All placed their hands over their hearts. Lorkin followed suit. The queen bent into a nod toward the audience, then toward the Speakers, and then she sat down. The Speakers took their seats.

"We begin the judgement of Speaker Kalia, who is accused of abduction and forcibly reading the mind of a Traitor. I call forward Lorkin."

All eyes turned to Lorkin as he walked forward and stopped before the Speakers.

"Tell us what happened to you."

Lorkin told his tale from the point where he was pounced upon in the dark. He described waking to find himself bound, blindfolded and unable to call out mentally. Holding out his arms to show the cuts—Tyvara had told him not to Heal them away—he explained that his captors had kept him weak by draining him of power frequently.

He pushed aside reluctance to describe Kalia reading his mind, recalling how she had extracted knowledge of how to Heal with magic as well as searching through his memories for anything that might be used against him. This roused a muttering among the audience. He went on to tell them of Kalia's intention to kill him and claim he'd left Sanctuary. This, strangely, caused the room to fall silent. He saw shock on many faces, but disbelief on others. He finished by relating how Tyvara and Savara had found them.

"You did not give or insinuate permission for anyone to take magic from you, or read your mind."

"No."

"Were you given food and drink?"

"No."

"How many magicians watched over and drained you?"

"I don't know. Two were always there, but I don't know if they were the same two. They must have been working in shifts, as the draining continued through the nights."

Riaya gave the Speakers a meaningful look, then turned back to him.

"Will you consent to a mind-read to prove your story?"

He considered the question. While the idea of having another person roaming about his memories sent a chill down his spine, he'd rather endure that than risk that Kalia might remain free and unpunished for her crimes. Every Traitor he let into his mind was another who would gain knowledge of Healing, but that knowledge was already stolen. Had Kalia passed it on? Perhaps she hadn't had a chance to. But if she allowed a mind-read, the knowledge would be given to another anyway.

He could feel eyes on him. *Gain some time*, he told himself. *Make them try other ways of gaining the truth first.*

"I will, but only if there is no other way," he replied.

Riaya looked at the Speakers again. "Any further questions?"

The women shook their heads. Riaya nodded to Lorkin. "You may go."

He walked back to stand beside Tyvara. She gave him a nod and a smile.

"I call upon Speaker Savara to tell her part in this."

Savara stood. As she spoke, Lorkin learned that Evar had alerted her to his disappearance. She had investigated whether he had left Sanctuary and searched for him within it, but also arranged for any person who had been heard speaking against him recently to be followed. This led her to an abandoned cave near an unstable part of the city, where she found Kalia in the process of reading Lorkin's mind.

The Director told Savara she could be seated, then turned to Kalia.

"Speaker Kalia, step forward and be judged."

Kalia strode to the centre of the room and turned to face the Table. Her back was straight and her expression haughty.

"Is Lorkin's account true?" Riaya asked.

Kalia paused and nodded. "Yes."

"Are you innocent or guilty of abduction of a Traitor, and reading a Traitor's mind against her or his will?"

"Guilty—if you consider him a Traitor, that is."

Riaya folded her hands together. "Then there is no need to investigate the matter further."

"May I address the people?" Kalia asked.

Riaya looked at the Speakers. The six women did not look surprised. They all nodded, some eagerly, some with resignation.

Kalia turned to face the audience. "My people, I felt driven to break our laws for your sakes. I have a duty, as your Carer and Healer, to ensure that when you come to the Care Room no harm is done to you. Recently Lorkin the Kyralian has taken to administering magical Healing, a skill he has refused to teach us. How could I be sure what he was doing was safe? That it would not do more harm than good? He claimed that it has limitations, but how can you or I know if this is true, should his magic ever harm or kill one of us?

"I have taken him in and given him occupation out of kindness to a newcomer. I have offered him all the lore and training that I and my predecessors have always shared. In return he has disobeyed and defied me, using untested magic without guidance or permission.

"If he refuses to follow Traitor custom, is he truly one of us? I say he is not. And if he is not a Traitor, then what I did was not unlawful. It was justified and necessary, in the defence of our people."

Lorkin saw many thoughtful expressions among the audience. He looked at the Speakers, who were frowning.

"May I speak, Director?"

The voice was Savara's. Kalia turned to stare at her enemy with narrowed eyes.

"You may, Speaker Savara," Riaya replied. "Speaker Kalia, please leave the floor."

Once again, Savara rose. Her mouth was set in a

determined line. She waited until Kalia had returned to her former position, then lifted her chin.

"When Lorkin decided he would come to Sanctuary I had my doubts about him," she began. "Why would a magician from a sophisticated, powerful nation sacrifice the wealth and power that he possessed and accept the restrictions we would put on him? He knew little about us. It was a great risk he took, trusting that we were a fair and good people.

"Why did he do it? To defend a Traitor. To save someone of a nation that was not even his, simply because it was the right thing to do. How many of us would do that?

"The secret of Healing is not his to give. If one of us were in the situation he is in, we would not expect to give away our secrets. We would expect our hosts to respect that, and not demand or steal them."

Savara's voice grew loud and stern. "This is not only a crime of an individual against another. This is an unlawful act of one nation against another. Kalia has not only stolen knowledge from Lorkin; the Traitors have stolen secrets from Kyralia, and the lands Kyralia is allied with—one which lies just over the mountains. Lands that are not our enemies, though they would be justified in considering us one after our treatment of Lorkin. Let's hope that Kalia has not secured us a long future of hiding from lands on all sides, instead of just the rest of Sachaka."

Faint whispers were all that stirred the quiet that followed. Savara sat down and nodded to Riaya.

"Speaker Kalia admits to the crimes she is accused of," the Director said. "We Speakers must now discuss her punishment."

As the Speakers and Director began to talk, the room

exploded with sound as all discussed what had been said. Lorkin felt Tyvara's shoulder brush his as she leaned close.

"Don't get your hopes too high," she murmured.

He looked at her. Her expression was sour. "What do you mean?"

"They won't execute Kalia," she told him, looking away.

"Well..." He looked over at Kalia and shuddered. "That's probably a good thing. Even if she did plan to kill me. It means the rest of the Traitors are better people than she is."

A bell rang out and he looked over to the Speakers in surprise. *That was quick.*

"We have decided," Riaya declared when the room quietened. "Speaker Kalia will be stripped of her title, and will never be considered for a Speaker's position again. She will be given menial duties for a year, for the benefit of the city. She is forbidden to use or teach Healing magic unless ordered to. If she is deemed to be trustworthy, she may apply to return to working in the Care Room, but never in a position of leadership."

Protests were voiced in the audience. Lorkin felt as if someone had punched him in the stomach. *That's not a punishment. It's a delay. Eventually, when they've made a good enough act of looking contrite, they're going to let her use the knowledge she stole from me.* He felt betrayed. Tricked. *Maybe this was the plan all along.* He thought of Tyvara's warning...

The protests stopped and he looked around to see the cause. The queen had risen from her seat, one hand on the arm of the chair to steady herself.

"In compensation for the abuses he has suffered," she said, "and the secrets that were taken, Lorkin is to be taught the art of stone-making."

Lorkin stared at the queen in surprise. She met his gaze, her eyes bright with amusement. Realising he was gaping at her, he quickly stopped himself and lowered his gaze. A thrill of excitement ran through him. *At last! New magic to bring back to the*... As quickly as it had come, the excitement faded. He could not take the knowledge to the Guild. He was stuck here in Sanctuary, forbidden to leave. *And besides, leaving Sanctuary would mean leaving Tyvara.*

With the Traitors in possession of Healing, he no longer had anything to use to lure them into trading with the Guild and Allied Lands. Looking at it that way, he realised he had failed. The Traitors had gained Healing, the Guild still did not have stone-making.

But I must not lose hope. Perhaps, one day, they'll let me go. I could run away, but if I fail they will never trust me again. I must be patient.

He looked up at the queen again. She nodded once, then turned back to the Speakers.

The six women wore vastly different expressions. A few looked aghast, a few approving, and Savara actually looked surprised and a little worried. The audience was abuzz with chatter. Lorkin caught looks of worry and disgust, as well as smiles of agreement.

Riaya's bell rang out again. She stood up.

"The judgement of Kalia is made. The punishment decided. This trial is concluded and the laws of Sanctuary upheld. May the stones keep singing."

The audience murmured the reply with enthusiasm,

then a cacophony of voices and footsteps filled the room and people began to move toward the doors. Lorkin heard shouts from outside the room as news was passed along the corridors.

"Well, I'm glad that's over with," he said.

"Not quite," Tyvara replied.

He looked at her.

"Someone has to teach you stone-making."

"You?"

She shook her head. "You don't teach your greatest secrets to the people you send out to live as spies among the enemy. And I never had the patience for it."

"You preferred pretending to be a slave than stone-making?" He frowned. "How difficult is it?"

She patted his arm. "Don't worry. It's really not that dangerous, once you know what you're doing. Come on. Unlike you, I haven't had an enormous breakfast and a sleep-in. Let's get some food."

She hooked a hand under his arm again, and drew him into the stream of people pouring into the corridor where, to his surprise and delight, he received many apologies and sympathetic pats on the shoulder. For all their faults, they were a good people, he decided. Especially when he remembered that what Kalia had done to him was done to thousands of slaves every day down in the rest of Sachaka.

"And yes, I am allowed to see you now," Tyvara told him. He grinned at her, and she smiled.

Sonea knocked on the door of the treatment room. It opened and, to her amusement, Dorrien looked relieved.

"Ah, good," he said. "End of my shift, then?"

"Yes. How are you doing?" she asked.

He sighed. "It's quite draining, isn't it? By the end of the day I can feel how depleted my reserves of magic are."

"Yes, on busy days." Sonea shrugged and sat down on one of the chairs for patients. "If we don't use our power each day, it goes to waste." *Though if he is draining himself too much he will be of no use to me should we confront Skellin. I must have a chat to the Healers here about his work load.*

"Oh, I'm not complaining. I agree. I'm just not used to it." He grimaced. "Alina and the girls aren't used to it either."

Sonea frowned. "You need to use magic at home? I guess we could reduce—"

"No, that's not it. I'm...I guess being tired makes me a little grumpy. Alina can be..." He waved a hand, frowning as he searched for the right word. Sonea waited. Though there were a few words that came into her mind—*jealous, possessive, insecure*—they weren't exactly the polite way to describe his wife's manner.

"She has a lot to adjust to," Sonea told him. "A tired husband who is absent more than he used to be, a city she doesn't know, being far from people who know and understand her—and I'm sure she's not a little afraid for you."

Dorrien nodded. "Sometimes..."

Sonea waited, but Dorrien looked pained and shook his head.

"Sometimes what?" she urged gently.

He looked down at the table. "Sometimes," he said in a low, guilt-ridden voice, "I wish I hadn't married her."

Sonea stared at him in surprise. She had urged him to speak because she had assumed he wanted to admit he was afraid as well. He looked up at her, his eyes shadowed and unreadable.

"I should have married a magician. We'd have had... more in common."

Looking away, Sonea grabbed at the first thing she could think of to shake him from this line of thinking. Much as she didn't like Alina, she did not want to see Dorrien hurt his family. Moving to the city had highlighted the differences between him and his wife. They had distracted him from the similarities.

"You have the village in common and the love of the country. That may seem less significant now, but it is where you have always felt you belonged."

Dorrien gazed at her unhappily, then his shoulders dropped and he nodded. "You're right. It's like Alina's distrust makes me wonder if she sees something I can't. I'm tired of her questions."

"About the hospice? And the search?"

He nodded. "Among other things."

"Then bring her here one day. Show her what we do. At least you can take the mystery out of one aspect of your work."

A thoughtful look crossed his face, then he looked at her and got to his feet. "Well, I guess we should swap places."

She nodded and stood up, waiting until he had stepped out from behind the table before she slipped past and sat down in the chair he'd been sitting in.

"No messages from Cery?" she asked.

"No," he replied.

She sighed. "The Administrator has decided to check on our progress as many times a day as he can," she warned him. "Don't be surprised if he drops by your home."

Dorrien winced. "Alina will *love* that. Goodnight, Sonea."

She smiled. "Goodnight, Dorrien."

When the door closed behind him, she looked around the room once to ensure she had all the cures, bandages and tools at hand that she might need, then she sat down again. Before long the first knock came at the door.

Drawing magic, she sent it out to the door. To her surprise, Dorrien stood there with Healer Nikea.

"A message just arrived," he told her.

"Bring it in."

Nikea handed a slip of paper to Dorrien, then smiled at Sonea and headed back down the corridor. Dorrien stepped into the room and closed the door behind him. He handed the paper to Sonea.

Big meeting tonight. Come for dinner. Bring sweets.

She looked up at Dorrien, her heartbeat quickening.

"This is it," she said. "The opportunity we've been hoping for."

She'd agreed with Cery that they'd refer to any confirmed arrangement between Skellin and Anyi's new boss, or the Thief that he worked for, as "big." "Dinner" meant an hour after sundown. A request for sweets meant to join him at the room under the sweet shop.

"I should be more pleased about that than I feel," Dorrien murmured.

Sonea smiled grimly. "Don't worry. I'll see if one of the Healers here can join us. I'd rather send for someone at the Guild, but we don't have the time. Though perhaps we can send a message anyway, to see if someone from the Healers' Quarters of the Guild can help out here tonight."

Dorrien nodded. "Worth a try."

Lilia felt much calmer about everything now that she'd had a few hours' sleep and a meal among people who she hadn't recently seen beat a man half to death. Worries about the consequences of not returning to the Lookout were easier to push to the back of her mind. Instead, worries about the people she was trusting began to seem more important.

While she felt confident that they couldn't hurt her, since she had magic, there could be other ways they might take advantage of her. She could only hope that Lorandra would stick to their deal. Though the old woman appeared to be doing that, Lilia doubted she would continue to do so if the search for Naki brought her into conflict with an ally, or came with too high a cost.

The effort she is going to, to help me, seems to be greater than what I did to help her. All I did was bust her out of prison. I didn't need to ask favours of anyone. Now that I've seen the world she belongs to, I don't think she's going to value the sacrifice I made by doing something that'll get me in more trouble with the Guild. She doesn't understand that I want to return, and hope to rejoin the Guild some day, because she never wanted to join it in the first place.

The Thief, whose name was Jemmi, had arranged a meeting with another Thief who might know where Naki was. He, Lorandra, Lilia, and a man and a woman who appeared to be bodyguards had left an hour or so ago and travelled an underground route to a warehouse. From there they'd emerged into dark streets and huddled in heavy, hooded coats as they walked through the rain to a bolhouse.

All filed up a flight of stairs and into a small room containing two small chairs and a table. It was cold in the room and Lilia was tempted to warm the air, but Lorandra had warned her not to use magic unless she had to. The male bodyguard moved closer to Jemmi and said something. The Thief frowned and turned to Lorandra.

"We need to discuss a fee before we move on."

"What fee?" Lorandra's odd-shaped eyes narrowed. She looked at Lilia. "Stay put," she said. "We won't be far away."

She headed for the door. Jemmi looked at the male bodyguard and jerked his head to indicate he should accompany him out. The bodyguard looked at his female colleague and made a quick signal, before stepping into the corridor and closing the door.

Bemused, Lilia sat down in one of the chairs.

The female bodyguard moved to the door, clearly listening to the faint voices beyond. Lilia watched her, wondering how a woman could end up in a job like this. *She's younger than I first thought*, Lilia mused. Looking even closer, she noted a few scars on the woman's hands and one on her neck. The way the fabric of her coat hung and moved suggested that objects were contained within. *Knives, perhaps? Surely not a sword...*

The woman turned to look at Lilia. Her expression was one of indecision. She shook her head, then sighed.

"Do you know who you're about to be given to?"

Lilia blinked. "Me?"

"Yes. You."

"They're taking me to see another Thief."

"So that's how they put it." The woman's lip curled. "The Thief's name is Skellin. Do you know who he is?"

Skellin? Lorandra's son was a Thief? Lilia felt cold fear prickle her skin. *Why hasn't Lorandra told me she is taking me to her son? Did she think I'd realise he was a magician, and be scared and try to run away?* She swallowed. *I suppose she's right. He is scarier than she is, because he has control of his powers.*

The woman was staring at her expectantly.

"I thought she'd help me find Naki before joining him," Lilia explained. "She said we were going to meet someone who would have a better chance of finding her, and maybe he is the best—"

"Skellin is a magician." The woman moved away from the door and grasped the arms of Lilia's chair, staring down at her.

"I know—"

"And *you* know black magic. Do you really think he's going to find your friend for free? He's not going to do anything for you until you teach him black magic."

"I'll refuse unless he finds Naki."

The woman's stare was unfaltering. "Assuming he lets you, what then?"

Lilia could think of no good answer. The bodyguard glanced back at the door, then sighed again.

"You don't need to betray everyone to find your friend," she said. "There are others who can help you. Others who won't blackmail you, because they know it's better for everyone if the Thieves have no access to magic. Especially black magic."

"I...I didn't know."

The woman let go of the chair and straightened. "I guess you wouldn't."

Lilia shook her head. She felt foolish and helpless and frightened. "I...it's too late now, isn't it? What else can I do?"

The woman glanced at the door, then at Lilia. "It's not too late." Her whisper was full of urgency. "I can get you out of here and introduce you to people who can find your friend without asking you to teach anyone black magic. But only if you come with me *now*."

Lilia looked at the door. Lorandra had agreed to help her. She'd made a deal and appeared to be sticking to it. *But to get Skellin's help...he'll probably want to make a deal of his own...if there's a chance I can get out of here, I have to try.*

"Are you sure you can find Naki?"

"Yes." The woman's gaze was steady and her voice full of confidence.

Hoping she wouldn't regret it, Lilia got to her feet.

"All right."

The woman gave her a feral grin.

"Follow me."

In one graceful movement, she stepped up on the table, then reached to the ceiling. Lilia hadn't noticed the hatch there. It opened silently. The woman held a hand out to Lilia and helped her up, then grabbed her by the thighs and lifted. Lilia bit back a gasp of surprise at being so man-handled. *Or is that woman-handled?* Her head and shoulders were in a roof space. She braced herself on the frame of the hatch and, helped by a shove from below, pulled herself inside.

The woman appeared in the hatch opening, swung up

and pulled it closed. She put a finger to her lips, then slowly and silently crawled along the cavity to the far wall. Following, Lilia concentrated on placing her hands and knees gently on the ceiling panels and not scraping her feet on them. She listened for sounds that might indicate their absence had been discovered, but no shouts or calls reached her.

What am I doing? I should have stayed with Lorandra. But something told her that this woman was right. Lorandra might have been able to help her find Naki, but the cost would have been terrible. *This bodyguard had better be right, though. If she can't find Naki I will tell her to take me back to Lorandra.*

At the end of the building they reached a triangular wall. A single window opened in the centre of this and the woman headed for it. Cold air and wind-blown rain rushed inside as it swung inwards like a door. The woman rose into a crouch and put one leg through, bending almost double against her other leg as she carefully backed out through the gap.

Lilia followed and found herself on top of another roof. The bodyguard drew her coat close and walked along the peak, dropping back into a crouch as she neared the edge. Judging by the gap between the roof and the wall of the next building, Lilia guessed there was a road below. She chose her steps carefully. The rain had made the roof tiles slippery. The woman stepped back from the edge of the roof as Lilia reached her.

"I'd like to get us into that building." She pointed across the road to a three-storey stone building. "See those ropes?"

The woman was pointing to a couple of ropes strung

across the gap a few houses further along the road. Lilia nodded.

"We can get across on them, then make our way back across the rooftops, and in through that attic window you can just make out down the side there."

Lilia looked at the ropes and felt an unexpected wave of admiration for the woman.

"You do this all the time, don't you?"

The bodyguard smiled. "We put them there. Never know when you'll need to get away from somewhere."

Lilia nodded toward the road. "Anybody watching?"

The woman leaned toward the edge, looked up and down the street, then shook her head.

"Then I have a better way for you," Lilia told her. "Hold on to me and don't shout."

She drew magic and created a disc of it beneath their feet. The woman threw her arms out, unbalanced, and Lilia caught them to steady her. Willing the disc to rise, Lilia carried them out across the road to the roof on the other side. The woman was staring at her as their feet met the tiles.

"Rek was wrong. You *do* have your powers back."

Lilia nodded, then looked back at the bolhouse roof. "She doesn't."

"That's the best news I've had all night." The woman moved to the attic window. It was boarded up on the inside. She unblocked it with one quick kick. As Lilia followed her into the dark room, she hurried to the door, opened it and listened. Then she crept further into the house, peeking through doors. "Nothing. Doesn't look like anybody is home. That's the second best news I've had all night."

"You broke in without knowing if anyone was home?"

The woman shrugged. "I could have handled it."

Lilia decided she didn't want to know how. She followed her rescuer into a bedroom. The woman approached the window cautiously.

"Don't get too close," she warned. Then she tensed. "Ah. There they are. If we'd taken any longer, they'd have spotted us."

Lilia moved to the side of the window and peered out. Figures roamed the street below. A movement higher up drew her attention to the roof, where two people were balancing, one pointing at the ropes and another staring around at the rooftops.

"I better go cover that window again," the woman muttered. She hurried upstairs and Lilia soon heard a muffled banging she hoped wasn't audible from the outside. Fortunately, the rain had begun to come down harder. Perhaps it would mask the sound.

The woman reappeared, this time carrying two chairs, which she set down either side of the window. She dropped into one, and Lilia took the other.

"We're going to stay put," she told Lilia as she scanned the street outside again. "They're heading off along the known routes, not searching houses." She grinned. "I suppose if I'd known you had your powers and Lorandra didn't we could have just walked out of there, but then they would have followed us. And there's something satisfying about disappearing from and then hiding right under the enemy's nose." Abruptly her smile faded and she frowned as if something bad had occurred to her.

"What is it?"

The woman grimaced. "Aside from just losing my job,

I had other things I was supposed to be doing. People are going to be waiting for my message, and when it doesn't come they'll worry about me."

"Oh." Lilia felt a pang of guilt. "Well...thank you for helping me—and for offering to find Naki. You're *sure* you can find her?"

"We will. We won't ask you to betray the Allied Lands in the process." The woman straightened. "In the meantime, we haven't been formally introduced. Though I've guessed who you are."

"Yes. I'm Lilia, the novice who accidentally learned black magic," she said wryly.

"Honoured to meet you, Lady Lilia." The woman bowed slightly. "My name is Anyi."

CHAPTER 20

NO RETURN

It had been a rough night at sea, and Dannyl had been relieved when the *Inava* had turned into a small, sheltered bay in the early afternoon. Though Achati had planned for them to spend most nights on land, the further north they sailed the greater the distance was between port towns. Tayend had taken an extra dose of the seasickness cure the night before and promptly fallen asleep, something which Dannyl had eventually begun to envy. Though Dannyl could Heal away the ill effects of sea travel, the heaving of the ship meant that staying in bed sometimes took some effort. Finally, a few hours before dawn, the storm passed and he got some sleep, but all too soon they had to get up again.

Achati had arranged for them to stay at the estate of a friend, who was currently visiting the city. They had the place all to themselves—bar the slaves of course. The slaves, who had been told to treat their master's guests well, had a delicious meal ready and escorted them to baths built around a natural hot spring that Achati said were not to be missed.

It looked like Tayend would miss them, however. He had to be half carried off the ship by a slave, then lifted into the waiting carriage. He'd snored loudly all the way to the estate and roused himself only long enough to follow a slave to the guest quarters. The slaves reported that he fell asleep as soon as he reached a bed.

Achati and Dannyl headed for the baths together. These turned out to be one long room, a door at each end, with no windows but with an opening in the ceiling that revealed the starry night sky. Steaming pools of water ran down the room's length, each pouring into the next, with a path that wound beside and, in one place, over a pond via a curving bridge. A metallic, salty tang hung in the air.

"The closest pool is warm," Achati said as he began to strip off his clothes. "It's for cleaning, and drains separately. Once you are clean, you can start at the next pool and move down the room until you find one that suits you. The ones at the centre are hot, then they grow cooler again until the last, which is cold."

"They finish with a *cold* pool?"

"Yes. To wake you up. It's very refreshing. But if you wish to go to sleep straight after a bath it is recommended you get out of one of the warmer pools. There are absorbent coats down there to put on to keep yourself warm." Achati, who was down to just his trousers, looked at Dannyl, who hadn't begun to undress. "The slaves will clean your clothes and take them back to your room."

Dannyl nodded, then began removing his clothes. Public bathing had gone out of fashion in Imardin a hundred or so years ago. It was well known that baths (and some records rather snarkily claimed bathing as well) had been introduced by the Sachakans when they had conquered

Kyralia. Bathing had remained popular, but not the public
aspect. The Guild's baths were divided into private rooms,
as were the facilities in the city—though he'd heard that
some bathhouses associated with brothels had larger
pools for mixed bathing.

Elyne still had a few public baths, but men and women
used them separately, and wore a modest shift of heavy
cloth. Dannyl had visited them a few times with Tayend,
when he had been Guild Ambassador to Elyne. It had
been fashionable to lament the passing of the good old
days of nude bathing, but nobody tested the apparent
common opinion that it was better stripping off completely.

*Of all the more confronting Sachakan habits—
slavery, black magic—surely this should be the easiest to
adapt to. Though I haven't heard of any public baths in
Arvice. Maybe it has gone out of fashion in Sachaka, too.
I can't imagine them allowing their women to bathe
publicly.*

Achati had removed all his clothes now, and was stepping into the first pool. His darker skin was suddenly
more obvious, and though Achati was smaller in size than
the average Sachakan man, he had the same broad shoulders and sturdy frame. Taking a deep breath, Dannyl
shrugged off the outer magician's robe and stepped out of
his trousers. He made himself turn around, walk to the
pool and step into the water.

He'd been expecting heat, but the water was tepid.
Achati's expression was neutral as he indicated a bowl at
the pool's edge that contained bars of soap. He was surrounded by a slick of soapy residue, which concealed his
body beneath the water. The pool was large. Plenty of

room for the both of them—possibly enough for four. Dannyl concentrated on the details, not wanting to think too much on the fact that he was naked in the company of a man who had indicated he wanted there to be more than just friendship between them.

The soap was strange. It contained grit, which scratched Dannyl's skin and left red lines. As Achati stepped out of the pool, Dannyl noted that any such marks weren't as noticeable on the Sachakan's skin.

He finished scrubbing himself, then rose and followed Achati to the next pool.

This one was hot. Seats had been built into the sides. Dannyl felt his skin smart at the temperature. Achati did not stay there for long, but moved from pool to pool until he found one that he proclaimed the most comfortable.

"Hot enough?" he asked Dannyl.

Dannyl nodded. "Very."

"Go on to the next one. I'll stay here. We can claim one each and still chat."

So Dannyl stepped down to the next pool, which was pleasantly warm. "Ah. Yes. That's the one." He settled into a seat alcove from which he could easily turn and talk to Achati. Though he was growing used to being unclothed, he had to admit to feeling a little relieved that they were now separated by the low wall of the upper pool.

Achati chuckled.

"What is it?" Dannyl asked, when his companion didn't explain the source of his humour.

The Sachakan smiled crookedly. "You. I thought you'd turn and run."

"From this?" Dannyl shrugged. "I'll admit it's a new experience, and not a completely comfortable one."

"And yet you managed it. With me here, as well."

Dannyl tried to think how best to answer that, but before he managed to, Achati continued.

"You've been doing very well keeping me at arm's length."

Dannyl couldn't think of anything smart to say to that, either.

"Have I?" he managed.

"Yes. Having Tayend ask to come along was a clever move."

Dannyl straightened in surprise and indignation. "I didn't have Tayend ask to come along." He scowled. "He came up with that idea all by himself."

Achati's eyebrows rose. He looked at Dannyl thoughtfully. "I think I believe you."

"It's true," Dannyl told him, trying to avoid sounding offended, and not quite succeeding. "Though it's also true I've been keeping you at arm's length."

"Why?"

Dannyl looked away and sighed. "Consequences. Conflicting loyalties. That sort of thing."

"I see," Achati said quietly. He was silent for a while, then suddenly rose and moved into Dannyl's pool. Once settled, he sighed deeply. "That is better." Then he looked at Dannyl. "You're worrying about the wrong things, Ambassador Dannyl."

Dannyl met Achati's eyes. "Am I?"

"Yes. My loyalties lie first with Sachaka and my king." Achati's eyes flashed. "Yours are with Kyralia, your king, the Guild and the Allied Lands—though not necessarily in that order. Nothing will ever change that, and nothing should." He smiled thinly. "Think of it this way: if my king ordered me to kill you, I would. Without hesitation."

Dannyl stared at the man. Achati's eyes were hard and his expression challenging. *He means what he says, but then, wouldn't I do the same, if we became enemies? Probably. I would feel bad about it, but... how likely is it?* He pushed that thought aside. *What is true is that I'd feel bad about it no matter how close we were, and it's not that we could ever do anything to make others doubt our loyalties, like having children or getting married...*

It wasn't as if Achati wanted any commitment. For once, that appealed. While Dannyl ought to have been repelled by the man's admission that he'd kill him if ordered to... it was strangely exciting.

"So... you wouldn't hesitate? Not even a little bit?" he asked.

Achati smiled and pushed away from the wall, moving to the centre of the pool.

"Well, maybe a little bit. You could come here and convince me how long I should hesitate for."

Chuckling at his friend's invitation, Dannyl moved to the middle of the pool. For a few heartbeats they stared at each other. Time seemed to slow and stop.

Then both froze as muffled voices came from the direction of the bathhouse entrance. They quickly moved apart and stood up so they could see who was there. Dannyl was relieved to see the door was still closed.

The voices fell silent, then there was a tapping at the door. Achati glanced at Dannyl, his annoyance gratifyingly obvious. "I gave the slaves orders that we weren't to be disturbed unless it was urgent."

"You had better find out what's wrong," Dannyl replied.

Achati stepped out of the pool and brought a coat to him with magic. He shrugged into it and moved to the door.

"Come in."

The door opened. Dannyl quickly schooled his face as he saw Tayend peer around it. *The more annoyed I look, the more he'll suspect.* Inside he felt as if his blood was boiling with fury.

"Am I interrupting?" Tayend said. "The slaves said you were here, and after you said we had to try these baths it seemed rude not to come and see them."

"Of course not," Achati replied. He waved Tayend toward the cleansing bath and explained the procedure.

Then, as he walked back to join Dannyl, he smiled and silently mouthed a promise.

Later.

Not long after arriving at the Care Room, a magician came to escort Lorkin to the stone-makers' caves. He was a little reluctant to leave, as the woman who had replaced Kalia was still working out where everything was stored and learning which ailments the patients occupying the beds were recovering from. But she shooed Lorkin away when the escort arrived.

"Go," she'd ordered. "I will work it all out."

"I'll come back later," he promised.

The magician escort had smiled shyly at him and said little as she led him to the caves. It was so unusual for a Traitor woman to be shy and awkward that he resisted trying to draw her into a conversation. If growing up in a place where women were powerful hadn't helped to make her bold and confident, then the awkwardness must run very deep—and challenging it might do more harm than good.

She led him deep into the city, further inside the mountain than most Traitors liked to live. The passage became winding, and they passed openings into caves on either side. He'd figured it prudent not to show too much interest in them the last time he'd passed, when being escorted out of the cave Evar had shown him. Now he was free to glance inside.

The caves were of varying sizes and shapes. Some effort had obviously been put into levelling the floor in places, but the uneven and angular walls had obviously been left untouched. In a larger room, Lorkin noted that walkways had been fixed to the walls to allow access to higher parts of them.

In all of the caves he saw spreads of glittering colour, on walls, ceilings and even, in a few instances, on floors.

None of the caves had doors. It seemed a strange omission in a part of the city that contained such magical secrets. *But perhaps the secrets can't be extracted from the stones. Perhaps they can only be passed on mind to mind, like black magic.* Or perhaps they were kept in books in a secure room somewhere.

The winding corridor ended at another cave. The guide continued through it, to where another cave joined it, then another. There had been fissures in the walls and floor of the passage, easily stepped over. Now they passed over bigger cracks via bridges made of slabs of the same stone as the walls.

And then they arrived at a door.

The escort knocked, then smiled at him and walked away quickly, before he could thank her. He turned back to find the door open. A voice called out.

"Come in Lorkin."

He recognised the voice as Speaker Savara's. Stepping inside the room, he saw that she and Speaker Halana were sitting in two seats of a ring of five. Savara gestured to one of the chairs, and he sat down.

"Are you aware of the responsibilities of each of the Speakers?" she asked.

He nodded. "Yes. Well, at least some of them. Speaker Riaya organises meetings, elections, judgements and such, Speaker Kalia oversaw health, Speaker Shaiya controls the production of food and supply of water, and you are in charge of defence."

"That is correct. Speaker Lanna's responsibility is living arrangements and Speaker Yvali's is education. Speaker Halana's," she nodded at the other woman, "is stone-making."

He looked at Speaker Halana and inclined his head in respect. "So you will be my teacher?"

The woman nodded. "I will. If you agree to it."

He smiled. "I can think of no reason why I would not."

Halana did not return his smile, though there was a hint of amusement in her eyes. Something about her expression sent a warning chill up his spine. He frowned and looked at Savara.

"*Is* there are a reason why I would not?"

She smiled wryly. "Possibly. I may have mentioned before that I once travelled to Kyralia. I visited Imardin for a while, before and during what you call the Ichani Invasion."

He stared at her in surprise. "You saw the invasion?"

Her expression was serious now. "Yes. We keep an eye on the Ichani, since they are always on the move and sometimes venture too close to Sanctuary. Mostly they are harmless, too occupied in fighting each other to cause us trouble. But any signs that they are uniting, as you can imagine, are alarming. Fortunately for us, the last time they did that their intent wasn't to cause us trouble. Unfortunately for your people, their attention had turned to Kyralia.

"We noticed that they were sending slaves into Kyralia, so I went to investigate their purpose. The events that I witnessed made it very obvious that the Guild does not use, and in fact forbids, higher magic."

Lorkin nodded and looked down. "It is called black magic. And it is no longer forbidden."

Her eyes narrowed. "And yet its use is restricted. Only a few know how to use it."

"Yes."

"And if our spies are correct, the knowledge that those few have is incomplete, too."

He met her eyes. "I don't know, since I'm not one of the few allowed to know it."

"You're *not*," she said, holding his gaze, "or *weren't*?"

He looked away. She was asking... what was she asking? If he still considered himself a Guild magician. But there was an unspoken question behind the one she'd asked him: did he want to retain the option of being one again? If he learned black magic, he might never be able to rejoin the Guild.

She could be simply offering to teach it to him *instead* of stone-making, but he doubted that.

This could be a test to see if he meant to take the stone-making knowledge straight back to the Guild. But that didn't make sense. The queen hadn't said anything about him not being allowed to pass on the knowledge. But she hadn't said he could, either.

"I am asking you this," Savara said quietly, "because to teach you stone-making, we will have to teach you higher magic."

He looked up at her in surprise. "Oh."

"And I'm asking if that would prevent you from ever returning to the Guild."

"I see…" Suddenly it all made sense. The queen felt that he was owed something of equal value in compensation for the Healing knowledge that had been stolen from him. The only magic he did not have was black magic and stone-making. Since he needed the former in order to achieve the latter, they both came at the same price: he could never go home. *And that must mean they have considered the possibility that one day they might let me go…*

How would the Guild react to him knowing black magic? Would they forgive it, when he revealed he had found a new way for them to defend themselves? Then his heart sank. *I was hoping to find a way that would replace black magic, not use it. If stone-making involves using black magic, then I have failed. The Guild might not accept it.*

He realised, then, that he didn't truly believe that. The Guild would never turn down the opportunity to learn a new kind of magic, especially if *using* the stones didn't involve using black magic. It would only have to restrict who could *learn* it.

If they wanted the benefit of the magical gemstones,

the Guild would have to accept that Lorkin had learned black magic in order for them to have it. If they didn't... *well, they can have me and gemstones, or neither. Just as I have to accept that I can have stone magic and black magic, or nothing at all.*

And if the Guild rejected him... well, he would return to Sanctuary. Traitor society was not without its flaws, but what land or people was? Yet the thought of never returning to Imardin brought a pang of regret. There must be some way he could visit his mother, Rothen and his friends.

That is something I'll have to work out later. This is more important. It could be disastrous if the Ashaki gain this magic before the Guild does. I can't contact Osen and ask him to hold a meeting to decide. I have to take this opportunity to learn stone-making, and hope that the Guild doesn't reject me for it.

He looked at Savara.

"Knowing black magic might prevent me from returning permanently," he told her. "I may only ever be able to visit. I'm willing to take that risk, if you assure me that there will always be a home for me in Sanctuary."

She met his eyes levelly, then looked at Halana. The other woman nodded. Savara turned back and smiled. "So long as you never break our laws, you will be welcome to live among us."

"Thank you."

"And now," she said, standing up and gesturing to Halana. "Now it is time we completed your education." She patted him on the shoulder as she passed. "No doubt you're more worried about the higher magic. Don't worry. It's the easy part."

Halana rolled her eyes and clucked her tongue. "Don't pay any attention to her," she said. "She's right that higher magic is easy to learn but stone-making really isn't that difficult, if you have patience, diligence and focus."

Lorkin glanced back at Savara to see the woman shake her head in disagreement before she closed the door. "And if you don't?" he asked, turning back to Halana.

The woman shrugged. "That depends on the stone you're raising. If it's meant to produce heat and you lose concentration...can those Healing powers of yours treat burns?"

He swallowed. "Yes."

She smiled. "Well, then. With an advantage like that, you've got nothing to worry about."

It hadn't surprised Sonea to find that Cery wasn't waiting under the sweet shop, and that instead there was a message instructing them how to find him. She, Dorrien and Nikea had disguised themselves as a couple and their daughter looking to expand their trade in gathering and preparing rag for paper production. The message led them to a bolhouse, through a small night market and a bath-house, before they found themselves climbing out of a basement to find that Cery had taken over a neat and surprisingly well-decorated home for the night.

Where the occupants were, Sonea was reluctant to ask. Signs of them were everywhere, from the toys visible through the open door of a bedroom, to the food half eaten at the table. They found Cery in a darkened room, sitting by a window. Gol had met them in the basement, and warned them not to create any lights.

"The meeting is supposed to take place in that room

over there, on the second floor," Cery told them, pointing out of the window.

Looking across, Sonea saw the lamp-lit guest room of a house across an alleyway. The alley was so narrow she could have stepped into the other room in a few strides, if there hadn't been two walls between them.

They discussed how to approach the other building, and cut off the obvious escape routes. Cery hadn't been able to get anyone close enough to check for hidden escape routes without them risking being seen. The house they were in got them as close as he dared. It was up to the magicians to find their way over to the room opposite, once the meeting began.

Sonea thrashed out a plan with Dorrien and Nikea, but they hadn't a chance to put it in action. The room opposite remained empty.

The night passed slowly, and at every hour Cery grew increasingly withdrawn. He spoke less and less, and eventually they all remained silent, not wanting to voice their fears. Shoulders drooped and faces sank in disappointment as it became clear there would be no meeting, and no capture of Skellin or anyone else. When the walls outside the window began to lighten, Nikea finally broke the silence.

"What do you think? Should we conclude that the meeting was called off?"

All exchanged glances except Cery, who was staring at nothing.

"We'll wait for news," Sonea told him.

"If Anyi managed to slip away, or send a message through someone, where would they go?" Dorrien asked Cery.

Cery's frown deepened. "She wouldn't come here, or send a message here, in case it drew attention to us." He rose, a movement that seemed abrupt after hours of stillness and silence. "Follow me."

They obeyed, returning to the basement and retracing their steps to the bathhouse. There, the middle-aged woman who ran the house approached Cery nervously and handed him a slip of paper.

"I'm sorry. It came a few hours ago," she said. "I didn't know what to do with it. You never said I might get messages, or where to send them."

"I never expected you to have to," he said. "But thank you for keeping it safe."

She looked relieved and made a quick retreat from the room. Cery read the note and sighed with relief.

"She's alive and safe," he told them. "But they've discovered that she was a spy." He shook his head. "I wish I'd been able to arrange writing lessons for her." He held out the slip of paper, with two scrawls on it. "We worked out a code, but it doesn't give much detail."

"You'll be able to meet with her and find out what happened?" Dorrien asked.

Cery nodded. "How soon will depend on how much her employer and the Thief that controls him know about her, and if they are hunting for her." His expression became grim again. "I'll let you know as soon as I find out."

Sonea put a hand over his. "I hope she's all right. And pass on our thanks to her."

He managed a wan smile. "All this, and we didn't catch Skellin."

"Well, let's hear what she says before we call it a

complete failure. Maybe she's picked up some information we can still use."

He nodded. "Then I had better get you back to the Guild with your own identities still concealed." He beckoned. "Come on. I've made some arrangements."

CHAPTER 21

LIES, HIDDEN TRUTHS
AND DELUSIONS

After a nervous night waiting silently in the attic of the house they'd broken into, when the occupants—a family with noisy young children—had returned, followed by a day of restless sleep in a tiny room below a bolhouse, Lilia was beginning to wonder if her life was going to permanently switch to a nocturnal routine.

If it was, then she hoped that she would adjust to it quickly. Though Anyi had assured her that she knew the bolhouse owner, and was confident enough to fall asleep straightaway on one of the narrow beds, Lilia woke at every noise. And sleeping under a bolhouse meant there were a lot of noises to wake her. She must have grown used to it, because Anyi eventually had to prod her into waking up.

"Time to get up," Anyi said. "I've got some clothes for you, then we'll be having dinner with the woman that runs this place."

Lilia sat up, yawned, then picked up the topmost piece of clothing in the pile at the foot of the bed. A heavy tunic top. She frowned. It was clean, but threadbare at the elbows.

"Your clothes are too good," Anyi told her. "People will spot that you're out of place as soon as they see you. If you want to stay hidden until we find your friend, you're going to have to dress like you belong here."

Lilia nodded. "If Black Magician Sonea can do it, so can I."

Anyi chuckled. "I'll slip out while you get changed."

The old clothes smelled of wood smoke and soap. Though they were of coarser fabric than the clothes Lilia had been given to wear at the Lookout, something about them brought a feeling of comfortable familiarity.

They remind me of my life before I became a novice. They are like the clothes the servants wore who did the rougher, dirtier duties.

Once she was done, she moved to the door and opened it a crack. Anyi was waiting outside, and beckoned as she saw Lilia.

"Come upstairs," she said. The little room was underneath a staircase, and they climbed to a floor two storeys up. Anyi knocked on a door and a voice called out, "Come in." Smiling at Lilia, she opened the door and moved inside.

"Here she is, Donia," she said, waving at Lilia. A middle-aged woman was standing in front of a half-circle of guest room chairs. "This is Lilia."

The woman bowed. "Lady Lilia, I think is the correct title."

Lilia flushed. "Not exactly. I'm not a magician any more. At least, not a Guild one."

Anyi gestured to the woman. "This is Donia, the owner

of this bolhouse and a childhood friend of Black Magician Sonea."

Lilia glanced at Anyi in surprise. "Is that true?"

"Not exactly." Donia shook her head and smiled sadly.
"I became the wife of one of her friends, and he died some
years ago. Please sit down. I'm having some food brought
up. Would you like some wine?"

Lilia hesitated. The last time she'd drunk wine had
been the night before Naki's father had died. Memories of
that night were interrupted as Anyi shooed her toward the
seats. Lilia let herself be herded into a chair.

"I'll have some bol," Anyi told Donia. "If you're
offering."

Donia smiled. "Of course. Would you prefer bol, Lilia?
I'm afraid the water here isn't as drinkable as it is in the
nicer parts of the city."

"Wine would be nice," Lilia replied, remembering the
sickly sweet drink the thugs had given to her and managing not to shudder.

Moving to a narrow table, Donia tapped a small gong.
Footsteps sounded outside the door, then it opened and a
younger woman peered inside, an eyebrow raised in
question.

"A mug of bol, two glasses and a bottle of the good
wine," Donia said. The woman nodded and closed the
door. With a sigh, Donia sat down. "She won't be long.
So...Lilia. Can you tell us how you came to be in the city,
heading for a meeting with Skellin?"

The question was asked gently, and Lilia guessed that
if she said she couldn't answer, the woman would accept
that. But she felt an urge to speak, to tell somebody what
had happened to her, and to find out if her decisions had

been right or not. Was it wise to talk to this stranger? It seemed that every time someone wanted her to do something, it brought more trouble. First it was Naki, urging her to try to learn black magic, then it was Lorandra, talking her into escaping from the Lookout.

I don't know Donia. I don't know Anyi either, yet for some reason I trust her. She could have taken me straight to the Guild, but she didn't. Doing what Anyi had told her to do had actually got her *out* of trouble, so far. *I don't have much choice but to trust her, anyway. It's that, or try to find Naki on my own.*

"You can trust Donia," Anyi said. "She's looked after me for years. The more we know, the better chance we'll have of finding your friend."

Lilia nodded. She started at the night she and Naki had gone to the library and tried the instructions on using black magic. She started there, because she had to tell them about the murder of Naki's father, which might be connected to Naki's disappearance. From there she told them everything up to the point where Anyi had rescued her from the impending meeting with Skellin. The only times she paused were when the servant woman returned with the drinks, and two male servants brought in the food. The wine loosened her tongue even more, and she confessed to some darker thoughts that she had kept to herself, like the fear that she *had* killed Naki's father and somehow the roet and wine had made her forget it.

"Rot," Anyi said with unhidden disgust. "It wouldn't surprise me if it made you kill him."

Lilia winced. "So you think I did?" she asked in a small voice.

Anyi's eyes widened. "No! I don't think you could do that. It's just...it makes people do things they wouldn't normally do. I don't think it makes them forget that they've done it, though." Then her expression became thoughtful. "Have you had any rot since that night?"

Lilia shook her head.

"And do you...want more. Do you crave it?"

Lilia considered, then shook her head again.

Anyi's eyebrows rose. "Interesting. It's not supposed to be different for magicians."

"Some people aren't as affected by craving as others," Donia said.

Anyi looked at the woman. "You sound sure of that."

Donia nodded. "I've seen it with the customers. Some people can't stop, others can. It's the same as drinking, though I'd wager that rot hooks more people than drink does." She shrugged. "It's rotten luck if you're one of those people, or their family." She looked at Lilia, and her brows creased in consideration. "That's quite an adventure you've had. Lots of things don't make sense. You say you learned black magic easily, but your friend followed the same instructions and didn't. Her father was killed by black magic, but neither you nor your friend did it—which must be true because Sonea read her mind, too. There are only two other black magicians, but the Guild doesn't think they did it. So there must be another black magician out there."

"If there is, Skellin isn't controlling them or Lorandra wouldn't have been so keen to get Lilia to him," Anyi reasoned. "And he can't be the black magician, for the same reason."

"Naki's father was killed after Lorandra was imprisoned," Donia pointed out. "If Lorandra knew Skellin had learned black magic, Sonea would have learned that when she read her mind. If Skellin learned black magic *after* her capture she wouldn't know about it."

Anyi's eyes widened. "I hadn't thought of that. Who knows what he would have done with Lilia if he hadn't needed her? Probably killed her."

"If he could. She is a black magician, too," Donia reminded her.

"Ah, but Lilia hasn't been strengthening herself by taking magic from others." Anyi turned to Lilia. "Have you?"

Lilia shook her head.

"And this other black magician has, because he killed Naki's father." Anyi grimaced. "Maybe it is a good thing the meeting didn't take place. What if there had been a black magician there, and he was stronger than Sonea and the other magicians?"

Donia spread her hands. "What's done is done."

Lilia looked from the older to the younger woman.

"*Sonea* was going to be at the meeting?"

Anyi winced. "Yes. Well, not so much *at* the meeting as interrupting it. You see, I was working as a bodyguard for Rek so I could spy on him. My real employer—the person who is going to help you find Naki—has been helping Sonea search for Skellin."

Lilia frowned. "You work for the Guild?"

"No. I work for someone who works for the Guild—but don't worry. I'm not going to turn you over to them."

"Why not?" Lilia asked.

"Because...because I promised to find Naki for you,

and I don't break promises." Anyi smiled crookedly. "She must be very special to you, for you to risk so much for her."

Unexpectedly, Lilia's face began to warm. She nodded and looked away, pushing aside the memory of a kiss. "She's my friend. She'd do the same for me."

"You need to tell Cery," Donia said.

Anyi sat up straight. "No. He'll just hand her over to Sonea."

Donia smiled. "He'll want to, but you'll have to convince him otherwise."

Leaning back in her chair, Anyi brought her hands together and drummed the tips of her fingers against each other. "I'll tell him I promised Lilia he'd find Naki. Surely he wouldn't want me to break a promise."

Donia chuckled. "You clearly haven't got to know him well enough yet, if you think that will work. You need to point out how keeping Lilia around will be more useful to him than giving her over to the Guild."

Lilia regarded Donia with dismay. This person named Cery sounded more ruthless and self-serving than what Anyi had led her to believe.

Anyi's eyes narrowed. "I can do that." She looked at Lilia and an expression of concern crossed her face. "Don't worry. It won't involve using black magic. Or anything you're not allowed or willing to do."

Donia looked at Lilia and nodded. "She's right. Unlike most men in his position, he has lines he will not cross."

"They're just a little more flexible than most people's." Anyi grinned and looked up at Donia. "Can Lilia stay here in the meantime?"

"Of course." Donia looked at Lilia and smiled. "If you'd like to, you're welcome to stay. You'll have to sleep under the stairs again, though. We don't have any other spare beds."

Lilia looked from Anyi to Donia, then nodded. "Thank you. I'll stay, and if there's anything I can do to pay for my stay and food…"

Donia waved a hand dismissively. "A friend of Anyi is a friend of mine, and I'd never consider charging a friend."

Anyi snorted. "I should tell Cery you said that."

The woman narrowed her eyes at Anyi. "Not unless you intend to pay for the bol."

Back in the main room of the guest wing, Dannyl was listening to Achati's description of the escapades that he and the estate's owner had got themselves into as young men. A movement at the door caught Dannyl's attention, and he beckoned as he saw a slave hovering there.

The man threw himself to the floor. "Dinner is ready, master, if you wish to eat now."

"Yes!" Achati said. He looked at Dannyl. "I've worked up quite an appetite."

Dannyl smiled to himself, thinking of Achati's silent promise. Though Tayend had kept the Ashaki occupied all day, he had to sleep some time.

Perhaps a liaison with Achati would be short, perhaps it would have awkward consequences in the future, but, for now, it felt right. *Besides*, Dannyl reasoned, *Tayend and I were together for years, and it still ended. And not without some pain and regret.*

As if summoned by his thoughts, Tayend emerged

from his room. He blinked at them, his gaze moving from Achati to Dannyl. "Aren't you getting changed?"

Dannyl looked down at the bathhouse coat. Achati hadn't made any move to return to his usual elaborate clothing, so Dannyl hadn't either—and he was enjoying being dressed in something other than magician's robes.

Achati chuckled. "There didn't seem much point getting dressed. We'll be retiring to bed in a few hours."

Tayend's nose wrinkled. "I reckon I'll stay up. I've been sleeping so much lately."

Dannyl felt his good mood beginning to sour as a suspicion came over him. He resisted the urge to look at Achati, to see if the other man was thinking the same thing. If Tayend stayed up late...

"Dinnertime!" Achati interrupted, beckoning as another slave appeared in the main room's doorway. "Are you hungry, too, Tayend?"

A delicious smell wafted into the room. Tayend's expression changed to one of interest as he eyed the tray in the slave's hands.

"I am."

"Then sit and eat," Achati invited.

Tayend settled on a stool and they all began to eat and talk.

"How are you feeling?" Achati asked Tayend after a while. "No problems with the seasickness cure?"

"No." The Elyne shrugged. "I was a bit foggy when I first woke up, but it wore off after the bath. When are we leaving again?"

"Tomorrow morning."

Tayend nodded. "Let's hope there are no more storms."

"Indeed."

"I'll probably read tonight. I haven't had much chance to since we set off."

"Do you need anything to read?" Achati asked.

Dannyl listened as they discussed books and the record of the attempt to subdue the Duna tribes that Achati had been given. Achati was giving Tayend his full attention, but then it was likely Tayend would sleep all the next day, and any day they were onboard ship. If he kept up this pattern he wasn't going to get many chances to talk to Achati or Dannyl.

Which, I have to admit, I'm selfishly pleased at. I have most of Achati's attention, even if we aren't alone, since Tayend is mostly asleep when we're awake, thanks to that seasickness cure.

A cure which Achati had given Tayend. *I don't suppose... Could Achati have intended this? Was it a clever way to keep Tayend out of his way? Our way?*

Perhaps it was just a convenient side-effect. After all, Achati had said that not all people were affected so potently by the cure. Dannyl had offered to Heal away Tayend's seasickness, but the Elyne had declined. Tayend was too proud to come to him for magical relief. Not when there was an alternative. Had Achati guessed this about him?

What would Tayend say if he knew what Achati and I discussed at the bathhouse? Dannyl felt a small pang of guilt, but he wasn't sure if it was from the possibility that having a new lover might upset Tayend, or from ignoring Tayend's warning about Achati.

Eventually Tayend is going to work it out, or else I'll have to tell him. For now, Achati is right: it would be better Tayend was told once we are not spending hours cooped up in a ship together. I'm sure Tayend will have some disapproving things to say about it. I'll just have to explain that I understand, and that it's an "as long as it lasts" arrangement.

Dannyl felt a twinge at the last thought. What if it stopped being an "as long as it lasts" arrangement?

I'll worry about that if it happens, because otherwise I'm not going to be much fun to be around. Again.

The hospice storeroom felt crowded with all the people in it, despite being a large room. All were standing around a table near the door. Sonea and Dorrien stood on one side, Cery and Anyi on the other. Nobody had bothered sitting down in the sole chair. The other chair was missing. Sonea made a mental note to tell one of the Healers.

"I only wish I'd known Lorandra had not regained her powers," Anyi lamented. "Then I wouldn't have left, and you might've caught both of them. But I didn't know if you'd be able to take on the two of them. I had to warn you."

Sonea smiled. "You couldn't have known," she said. "It must have been a shock to find yourself in the same room with her. Are you sure she didn't recognise you from the Hearing?"

Anyi frowned. "I don't *think* so. She didn't behave as if she did, but she might have been pretending, so that I would stay. Then, once we met Skellin, she'd get him to take care of me."

"If so, she couldn't have had much confidence that Jemmi and Rek would believe her if she told them you were a spy."

"Maybe they convinced her that I'd turned on Cery."

"If I was in her place, I'd have insisted Jemmi find different bodyguards," Cery said.

"Since she didn't, it seems more likely she didn't recognise Anyi," mused Dorrien. "She would surely have been uneasy, otherwise, being around someone she knew had worked for the Guild in the past, even indirectly, especially when she was meeting her son."

"Whatever the reason, our chance to catch Skellin was lost," Cery said, sighing. He looked at Sonea. "Can Skellin remove the block on Lorandra's mind?"

"Probably." Sonea looked at Anyi. "Did anybody mention Lilia?"

The girl shook her head.

"Well, let's hope that means Lorandra dumped her once she wasn't useful any more. Or that Lilia had the sense to get away from her."

"And that Lorandra didn't kill her once she wasn't useful any more," Dorrien added grimly.

Sonea grimaced. "At least it means Lilia didn't tell Lorandra that she had learned black magic. Or if she had, then Lorandra hadn't realised this meant Lilia could instruct her. She would not have let Lilia go, if she'd known."

"Lorandra wouldn't have known what Lilia was imprisoned for unless Lilia or one of the guards told her," Dorrien added thoughtfully. "But now that rumours about the pair escaping are spreading, Lorandra will soon learn what Lilia knows. We have to hope that she doesn't know where Lilia is, and go back to fetch her. We have to find Lilia as soon as possible."

"No. *We* don't." Sonea sighed as all turned to look at

her. "Black Magician Kallen does. I'm supposed to be finding Skellin."

"I suppose this means you need to meet with Kallen and tell him what happened last night," Cery guessed, giving her a sympathetic glance.

"Yes. Without delay."

He nodded and made a shooing motion. "Go then. We have nothing else to tell you." Anyi shook her head in agreement.

"Go yourself," Sonea replied, copying his shooing motion. "You're in *my* hospice, remember?"

He grinned. "Oh, that's right."

Turning away, he led Anyi back to the hidden hatch by which he'd entered the room. Sonea waited until the pair were gone and the hatch was closed, then she turned to Dorrien. "Have you been introduced to Kallen before?"

He stepped forward and opened the door for her. "No. Anything I should know before I meet him?"

She stepped out into the corridor, saw a Healer approaching and changed her mind about what she intended to say.

"Only that he doesn't have much of a sense of humour."

"I have heard that noted before," Dorrien said as he followed her down the corridor. "Though now that I think about it, it was said by you."

"He takes his job very seriously."

"That surely is a good thing."

Sonea looked at him. He grinned. She shook her head. "There are limits."

"To taking a job seriously?"

"To teasing me and getting away with it," she replied tersely. They made their way through to the carriageway next to the hospice. The carriage she had arrived in was waiting, as she usually insisted that Dorrien finish his shift and go home once she'd arrived. She told the driver to head back to the Guild, then climbed in after Dorrien.

"Something about this doesn't seem right," Dorrien said, after the carriage had entered the street.

Sonea looked at him. "Something about what?"

"Last night." He frowned. His gaze was fixed outside the window, but in a way that suggested he was lost in thought. "Anyi's story. Maybe it was the way she told it. She kept rephrasing things, or stopping in the middle of sentences, as if she had to stop herself from saying something."

Sonea thought back to the meeting. She hadn't detected anything odd in Anyi's behaviour. The girl's description of the events had been halting, but Sonea had assumed it was from a difficulty in putting her suspicions, and the spontaneous decisions she'd made, into words.

"Maybe she was nervous," Sonea said. "She knows I used to live in the slums, but you are from one of the Houses." That didn't seem likely, but perhaps Anyi's usual forthright manner depended on who she was with.

Dorrien's frown didn't ease. He shook his head. "Perhaps. But I think there's more to this than what she told us. Do you think it's possible she's being blackmailed?"

Sonea felt her stomach clench. Oddly, the suggestion brought Lorkin to mind. *Though he said he was going to join the Traitors willingly, it still means his life is in some-one else's hands. I wish I had some word from him.*

"Anything is possible," she replied. "But I'd have expected that if Skellin wanted to blackmail anyone it

would be Cery. And if he was blackmailing him, he'd
have locked Anyi away somewhere and threatened to kill
her if Cery didn't do what he wanted."

Dorrien looked unconvinced, but didn't say anything
more. The streets of Imardin were quiet. Those people
who had the choice were inside, keeping warm. As the
carriage swung through the Guild gates a light snow
began to fall.

They made their way through the University, across
the courtyard and to the Magicians' Quarters. Sonea led the
way to Black Magician Kallen's door and knocked. As the
door swung inward, a fragrant, smoky smell reached her
nose.

A chill ran down her spine. She had never encountered
roet smoke before, but she had smelled its residue on clothing many, many times. Remembering Anyi's story of seeing
Black Magician Kallen buying roet, she felt shock change
to disgust as she saw that Kallen and two of his magician
friends and assistants were sitting in his guest room, sucking on elaborately decorated smoking pipes. Kallen
removed his from between his teeth and smiled politely.

"Black Magician Sonea," he said, standing up. "And
Lord Dorrien. Come in."

Sonea hesitated, then forced herself to walk into the
room. Knowing what she did about roet, she did not want
to breathe any of the smoke, even if it was probably too
thin to affect her mind.

"What can we do for you?" Kallen asked.

"We came to tell you of a failed ambush we attempted
last night," Dorrien said. Sonea glanced at him, and he
returned her look with a shake of his head.

Turning her mind back to their reason for visiting, she

described the planned meeting and why it had failed. Kallen asked all the questions she expected, and she was relieved when it was clear they were done and she could leave. Kallen thanked her for filling him in, and assured her he was doing all he could to find Lilia and Naki.

Back in the corridor, Sonea let her grip on her anger loosen.

"I can't believe he was sitting there smoking roet in *his own quarters*!" she said, intending it to be a whisper but it coming out instead as a hiss.

"There's no law against it," Dorrien pointed out. "In fact, those pipes almost make it look respectable."

"But ... doesn't anybody grasp how dangerous it is?"

He spread his hands. "No. Even those who see that it has a bad effect on common people assume it's no worse than drink if taken in moderation, by sensible people—like magicians." Dorrien looked at her. "If it really is dangerous, then Lady Vinara ought to state it clearly."

Sonea sighed. "That isn't going to happen unless magicians agree to be tested. The ones who use roet refuse, and it isn't fair to ask those who don't use it to risk being permanently affected."

"That might change. All you need is for a magician to try to stop taking it, and find that they can't." He looked thoughtful. "I'll ask around. It could be that there are a few already at that point, too embarrassed to say anything."

She managed a wan smile. "Thank you."

"As if you need another urgent matter to tackle," he added. Then a wary, hesitant look crept over his face.

"What?" she asked.

"It's just ... Well ... Did you know that the perfume you wear is made from roet flowers?"

Sonea stopped and stared at him. "No..."

He looked away guiltily. "I should have told you earlier. I was in a perfumery a week or two back, and I recognised the scent. So I asked what it was."

She closed her eyes and shook her head. "Of all the perfumes I happened to buy. On a whim. Just because I needed to look occupied. I guess I should throw it away."

"That would be a shame."

She blinked, and looked at him questioningly. To her amusement, he avoided her gaze.

"You like it?"

He looked at her, then away. "Yes. You never used to wear perfume. It's ... nice."

Smiling, she started walking again. They left the Magicians' Quarters and made toward the University.

"So why were you at a perfumery? Buying a present for Alina?"

He shook his head, then seemed to catch himself.

"Seeing what I might get for Tylia. For her Acceptance Ceremony."

"Ah." She nodded. "Not the usual fancy pen, then?"

"No."

He was silent for the rest of the way to the carriage, probably contemplating having a daughter grown up enough to become a novice. She remembered how she had felt when Lorkin had made his vow and received his first set of robes. The pride she'd felt had been tinged by the memory of how she had broken that vow, and of the day the entire Guild had filed past, tearing her and Akkarin's robes in a symbolic gesture of rejection, before sending them both into exile.

As then, she pushed that memory aside. Lorkin might

have gone to live in a hidden city of rebels, but there had been no serious discussion about exiling him because of that decision. Which was reassuring. If the Guild still believed he would find his way home, then it was much easier to believe the same thing herself.

CHAPTER 22

IN GOOD COMPANY

Something brushed against Lorkin's senses. He ignored it, but the sensation came again and something about it made his skin prickle. The interruption was annoying but, as he had been taught, he accepted it and carefully disengaged his mind from the growing gemstone.

As awareness of his surroundings returned, he opened his eyes and looked around the cave for the source of the distraction. It wasn't the stone-makers sitting nearby. They were glancing around in the same way as he was. He was fairly certain that it wasn't the two magicians standing by the door, though their postures hinted that they had been talking. He'd learned to block out nearby conversations days ago.

He listened, and realised he could hear a faint, low noise. At the same time he noticed that he could feel, under his hands, feet, and through the chair, a vibration.

At once his heart began to race, and he quickly drew magic and surrounded himself with a strong barrier.

A tremor, he thought. *I wonder how bad it is.*

Not bad enough to send the other magicians fleeing the city, he noted. Were the non-magicians evacuating right now? The last time he'd seen the valley outside, it had been covered in a deep blanket of snow. The thought of what might happen should the entire city collapse and strand thousands of people out in the savage cold made him shudder.

The city had survived, albeit with a few cave-ins, for many hundreds of years. That didn't mean there would never be a day when a tremor was severe enough to destroy it, but it did reassure him that the odds of not having to somehow dig his way out from these deep tunnels under the mountain were in his favour.

Still, it does highlight why some people here believe the Traitors must eventually leave Sanctuary.

He looked around the room. Walls glistened with crystalline points of reflected light. No longer were these outcrops a colourful mystery to him. He knew what each patch was destined to be—which magical task it was being trained to do.

Two kinds were made: patterned and powered. The patterned stones had merely been imprinted with a way to shape magic. The user sent magic into the stone, and it shaped that power into something physical: force, heat, light and various familiar combinations. The intensity of the output was controlled by how much magic was put into the stone. This was what magicians did when they channelled magic out of themselves, so the patterned stones were of not much use to a magician unless he or she hadn't learned how to do a particular task yet, or could not do it well. They were also of no use to a non-magician, since they couldn't channel power out of themselves, and had very little or no power to channel anyway.

It didn't take me long to work out how useful it would be to train gemstones to Heal, so I imagine it's already occurred to a few Traitors. But there seems to be a limit to the complexity of the task a stone can be trained to do, so if any Healing stones were made they'd only be able to perform basic tasks.

The second type of stone—the powered ones—were far more useful to a magician. They were taught to do the same sorts of tasks, but in addition the maker infused them with their own store of magic. However, this magic was depleted with use. If well made, stones could be re-infused. Less successful stones were single-use. Sometimes they were made to be single-use deliberately, if what they were used for destroyed them, but the majority of powered stones were meant to be re-infused.

Which is so similar to the way the Guild keeps the Arena, and any magically strengthened buildings, strong. The buildings lose magic very slowly, but the Arena and the barrier around it is occasionally battered during Warrior lessons and practice, and has to be strengthened constantly.

The two kinds of magic—the strengthening of buildings and stone-making—were so similar that Lorkin was amazed the Guild had never stumbled on the latter before, until it occurred to him that there were no caves full of naturally occurring gemstones in Kyralia. Neither could they work with imported stones, since by the time these reached the hands of magicians, as jewellery, they were too old to be imprinted effectively.

The other impediment was that the architect who had

invented the method of strengthening stone with magic had lived during an era when black magic was banned. Lorkin felt a chill as he remembered how easily and quickly he'd grasped the ideas behind black magic. In less than an hour he'd broken his vows as a magician and a centuries-old taboo.

And for all that, it's been a bit of a disappointment. I haven't got any stronger. It hasn't given me any new skills. All it's done is enable me to more easily understand and apply the process of stone-making—which will be of limited knowledge to the Guild unless they manage to find some gemstone caves in Kyralia, or work out how to create them another way.

Learning black magic had given him a more realistic view of the magic within him, and his own strengths and vulnerabilities. He suspected it was possible to raise a stone to perform a task without knowing black magic, but it would have been like working blind—impossible to tell if he was getting it right, how much magic the stone could hold, or when it was ready to use.

He looked down at the small green gemstone in his hands. For most of the process, he'd had to work with it while it was still attached to the wall, and a few times he'd lost it among the masses of stones there. When he'd established enough of an imprint upon it, he'd been able to remove it and refine its training at a table.

Long periods of unwavering focus were required. He understood, now, why Tyvara had said she didn't have the patience for stone-making. Speaker Halana had also told him that making stones that produced heat or explosive force could be dangerous, if the maker's concentration broke, too much magic was stored in it or the stone was flawed. That was why some stone-making was done in remote caves, where entry was forbidden except by the invitation of the stone-maker who worked there.

Lorkin was making a light-producing stone. Though it was more difficult, he was also being taught how to infuse it with magic. It was also more dangerous because a learning stone-maker could easily infuse it with too much power, or lose concentration. He could have been given a duplication stone to use. These could create endless copies of the pattern held inside them—particularly stones to be trained in complicated magic. Speaker Halana, however, insisted that all students first learn how to create a stone without the help of duplication stones, so that they did not come to rely on them too much.

The vibration had stopped now. Lorkin glanced around the room. The other stone-makers had returned to their work, heads bent over tables. He drew in a deep breath and started a mind-calming exercise. He did not know if the Traitors had similar exercises, but the simple ones he'd been taught at the University were coming in very handy now.

As he was about to send his mind out to the stone again, he heard his name murmured. He looked up. Speaker Halana was walking toward him.

"How is it going, Lorkin?" she asked as she reached his table.

"Good, Speaker Halana," he replied. "Well, nothing has gone wrong yet."

She smiled crookedly, with a now-familiar dark humour, and picked up the stone. All but the newest stone-makers had a similar fatalistic humour, he'd noted. Though accidents were rare, they did happen. Lorkin had

seen some badly scarred women making their way
through the caves. Once, one of the newer makers had
whispered to him that some of them worked alone not just
to avoid dangerous distractions, but because they preferred that others didn't see their scars. Some of them ate,
slept and worked in the inner caves permanently, almost
never leaving.

After staring at the stone intently, Halana put it down
again. "You're doing well," she said. "It's a little better
than most first stones. In a few days we should be able to
activate it."

He smiled. "And then?"

She met his eyes and paused, then shrugged. "Then
you'll move on to bigger tasks. I'll check on you again
tomorrow."

With that, she turned away and moved on to the next
student. Lorkin watched her, wondering at the pause after
his question. It was almost as if the question had surprised
her, and she'd assumed that he had known already.

*Perhaps she hadn't thought that far ahead. Or she's
not used to students wanting to know what they'll be
learning next. Or the answer is rather obvious.*

Shrugging, he turned back to the stone and, as he was
growing quite skilled at doing, resolved to think about it
later.

With a little magic, Lilia gently warmed the water in the
bucket. She dared not heat it too much in case other servants noticed it steaming, realised that Lilia hadn't gone
to the kitchen to heat it, and started to wonder about her.
Kneeling on the floor, she dipped a cloth in the water and
began to wipe and scrub.

For a week Lilia had been living in the bolhouse, sleeping under the stairs and pretending to be a cleaner. Donia had been surprised when Lilia had suggested the disguise, until she learned that Lilia's family were servants. Anyi had disappeared after the first dinner, and when she reappeared the next morning she'd been angry to find Lilia scrubbing pots in the kitchen. Lilia had needed to talk her out of telling Donia off.

"You're a magician," Anyi had said, her voice low so the other servants wouldn't hear. "It shouldn't matter that you were born a servant."

"Actually, I'm not a magician—not a Guild one, anyway," Lilia pointed out. "They threw me out, remember? I don't mind doing this, and I could hardly expect to stay here for free."

Anyi had told Lilia of her meeting with Cery. He'd agreed not to tell the Guild that Anyi had rescued Lilia and knew where she was. Lilia could not help feeling curious about him. Anyi had strong opinions about what was right and wrong, and Lilia couldn't imagine her working for anyone who didn't agree with her ideals. From what she had said about Cery, he was working at great risk to himself to keep magic out of the hands of the underworld. Donia, on the other hand, seemed to think Cery was more pragmatic—perhaps even ruthless—than Anyi believed.

A booted leg appeared beside her. Startled, she jumped and a yelp escaped her. Looking up, she was relieved to see it belonged to Anyi.

"You startled me," she said reproachfully, throwing the cloth back into the bucket. "Can't you make a small bit of noise when you walk up behind me?"

"Sorry." Anyi didn't look sorry, though. She looked smug. "Part of my job. I forget that I'm doing it." She looked at the bucket and wet floor. "Looks like my timing has been good. What have Donia's guests left for you to clean up this time?"

Lilia grimaced. "You don't want to know. And it would have been good timing if you'd got here *before* I had to clean it up."

"Sorry about that. I'll try to be early next time." She grinned. "Are you done? We have a meeting to get to."

Lilia felt her heart skip. "With Cery?"

"Yes." Anyi's eyebrows rose. "You look eager to meet him."

Lilia stood up. "Only because you make him sound like an interesting person."

"Do I? Well, don't tell him that." Anyi bent to pick up the bucket, but Lilia moved it out of reach with magic.

"*I'm* the servant, remember. I'll just drop this off before we go." She picked it up and headed downstairs. Anyi grumbled quietly as she followed.

Once the bucket had been rinsed and returned to the stack, and Lilia had borrowed a heavy coat from Donia, Anyi led her out of a back door into an alleyway after checking if anybody was watching. The air was very cold and Lilia had to resist the temptation to warm the air around them. To add to her discomfort and frustration at not being able to use magic, it began to rain.

The alley was empty of people, though full of rubbish and boxes.

"You need to know some things," Anyi said quietly. "I've been trying to prevent this meeting, for two reasons..."

She paused as they reached the end of the alley, checking the cross street before they walked over it into another, narrower alleyway.

"Firstly, my employer is in hiding, too. Bringing you to meet him is a risk. Seems to me that bringing two wanted people together doubles the risk of them both being found. But it is safer bringing you to meet him, rather than the other way around. The people who want to find you want to lock you up. The people who want to find him want to kill him."

"Skellin wants to—"

"Shh. Don't say his name. The rain covers our voices, but some words attract more attention than others. But... yes." Anyi peered around a corner, then continued around it. "He's very powerful, you know," Anyi glanced at Lilia. "The most powerful Thief in the city. Got allies everywhere, high and low."

"So... if your employer is in hiding, and the most powerful Thief—who is also a magician—is after him, is he going to be able to help me find Naki?"

Anyi stopped and turned to face Lilia. "He has allies, too. Not as many, but they're reliable people. The rest would hand you over to *him* straightaway."

Lilia stared back at the woman. She'd obviously offended Anyi by questioning Cery's abilities. *Which is fair enough... but something tells me there is more to her relationship with this Cery than she's letting on.*

"You're very loyal to him, aren't you?" she observed.

Anyi sucked in a deep breath, then let it out again. "Yes. I guess I am." Her expression was oddly thoughtful, but only briefly. She started forward again.

Lilia realised that the rain had stopped, which would

have been a relief except that it was now snowing, and even colder. She shoved her hands deep into her coat pockets, then regretted it as her fingernails filled up with grit caught in the bottom.

"Good," Anyi said, more to herself than to Lilia. "I was hoping for snow. It'll keep people off the street." She flipped the hood of her coat up over her head.

"So what's the second reason?" Lilia asked.

Anyi frowned. "Second reason for what?"

"For avoiding this meeting."

"Oh. Yes." Anyi grimaced. "Even though he said he wouldn't, I wasn't completely sure he wouldn't hand you over."

To the Guild, Lilia finished. "So you're loyal, but you don't trust him."

"Oh, I do," Anyi assured her. "I'd trust him with my life. Trouble is, I wouldn't trust him with most other people's."

"That's not very reassuring."

"I realise that. But you should know. He is what he is."

A possibility flashed into Lilia's mind.

"A Thief?"

Anyi glanced at Lilia and frowned. "Was I that obvious?"

Lilia smiled. "Either that, or I'm getting better at this."

"Do you mind?"

"No. I figured I'd have to work with some shady types in order to find Naki."

"I thought you might, since you were willing to trust that murderous woman even though you knew who she was."

"I didn't trust L—...that woman," Lilia corrected. "I

took a chance, because I couldn't think of any other way to find Naki." She looked at Anyi. "So how do you know Cery won't hand me over to the Guild today?"

Anyi chuckled. "I gave him a good reason to keep you."

"What's that?"

"We're going to use you as bait to trap Skellin."

Lilia stumbled to a halt. "You're going to—"

"Anyi!"

A woman had stepped into the alley ahead, where it met another street. They both turned to stare at her. She was tall and very thin, and other than a cursory glance at Lilia, her attention was fixed on Anyi.

Anyi cursed quietly, then trudged forward.

"Heyla. Are you following me?"

The woman's stare was unwavering. "Yes. I want to talk to you."

Anyi crossed her arms. "Talk then."

Heyla glanced at Lilia. "Privately."

Sighing, Anyi walked to the corner and stopped. "This is private enough."

The woman looked like she might protest, then shook her head and hurried over to join Anyi.

The pair began to talk quietly. Lilia was only able to make out a few words. Heyla said "I'm sorry" several times. Watching the woman's face, Lilia read guilt, regret and, oddly, hunger. The woman's shoulders slumped. Her hands moved quickly, and at one point she reached out toward Anyi, only to snatch her hand back.

Anyi, on the other hand, looked calm and attentive, but something about the tension in her jaw and the narrowing of her eyes suggested she was holding back anger. The longer Lilia watched Anyi, the more she grew convinced she was seeing something else in her rescuer's face. She couldn't decide if it was hope or pain. Then the woman said something, and Anyi winced and shook her head.

The woman suddenly pointed at Anyi aggressively and said something in a low voice.

Anyi laughed bitterly. "If you can find him, tell him he's a bastard. He'll know why."

The woman turned to look at Lilia again. "What about her? Is she a client? Should I warn her to keep her bedroom locked? Or is she my replacement?"

"Well, she hasn't turned into a traitorous, thieving rot-addict yet," Anyi snarled in reply.

Heyla whirled around to face Anyi, one hand curling into a fist, but Anyi, with the slightest shift of her stance, was suddenly poised and ready for a fight. Heyla paused, and stepped back.

"Whore!" she spat, then stalked off down the street.

Anyi watched the woman until she had disappeared far down the thoroughfare, then she beckoned to Lilia. "We'd better keep an eye out," she said. "She might try to follow us—or have someone else watching."

She headed back down the alley, then took a narrow, covered route between two buildings into another alley.

"Who is she?"

"An old friend, believe it or not." Anyi sighed. "We were close once, until she tried to sell me off to our enemies for money to buy rot."

"What did she want?"

"Money. Again."

"She threatened you?"

"Yes."

"If you'll forgive me saying this," Lilia said. "But you're having about as much luck in choosing who you associate with as I am."

Anyi didn't smile. Instead she looked sad, and Lilia regretted her words.

"I'm sorry."

"It's fine. I'm over her," Anyi said. She quickened her pace. Lilia lagged behind, then forced her legs to move faster so she could catch up.

"*I'm over her*," she thought. *That sounds like what people say when… Wait. What was it Heyla had said? "Should I warn her to keep her bedroom locked? Or is she my replacement?" That could mean something else but…*

As another possible meaning behind the woman's words dawned on her, she could not help looking ahead, at her guide, and speculating. *Perhaps I'm wrong about her and Cery.* Anyi was no great beauty, but she was… *impressive*. Poised, strong and smart. *In fact, if it weren't for Naki… no, don't think that.*

Because not only was it disloyal to Naki, but it would make working with Anyi much too distracting.

Looking pale and ill, Tayend moved to the railing to join Dannyl and Achati. He'd decided that morning that he would only take a half-dose of the seasickness cure, so that he wouldn't be groggy when they arrived at their destination. Dannyl knew with fatalistic certainty that Tayend would be wide awake by the evening, and keeping him and Achati from having any private time together. *Not that any private time would come to much, since Achati warned us that our next host is a… how did he put it?… a "disapproving prude."*

"Welcome to Duna," Achati declared, gesturing toward the port ahead.

The *Inava* was sailing toward a wide valley. On either side, cliffs rose in staggered, weathered layers. In the centre, a wide, muddy river poured out into the sea, the grey-brown water cutting a swathe through the salt water for some distance before it mixed with the ocean.

Achati had been not entirely accurate in his declaration. The valley was not the beginning of the Duna lands. The ship had been sailing past them for the last few days, though there was no agreed boundary point. The valley ahead was where most visitors disembarked when they arrived by sea, and it was the closest thing the Duna had to a capital city.

Unlike the dry land and rough cliffs they had seen to their left for most of the journey, the valley was green with vegetation. Houses had been built on high stilts, the level of floodwaters suggested by stains on the wood high above the height of a man. Ladders provided access to some, while rough staircases made of bundled and bound-together logs had been added to others. The gathering of huts was called Haniva, and the valley was known as Naguh Valley.

The captain called out to the slaves, who began to scamper around the ship. The anchor went down and sails were furled.

"We can't come any closer," Achati explained. "The silt from the yearly floods makes the water too shallow. Occasionally storms pass through and wash the build-up away, but since they'd probably destroy any dock we might build it's not worth trying to keep the bay clear with magic."

When the ship was secure, the slaves lowered a smaller row-boat down to the water. Dannyl, Tayend and Achati thanked the captain, then climbed down a rope ladder into it. Once on shore, they waited for the slaves to return to the ship for their travel trunks and followed as they carried these into Haniva.

The town had no streets, just trails kept clear by the passing of feet, and the houses appeared to be randomly placed—often in groups connected by narrow walkways. Floods were obviously not expected for some time, Dannyl guessed from the crops growing around the houses. These were planted in a way that allowed room for the enormous trees, from which fruit hung in bunches. Each was a single smooth trunk topped with either an umbrella-like mass of branches, or an explosion of huge leaves. Tall spikes shooting from the ground puzzled Dannyl at first, until he saw a few larger ones sprouting leaves, and realised they were the sapling versions of the trees, throwing all their energy into growing tall enough to escape floodwaters before putting out foliage.

As they passed people walking in the field, he noticed that their skin and build was somewhere between the stocky brown typical of Sachakans and the grey slim build of the tribesmen. He assumed there had been some interbreeding of the races over the centuries. Settling in towns was not the usual habit of the Duna tribes, from what Dannyl had read or been told. They were a nomadic people.

Perhaps these people could be considered another race, he thought. *Maybe called "Naguhs" or "Hanivans."*

After they had passed a few dozen houses, the slaves headed toward a group of buildings standing alone in a field. It was immediately obvious that these were different, despite being constructed of the same building materials and raised on stilts. Their arrangement was symmetrical, with one house in the centre three times the size of the local homes, and smaller buildings arranged around the sides and rear, all accessed by a walkway. A single wide stairway led up to the central house, and the path that led to it was straight. As the slaves reached it they stopped and waited for Achati, Dannyl and Tayend to climb up ahead of them.

Climbing the stairs changed not only the view of the town, but the way Dannyl viewed it. He could see more houses, and the people in them, as well as the workers in the fields. Suddenly Haniva felt far more populated and town-like.

A house slave emerged and threw himself face down on the wooden deck at the top of the stairs.

"Take me to Ashaki Vakachi, or whoever speaks for him when he is absent," Achati ordered.

The man leapt to his feet and led them inside. The inner walls had been painted white and led down a corridor to a large room. *Like a typical Sachakan home, except the walls are straight.* In the Master's Room, a man stood waiting for them. His skin had a hint of dusky grey to it, and his shoulders were narrow, hinting at a touch of Duna in his blood.

"Welcome, Ashaki Achati," the man said, then as Achati thanked him he turned to his two companions. "And you must be Ambassadors Dannyl and Tayend."

"We are," Dannyl replied. "And we are honoured to be staying with you."

The man invited them to sit. "I have arranged for a

light meal to be served, then you each will be taken to your own *obin*—one of the detached houses you no doubt noticed on your arrival. They are a local idea, usually added for the use of a son after he is married, or an elderly relative after the son inherits the house, but also to keep an eye on unmarried young men and women."

"Is this a Duna tradition?" Tayend asked.

Vakachi shrugged. "It is and it isn't. The tribe of Naguh Valley have their own traditions, different to the rest of the Duna. Though they are a settled tribe, and more civilised than their cousins, they are regarded as inferiors and pay tribute to those of the escarpment."

"Is it possible that any of them are Keepers of the Lore?" Dannyl asked.

Vakachi spread his hands. "I couldn't say for sure. Since the Keepers remain hidden by living ordinary lives and saying nothing of their status, there could be some here but nobody knows it." He smiled. "No, your best chance to meet one is to climb up to the escarpment and seek one among the full blood tribes. Not that your chances are good even then. The Duna have a unique and effective habit of being uncooperative."

"So I have heard, and read," Dannyl said.

Vakachi nodded. "Still, it's possible a foreigner will have greater luck than a Sachakan. I have arranged transportation to the escarpment for you all, setting out tomorrow. It will take a few days. In the meantime," he gestured to the slaves filing into the room, "eat, rest and be welcome."

CHAPTER 23

GOOD NEWS, BAD NEWS

As Sonea entered the treatment room, Dorrien looked closely at her and frowned.

"You look pale," he said.

"I'm fine," she told him as she sat down.

"How long has it been since you saw sunlight?"

Sonea considered. She'd been working the night shift for some weeks now, only taking time off to meet with Cery. The morning after the failed attempt to catch Skellin had been the last time she'd seen sunlight, though surely—

"If it's been so long you have to think about it this much, it's been too long," Dorrien told her sternly.

Sonea shrugged. "The short winter days mean it's dark when I leave the Guild."

"If you wait until the days get longer, you might not see the sun for weeks." He crossed his arms. "You're like some sort of creepy nocturnal creature, and the impression isn't helped by the black robes and black magic."

She smiled. "You're not scared of me, are you?"

He chuckled. "Not one bit. But I'd hesitate to invite you over to dinner. You might scare the girls."

"Hmm...it's probably my turn to host a dinner."

"You don't have to take a turn," he told her. "You've got too many other things on your mind. Have you heard from Cery lately?"

She shook her head. "Just a few cryptic messages. He believes Lorandra will have joined Skellin by now."

"How is Kallen's search for Lilia and Naki going?"

"He and his assistants have printed out flyers with drawings and descriptions of the girls, and hired people to hand them out around the city. A few have reported seeing one or both of the girls, but none of the sightings has led him to either of them."

"People have seen Naki? At least that means she's alive."

"If the girl they saw *was* Naki. Still, the Guard hasn't found any bodies of young women that look like her."

Dorrien looked thoughtful. "We should put some of those flyers up in the hospices."

Sonea nodded. "That's a good idea."

"I'll send a messenger to Kallen before I leave. Pity we didn't get a picture drawn of Lorandra before she escaped."

"Her appearance is much more distinctive than the girls', and so is Skellin's, but the descriptions we put out of those two haven't attracted any reports of sightings."

"No, I suppose—"

A knock at the door interrupted him. Sonea turned in time to see it swing open. Healer Gejen nodded to her politely.

"Black Magician Sonea," he said politely, before

turning to Dorrien. "Your wife is here to see you, Lord Dorrien."

"Tell her I'll be out as soon as I've finished briefing Sonea," Dorrien replied.

As the door closed, Dorrien sighed. "I was wondering how long it would take before she gathered the courage to check on me here."

"Check on you?"

"Yes. To make sure we're not up to anything she wouldn't approve of."

Sonea shook her head. "I don't understand. What does she think we do here? Is she afraid I'll corrupt you?"

"In a way."

"She thinks I might teach you black magic?" Sonea threw up her hands in exasperation. "How can I convince her to trust me?"

"It's not that she distrusts you. She's in awe of you. And she's jealous."

She looked at Dorrien. He wore an expression she had seen before. Before she could put a name to it, he spoke again.

"It's me she doesn't trust."

"You? Why ever not?"

"Because..." He paused, then looked at her as if meeting her gaze was difficult. "Because she knows that if there was ever a chance you and I could be together, I'd take it."

She stared at him, surprised and shocked. Suddenly she understood the look on his face. Guilt. *And a cautious longing.* An answering guilt rose up within her and she had to look away. *All these years, and he has never stopped wanting me. I thought he had, when he met and married Alina. I was relieved to be free of the burden of not returning his feelings.*

She had been caught up in grief then, still in love with a man she had lost. There had been no room in her heart to consider another.

Was there now?

No, she thought, but a traitorous feeling rose to contradict that thought. Panic rose but she pushed it aside. *I can't desire Dorrien*, she told herself. *He is married. It will only make things awkward and painful for all of us.* She needed to say something that would end the possibility before it had a chance to take root in her mind. Something tactful, but clear. Something...But she couldn't think of the right words.

Dorrien stood up. "There. I've said it. I..." He broke off as she looked up and met his eyes, then smiled crookedly. "I'll see you tomorrow," he finished. He moved to the door, opened it and left the room.

It doesn't matter what I say, she realised. *This is already awkward and painful, and has been for months. I'm just a latecomer to the situation.*

Cery's home was a hole in the ground. However, it was a surprisingly luxurious hole, with all the comforts of an Inner City mansion. It was so luxurious that it was easy for Lilia to forget that she was underground. The only reminder was the small size of the place—it contained only a few rooms—and lack of servants.

Hiring servants would have meant people coming and going, and that would defeat the purpose of having a secret location. Cery's bodyguard, Gol, had assured her that there were food supplies like dried beans and grains, salted meat and preserved fruit and vegetables stored here in case it became too dangerous to leave. She had never seen anyone cook them. Instead, Gol brought fresh food to the hideout every few days.

Now that Lilia and Anyi were staying there, he had to bring more food more often, which must have made it harder to keep the hideout location secret, or perhaps just increased the risk that someone would recognise and follow him. Cery had been very insistent that they stay, however. Anyi had argued with him, and lost.

It had amazed Lilia to see how uncowed Anyi was around her employer, considering that he was a Thief. The young woman expressed a mix of loyalty, protectiveness and defiance, and he tolerated the latter with surprising patience. Instead of exerting his will with orders and discipline, he deftly skirted around her demands or objections.

To get Anyi to agree to stay, he didn't bother trying. He simply turned to Lilia and suggested a deal: he would help her find Naki and keep her hidden from both the Guild and Skellin in exchange for her protecting him and Anyi. She had agreed.

The best way to protect Anyi, it turned out, was to make her stay in the hideout. The easiest way Lilia found to ensure that was to stay in the hideout herself. However, it wasn't *that* easy. The more Anyi felt cooped up, the more she spent her excess energy on arguing. Gol's return with the evening meal had her circling him eagerly.

"Have you seen any sign that Lorandra or Jemmi or Rek are looking for me or Lilia?" she asked.

"No," he replied, stepping around her and placing a sack on the low table between the guest room chairs.

Anyi turned to Cery. "See? Surely if they'd made the connection they'd be looking for us."

"Skellin's not stupid," Cery replied. "He knows that either you're with me or out in the city on your own. If you're on your own the chances are greater that someone will see you and report it to him. If you're with me… well, he's already got plenty of people looking for me."

"But what if Rek didn't tell Lorandra that I used to work for you?"

"What else is he likely to tell her, and Jemmi, to convince them that you taking Lilia away wasn't his idea in the first place?"

"He might only have told Jemmi."

Cery pointed at a chair. "Sit, Anyi," he ordered.

She obeyed, but continued to stare at him while Gol began removing well-wrapped packets out of the sack and tearing them open. The extra wrapping was to reduce the smell of food escaping and acting as a trail through the tunnels to the hideout. Delicious smells filled the room.

"Jemmi will have told Lorandra you must have been my spy, in the hopes of convincing her there was no plot," Cery continued. "Like it or not, Anyi, they know your betrayal was faked. You're stuck here with me."

Lilia felt a pang of sympathy as Anyi's shoulders slumped. Not the first time, she wondered if Anyi had told Cery of her encounter with Heyla.

"I didn't hear that anyone is looking for you," Gol told Anyi. "But I heard that people are looking for someone who, from your description, sounds like Naki. They're not our people, or the Guild, I think. They're people she really wouldn't want finding her, I reckon."

Lilia sat up straight. "Someone else is looking for her?"

Gol nodded, then looked at Cery. The Thief's eyes narrowed.

"So the race begins," he said.

"Who is looking for her?" Lilia asked. "And why?"

"Skellin," Cery answered. "It's no secret that Naki is missing, and that she and Lilia tried to learn black magic. The fact that Naki didn't succeed only makes her a slightly less appealing captive than Lilia. She can still tell Skellin everything she read and did. After all, if Lilia succeeded with the same information, there's a chance he would too. If he doesn't," Cery looked at Lilia and grimaced, "he knows Lilia cares about Naki. He'll try to blackmail her into teaching him, in exchange for Naki."

"We have to find Naki first," Anyi said.

"Yes." Cery smiled thinly. "Skellin's search for her might help us. I have people watching his people. If his look like they've found answers, mine will ask the same questions. If his look like they're about to search somewhere, mine will be watching, ready to help Naki escape."

A bell chimed somewhere behind the walls. Cery looked at Gol, who gave the opened packets of food a look of regret.

"We'll save you some," Cery promised.

The big man sighed and hurried to the hidden door built into the panelling in the room. Anyi rose and grabbed some plates and cutlery from a side cabinet, handed them out, then joined in as Lilia and Cery began to serve themselves and eat. Gol had brought several river fish baked in a salty-sweet sauce, plus roasted winter vegetables and freshly baked bread.

Soon afterwards, Gol returned. This time it was Cery

who looked disappointed, as he and Gol left. Once they were alone together, Lilia looked at Anyi.

"Do you think Heyla is out there, telling people she saw us?"

Anyi's expression darkened. "Probably. She's done it before. She'll get herself into more trouble than she realises if she does."

"Does Cery know about her?"

"Kind of." Anyi looked pained. "I started working for Cery after Heyla and me weren't friends any more. I told him a friend had tried to sell me out, but I didn't tell him who she was."

"If you weren't working for Cery, how did she know about him?"

Anyi paused, then shook her head. "Oh, I knew of him. Distantly. Anyway . . . I'd rather not talk about her."

Lilia nodded. "Your secrets are safe with me."

Anyi looked up at Lilia but didn't smile. Instead she regarded her with a thoughtful expression that contained a hint of speculation.

"What?" Lilia asked.

"Nothing." Anyi looked away, then back. "How close are you and Naki?"

Lilia looked down at her plate. "Very close. Well, not so close after she thought I'd killed her father."

Anyi grimaced in sympathy. "Yes, that *would* test a friendship. Not just for her, thinking that you had done it. It must equally have hurt you that she could even suspect you of having done it."

Lilia glanced at Anyi reproachfully. The pain of knowing that a friend could believe you'd killed someone was surely nothing like the pain of thinking a friend *had* killed a loved one. *But she does have a point*, Lilia found herself thinking. *How could Naki have thought I'd done it? Especially after Black Magician Sonea read my mind and said I hadn't.*

The usual pattern of chimes and knocks warned them that someone was approaching the hideout. Anyi leapt up, knocked and tapped in reply, and worked the mechanisms to let Cery and Gol back into the room.

"That was a messenger," Cery told them. "From the Thief, Enka, who is one of the few not completely owned by Skellin yet. He wants me to help him deal with a problem he has with his neighbour, who he says has a magician working for him. He thinks I can arrange for the Guild to find her."

"Her?" Lilia asked, her heart skipping. "Is it Naki?"

"He says it's a woman," Gol replied. "His description of her sounds nothing like Lorandra."

"Lorandra hasn't got any magic," Anyi pointed out.

"She probably has now," Lilia told her. "Skellin could have removed the block. But Naki's powers *are* blocked."

Cery frowned. "Perhaps she has removed the block herself as you did."

"I was only able to do that because I'd learned black magic. Naki hasn't."

"Then she must be relying on her reputation to intimidate people, and perhaps using tricks to convince people that she has her powers back. Enka did say he hadn't seen her use magic yet. We should make sure it's her before we show ourselves, of course, and be prepared in case it's a trap set by Skellin. At least we know that he and Lorandra won't turn up because he'll expect Guild magicians to arrive. We have Lilia to protect us from non-magical attacks," he added, bowing to her.

"Why don't you tell the Guild?" Gol asked, frowning. "Save us the trouble and risk."

Cery smiled and looked at Lilia. "Because if Lilia rescues Naki, the Guild will look more kindly on her escaping from the Lookout."

Lilia smiled in reply. *I can't believe I'm thinking this about a Thief, but I'm really starting to like Cery.*

The Thief rubbed his hands together and moved back to the chairs. "Come on you lot. Let's finish eating. We have cunning plans to hatch."

"So," a familiar voice said. "I hear you finished your first stone."

Lorkin turned to see Evar walking along the corridor behind him. He grinned and slowed down to join his friend.

"News travels fast in the stone-makers' caves," he observed.

Evar nodded. "We were curious to see how you fared. Stone-making isn't suited to everyone."

"I can see why. It takes so much concentration." Lorkin looked at Evar critically. The young man appeared to be healthy and relaxed. "I haven't seen you in a while. I thought we'd run into each other in the caves."

Evar smiled. "You won't find me in the students' caves. I'm working on much more sophisticated stones."

"Too busy to drop by on a friend?"

"Perhaps."

Lorkin checked his stride. "Wait a moment. You're a man, so you don't know bl—...higher magic. How can you be making stones?"

The smile fled from Evar's face. He bit his lower lip, then looked apologetic. "Uh...I might have exaggerated my role here."

Lorkin stared at his friend, then burst out laughing. "What do you...? No, actually, I'll save you having to answer that by not asking."

"I'm an assistant," Evar said, lifting his chin in mocking haughtiness. "Sometimes I provide extra magic."

"And at other times?"

"The caves don't heat themselves, and stone-makers have an annoying habit of forgetting to eat."

Lorkin slapped him gently on the shoulder. "All essential to the process."

"Yes." Evar straightened. "It is."

They walked along in companionable silence, turning from the smaller passage into a wider, busier thoroughfare. Lorkin had taken only a few steps when he heard his name called. He looked around and saw the magician he'd seen guarding the queen's room weeks ago beckoning to him.

"Got to go," he told Evar. "Perhaps I'll see you tomorrow?"

Evar shrugged. "I doubt it. Early start. We're quite busy right now."

Lorkin nodded, then hurried to meet the magician.

"You're to see the queen," she informed him. She turned and set a pace that had them weaving through the people walking along the corridor. At one point she led him through a door that opened onto an empty narrow passage.

"I didn't know that existed," he murmured as they emerged into more familiar parts of the city.

"Short cut," she said, smiling briefly.

A few turns later they arrived at the door of the queen's rooms. The magician knocked, then stepped back as the door opened. To Lorkin's surprise and pleasure, Tyvara stood there. His mood instantly lifted, despite the fact that he'd already been in a good one.

"Tyvara," he said, smiling.

Only the corners of her mouth twitched upwards, as they did when she was trying to maintain a serious demeanour.

"Lorkin. Come inside."

As before, the queen was sitting on one of a circle of plain chairs. He placed a hand on his heart and, unlike in the previous visit, she nodded in the formal response.

"Please sit down, Lorkin," she said, gesturing to the chair beside her.

He obeyed. Tyvara sat at the other side of the old woman. A movement in the doorway to the inner room caught his eye. He looked up to see the queen's assistant, Pelaya, peering in. She smiled at him, then moved out of sight again.

"I hear you completed a stone," the queen said.

News does travel fast. "I did."

"Show me."

He reached into the pocket of his tunic and drew out the tiny crystal. The queen extended a withered hand, so he dropped it into her palm.

She stared at the stone for a moment, and it began to glow. A satisfied smile spread over her face and she looked up at him, eyes bright.

"Well done. Not many students accomplish a flawless stone on their first attempt. Some here would say you have stone in your blood." She shrugged. "Obviously not literally." She handed the stone back. It was already fading. "I am pleased, and not only that you were able to receive what we offered in compensation for the knowledge that was taken from you. I have a task for you."

He blinked in surprise, then felt his heart sink a little.

"You hesitate," she noted, her eyes narrowing. "What is it?"

"Nothing," he said, then because it was clearly not so: "I was looking forward to making another stone. Learning more. But that can wait."

Zarala chuckled. "Were you? Well, what Kalia took from you was a basic understanding of Healing. We have given you a basic understanding of stone-making. I'm afraid you, as she, will have to learn more through experimentation, without the aid of generations of knowledge."

Lorkin nodded, though he was not happy. Not only would he not be taught any more, but Kalia would be allowed to use what she had taken from him.

"Besides, there is no time for you to learn all we know about stone-making," she told him. "There are more pressing matters to attend to. That is why I am ordering you to leave Sanctuary and return to Kyralia."

He looked up at her in surprise and, unexpectedly, dismay. He did not want to leave. *No, that's not entirely true. I do want to leave. I want to be able to see my mother and friends again. But I want to be able to return to Sanctuary, too.* He looked at Tyvara. *Will I see her again?* She smiled. It was a reassuring smile. It seemed to say "wait and see."

The queen's expression was knowing, and perhaps a little mischievous. She looked at Tyvara, then back at him. Her expression became serious again. "When you arrive, and if you are received well, you are to begin negotiations between us and the Allied Lands for an alliance."

Lorkin could not help letting out a small gasp of amazement. *This is what I hoped for! Well, I hoped the Traitors and Guild would trade magical knowledge* after *an alliance, not* before *it, but…*

"Tyvara will guide you out of the mountains, then you will journey to Arvice to rejoin the Kyralian Ambassador. To keep what you know of us secret, we will give you a blocking stone. Though it would be politically harmful for the king and Ashaki if anybody read your mind against your will, they may decide it's worth it for the chance to find us. We would take you straight to the pass into Kyralia, but the mountains are too dangerous for travel at this time of year, with the Ichani growing bolder out of hunger." She fixed him with her bright eyes. "Will you do this?" she asked.

He nodded. "Gladly."

"Good. Now, there is something I must give you."

She picked up a small bag that he hadn't noticed lying on her lap. Loosening the ties, she upended it and a rough, chunky ring fell into one palm. Holding it up, she regarded it, her expression thoughtful and sad, then extended her hand to him.

He took the ring. The band was gold, but very roughly fashioned, as if made of clay by a child. Set within it was a dark red gemstone.

"Your father gave this to me a long time ago. In fact, I instructed him on how to make it. Of course, it no longer works."

A chill ran up Lorkin's spine, and his heart missed a

beat. *Father made this!* He turned it over and over, the stone catching the light. *Did Father know stone-making? Surely not.* The answer was suddenly clear to him. *It must be a blood gem.* The implications of that hit him like a slap. "You were in communication with him all along!"

Zarala nodded. Her eyes were misty. "Yes. For a time."

"So you know why he didn't return here!"

"If he ever made a decision about that, he never told me." She sighed. "I know he returned home out of fear the Ichani would invade, and I disagreed with him. I didn't believe the danger was immediate. Afterwards...there was always something that prevented him leaving Kyralia. And there was more to our deal than an exchange of higher magic and freedom for Healing." She shook her head. "I was never able to uphold one thing I agreed to. Like him, the situation at home was more difficult to overcome than I'd hoped. After my daughter died, I...I stopped contacting him. I knew I was partly to blame for her death, for asking too much from him, and agreeing to give too much in return."

The old queen drew in a deep breath, then let it out again. Her thin shoulders rose and fell.

"We were both young and idealistic, thinking we could do more than we could. I believe he intended to return. My people didn't agree and I couldn't convince them otherwise without revealing what it was that I'd failed to do." She reached out, cupped her hands around Lorkin's and bent his fingers in around the stone.

Over their hands, she looked at him and her gaze was steady.

"Sending you to Kyralia will go some way toward me doing what I agreed to do. I only hope that, unlike your

father, I live long enough to keep my promise. Now go."
She released his hands and straightened. "Tyvara has
made the preparations and it's a clear night outside. Be
careful and be safe."

Rising, he bowed in respect. Then, with Tyvara leading, he left the room and the city he had expected to make
his home for a lot longer than a few short months.

CHAPTER 24

A MEETING

The horses that carried people up the road to the escarpment were short, sturdy creatures. Dannyl was sure his feet would have been scraping the ground if his mount had not had such a broad girth. The beasts didn't often carry people, since visitors to Duna—or to the dryer areas—were rare. They were more used to carrying food and other supplies.

Carriages were too wide for the narrow road, which twisted and turned on itself at angles impossible for a vehicle to manage. The high side of the slope was so close that Dannyl had occasionally scraped his boots on the rock wall. His other boot hovered over a near-vertical cliff plunging down either to a stretch of the road below, or to the distant valley floor.

Though he had no fear of heights, he'd found that the constant threat of such a precipice put him on edge. Achati appeared to grit his teeth and resolutely set his gaze on the road ahead. Tayend, despite not having the reassurance of magic to call upon should he or his horse slip, didn't appear to be bothered at all.

The benefit of the exposed, precarious journey was the view.

The road had begun about mid-way along the valley, the wider end of which spread out behind them, divided into fields dotted at the edges with clusters of houses. A pale band of grey sand separated the green land from the blue ocean. Ahead, the valley narrowed, the cliffs undulating as they drew closer to each other. A ribbon of water threaded through it all, glistening whenever the sun reflected off its surface.

Looking ahead, Dannyl saw that there were several people standing at the next turn. The only places on the path wide enough for travellers to pass each other were bends where it switched back on itself. The people waiting were clearly Duna: slim, grey-skinned, and dressed in only a cloth wrapped about their waist and groin. They were carrying large sacks across their shoulders.

The guide called out a greeting as he neared. The tribesmen—there were no women among them—did not reply or move. Perhaps they made some sign of greeting, because the guide was smiling as he turned and started up the next section of road. Achati was next to turn, and his expression did not change from the same look of grim determination he'd worn since they'd started the climb. Dannyl smiled at the men as he passed. They stared at him in return, their faces impassive but showing neither hostility nor friendliness. He wondered if they felt as much curiosity about him as he did about them. Had any Kyralians visited their lands before? Had any Guild magicians?

I might be the first.

He looked back to see Tayend smiling as his mount turned in behind Dannyl. The Elyne saw Dannyl watching and grinned. "Exciting, isn't it?"

Dannyl could not help smiling in reply. As he turned away he felt an unexpected wave of affection for his former lover. *He embraces life as if it's all a big adventure. I do miss that about him.*

"And we're nearly there," Tayend added.

Looking up, Dannyl saw that the next stretch of road was short. He felt his heart skip a beat as he saw the guide turn to the right and disappear. Achati followed, and then it was Dannyl's turn.

After a full day of riding, the change of surroundings was so abrupt it left Dannyl feeling disorientated. Suddenly the horizon had returned. The land was so *flat* there was nothing between Dannyl and the line where the grey earth met the sky.

Nothing except a whole lot of tents, he corrected himself, as his horse turned to follow Achati's. Even then, the gathering of temporary homes blended with the colour of the land. It looked like a tangle of cloth and poles.

"It's hot up here," Tayend said, riding up beside Dannyl. "If this is what winter is like, I'm glad we didn't come in summer."

"We must be about as far north as Lonmar," Dannyl replied. "The difference between seasons there isn't as great as it is in the south. Duna may be the same."

He didn't add that it was the end of the day, and the heat given off by the sun now hanging low in the sky would not be as strong as at midday. As in Lonmar, the air was dry, but here it had a different taste.

Ash, he thought. It blew into his face, finer than the sand that got into everything in Lonmar. *I wonder if they have the same fierce dust storms.*

The edge of the tents was a few hundred paces from the precipice. As the riders approached, the Duna stopped to stare at them. The guide called out the same greeting, then pulled his horse to a stop a dozen paces from the audience.

"These people have come to speak to the tribes," he said, his voice lower and respectful. "Who has the Voice?"

Two of the men pointed toward a gap in the tents. The guide thanked them, then directed his mount into the opening, Achati, Dannyl and Tayend following. Every ten or so tents the guide repeated the question, and each time set off in the direction the Duna pointed in.

Soon they were surrounded by tents. Dannyl could not make out where the camp stopped. Some were tattered and well patched. Others looked newer. All were coated in grey dust. Of a similar size, they appeared to be occupied by extended families, from small children to wrinkled old men and women. Everyone in between was occupied in some task—cooking, sewing, weaving, carving, washing, mending tents—but all with slow, steady movements. Some stopped to watch the strangers pass. Others continued on as if visitors were of no interest.

A small crowd of children began following them. It rapidly swelled to a larger one, but although the children giggled, talked and pointed, they were not rowdy or noisy.

The sun had dipped close to the horizon by the time

they found what they were searching for. Outside a tent no more extraordinary than the rest sat a ring of old men, cross-legged, on a blanket on the ground.

"These people have come to speak to the tribes," he told them, pointing at Achati, Dannyl and Tayend. "They have questions to ask. Who has the Voice? Who can answer the questions?"

"We are the Voice today," one of the old men answered. He stood up, his eyes moving from the guide, who was dismounting, to Achati, Dannyl and Tayend as they followed suit. "Who asks the questions?"

The guide turned and nodded to Achati. "Introduce yourselves," he instructed quietly. "Only you, not your companions."

Achati stepped forward. "I am Ashaki Achati," he said. "Adviser to King Amakira and escort to . . . these men."

Dannyl moved forward to stand beside him, then inclined his head in the Kyralian manner. "I am Ambassador Dannyl of the Magicians' Guild of Kyralia."

Tayend followed with a courtly bow. "I am Elyne Ambassador Tayend. An honour to meet you."

The old man exchanged a look with his fellows, who nodded. They shuffled outward to widen the circle. "Sit," he invited.

"We have brought gifts," Achati said. He moved to his horse's saddle-bags and removed a package, then returned and set it down in the middle of the circle.

"You know our customs," the speaker observed. "And follow them." The last was said with a hint of wry surprise. One of the other old men reached for the package and opened it. Inside were finely made knives, a box containing a glass lens, a roll of good-quality paper, and a writing set with pen and ink. The old men hummed with pleasure. From the way they handled the items it was clear they were familiar with their uses, despite the fact that they would not be easily obtainable in Duna. The speaker nodded.

"Ask your questions. Know that we may not answer at once. We may not answer at all."

Achati looked at Dannyl and nodded. Dannyl ran through all the approaches he'd considered during the journey.

"Many years ago I began a task," he began. "To write a history of magic. I have sought the answer to many questions, concerning both ancient and recent events, and..." he sighed, "the answers have led to more questions."

A few of the old men smiled a little at that.

"The most puzzling discovery I made was that my people, many hundreds of years ago, possessed something called a storestone. It was kept in Arvice until a magician, through avarice or madness, stole it. The records of that time suggest that he used it, perhaps in a confrontation with his pursuers, perhaps by mistake, perhaps even deliberately, to create the wasteland that borders the mountains between Sachaka and Kyralia."

The old men were all nodding. "We know of this wasteland," the leader said.

"My questions are... what was this storestone? Do any more exist? Does the knowledge of how to make one still exist? If it does, how could any land defend itself against its use?"

The spokesman chuckled. "You have many questions."

"Yes," Dannyl agreed. "Should I limit them?"

"You may ask as many as you wish."

"Ah, that's good." Dannyl smiled in gratitude. "I have a lot. Well, I mostly want to ask about magical gemstones. Not for the secrets of how to make them, of course. But they are a new kind of magic for me. What can they do? What are their limitations? A Duna tracker named Unh told me that the Traitors stole some of this knowledge from you. How much do they know?"

The old man looked at Achati. "That is a question you would like the answer to as well."

Achati nodded. "Of course. But if you wish to speak to Dannyl alone, then I will leave."

The old man's eyebrows rose. He looked at each of his fellow tribesmen in turn. They made no signal that Dannyl could detect, but somehow they communicated their feelings to him. As he finished gazing at the last of them, he looked up at Dannyl.

"Are these all the questions you have?"

Dannyl nodded, then smiled wryly. "Unless the answers raise more questions."

"We must discuss and decide what answers we may give you," the man said. "And some questions can only be answered by a Keeper of the Lore, who may not agree to speak to you. There is a tent here for guests that you are welcome to sleep in, while you wait."

Dannyl looked at Achati, who nodded. "We would be honoured—and very grateful," Dannyl replied.

The old man called out, and a young man hurried out of a tent. "Gan will take you there," said the spokesman, gesturing towards the newcomer.

Achati, Dannyl and Tayend climbed to their feet, and joined their guide as he followed the young man into the forest of tents.

• • •

The late-afternoon sun cast a cool light over the Guild gardens. Trees and hedges cast deep shadows, and it had taken Sonea a while to find a bench still in sunlight. Fortunately there were few magicians occupying the gardens, since the air still had a crisp winter chill to it. She could feel the cold of the wooden slats through the cloth of her robes.

It had been two days since she had spoken to Dorrien. The previous evening she had delayed her arrival at the hospice so that he was already gone by the time she arrived. It had been cowardly, she knew.

But I haven't decided what to say to him. She knew that she should tell him she could not have a relationship with him other than friendship. *But he'll see the evasion in that. "Could not" was different to "would not."* He would want her to make it clear that she did not feel the same way about him as he had admitted he still did about her. *And if I tell him that, he'll pick up on my uncertainty and doubt.*

When she considered the idea she felt a traitorous longing, but she was unsure about the source of that, too. *Am I just craving company? Someone to come home to?* Was she simply wanting physical contact?

So much for telling Rothen I don't want a husband. And yet . . . I don't.

Company and desire weren't all that a relationship of that kind needed. There must be love, too. Romantic love. *And that's where I falter. Do I love Dorrien? I don't know. Surely I would know, if I did. Maybe it isn't so obvious, for older people.*

The other ingredient she considered essential was

respect, and that troubled her the most. *Dorrien is married. If he was unfaithful to Alina with me, I would lose respect for him. And myself.*

When she pictured herself telling him this, she felt such a reluctance to spoil things that she was beginning to doubt her own doubts. How could she be unsure whether she loved him, and yet so resistant to ending all possibility of love between them?

How I wish I could talk to Rothen about this. He would disapprove, she knew. At the same time he would point out, perhaps not directly, that it was all her fault for missing her chance with Dorrien. It would upset him that Dorrien and Alina were not getting along.

I wish Dorrien would just take his wife back to the village, she thought, then she immediately felt guilty. *At least Alina would be happier,* she couldn't help adding. *Dorrien would be too, after a while. It's where he's always felt he belonged.*

He had adjusted to living in the city remarkably well, though. Perhaps he wasn't as wedded to the country as he'd always maintained he was. It was fortunate, since she so badly needed his help finding Skellin.

Or do I? Cery still does most of the work. A couple of magicians were never going to match a Thief's spy network. But I still need someone to help me capture Skellin—even more so now that Lorandra has escaped. I can't let anything between Dorrien and me prevent us from capturing the rogues.

Not talking to Dorrien was doing exactly that.

The shadows were so long now that only her shoulders were in sunlight. Sighing, she stood and started toward the path that ran alongside the University. *I may as well get this over and done with.* She reached the path and started walking toward the front of the building. If she left now there would be an hour or two before her shift officially started. Plenty of time to sort this out.

The wait for a carriage and the journey to the hospice seemed to take longer than usual. Her heart was beating a little too fast as she walked down the corridor to the room Dorrien was working in. She knocked on the door and took a deep breath as it opened.

"Black Magician Sonea," an unexpected voice said behind her. She glimpsed Dorrien's face—looking both hopeful and guilty—before she turned to face the speaker. It was a young Healer—a shy Lonmar who had decided upon graduation to gain some experience with working among the common people before returning to his home.

"Yes?"

The man bowed, handed her a folded slip of paper, sealed with wax, then flushed and hurried away.

She broke the seal and read the letter. A shiver of anticipation ran down her spine as she read Cery's instructions, despite the fact that messages like these had led to disappointment in the past. She turned to Dorrien, who was eyeing her thoughtfully.

"You're finished here for the day, Dorrien," she told him. "But you'd best send Alina an apology for missing dinner. We've got work to do in the city."

"Wait here."

Though short and thin, the man sent to guide them to the meeting place by the Thief called Enka had exhibited a coldness and efficiency that made him more intimidating to Lilia than Cery's big bodyguard.

There's something about him that disturbs me, she found herself thinking. *I reckon he'd do anything his boss told him to, and it wouldn't bother him. Anything.*

He'd led her, Anyi, Cery and Gol to a half-ruined empty warehouse on one of the less-used wharves of the marina. Anyi had assured her that there were more of Cery's people involved, following at a discreet distance. They would be finding places to watch from, places they could emerge from quickly if Cery signalled for help.

"Where should we position ourselves?" Anyi asked. She was looking up. "Pity we can't get up there."

Lilia followed the woman's gaze. The frame of the warehouse was exposed, and the huge beams looked more than solid enough to keep the building standing for a long while yet. The end of the building had once had a mezzanine floor, complete with a row of windows, but the floorboards had rotted away or been salvaged. She could see why Anyi thought it a good vantage point. The windows would allow a view of the rest of the dock.

Moonlight shone through the windows, making it hard to distinguish details of the wall. Shading her eyes, she saw that one of the large beams ran along bricks where it had once supported the floorboards.

"If we could, do you think we could balance on that beam?" Lilia asked.

Anyi moved closer, then shrugged. "Easy." She looked at Cery and Gol. "What about you two?"

Cery looked at her and smiled. "I reckon I'd manage. Gol?"

"I s'pose. But how are we going to get up there?"

"Easily, with Lilia's help," Anyi said.

Lilia looked from Anyi to Gol and hid a smile. This wasn't the first time she'd picked up a little competitive rivalry between the two of them. She followed Anyi to the wall with the first-floor windows. Then Anyi turned and grabbed Lilia's arms.

"Do your thing, Lilia."

Creating a disc of magic under their feet, Lilia lifted them both up to the beam. Anyi stepped onto it, grinning. Lilia descended again.

With the merest of shrugs, Cery took hold of Lilia's arms. She levitated him up to the beam and when he was safely perched on it, holding the frame of the nearest window to steady himself, she dropped back down again.

Gol looked at her, then up at Cery, his eyes wide. He took a step back, palms outward.

"I'm not—"

"Get up here, Gol," Cery ordered tersely. Lilia glanced up. Cery was peering around the frame of a window, looking outside the building.

She heard Gol step closer and turned her attention back to him. He was hesitating again. She heard footsteps outside the warehouse.

"Now," Cery hissed.

Someone was coming.

Lilia stepped forward and grabbed Gol's arms, hoping he wouldn't cry out in protest or fear. She lifted them both upwards. To his credit, he made only a quiet yip of surprise. She moved to a place on the beam where an upright would give him something sturdy to grab hold of, and he immediately wrapped his arms around it.

With her own feet on the beam, she expanded the disc to form a shield surrounding them all, taking care to make it invisible.

The door below opened. Three men moved inside.

"Silent," one man said. "The hinge has been oiled."

"For this, or another meet?"

Nobody answered, and the three looked around the warehouse. One even glanced up at the windows, but didn't appear to see them. *Probably half blinded by the moonlight, like we were.*

The men left. Lilia let out the breath she had been holding and moved to a window. The openings had long ago lost both glass and mullion framework. She peered around the edge of the hole, and what she saw outside made her heart stop.

A fishing boat was moored to the wharf. The three men who had inspected the warehouse were walking toward two pairs of people. The first pair was a slim old man who she guessed was Enka, because his companion was the man who had been their guide.

The other couple consisted of a rather fat, well-dressed man and a slim woman who, if anything, was more beautiful in the moonlight than daylight. Lilia's heart felt as if it had begun to glow inside her.

Naki! I've found her at last!

Beyond the two groups were more men. She could not tell if they belonged with Naki's Thief or Enka.

It doesn't matter, she thought. *They're not magicians. They can't stop me.* She put a foot up on the sill of the window, then paused.

"Go on," a voice whispered at her side. She turned to see that Anyi had shuffled along the beam to stand next to the window. "Cery says don't forget to protect Enka and his second."

Lilia nodded in gratitude, then drew magic and sent it out in two directions to surround Cery's allies and Naki. She climbed up onto the sill, crouching to duck under the lintel, and stepped out.

The people outside didn't notice her float to the ground, but Naki was looking around, having detected the shield around her as it bumped up against her own. *Oh good*, Lilia thought. *She can protect herself.* She let the shield drop. Something about Naki's shield nagged at her, however. She began to walk toward the people, half hidden behind the three men who had investigated the warehouse.

"There's another magician here," Naki said in a warning tone.

At once all began to cast about, and spotted Lilia quickly. The three men parted, backing away in fear and uncertainty as Lilia passed between them.

"Naki," Lilia said, then smiled. Her friend was staring at her in surprise. "It's so good to see you. What trouble have you got yourself into this time?"

"Lilia." Naki did not speak the name with hatred or accusation, to Lilia's relief. But she didn't speak it fondly, either. "Why are you here?"

"To help you."

Naki sent a flash of light through her shield. "As you can tell, I don't need your help."

Lilia gazed at her friend and realised this was what had been nagging at her. *She's right. She doesn't need my help. She has magic. Somehow she or someone else has removed the block. That's what was so strange about her shield—she shouldn't be able to raise one.* And then the real meaning behind Naki's words hit her.

Naki did not want to be rescued.

She's quite happy working for a Thief. In fact, she probably disappeared deliberately. Unless...? Lilia did something risky then. She spoke with her mind, as softly as possible in the hope that nobody in the Guild would hear.

—Are you being blackmailed?

Naki laughed. "No, you slow-witted fool. This is what I planned all along: get away from the Guild and all their rules and suffocating judgement and be free to do whatever I want."

Her stare was full of hatred now. Lilia felt a familiar wave of guilt, but she resisted the urge to look away. *I did not kill her father,* she told herself. *She has no reason to hate me.* But uncertainty remained. Naki clearly did not want to be rescued. *What do I do now?*

Naki was breaking the law—but she knew that. Pointing it out was not going to persuade her to return to the Guild. However, if she knew Skellin was after her she might. She'd need the protection of the Guild. Unless... what if Naki was happy to switch from one Thief employer to another? Lilia realised that she needed to take a different approach. One that appealed to Naki's nature.

"Are you truly free?" Lilia asked. She looked at the fat Thief pointedly.

Naki smiled. Clearly she had expected this argument. "As free as I want to be. Freer than I'd be in the Guild."

"But for how long?" Lilia asked. "There are people after you. Not the Guild. Powerful rogue magicians."

"Great." Naki shrugged. "Then we'll have a drink and swap stories."

"They're not after conversation," Lilia told her, annoyed at Naki's refusal to see the danger. "They'll force you to tell them what was in the book, then they'll kill you."

Naki frowned. "The book?" A piercing whistle rang out from the direction of the warehouse, and the girl glanced in that direction before turning back to Lilia. "Oh, you mean black magic? Really, do you think I'd teach them that?"

Something began to bang against the shield Lilia was holding around Cery's allies. She glanced to the side to see that Cery's Thief friend and his companion were trying to get out of the barrier. Then she noticed that the fat Thief and his men were moving away toward the fishing boat. Hoping that there was nobody left to harm Cery's allies, she let the shield around them fall.

Naki was walking toward her. The shadows made her smile look like a crazed grin.

"You know..." She tilted her head to one side and her expression became thoughtful. "...if the price was right, working with the rogues might be tempting."

She was a few steps away. Her stare was predatory and dangerous. Lilia found herself backing away and strengthening the shield around herself.

"You wouldn't."

"Oh, of course not. It wouldn't be smart, would it? I'd be creating potential enemies as powerful as me."

"As powerful as..." Lilia stopped backing away. "You *did* learn black magic that night!"

"No." Naki's beautiful mouth widened into an

ugly, self-satisfied smile. "I taught myself before we even met."

She spread her fingers, and a bolt of magic clashed against Lilia's shield. This was no cautious practice strike in Warrior classes. It was a blast that forced Lilia back, then to desperately draw forth more power than she'd ever needed to before to hold her shield up.

I ought to strike back. Lessons returned to her. A shield took more magic than a strike. If two combatants were equal in strength, the one who shielded more would fail first. *But this is Naki. What if I hurt her? What if I kill her?*

Clearly, Naki wasn't having any of the same doubts. Her words echoed in Lilia's mind. *"I taught myself before we even met."* That meant Naki had known the instructions in the book would work. She had known she was ruining Lilia's life. Lilia felt her heart shrivel away from the thought. Why would Naki do that? To share the crime with another? Which meant Lilia hadn't been the only person in the house who knew black magic the night Lord Leiden had died.

But surely she wouldn't kill her own father...

Who else could it have been? Suddenly Lilia had to know for sure—and the only way she could do that was to ensure Naki was captured, so that Black Magician Sonea could read her mind. *Or me. I could read her mind.*

The best chance she had at that was to fight back. Carefully. She'd never know the truth if Naki died. So she threw magic back at Naki. At first the strikes were meagre things compared to Naki's, and the other girl laughed, but Lilia found she rapidly grew used to using this much

power. Naki's strikes were careless, which sent a trickle
of fear through Lilia.

*If she's known black magic for so long, has she been
strengthening herself? I haven't used black magic once.
I'm only as strong as I naturally am, and I've been levi-
tating a lot...*

That thought sent a rush of panic through Lilia. She
pushed it aside as best she could. Though she could feel
herself trembling, she managed to keep her strikes accurate and her shield steady. A part of her was amused to see
that Naki, despite being best at the Warrior discipline, wasn't bothering to do anything tricky or cunning,
but her amusement fled as she realised this was because
she didn't have to. She wanted this over as soon as
possible.

Abruptly, Lilia reached for power and found her
strength depleted. She gasped with horror and disbelief as
her shield faltered, and braced herself for the blow that
would kill her. Naki gave a crow of triumph, but the strike
did not come. To Lilia's immense relief, the girl stopped
striking and started toward her.

"You haven't taken magic, have you?" Naki said, snak-
ing a hand out and grabbing Lilia's arm. She shook her
head. "All this time you were free and you never took
power. You always were stupid and gullible." With a push,
she turned Lilia around and twisted her arm behind her
back. Pain shot through Lilia's arm and shoulder.

"If you're so smart, why are you working for a Thief?"
Lilia replied. "Why isn't he working for you?"

Naki laughed quietly. "Oh, I'm just learning the ropes."

She shifted, and something cold and sharp touched
Lilia's neck. In the corner of her eye Lilia could see the

moonlight catch the edge of a knife. A chill rushed
through her body as she realised what Naki intended to
do, followed by a deep, rending hurt in her chest. *She's
going to kill me after all. All along I've been hoping she
has been caught up in one of her crazy schemes. That
she's being reckless, and doesn't really want to hurt me.
But she doesn't love me. She probably never did.*

She's right. I am a fool...

Then Naki yanked Lilia backwards and let her go.
Lilia heard a crack as she staggered, off balance, tripped
and fell onto her backside.

From somewhere nearby, someone uttered a curse.

Shouts rang out, then the sound of running. Looking
around, Lilia saw Anyi, Gol and Cery hurrying toward
her. From another direction came a magician, black robes
snapping.

Sonea?

The Black Magician did not look at Lilia as she ran
past. Turning, Lilia saw Sonea throw herself onto her
knees next to Naki, who was lying on the wharf, and
grasp the girl's head. Which was bent at a strange angle.

As she watched, the head slowly moved back to a natural position, colour returning to Naki's face. The girl
groaned and opened her eyes. She looked up at Sonea and
groaned again.

"Yes. Me." Sonea's expression changed from relieved
to grim. She got to her feet. "You may not want to thank
me for saving your life."

Naki sat up and rubbed at her neck. "Why should I?
You nearly killed me."

Sonea looked at her as if she wanted to say more, then
changed her mind. She took hold of Naki's arm and

hauled her to her feet, then turned to Lilia. "Cery assures me you'll come back to the Guild willingly now."

Following her gaze, Lilia saw that Cery, Anyi and Gol were standing right behind her, along with two other magicians in green robes who she had never seen before.

"Yes," Lilia replied. "Now that I've found her." Anyi held out a hand and helped Lilia climb to her feet.

"Anything broken?" Anyi murmured.

"Just my pride."

"And your heart, I think."

Lilia stared at Anyi, who gave her a knowing look before stepping away. "Well, I guess you'll be going back to the Guild now. Drop around from time to time. You'll always be welcome."

Lilia winced. "I don't think I'm going to have much chance of visiting anybody."

Anyi's smile faded. "Well then...we'll just have to drop in on you."

Sonea looked from Anyi to Lilia thoughtfully, then turned to Cery. "You and I need to have a little chat."

He smiled. "Always do. I'm happy to wait until you haven't got your hands full, and I'm sure the Guild will be keen to have this one back in their hands as soon as possible." He gestured towards Naki.

Sonea gave him a level look. "Another time, then."

He nodded, stepped back and waved a hand. "Goodnight, then."

As the Black Magician stepped away, Anyi patted Lilia on the shoulder. "They'd better treat you right, or I'll come bust you out myself."

"I'll be fine," Lilia told her, though she wasn't sure if that was true.

As she joined Sonea, Naki and the other magicians, Cery, Gol and Anyi started toward the warehouse. Then something occurred to Lilia. She'd left the trio stranded there so… "How'd you get down from the beam?" she called after them.

Anyi paused to look back, grinning. "With not as much difficulty and swearing as the others." Then she disappeared into the shadows, leaving Lilia wondering if she would ever see her rescuer again.

CHAPTER 25

GIVING AND WITHHOLDING

The environment outside Sanctuary had changed so much since Lorkin had last travelled through it that he could imagine the city had been lifted up and deposited in a new place. Everything was covered in snow. It gathered in deep drifts, and clung to rocky slopes. Icicles hung from every overhang and wind-twisted tree.

When they had left the city, Tyvara had blindfolded him and led him out of another secret entrance via a long passage. Once outside, they'd kept to the valleys and avoided the treacherous snow on the ridges, which was likely to slide off under the press of a foot. Their mode of transport was also different. Each of them had a smooth board, curved at the front and with supplies strapped onto the back, used as individual sledges. Sliding downhill was exhilarating, and definitely preferable to hauling the sledges uphill while trudging through the snow.

For three days they had travelled this way, their progress slow but steady. Each night they unrolled the mattresses that were part of a Traitor's travelling kit and slept under the stars, keeping themselves warm with magic. They talked from time to time, when sledging or the effort of slogging through the snow didn't prevent them from doing so, but at night they were both too exhausted for conversation.

They had not been travelling long on the third day when the sky darkened and wind began to batter them. Falling snow soon thickened to a whirling curtain that reduced their view to a few paces. Tyvara led him onto a narrow path along a cliff face—more a natural fold in the rock—that led downward. They had to carry the sledges, which made the descent even more precarious. He wondered why Tyvara didn't stop and find somewhere sheltered to wait out the storm, but before he could call out and suggest it, a cave mouth appeared ahead of them.

They hurried through into darkness. Tyvara paused to create a globe light, revealing a tunnel-like cave. A wall of ice ran along one side. *This is probably an overhang that's been buried*, Lorkin thought as he followed Tyvara along the cave. She moved to a flat area and set down her sledge. He dropped his next to hers and sighed with relief.

"We may as well stay here until the weather clears," she said.

Lorkin nodded in agreement. As Tyvara unrolled their mattresses on the floor, he felt his mood lift. At least they could now spend a little time together, not exhausted or occupied in moving. And it would delay the moment they had to part.

Sitting on his mattress, he busied himself with heating a little water and making some raka. She smiled as he handed her a steaming cup.

"This is the start of a larger valley that stretches down to the Sachakan plains," she told him. "You'll be able to make your way down it easily, to the road."

"So this is as far as you're going?"

She looked at him, her expression unreadable. "Yes."

What then? he wondered. *Will we ever see each other again? Will she even miss me?* A mix of emotions welled up into his throat: longing, doubt, regret, even bitterness. He wanted to somehow convey all of it, but he remembered Chari's appraisal of Tyvara. She did not want to be encumbered. To seek a bond with her would only drive her away.

"I am..." she began. He waited for her to continue, but she frowned and fell silent.

"Yes?" he asked. *Not seeking a bond is one thing, but I'm not going to let her get away with mysterious unfinished sentences.*

Tyvara shook her head. "I knew this would happen. I didn't want to become attached to you because I knew, if I did, something would take you away."

Suddenly he couldn't stop smiling. She looked up and frowned.

"What's so funny?"

"I love you, too," he said.

She stared at him, then a smile slowly spread across her face. "I'm not very good at this, am I?"

He shook his head. "Appalling."

"Well...there it is. What a pair we are. Except we're not a pair, since you're heading home and I'm...well, I am too."

"If it makes you feel any better, I'll promise to come back."

She put a hand out and touched his mouth. "Make no promises."

He made a sound of protest, then took her hand. "No promises? I'd at least like to know you're not going to tuck up in bed with someone else while I'm gone."

She gave a short laugh. "Despite all our efforts to adopt the roles that men have in other societies, we Traitor women haven't managed to match all of their despicable ways. Though I'll admit there are certainly a few women who seem bent on bedding every man in Sanctuary," she added, with a grimace.

He looked at her. "That's no promise."

"That's all you're going to get," she told him.

He shrugged and sipped his raka. *Well, it isn't as if I've asked her to marry me. I'm not even sure how that works here. Women choose their men, so I gather she's supposed to ask me.*

"You should take power from me before you go," she said quietly.

Surprised, he looked at her. "Using black magic?"

"Of course. You haven't noticed, since it's done privately, but non-magician Traitors regularly donate power to the magicians. There was no time to arrange this for you before you left. I have plenty of extra power, and I can replace it easily enough when I get back. You shouldn't venture back into Sachaka without first increasing your store of it. The Ashaki might be suspicious of a Kyralian magician wandering about not wearing robes. They might recognise you and, knowing where you've been, treat you as they would a Traitor. The mind-blocking stone will stop them discovering anything about us by reading your mind, but it won't stop them trying to get the information out of you in other ways. Taking a little extra power from me won't hold them off long, but it may be enough to get you away from them if they're not expecting it."

Lorkin felt a chill run down his spine. He looked away, hoping his fear didn't show.

"Is it... am I... allowed to take it?" he asked.

"Of course you are. In fact, the queen suggested it. She also suggested I teach you Lover's Death."

He turned to stare at her, then felt his face warm. "With... you?"

She smiled. "Who else is there?"

"But..." She obviously didn't want him to kill her and he certainly hoped the queen didn't mean for Tyvara to kill him.

Tyvara smiled. "Don't worry," she said. "The name isn't appealing, but it's not only useful for killing people or draining them to the point of exhaustion. For most couples or lovers it's a much more enjoyable way to give or receive power." Her eyebrows had risen on the words "much more enjoyable," and now she was regarding him coyly, her eyes dark and inviting.

His heart began to race. He hoped he understood what she was suggesting. But he could be wrong...

"So. Do you want me to teach you?"

He nodded.

"It takes a certain self-control for a man to bring a woman to the point where he can take power from her. You think you can manage that?"

He smiled and nodded again.

"Well then, let the lesson begin."

For the next who-cares-how-long, more than an exotic kind of magic was learned. As instructed, he attuned himself to the whole new awareness of the power within his body, and where it brushed up against hers. When he sensed her natural barrier falter ... it was fascinating in all kinds of ways and he nearly forgot to try drawing power from her.

And then he saw how it prolonged the moment for her, and he knew why Evar hadn't been so bothered by his draining. Suddenly he was really looking forward to learning what it was like to give power. He stopped drawing from her, reasoning that he did not know how much power he could safely take.

"Do you trust me?" she asked, when she had regained her composure.

He nodded rapidly. She laughed, then taught him why giving was even better than taking.

Despite the hard, narrow beds and Tayend's snoring, and the constant, irritating sensation of dust in his nostrils and lungs, Dannyl slept soundly and woke to find sunlight filtering through the half-closed flap of the tent. He rose and stepped outside. A blanket was spread out in front of the tent, and he shook the dust off it before sitting down to watch the activity in the camp.

Not long after, a woman peered around a tent at him, smiled and disappeared. She soon returned carrying a sling-like woven bag full of food, and a bowl of water. The food was the same sort of fare that the guide had provided—fruit and preserved meats grown and prepared in the canyon below. *There can't be much grown up here, and though I've seen some domestic animals I've seen nothing growing around here that they could eat.*

He puzzled over how the Duna of the camp fed

themselves and their animals until another two occupants of the tent emerged. Tayend and Achati blinked in the morning sunlight, then joined Dannyl on the blanket, with Achati pausing long enough to wake the guide.

The man came out grumbling, but cheered up when he saw the bag of food. He headed off through the tents, then returned with a pack full of utensils. When mugs and a pack of raka powder appeared, Dannyl took them and began preparing the drink, first heating the water with magic, then pouring it into mugs over spoonfuls of raka.

They ate. They waited. The sun climbed higher and they had to retreat into the tent to escape its heat. Inside, it was stifling as well as hot, but at least their skin did not burn.

Some time after the sun had passed its zenith, the tribesman elder who had spoken for the group the previous night stepped into the tent.

"When we speak as one voice we are nameless," he said. "But I now speak as one. I am Yem." One bony hand touched his chest briefly, then his expression became serious. "We talked until the sun came back, then we decided. We put our decisions to the test of sleep and a second talking. They remained the same. We will give our answers to one only." He turned to Dannyl. "Ambassador Magician Dannyl."

Dannyl looked at Achati, who shrugged. *I suppose he can't be surprised by that. The Duna hardly have reason to trust him. But then, they don't have reason to trust me, either.* Tayend had opened his mouth as if to protest, but said nothing. Yem's gaze shifted to him.

"Do you have questions as well?"

Tayend shook his head. "No. I'm just curious to hear the answers."

"It will be Ambassador Magician Dannyl's choice if you may hear them," Yem said. He looked at Dannyl expectantly.

Dannyl grabbed his notebook and stood up. "I am honoured that you have chosen me to hear them from you and your people."

Yem smiled, then beckoned and stepped out of the tent. Glancing back once, Dannyl saw that Achati was smiling his encouragement, and Tayend already looked bored. He turned away and followed Yem through the tents.

"We have found a Keeper of the Lore willing to speak to you," Yem told him. "Do you swear not to seek her name or tell others of her?"

"I swear I will not seek or reveal her identity," Dannyl replied.

They rounded yet another tent and suddenly were striding out into the grey desert. Ahead, Dannyl could see that a shelter had been erected out of poles with a large sheet of cloth stretched over them and tied at the corners to stakes in the ground. The soil beneath his feet was hard and dusty. *Is it technically a desert, if there isn't any sand?* Dannyl wondered.

The sun beat down mercilessly. Dannyl felt sweat break out on his forehead and wiped it away with the back of his hand.

Yem chuckled. "It is hot."

"Yes," Dannyl agreed. "And yet it is winter."

The old man pointed to the west. "Long way that way the volcanoes are covered in snow. It is high and cold."

"I wish I could see that."

Yem's shoulders rose. "If the volcanoes wake, the snow melts. Then we have floods. Very dangerous. Not as dangerous as the floods of molten rock." He glanced at Dannyl. "We call the floods 'volcano tears' and the red rivers are 'volcano blood.'"

"And the ash?"

"Volcano sneezes."

Dannyl smiled in amusement. "Sneezes?"

Yem laughed—a quick bark that reminded Dannyl of Unh. "No. I lie. We have many names for ash. There are many kinds of ash. Hot ash and cold ash. New ash and old ash. Ash that falls dry and ash that falls wet. Ash that fills the sky. We have a Duna name for each kind. More than fifty winters ago one of the volcanoes exploded, and the sky was full of ash for many months."

"That must have been the eruption that caused the long winters in Kyralia."

"Its reach was that great?" Yem nodded to himself. "It is a powerful volcano."

Dannyl did not answer, for they had reached the shelter. He sighed with relief as he stepped into its shadow. The same old men that he'd spoken to the previous night sat in a ring on a blanket, but there were two male additions and one old female. Yem indicated that Dannyl should sit in a gap between two of the men. He himself moved around the circle to fill a gap on the opposite side.

Yem looked around at each of the men, then turned to the woman.

"Speak, Keeper. Give Ambassador Magician Dannyl your answers."

The woman had been staring at Dannyl, her gaze keen and assessing. Though her expression was unreadable, there was something anxious and disapproving in her demeanour.

"You wish to know what stones can do?" she asked.

He nodded. "Yes."

"They do whatever a magician can do," she told him. "They turn magic into heat. They can be like a dam or shield. They make light. They can hold something still." Her eyes focused on a distant point, and her voice took on the tone of a teacher reciting a familiar lesson. "Two kinds of stone may be made. One can be taught a task, but the magic must come from the holder. One can be taught a task, and holds magic for the task. Both can be made to use once, or many times, but the store must be filled again when it is emptied." She blinked and looked at him. "Do you understand?"

"I think so," he replied. "So if a stone can hold a store of magic, is it a storestone?"

Her chin rose. "Not such a stone as you spoke of last night. A careful stone-maker makes a stone hold only enough. Most stones hold only so much, then they break. So to stop the breaking, they are made to hold only enough." She cupped her hands together. "The stone you spoke of had no stop to it." She threw her arms wide, fingers splayed. "Stones that don't break are rare. We do not know how to tell if they won't. And even if they don't, they are still dangerous. The more magic inside, the more dangerous—like if a magician takes and holds too much power it is dangerous. Easy to lose control."

Dannyl straightened in surprise and interest. "Are you saying that a black magician—a magician who knows higher magic—can take so much power that his control over it starts to slip?"

She paused, obviously taking time to translate the less familiar words he'd used, then nodded.

"Long, long ago many peoples lived where the Duna and Sachakans are. They had cities in the mountains where the stones were made, and were always at war with each other. Whoever had the most stones was strongest. One queen lost her stone caves and sought to be a stone herself. She took more and more magic from her people. But she lost control of that power and burned, and that was when the first volcano was born. It turned her people the colour of ash." She pinched the skin of her arm between finger and thumb and smiled. "Storestones are like magicians. Better to keep a little power, then use, then restock."

I wonder how much power it takes for a black magician to lose control, Dannyl thought. *Clearly more than what Sonea and Akkarin took to defend Imardin. Hmm, I had better let Sonea know about this. We don't want Imardin turning into a volcano.*

"Do not fear," the woman said, mistaking his worried look. "Nobody makes storestones any more. They stopped trying because it was too dangerous, and then they forgot how to."

He nodded. "That is good to know." Then something occurred to him and he frowned. "If a stone can be taught anything a magician can do, can it be taught black magic—what Sachakans call higher magic? Can a stone *take* magic from a person?"

She smiled. "It can and it can't. A stone can be made to take magic, but it would not work unless the skin of the person touching it was cut or they were tricked or forced into swallowing it. It will only take as much magic as it is made to take, or it would break. It would have to be able to hold much magic to kill a magician."

Dannyl shuddered at the thought of having a black-magic-wielding stone in his stomach, sucking out his life. But perhaps it wouldn't be able to take enough power from him to kill him, and it would soon pass through his system. *Still, it would weaken a person, and might do a lot of damage to their insides if it broke.*

"What happens when a stone breaks?" he asked.

"It may break into many pieces," she said, flaring the fingers of both hands. "Or it may crack. If magic is stored, it can go out in many ways. Maybe how the stone meant to send it, maybe unshaped, maybe shaped in another way."

Dannyl nodded. *So either you'd get a warm glow inside or be cut to ribbons and burned up. Nice. Seems to me that these stones could give us as many more ways to do harm as good.*

"How much do the Traitors know of making stones?"

Her eyebrows lowered. "All that we know, and more. They once traded with us, but broke our trust by taking the secrets from us."

He nodded in sympathy. So it was true. He considered what to ask next. He wanted to know how easy or time-consuming the stones were to make, but he figured that would be asking for too much detail. If the stones were difficult to make, that knowledge could be used against the Duna. No, if he was to ask any new questions, he ought to take the opportunity to seek information that might add to his book.

"How do the Duna believe the wasteland was created?"

"Only what you have told us," she said, shrugging. "Before then we knew only that the Guild made it."

What else could these people tell him about the history of magic? He'd like to know more about their own origins. Perhaps they could tell him about other ancient peoples who lived in the mountains. Perhaps those who once occupied the ruins of Armje in Elyne.

"I would like to know more about the people you spoke of, who lived in the mountains long ago."

"What we know are only tales," she warned him.

"Even so, they are all we have of those times, and tales that last as long as these are usually good ones."

She smiled. "Very well." She looked at Yem. "But there are many, many stories. Maybe I tell you another time."

"After this meeting is done," Yem agreed. He looked at Dannyl appraisingly. "There is more we wish to tell you," he said. "Other things than answers to your questions."

Dannyl looked around at the old men, all of whom were now watching him intently. "Yes?"

"You know that the Traitors stole our secrets. They have grown their knowledge more than we ever have. We are able to make stones that will block a magician from reading a mind. They have stones that can make that magician see thoughts he expects."

Dannyl's heart skipped. *So that's how their spies avoid discovery and keep their home hidden!* Then a cold sensation flowed over him. *If Achati heard this... He would tell his king and then perhaps other Ashaki. All would search their slaves for stones and remove them. They'd kill thousands of slaves—after reading their minds. The Traitor stronghold would be found and destroyed—and Lorkin with it.*

Which meant he could not tell Achati. Even if Lorkin was safe, Dannyl could not be responsible for the deaths of so many people. *A decision that important is not mine to make, anyway.* He felt a guilty wave of relief. *It is one for the Guild, and they would most likely defer to the wishes of the Kyralian king, if not all the rulers of the Allied Lands.*

If the tribesmen and woman had noticed Dannyl's surprise and shock, they did not comment on it.

"A half moon cycle ago the Traitors came to our stone caves and broke all the stones," Yem continued. Dannyl looked up and met the old man's eyes as he realised what this must mean for the Duna. "We fear they are planning to make war. Maybe to invade Duna. Maybe to fight the Ashaki."

"Why would they break your stones if they want to start a civil war with the Ashaki?"

"To be sure no magic stones can be used against them."

"If they invaded Duna the Ashaki would do something about it."

Yem nodded. "A fight with Duna is a fight with the Ashaki, whether we wish it so or not."

Dannyl considered the news. *Surely the Traitors won't bother invading Duna before attacking the Ashaki. But perhaps there was a strategic reason for doing so.* He'd have to think about that. The Duna people's motives were clear, however.

"Did you tell me about the mind-read-blocking stones so that I'd warn the Sachakan king?" he asked.

"No," Yem said firmly. "We seek friendship with Kyralia and the Allied Lands."

Dannyl looked around the circle in surprise. All stared back at him expectantly.

Yem nodded. "We have long debated this. The Ashaki have learned that invading Duna is costly. The Traitors do not know this. But the Ashaki are more cruel than the Traitors. We know who we prefer as neighbours, but they do not want us." He smiled grimly. "If Kyralia and Elyne agree, maybe we can help each other."

Dannyl stared at the old man, who returned his gaze steadily. He thought about all that was being offered and predicted. *An alliance. With a people who have stone-making knowledge.* He smiled.

"I would be honoured to negotiate such an alliance," he said. "And it would give me great pleasure if I could forge such a friendship between our peoples."

The old man's answering smile was wide and toothy.

And as they began discussing how the two peoples might help each other, Dannyl found that a journey that had been purely for research purposes was suddenly about everything his role as Ambassador entailed.

None of the magicians in the Administrator's office made a sound when Lilia stopped talking. She looked around quickly. Some of them were staring at her, others looked distant and thoughtful. All were frowning.

Now that she had finished explaining everything that had happened since she had first spoken to Lorandra at the Lookout, she felt utterly drained. Her weariness wasn't from magical exhaustion, since her powers had mostly recovered from the fight with Naki. It wasn't phys-ical either, since she had used Healing to combat tired-ness from lack of sleep. She felt worn out from all the hope, fear, hurt, guilt, anger, relief and gratitude that had gripped her over the last day.

Her mood now was something between resignation and acceptance. She wasn't sure whether she simply didn't care what the Guild did to punish her for escaping from the Lookout and becoming a rogue, or whether she couldn't bring herself to consider it. She was tired of the secrets, and glad to be rid of them.

Though it occurred to her she could try to hide the fact she'd been able to break the mind block, she suspected Sonea had arrived early enough to see her fighting Naki. What that meant for her future, she couldn't guess. They could lock her and Naki up, but it wouldn't be easy to keep them there.

Her mind kept returning to Naki's betrayal.

"I taught myself before we even met."

Why had Naki befriended her? Were the rumours about her liking for other women even true, or were her kisses part of the deception? Why did she encourage— perhaps even trick—Lilia into learning black magic? Or had she killed her own father by accident and arranged for Lilia to take the blame?

That didn't make sense. For a start, Lord Leiden had been alive when Lilia had last seen him, and she'd been with Naki every moment subsequently until after their attempt to learn black magic.

Then she must have planned *to kill him and blame me.*

Surely Naki must have known that if Lilia didn't have memories of killing Lord Leiden, then there could be no proof she was guilty. Perhaps she hoped that the other evidence—blood on Lilia's hands—might be enough to convict her.

And how did the blood get onto my hands in the first place?

"How can there be so many differences between Lilia's story and what Black Magician Sonea read in Naki's mind after Lord Leiden's death?" Lady Vinara asked, voicing what had bothered Lilia all along.

"I can see only three possibilities, and none are likely," Administrator Osen replied. "Either Black Magician Sonea's mind-reading failed, or Naki is able to confound a mind-read, or Lilia is able to."

"Then I suggest that both young women's minds are read by Black Magician Kallen," High Lord Balkan said.

Osen looked around the room. All of the magicians nodded, including Sonea. Lilia suppressed a sigh and braced herself for another mind searching through her own again.

Whatever it takes, she thought. *I'll accept whatever punishment I deserve so long as I'm not blamed for anything I haven't done.* That was all she wanted, now that she was no longer in love with Naki. *I thought I was only telling myself I wasn't, but I think it's true. It's hard to love someone who's tried to kill you. Love isn't as unconditional as the songmakers say it is.*

"Have Naki brought here," Osen ordered, looking at the magicians closest to the door. He nodded to Kallen. "You have permission to read Lilia's mind."

Black Magician Kallen moved from the wall he was standing against and stepped around the chairs to where Lilia stood, in front of Osen's desk. He gave her a thoughtful look, then reached out and set his palms on the sides of her head. She closed her eyes.

This time the experience was subtly different to the last. His searching was slower, though that might have been because he was being more careful, knowing that

Sonea's mind-read had not picked up Naki's guilt. Kallen looked at all of her memories, but she sensed nothing from him and he did not once speak to her. The only indication of a reaction was the way he skimmed past her early feelings for Naki rather quickly, once he encountered them.

She only knew it was over when she felt the pressure of his hands cease. Opening her eyes, she looked up at Kallen. He was staring down at her, frowning.

"I see nothing that she hadn't told us," he said. "No deceit. Everything she has said, she believes to be true."

Kallen stepped aside. She saw that the Higher Magicians had turned to look toward the back of the room, and as she spotted what they were looking at, her heart wrenched. At the same time, she felt strangely panicky, and the disturbingly vivid memory of the sensation of a cold blade against her throat came into her mind.

"Bring her forward," Osen said.

Naki's face was pale and sullen. As she was pushed firmly into place by one of the two magicians who had been standing either side of her, she scowled. Her gaze flickered to Lilia. It became mocking and her lips curled into a sneer, but guilt didn't rise in response. *She's not beautiful any more*, Lilia realised. *Something has changed her. Something has changed in her.* Shocked and sickened, she moved away as far as she could without escaping the ring of magicians.

Kallen took hold of Naki's head and stared at her for some time. All watched and waited silently. Naki's eyes remained open, gazing somewhere beyond Kallen's chest. Her expression remained mostly blank as he began the mind-read, though there was a little crease of concentration between her brows.

After an unbearably long time, Kallen finally released her. He took a step back and frowned down at Naki, clearly not happy, before turning away.

"She learned black magic before Lord Leiden's death, by experimenting, but she didn't realise she had succeeded. Otherwise she would not have encouraged Lilia to try it. A Thief heard about her and blackmailed her into working for him. He also ordered her to kill Lilia."

"How did she remove the block on her magic?" Sonea asked.

"She thinks," Kallen turned to regard her, "that it was never properly done in the first place."

Sonea's eyebrows rose, but she said nothing to that.

"I think these two young women had best be returned to their temporary cells," Osen said. "Then we will discuss this in depth."

Naki was escorted out first, and Lilia was relieved when she had gone. Other magicians were summoned to take Lilia away, so that Sonea, who had brought her to the meeting, could remain.

Before long, Lilia was walking down the University corridor, barely noticing the two magician guards as she puzzled over the fact that neither Sonea nor Kallen had been able to see into Naki's mind.

And if they can't do so using black magic, should I really feel so bad that I couldn't either?

CHAPTER 26

RINGS AND STONES

L orkin woke with a jolt, to find his leg had slipped between the two sleeping mats and had come into contact with the icy stone below them. He rolled back onto the bedding and found himself staring up at the cave's roof. Light was filtering through the wall of ice, casting a cool, blue light over everything. Looking closely, he could see where the warmth of Tyvara's shield set the chilly external air steaming.

Tyvara...

He turned to look at her, half covered by the blanket. The covering wasn't necessary since the air within the shield was warmed with magic, but he had to agree that it gave an impression of protection that he'd appreciated as the storm winds whistled and wailed outside. His mind couldn't shake the conviction that it was cold, and that it wasn't sensible to leave his skin exposed.

His body, however, approved of Tyvara's lack of clothing. He longed to reach out and touch her, but resisted. The sooner she woke, the sooner they would have to part.

So he lay there and gazed at her, hoping the image would remain clear in his memory forever.

I will come back, he told himself. *If Father had had such a reason as this, I'm sure he would have returned, too.*

Since his conversation with the Traitor queen, he'd wondered if there had been anything between her and his father, but he'd decided it was unlikely. They had met so briefly and there must have been quite a difference in age between them. Perhaps there had been some kind of bond formed through the blood ring, but, if there had been, it sounded as though the death of the queen's daughter had ended it.

He considered the blood ring. It was useless now that the maker was dead. Yet the queen hadn't thrown it away. Perhaps it had symbolised the agreement she'd made with Akkarin. What had been her side of that agreement? What had she failed to do, but now hoped to achieve by sending Lorkin home?

Perhaps an alliance between our lands. That would have required her to convince her people that it was a good idea. Not an easy task to take on, but she was younger then and maybe she hadn't realised how hard it would be.

Tyvara's eyes fluttered open, and he felt his heart sink, but as she turned and smiled at him it lifted again. She rolled over and they kissed for a while. When he hoped this might lead to more, she pulled away and stood up, the blanket falling away. She turned to regard the wall of ice and sighed.

"We slept longer than we should have," she said, starting to get dressed. "I ought to have headed home as soon as the storm passed. You never know how long it'll be to the next one, this time of year."

Lorkin felt a pang of worry for her, not quite eased by reminding himself that she was a powerful magician, and well capable of surviving storms. He got up and began pulling on his clothes. "Do you often travel at this time?"

She shook her head. "No, not if I can avoid it."

He looked at her sternly. "Well, I'm glad to have a little longer with you, but if it means you might not get home safely then I'm afraid I have to insist you leave right now."

She laughed, then her smile faded rapidly. Moving close, she kissed him firmly. "You take care as well. You're not quite out of the mountains yet."

"I will," he told her. "Kyralia has snow and hilly parts too, you know."

Her eyebrows rose.

"Which you've never been to, except on the way to Sachaka, at a time of year when there was no snow."

"Darn. I shouldn't have told you that."

She shook her head and pulled away, moving to the sledges. "Do you need me to run through the directions on how to get back to Arvice?" she asked, packing away the sleeping mats and utensils from the previous night's meal.

"Take the sledge down the valley to the hunter's shack. Leave it there and walk to the road. Slaves will be waiting to take me to the local estate and arrange transport from there."

"That's right. If you don't encounter them for some reason, it's the estate with four big trees either side of the entrance road. You shouldn't encounter any Ashaki. They don't tend to travel at this time of year. If you do, tell them who you are and request to be taken back to the Guild House. They'll be politically obliged to help you."

While she sounded confident, there was a worried look in her eyes. *What's the worst that could happen?* he asked himself. *The Ashaki might toss political obligation aside, reason that I'm a Traitor now and not protected by any diplomatic rules, and try to kill me. But they probably wouldn't without first trying to read my mind.* He rubbed the base of his thumb, where the mind-read-blocking stone lay beneath the muscle. It still itched a little, though he'd healed the cut. Tyvara had recommended the position for it, since a newly inserted stone did tend to itch, and a slave rubbing at sore hands wasn't unusual.

He'd not had much time to learn how to feed fake thoughts to a mind-reader. *Even with Tyvara's magic, I doubt I could fend off an Ashaki attack for long. If the Ashaki then senses that his mind-reading is failing, he might try to torture information out of me. I don't know if I could withstand that at all, or for long. Better to get to the Guild House and into Ambassador Dannyl's protection unseen.*

"I'll do what I can to stay out of sight," he assured her. "And this time I won't have half the Traitor spies trying to find us and turn us over."

She nodded. "Be careful who you trust, even so. Kalia's faction may be weakened, but there are still Traitors who hate you for what your father did. They won't do anything to endanger Sanctuary, but they may make your life uncomfortable."

He shrugged. "I've slept in a hole in the ground. I can

cope with a little discomfort." Then he frowned. "I've been thinking...is it wise that Kalia is the only one who knows how to Heal with magic?"

Tyvara's eyebrows rose. "I'm sure the queen would rather Kalia wasn't the only one, but we don't have any choice about that."

"Well...you could have another choice...if I teach you Healing before you go."

Her eyes widened a little, then she smiled and shook her head. "No, Lorkin. We don't have time for that."

"We could stay another night."

Her smile widened. "As much as that appeals, I still must go now. There are other reasons I need to get back quickly. The fact that Kalia has that one little advantage over us is the only thing keeping her faction happy."

"Nobody has to know."

She chuckled. "Zarala said you might offer this."

"Really?" He felt strangely affronted. Was he *that* predictable?

"Yes. She told me to refuse." Picking up the tow ropes of the sledges, Tyvara handed one to him. "Let's go."

They moved to the entrance of the cave and stepped out into a landscape coated with fresh, undisturbed snow. Bright morning light made everything dazzlingly white. The walls of the valley were steep and close, but widened as they reached eastwards. He could make out the line of the path they'd taken to descend into the valley, and another narrow one continuing down to the valley floor and a frozen river.

They turned to each other. They stared at each other. Neither spoke.

Then a distant rumble drew both to look at the sky.

They were too deep in the valley to see the coming weather. Tyvara cursed under her breath.

"I'll go first, so that I don't toss snow down onto you," she said. "Try to get to the hunter's shack before the next storm."

He nodded. She strode away, pushing snow off the path with magic. He watched her go, feeling that every step she took stretched some invisible bond between them. She did not look back, and he could not decide if he was disappointed or relieved.

When she finally reached the top of the wall, she did stop. Looking down, she lifted an arm and waved. It was less a gesture of farewell as one of impatience. His imagination conjured her voice and expression. "*What are you waiting for? Get going!*" He chuckled and set off into the valley, like her shoving snow off the path with magic as he went. When he reached the bottom he looked up.

She was gone. He felt strangely empty.

Then his eyes were drawn to the wall of ice that had covered one side of the cave they'd spent the last day and night in, and he gasped. It was a curtain of water, frozen in place.

A waterfall, he thought. *It's beautiful.*

He wished Tyvara had been with him to see it. But then, she had probably travelled this path before, and seen it already. *Still, it would have been nice to share such a sight with her.*

He sighed. There was no point wishing things were otherwise, and he must put all romantic notions aside and concentrate on getting back to Kyralia. There would be rough and dangerous times ahead, and important meetings and negotiations to arrange if all went well.

He turned away and hauled his sledge toward home.

•   •   •

The journey down the path into the canyon seemed far more precarious than the journey up. It was much harder to ignore the dizzying drop to one side, and instead of facing into the wall when making one of the sharp turns, travellers were forced to face outward over the valley.

Achati was even more silent and tight-lipped than before. Tayend was uncharacteristically quiet. Nobody wanted to turn in their saddle to look at others in case the movement unbalanced the horses and they swayed closer to the edge.

This left Dannyl with many hours to think about what he had learned from the Duna.

It had been late when he'd rejoined Achati and Tayend the previous night, having spent many hours listening to and writing down the Keeper's legends and stories. He'd told them what he'd learned of storestones, and shared his relief that they were so difficult and dangerous to make and that stones capable of holding so much power were very rare.

He hadn't mentioned that the Traitors had stones that could block a mind-read and present a mind-reader with the thoughts he might expect. Concealing such information from Achati gave him twinges of guilt, but he knew he'd feel much worse if he passed it on and brought about the slaughter of thousands of slaves and rebels. Though Dannyl resented the Traitors for taking Lorkin away, they hadn't killed the young man and certainly didn't deserve to be hunted down and murdered for it.

There were plenty of strategic reasons for protecting the knowledge of how to make magical stones, too. If the Ashaki took such secrets from the Traitors, Kyralia's former enemy would be even stronger, and less inclined to change its ways in order to join the Allied Lands. The Duna had trusted him with the information in the hope that they could form friendly links with the latter. Perhaps they would exchange stone-making knowledge in return for something.

What could we offer in return? he wondered. *Protection? With the Ashaki between Duna and Kyralia, and most Guild magicians not using black magic, how could the Allied Lands ever help the Duna?*

They couldn't. Kyralia didn't have any caves full of stones, as far as he knew, so stone-making knowledge would be equally useless to the Guild. *There might be caves in Elyne, or other Allied lands, though. The Cavern of Ultimate Punishment might be such a cave.* But he had his doubts about that. It had looked too symmetrical to be natural. He suspected it had been built, or carved out of the rock, and the crystals attached to the walls later.

The Duna knew that they could not gain effective protection from the Allied Lands. They wanted trade. They would supply the Guild with magical stones—once their own caves recovered from the Traitors' attack. It was up to the Guild to find something the Duna might want in exchange.

The Keeper had told him how the Traitors had always worked to destroy or steal any magical stones the Ashaki had taken from the tribes, and warned him that the Traitors would try to stop any trade with Kyralia. The Duna did not normally allow their own people to take magical stones out of their secret hiding places. A way would have to be found to transport them without raising Traitor or Sachakan suspicions.

Such precautions taken by both Duna and Traitors explained why the Ashaki had all but forgotten that such things existed. *I wouldn't be surprised if a few have a secret stash hidden away in their estates. Maybe they pass down the knowledge of how to use them to their heirs, maybe they've forgotten that they own anything more than pretty jewellery.*

After all, if the Guild could forget that it had ever used black magic, it was possible the Ashaki had forgotten they had ever stolen magical gemstones from the Duna.

Dannyl hoped they had, otherwise getting the stones from Duna to Kyralia without the Ashaki finding out could be even more difficult. All it would take was one shipment to be discovered to put him in a diplomatically awkward and dangerous position. Achati's anger would be the least of Dannyl's worries.

He hadn't had a chance to contact Administrator Osen yet. He'd been tempted to try back at the tent, but had been worried that Achati would think he was in a greater hurry to report to his superiors than he ought to be, when he'd essentially learned that storestones weren't a threat and the rest of the information related only to his research.

What about now? he asked himself. He had to admit, he did not like the thought of transferring his attention elsewhere when a deadly precipice was a mere few steps away. The guide had assured them that the horses did not need directing. They knew the path and were as keen to avoid falling off it as their riders were. *I'll just have to trust mine won't sense my mind is elsewhere and pitch me off for the fun of it.* While the horses had so far only displayed a sturdy, placid temperament, he'd encountered enough contrary animals in his life to suspect that the species, as a whole, had a mischievous sense of humour and was inclined to play tricks the moment a rider's attention strayed.

Pushing aside reluctance, he reached into his robes for Osen's ring, slipped it on a finger and closed his eyes.

—*Osen?*

—*Dannyl!*

—*Are you free to talk? I have some information to pass on.*

—*We are waiting for a Hearing to begin, but I have a little time to fill. I may have to end the conversation abruptly, however.*

—*I will be as concise as I can.* Dannyl described his meeting with the tribesmen and the Keeper, and their proposal.

—*How interesting.* Osen's excitement was faintly perceptible, like the sound of a distant vibration. *A stone that blocks a mind-read and projects false thoughts.*

Dannyl felt amusement and a little frustration. He'd expected Osen to be more interested in the proposed trade with Duna.

—*As I said, if the Ashaki and Sachakan king find out about this, they'll—*

—*The Hearing is beginning. Sorry, Dannyl. I have to go. Please take off the ring.*

Opening his eyes, Dannyl slipped the ring off again and pocketed it. He felt a nagging doubt. Had Osen understood the significance of what Dannyl had told him? Had he seen the potential in trading with the Duna? More importantly, did he grasp the dangers in it, and in the Ashaki finding out about the mind-read-blocking stones?

I'll have to trust that he does—or will when he gets the chance to think about it. Dannyl pushed the doubt aside. *I do wish I could discuss this with someone, but I can't even confide in Tayend. Not now that he's an Elyne Ambassador.*

The only person in Sachaka with whom he could have discussed the stones was Lorkin, and he was far away in the mountains, a willing prisoner of the Traitors.

The Guildhall echoed with voices as its occupants waited for the Hearing to begin. Standing to one side of the Front, Sonea looked up at the Higher Magicians and noted the same mix of worry and impatience on their faces that was growing inside her.

Where is Osen? Why haven't Kallen and Naki arrived yet?

Beside her, Lilia seemed oblivious to the rising tension. The young woman's gaze was fixed elsewhere. Her expression was sad and resigned.

She's grown up a lot these last few months, Sonea mused. The confused, dazed young woman whose mind Sonea had read after Lord Leiden's murder had been naïve and short-sighted—as surely anybody would have to be to experiment with black magic without considering the consequences.

To be fair, she was addled with roet and completely besotted. Just one of those could lure most novices into doing things they'd regret later.

Lilia had matured, however. She had learned to stop and try to anticipate the effects of her actions. She was also less trusting. When she'd agreed to escape with Lorandra, she'd made a choice, aware that the woman might not be trustworthy. Though it was a bad choice, it had been, in her mind, the best chance to save her friend.

It's the fact that she was willing to sacrifice her own future—and perhaps her own life—to find Naki that impresses me. I only wish she'd trusted me over Lorandra. But then, maybe it's my fault for not convincing her that I was doing all I could to find Naki.

Which hadn't been much, Sonea admitted. She had left it to Kallen. She would not make that mistake again.

Even Cery didn't trust me to know that he had Lilia. Perhaps he was protecting us both. What I didn't know about, I didn't feel obliged to deal with. It does worry me that he sent Lilia to rescue Naki. Did he not consider that Naki might not want to be rescued? If I hadn't been there, Naki would have killed her.

She couldn't help wondering if Cery had hoped to keep Lilia for himself. Would Lilia have agreed to that?

As for Naki, the only crime she had admitted to was learning and using black magic. She had done that out of the same foolish urge that had led Lilia to learn it. Her story of blackmail and working for a Thief was a little shaky. Sonea, Dorrien and Nikea had heard her tell Lilia that she was "learning the ropes." Perhaps Naki had given up escaping the underworld and figured that her only future was in it—even to the point where she would obey an order to kill Lilia.

Clearly, whatever the Thief threatened her with if she didn't work for him, it wasn't to kill Lilia. What was the threat, then? Kallen never mentioned it.

After Naki and Lilia had left the meeting of Higher Magicians in Osen's office, Kallen had told them that Naki blamed the Guild for the situation she had been in, their forcing her to live outside the Guild leaving her vulnerable to blackmail and too easily accessible to criminals.

Sonea suspected that many would sympathise with that view. Though, like Lilia, Naki had learned black magic through foolish experimentation, she had been forced to work for a Thief. Lilia's position was a little more precarious. She had deliberately run away—and released Lorandra in the process. She could have argued that Lorandra had persuaded her to go—it was partly true—but that would cancel out the positive aspect of her devotion to finding her friend. Still, the fact that Lilia's only motive had been to find Naki, and that she was successful, would gain her considerable support.

Both young women knew black magic. If the Guild chose to punish them for that, the least they could expect was imprisonment. The trouble was, the block on their magic had failed. Sonea knew that some magicians were claiming she had done a bad job of it. *They wish it was so, therefore they believe it was so*, she thought. No doubt Kallen would do the deed next time. She did not think he would succeed.

What would happen when Kallen's block failed? If it proved that a black magician's powers could not be blocked, what would happen to the girls? They could still be imprisoned, but their guards would have to be magicians and...

The side door on the other side of the hall opened. A novice peered nervously around the hall, but as his gaze fell on Sonea he straightened. He pointed to her, then Lilia, then beckoned.

Her heart skipped. *Has Kallen had some trouble with Naki?*

Sonea looked at Lilia, who had obviously seen the novice and was looking worried.

"Come with me," Sonea said.

The buzz of voices dropped as they walked across the hall. The novice was a tall, lanky young man, who bowed then bent forward to whisper in Sonea's ear.

"The Administrator wants you to bring Lilia to his office, Black Magician Sonea."

Sonea nodded. She moved to the door, Lilia following, and slipped out into the Great Hall.

The quiet of the hall was dramatic after the noisy Guildhall. Sonea gestured for Lilia to stay beside her, then strode toward the front of the University. As they reached the entry hall, she turned through the archway to the right and stopped at Osen's door. It swung inward at her knock.

To her relief, Kallen and Naki stood there calmly. Kallen met her gaze, but he looked as curious and worried as she was. Naki looked bored.

"Black Magician Sonea," Osen said. "I've just learned something very interesting, and it has raised a question I want answered before the Hearing begins." He turned to Kallen. "Please remove Naki's ring."

At once Naki's eyes went round. She drew her hands to her chest, one covering the other, and looked from Osen to Kallen and back again.

"No! It's my father's ring. The only memento I have of him."

Osen's eyebrows rose. "Other than an entire mansion and all his possessions—apart from a certain book containing instructions on black magic, that is."

Kallen took hold of Naki's arm. She resisted as he

pulled the concealed hand away from the other. Something caught and refracted the light. Sonea heard Lilia draw in a sharp breath. She turned to the girl.

"What is it?"

"That's the ring that was in the cabinet with the book." She glanced at Sonea. "She said her grandmother owned it, and that it was magical."

Kallen pulled the ring off Naki's finger and handed it to Osen. The Administrator examined it closely. He slipped it on his own finger and a look of concentration crossed his face; then he shrugged and removed it.

"I cannot sense anything magical about it."

"Of course not," Naki said, giving him a forced smile. "She was a mad old woman who liked to spin tales for children."

Osen looked at her, his gaze hard and assessing, and the smile slipped from her face. His gaze rose to meet Kallen's.

"Read her mind."

Both Kallen and Naki stilled. Kallen looked surprised; Naki slowly turned white. She recovered first.

"No," she said angrily, tugging against the hand still holding her arm. "How many times do I have to have my head invaded?"

The two men exchanged looks. Osen's expression hardened and he nodded to indicate that Kallen should continue. Kallen drew Naki closer.

"Wait!" she exclaimed, panic in her voice. "Isn't it enough that I've been abducted by a Thief and forced to work for him? Isn't it enough that...that my *father* was *murdered*." She pointed at Lilia with her free hand. "By *her*. You should be looking into her mind again. You should..."

"If there's nothing new to see in your mind, then let Kallen read it," Osen told her.

"No!" Naki shouted. She cringed away from Kallen. "I'm grieving! I don't want you to see that. Leave me alone!" She covered her face with her free hand and started sobbing.

Kallen frowned. To Sonea's surprise, he looked up at her, his expression questioning. She met his eyes and saw the reluctance there. Turning to Osen, she was a little chilled to see no sign of sympathy. He reached out, grabbed Naki's free hand and pulled it away from her face.

There were no tears. Naki stared at them each in turn, eyes wide with fear.

"Do it, Kallen," Sonea said quietly.

Naki fought him with magic, but the struggle didn't last long. As he took hold of her head Sonea looked at Lilia, concerned that the girl might be frightened, but Lilia watched with a calm intensity.

After a long silence, Kallen let Naki go, releasing her with a sound of disgust. He looked at Osen.

"You were right to suspect. The ring hides the wearer's true thoughts and memories."

Osen looked down at the ring, his mouth tightening in grim triumph. "What was she hiding?"

Kallen drew in a deep breath and let it out again. "She *did* learn black magic before she met Lilia—deliberately. She resented the constraints put on her by her father and the Guild, and wanted to be free to do whatever she wanted." His face darkened. "She befriended Lilia and lured her into earning black magic so that she could kill Leiden and someone else would be suspected of it—drugging Lilia and wiping blood on her hands to make her look guilty." He looked at Lilia sympathetically, then back at Osen. "She was inspired by Skellin, who she admired for avoiding capture for so long. The mind-block wasn't something she'd planned for, but it was easy to get past—I suspect no ordinary block would have been effective on a black magician. Naki then found a Thief willing to teach her how to survive in the underworld in exchange for magical favours." Kallen turned to regard Naki with contempt. "He brought her people that nobody would miss, so she could strengthen herself, and ensured the bodies were never found."

Sonea stared at the girl, outrage at her callous manipulations and murder of her father turning into horror. *How could she have done it? To kill people who meant her no harm...* Naki was now standing with her back stiff and her arms crossed, her lip curled in sullen defiance. *All so she could do as she pleased.*

"Sonea," Osen said.

She dragged her eyes away and looked at him. He held up the ring.

"I want you to attempt to read my mind."

She blinked in surprise, then understood as he slipped the ring on again. Moving forward, she placed a hand on each side of his head and closed her eyes.

Sending her mind forth, she slipped past the defences around his and sought his thoughts. She detected a strong sense of his personality, but the few thoughts she picked up were vague and fragmentary. Drawing her consciousness back, she opened her eyes.

"That's...odd. Your thoughts were disjointed, as if you were having trouble focusing them."

He smiled thinly. "I was thinking about Lorlen."

She regarded him thoughtfully. Osen had admired and worked with the former Administrator for years, and grieved over his death deeply. There was no chance she would have missed those thoughts and the accompanying emotions, without some kind of magical interference.

"I didn't sense this disjointedness when I read Naki's mind the first time," Kallen pointed out.

"Nor did I," Sonea said, turning to face him. "Perhaps there is some knack or skill to using the ring."

"From what I've learned, that is exactly the case," Osen told them. He smiled as they both looked at him. "Ambassador Dannyl reported to me as I was readying to go to the Hearing. He has discovered the existence of mind-read-blocking stones, among other things. Since there were so many inconsistencies between what Sonea and Kallen read in Naki and Lilia's minds, I decided to check whether either girl was wearing a gemstone before we proceeded."

"What will we do now?" Kallen asked.

"Proceed with the Hearing," Osen answered, looking at Naki. She glowered back at him. He turned to Sonea. "You and Lilia return first. I will come afterwards with Kallen."

She nodded. He led the way to the door and, to her surprise, followed her and Lilia out, shutting the door behind him.

"Before you go," he said, his voice low. His gaze moved from Sonea to Lilia and back, indicating he was speaking to them both. "Do not mention the ring to anybody for now." He turned to Sonea. "Construct a barrier of silence and tell the Higher Magicians that Kallen has read Naki's mind after a block was removed that prevented a mind-read. Tell them they will be given the details after the Hearing."

She nodded, and as he gestured that they could go, hurried away with Lilia at her side.

"So," Lilia said, as they entered the Great Hall. "If Naki is guilty of murder... of murder using black magic..."

Sonea felt a chill run down her spine. The punishment would be execution. She looked at Lilia and felt a wave of sympathy. *She definitely chose the wrong girl to be infatuated with.* Lilia had not just had her heart broken, but had found out that the object of her desire had murdered others, set her up, and then tried to kill her. *Now it is likely her friend is going to be executed. I hope she is going to be all right. I should keep an eye on her...*

The girl looked away.

"The king may grant her a pardon," Sonea told her.

Lilia gave a short and bitter laugh. "That's not going to happen."

Sonea sighed. "No, it's not likely."

As they reached the door to the Guildhall, something else occurred to her that made her pause, her heart filling with sudden dread.

Then who will have to perform the execution?

CHAPTER 27

UNPLANNED ASSISTANCE

Standing outside the hunter's shack, Lorkin looked around and wondered what time it was. All he was sure of was that the sun was up, because the fog around him was too light for it to have been illuminated merely by moonlight.

Should I stay here until it lifts?

Because of the storm that had delayed him and Tyvara, he was running low on food. While he was willing to go hungry for a day, he knew that, down at the end of the valley, Traitors disguised as slaves were waiting to meet him. The longer he took to arrive, the more likely they'd be missed at the estate they belonged to.

So long as I always go downhill, I shouldn't get lost. Tyvara said I wouldn't go astray if I travelled at night, because the road crosses the mouth of the valley. She said to just walk until I find it, then turn left and follow where it leads.

Surely the same instructions would apply now.

He looked back at the hut, mostly hidden by the fog.

He'd buried the sledge under the snow, as instructed. Someone would take it back to Sanctuary soon enough, he guessed. He'd also left his pack and changed into the sort of clothes that hunters usually wore in winter— roughly made trousers and a tunic covered by a hooded cape of hides stitched together. His boots were made of skins with the fur on the inside. There were simple gloves—mere pockets of hide—as well. Hunters were another group of Sachakans that didn't quite fit into the simple division of slaves and Ashaki. They were free men, but they weren't magicians. They lived on estates in exchange for the pelts, meat and other products they produced, but they weren't considered slaves. Since they spent much of the year in remote places, it would be hard for a master to maintain control of them. They also had an understanding of sorts with the Traitors, who left them alone so long as they kept away from certain areas in the mountains. Some actively helped the Traitors by allowing use of their huts—though they may not have had much choice about that. If they wanted to be free to hunt in the mountains, they had to stay on the right side of the magicians that lived there.

A hunter's outfit was the perfect disguise for Lorkin. If any Ashaki saw him, they'd ignore him, and it wasn't too strange for a hunter to be out and alone. Not that anybody was going to see him today.

Turning his back on the mountains, he started walking. The fog was so thick he had to constantly watch the ground for obstacles. After stumbling into depressions and the edge of the river, hidden under the snow, he broke a branch off one of the scraggly trees and used it to probe the drifts in front of him as he walked. It slowed his progress, so he was not expecting to find the road for some time. After the relief of a flat stretch of ground was followed by a sudden drop, however, he stopped and looked around. Exploring left and right, he discovered that the flat area continued in both directions, and was of a consistent width. It had to be the road.

Tyvara said to turn left. If I'm wrong and this isn't the road, the flat area will soon end, or I'll encounter the side of the valley.

So he started along the direction she'd said. After several hundred paces he relaxed a little. The surface continued straight and, aside from the occasional rut or puddle, remained level. With no obstructions to beware of, he was able to look around and search the fog for some sign of the Traitors waiting to meet him.

After a while he began to worry that he would pass them, unnoticed. Though the fog had a deadening effect on sound, his footsteps crunching through the snow and finding the occasional puddle seemed loud to him, and he had to resist trying to be quieter.

At least I should hear a carriage coming soon enough to get off the road and hide. It won't matter either if there's nothing to hide behind. All I have to do is crouch down and stay still, and if anyone sees me they'll probably think I am a rock.

A voice called out behind him, and Lorkin froze. He could not make out what it had said, but it had definitely been calling to someone.

To me?

He considered what Tyvara had said about the likeliness of encountering Ashaki. *"You shouldn't encounter any Ashaki. They don't tend to travel at this time of year."*

He doubted anyone would willingly venture out in this fog, and he'd heard no sound of carriage wheels or hoof beats. The only people likely to be out in such weather were the people looking for him. The voice had come from behind him. Maybe they'd seen his tracks and realised he'd passed them.

The voice called out again, this time further away. He started forward. Within a few steps he saw something move. He made out a figure coming toward him. A man, walking confidently. Wearing trousers and a cropped jacket.

Ashaki.

He stopped, but it was too late. The man had seen him. Lorkin's heart began to race. Should he throw himself to the ground and hope the man thought he was a slave? But a hunter wouldn't do that.

"You're not Chatiko," the man said, stopping. He came closer, bending forward as he stared at Lorkin. "I know you. I've seen you before." His eyes widened with realisation and surprise. "You're that Kyralian magician! The one who went missing!"

There was no point pretending otherwise. Tyvara's words rose in his memory.

"If you do, tell them who you are and request to be taken back to the Guild House. They'll be politically obliged to help you."

"I am Lord Lorkin of the Magicians' Guild of Kyralia," he said. "I formally request that you return me to the Guild House in Arvice."

The man smiled and patted him on the shoulder. "Well, it's your lucky day. We're heading that way ourselves. We were going to wait until the weather cleared, but Master

Vokiro insisted we leave at first light. I am Master Akami."

Lorkin searched for something to say. *Two of them are Masters. They aren't as highly ranked as Ashaki. That could be to my advantage.* He managed a smile. "Thank you, Master Akami."

The Sachakan gave Lorkin a familiar amused look at his Kyralian manners, then gestured back down the road. "The carriage is this way. Master Chatiko stopped to relieve himself." Lorkin fell into step beside the man. "He was taking so long I went looking for him. See how lucky you are? We could have driven by and not seen you. Ah! He's back."

Another man stood by the carriage. As he saw Lorkin, his gaze moved from Lorkin's head to his feet, an expression of puzzlement and distaste on his face.

"Look what I found," Master Akami declared. "A lost Kyralian magician! And I bet he has some tales to tell. He'll keep us entertained all the way back to the city!"

No sooner had the trunks been hauled onto the deck of the *Inava* than the anchor was pulled up and sails unfurled. Dannyl, Tayend and Achati were ushered to the one place on deck where they were out of the way of the captain and his slave crew.

Achati looked at Dannyl.

"So, are you content with what you learned here, Ambassador?"

Dannyl nodded. "Yes, though I would like to return and record more of these Duna legends. I asked to hear the ones about magic, but there would be plenty more that aren't. I guess that's a book for someone else to write."

Achati nodded. "Perhaps your assistant might write such a book. She seems very interested in the tribes."

Dannyl felt a small pang of guilt for leaving Merria behind. *But someone had to remain at the Guild House.* "Yes, she is."

"And what about you, Ambassador Tayend?" Achati said, turning to the Elyne.

Tayend waved a hand in a vague gesture that might have meant many things. He looked a little pale, Dannyl noted.

"Have you taken the seasickness cure?" Achati asked.

"Not yet," Tayend admitted. "I did not want to miss our last sight of . . ." He gulped and waved a hand at the valley. "I'll take it once we leave the bay."

Achati frowned with concern. "There will be some delay before it takes effect, and it won't have a chance to if you can't keep it down."

"Ashaki Achati," the captain called.

They all turned to see the man pointing out over the northern arm of the bay, his eyes bright and a grim smile on his face. Black clouds darkened the sky, and the horizon was invisible behind streaks of rain.

Achati chuckled. "A storm is coming." He took a step toward the captain. "I will give you my assistance."

The man's eyebrows lowered. "You have experience?"

Achati grinned. "Plenty."

The man nodded and smiled again. As Achati turned away, his eyes shone with excitement. Dannyl's skin pricked.

"We're not turning back?" Tayend asked, with an edge of panic to his voice.

"No," Achati replied. "You'd best take that cure now."

"You and the captain are pleased about this, aren't you?" Dannyl asked as the Elyne hurried away.

Achati nodded. "We are. Storms are common at this time. We've been taking advantage of them for centuries. Any Ashaki who travels by ship—any who value their life, that is—learns how to ride them. With magic to hold the ship together and an experienced captain to steer it, you can sail from Duna to Arvice in a few days."

As if to emphasise the point, a blast of wind battered the ship as it emerged from the protection of the bay. Dannyl and Achati caught hold of the rail to steady themselves.

"Can I offer any assistance?" Dannyl asked. He had to shout to be heard over the wind.

Achati's laugh held a hint of both affection and scorn. "Don't worry. The king will ensure that what magic I and the captain use will be replaced."

In other words, only a higher magician has the strength for this.

It had never been so obvious to Dannyl that he was no black magician. Oddly, that made him reluctant to slink away to the protection of his cabin.

"I'll stay and watch, then," he said.

"Later," Achati said, shaking his head. "Seasickness cures can only do so much. Tayend is going to need your help."

Dannyl met the Sachakan's eyes. He saw concern there. Sighing, Dannyl nodded in agreement and set off after the Elyne Ambassador.

As Sonea neared the end of the corridor, she saw, through the University entry hall, a carriage pull up. In the brief time the vehicle's window was visible, she glimpsed a familiar face.

Dorrien.

She cursed under her breath. If she crossed the hall he would see her and want to talk. She was in no mood for such an encounter, rife with unspoken questions, guilt and desire. The dread that had settled on her during the Hearing had kept her on edge all day.

So she turned and moved back down the corridor again, slipping into the nearest empty classroom. The novices were long gone. The lines of tables and chairs brought back memories, both pleasant and unpleasant.

Or would it be more accurate to say tolerable *and* unpleasant? *While I did enjoy learning magic, I didn't have much fun doing it alongside my fellow novices, even when they weren't making life difficult, snubbing me or, in Regin's case, finding new and increasingly humiliating and painful ways to torment me.*

After she had been accepted back into the Guild, completing her training had been difficult, the lessons having to be taught without any teacher communicating more complicated concepts mind to mind. She'd managed it, despite that. And the grief of Akkarin's death. And being pregnant with Lorkin.

Regin has turned out all right, she found herself thinking. She smiled wryly. *I never thought I'd think that. Or miss him.*

Which she did, in a way. It had been better, during the initial search, having a helper who wasn't besotted with her. Things had become much too complicated with Dorrien. She wished they could hurry up and find Skellin and Lorandra. Or that Dorrien's daughter could join the

Guild sooner, so that he and Alina could return to the country.

I guess this means I'm not in love with him, she realised. *Perhaps I might have been, if there weren't so many factors spoiling everything. Or maybe... maybe if it were love then those things wouldn't be able to spoil it. People have affairs all the time, it seems. The idea of betraying a spouse or causing a scandal isn't enough to deter them.*

She sighed and moved to the classroom door. Dorrien should have passed through the hall by now. She paused as she heard voices and footsteps approaching, not wanting to be seen hiding.

"...*this* convinced you that you need to stop taking roet?" a woman's voice asked.

The voice was familiar. Even as she realised it was Lady Vinara's, she heard another voice reply and felt a shock of recognition.

"I am convinced, but this may not be the best time," Black Magician Kallen replied as they passed the classroom. "I don't need to be distracted by—"

"There is *never* a good time," Vinara replied. "Do you think I don't hear this every day from...?"

The Healer's voice faded out of hearing. The pair were striding quickly toward the entry hall, on the way to Osen's office. As Sonea had been.

She counted to fifty, then stepped out and continued on her way. Triumph and worry mingled as she considered what she had overheard. Triumph that she had been right: Kallen's use of roet *was* a problem. Worry that she was right: Kallen's use of roet was a *problem*. Which, because he was a black magician, made it her problem, too.

The door to Osen's office was swinging shut as she arrived, so she pushed through into the room. Rothen was there already. She smiled at him as she passed. The Heads of Disciplines were in their usual trio of chairs. Kallen stood by the wall. The Administrator was seated. He met her eyes and they exchanged a nod, then she took her usual place, standing to one side of his desk.

The few missing Higher Magicians arrived soon after, and Osen began the meeting by explaining what had happened before the Hearing—Dannyl's information, summoning Kallen, Naki, Sonea and Lilia, and what Kallen saw in Naki's mind once her ring was removed.

"The king has not granted Naki a pardon," Osen told them, when he was finished.

Silence followed that announcement. Sonea examined the faces of the magicians. Some were nodding and unsurprised. Others looked shocked. Rothen was watching her, his expression sympathetic and troubled. She felt her stomach sink and her mouth went dry.

What will I do if they ask me to perform the execution? She had already decided that she would not protest if they ordered it, but if they gave her the opportunity to avoid it, she would. *There is no right decision in this case. Either I do it and have another death on my hands, or I refuse and force another to take on that burden.*

The other would most likely be Kallen. He had never killed anyone before—certainly not with black magic, and if Naki was to die without her magic being loosed then her powers would need to be drained beforehand. Naki was no invader; she was a young woman and Kyralian. Despite Sonea's dislike of Kallen, she would not wish the burden of such an execution on him.

If I do it, people will see me in a different way. Ruth-less and cold. If I turn from that duty, they'll see me as disloyal and cowardly. They'll—

"I have discussed this with Black Magician Kallen and High Lord Balkan," Osen said. "Kallen will remove Naki's power, Balkan will apply the penalty."

Sonea blinked in surprise even as she felt relief flood through her. Exhaled breaths combined to create a soft hiss in the room.

"The king has agreed that it should not be a public execution," Osen continued. "Despite the deterrent effect one might have." There were nods of agreement all around. "It will occur later tonight. The existence of these gemstones that block a mind-read must remain a secret," Osen added firmly. "The knowledge of them must not extend beyond us here. The Sachakans are not aware of them and if they learn of this kind of magic the consequences could be disastrous."

He took time to meet the eyes of every magician, until he'd had a nod or murmur of understanding from them all; then he relaxed and invited questions. Sonea did not hear what was asked, too caught up in her own relief.

She realised belatedly the sense behind Osen's decision: Balkan, as High Lord, was the Guild's leader and trained as a Warrior, so it was fitting he should enforce the law. She and Kallen had been accepted as black magicians only so that they could defend the Guild against invasion. Kallen's removal of Naki's power was a practical measure, little different to what he and Sonea did for dying magicians to ensure they passed away without their remaining magic causing any destruction.

A foolish anxiety slipped into Sonea's mind. *Did they*

think I couldn't or wouldn't do it? Did they think I couldn't be trusted?

Oh, be quiet, she told herself.

The meeting finished soon after. Rothen joined Sonea as she left the office.

"Going to the hospice tonight?" he asked.

They walked into the entrance hall and stopped at the open doors of the University. They both gazed out at the forest, which was dusted in snow.

"I don't know," Sonea replied. "I didn't sleep today. I could go back to my rooms, but that won't achieve anything. I could go to the hospice, but I suspect I'll be...a bit too distracted."

He hummed. "I think we'll all be, until the deed is done."

"And for some time after. How long has it been since the Guild had to execute a member—or former one?"

He shrugged. "A long time. Long enough I'd have to look it up in a history book."

Sonea glanced behind them. The entry hall was empty, the Higher Magicians having all left now.

"I admit that I'm relieved at their choice of executioners," she murmured. "Though it will still be hard on Kallen to be there and take part. He's never...he's inexperienced."

"Many feel they have asked a lot of you already," Rothen replied quietly. "They feel guilty about Lorkin."

She turned to meet his gaze. *They* should *feel guilty about sending Lorkin off to Sachaka*, she thought triumphantly, but not without bitterness. Rothen's eyes were steady and hinted at more. She wondered how often the Higher Magicians discussed her.

"Is this why they haven't expelled Lorkin from the Guild officially yet?" she asked.

He nodded.

"Or is it they're afraid of what I'd say and do if they did?"

Rothen chuckled. "That, too." His expression became serious. "I haven't had a chance to tell you some sad news—about someone else, not Lorkin."

"What is it?"

"Regin's wife tried to kill herself."

"Oh! That's terrible."

"Apparently she's been attempting to for years. This is the first time it's been, well, unavoidably public. There had been rumours, but…" Rothen grimaced. "I didn't like to pay much attention to them."

"Poor Regin," she said.

"Yes. But…not for quite the reason you think, I suspect."

"What do you mean?"

Rothen sighed. "According to rumours, each time she had attempted suicide she did so after he found out about and chased off one of her lovers."

Sonea winced. "Oh."

"From the reports I've heard, he's on his way back to Imardin and has asked for rooms in the Guild. He has given his house in Elyne to one daughter, and his Imardin family home to the other."

"That is one angry man."

"Indeed."

Sonea felt a small, somewhat inappropriate and slightly treacherous spark of hope. *Also a man needing something to occupy himself—like a hunt for a rogue.* She hooked her arm around Rothen's and tugged him back toward the University corridor.

"Are there a lot of married people having troubles at the moment, or does it just appear that way to me?"

"Who else is having troubles in their marriage?" he asked.

She shrugged. "Just... people. As for magicians moving back home, there's something I wanted to talk to you about. Something that we should be able to achieve without causing offence if we work together."

CHAPTER 28

A WELCOME RETURN

To Lilia's relief, she was being held in a room within the University rather than the airless Dome. It gave her a small measure of hope that the Guild might be more forgiving of her more recent crimes, and that her intention to return to her prison after finding Naki had convinced them that she didn't need to be given a harsher penalty.

What weakened that hope was the fact she had been told nothing since the Hearing. Servants had brought her food and tended to her needs, but would not speak even when Lilia questioned them. The magicians guarding her door told her to be quiet if she knocked to get their attention.

She had little choice but to think about what Naki had done. Though her heart still ached, it was for a person who hadn't really existed.

How could she kill her own father? I suppose he wasn't her real father. He was just the man who married her mother. She told me he didn't believe her when she said her uncle would have abused her. Was that even true?

Maybe it was. I don't know if he deserved her hate. I guess I'll never know.

The hurt at being set up and betrayed by Naki was countered by anger. She was tired of being manipulated by people. First Naki, then Lorandra. At least Cery and Anyi had been honest about what they wanted of her. As far as she knew.

I'm not going to be used and deceived by anyone again. People have to prove they are trustworthy before I'll trust them. At least being locked away means I'll encounter fewer people to worry about on that score.

Footsteps and voices outside the door drew her attention away from her thoughts. The door opened and Black Magician Sonea entered. Lilia felt her heart soar with hope, only to crash down again as she saw the woman's expression. She rose and bowed hastily.

"Lilia," Sonea said. "It seems I must apologise on behalf of the Guild for keeping you ignorant of the events of the last day. The trouble is, we haven't yet decided what to do with you."

Lilia looked away. It could not be a good sign if they were struggling to decide. As far as she could see, their choices were to execute or imprison her, and since her powers couldn't be blocked, the latter would involve keeping two magicians occupied as guards. Permanently.

"I can assure you that nobody is suggesting you face the penalty of death," Sonea said.

Relief spread through Lilia like the warmth of a heated room after a walk in the winter cold. A gasp escaped her, then she blushed at the unintended show of emotion.

"What we can't agree on is what to do with you. Some

want you back in the Lookout. Others want you back in the Guild."

Surprised, Lilia looked up.

Sonea smiled wryly. "Under tight restrictions, of course."

"Of course," Lilia echoed.

"I am of the latter opinion. Which is why I have arranged for you to stay in my rooms until the decision is made."

Lilia stared at Sonea in disbelief. She couldn't decide if this was a good or bad thing. It would be more comfortable and less isolated than this room, and it indicated that the Guild might be willing to trust her not to attempt another escape. But she'd be staying with *Sonea*. A *black magician*.

Which is what I am, too, she reminded herself.

Even so, all novices found the two black magicians a little scary. She suspected that more than a few graduated magicians did as well. Sonea had *used* black magic. She'd *killed* with it.

Only in defence of Kyralia. Not like Naki has.

Sonea made a small beckoning gesture. "Come on. Let's get you settled in."

Not trusting herself to speak, Lilia nodded and followed the black-robed woman out of the room. The two guards eyed Sonea nervously, which did not make Lilia feel any better. She followed obediently through the passages and corridors of the University, out and across the courtyard, and into the Magicians' Quarters.

In the wide corridor within, they passed two Alchemists. The man and woman nodded to Sonea politely, but their eyes slid to Lilia. She expected disapproval or suspicion. Instead they looked grim and sympathetic.

Only when she reached the top of the stairs did she work out why.

"Naki," she found herself saying.

Sonea glanced at her. "I have news of her, as well. Come inside first."

At once a deep dread filled Lilia. *The news isn't going to be good*, she thought. *I shouldn't care what's happened to Naki, after what she did to me.* But she knew that she would.

They paused before a door, which swung inward. Sonea gestured for Lilia to enter first. Stepping through, Lilia took in the simple but luxurious surrounds and realised that someone was standing in front of the guest room chairs. As she recognised who it was, her heart leapt.

"Anyi!"

The young woman smiled, stepped forward and gave Lilia a quick hug. "Lilia," she said. "I *had* to see how you were doing." She looked at Sonea. "Have you told her yet?"

Sonea shook her head. "I was about to." She met Lilia's gaze, her expression serious and sympathetic. "You were right: the king did not grant Naki a pardon. She was executed late last night."

Though Lilia had expected it, the news sent a shock through her. She sat down in the closest chair. For a while all she could do was breathe.

Gone. Naki is gone. She was so young. As they say, she was full of potential. Maybe it's a good thing that her potential wasn't realised, though. Who knows how many more people she would have killed?

A hand touched her back. She realised that Anyi was

sitting beside her. The young woman smiled, but her eyes were full of concern.

"I'll be all right," Lilia told her.

"I'll leave you two to catch up," Sonea said. She opened the door and slipped out of the room.

Lilia gaped at the door.

"What's wrong?" Anyi asked.

"She left me here alone."

"Alone? I'm here."

Lilia shook her head. "Sorry. I meant unguarded. By magicians." She narrowed her eyes at Anyi. "Unless there's something you're not telling me."

Anyi laughed. "There's always something I'm not telling someone. That's a part of my job. But no, I'm not a magician. Not a shred of magic in me. I got myself tested once, when I was a child. I thought if I could get into the Guild it would be a great way to spite Cery."

"Spite Cery? Why would getting into the Guild do that?"

A look of surprise and then realisation crossed Anyi's face, then she cursed and smacked her palm onto her forehead.

"What is it? You just gave something away, didn't you?" Lilia considered Anyi's words. "You've known Cery since you were a child." No wonder Anyi was so loyal. Except that she had once wanted to spite him. As if... "He's your father!"

Letting out a groan, Anyi nodded. "I am clearly much better at being a bodyguard than keeping secrets."

"What's the problem with people knowing your father's a Thief?"

Anyi grimaced. "Skellin had Cery's second wife and my half-brothers murdered. Well, we think it was him."

"Oh." All Lilia's satisfaction at guessing the truth melted away. "So you're afraid that, if he finds out you're Cery's daughter, he'll try to kill you, too."

Anyi shrugged. "He'd kill me anyway if he had the chance, because I'm Cery's bodyguard. It's more likely he'd do something to me to hurt or blackmail Cery, if he found out we're related."

"Well... your secret's safe with me. Though if Sonea or Kallen ever read my mind—"

"Sonea knows. Kallen, on the other hand..." Anyi frowned, then regarded Lilia with one eyebrow raised. "I don't suppose you feel like running away with me? With Cery's help, I can take you somewhere the Guild will never find you."

Lilia's heart flipped over. "No. It's tempting, but staying is... the right thing to do. I never really cared much about that, but I do now."

"Even if they put you back in the Lookout? How is that right? It would be a waste."

"No." Lilia shook her head. "I broke a law, and my vow. I did it out of stupidity, not malice, but I need to be seen to be punished so that novices like Naki don't do the things she did." She shivered. "The last thing the Guild needs is to waste time and magic looking for me when it should be finding Skellin and Lorandra."

But if I did go, Lilia suddenly thought, *I could help protect Anyi. And Cery. It would be like returning the favour they gave me...*

Anyi nodded slowly. "Well, it's your decision." She placed a hand on Lilia's and squeezed. "I hope they don't lock you up, because I've got rather fond of you. I'd like to see you again."

Lilia smiled in gratitude. "I'd like to see you again, too."

A tap at the door drew their attention. Anyi let go of Lilia's hand and stood up as Sonea entered.

"Sorry to interrupt," Sonea said. She looked at Anyi. "A rather cryptic message just arrived from Cery." She handed over a small slip of paper. "I think he wants you to return."

Anyi read it and nodded. "He wants me to pick up some sweet buns on the way." Anyi turned back to Lilia and smiled. "Good luck."

To Lilia's amusement, Sonea beckoned and took her into a small bedroom, closing the door.

"This is where you'll sleep," Sonea told her. She bent to the door, obviously listening. "Cery always has another way of getting into the room than the corridor and I assume Anyi used the same method," she explained. "I don't want to know how, in case my mind is ever read."

Lilia heard a dull thud. It must have been a signal, for Sonea turned the handle and opened the door. The guest room was now empty. Sonea turned to regard Lilia.

"Are you all right?"

"Yes." Lilia nodded. Though learning of Naki's execution had been a shock, she felt better than she had expected. Not happy, but accepting of how things had turned out and hopeful that the future would be better.

"I'm fine," she said. "Thanks. Thanks for letting me stay here."

Sonea smiled. "Hopefully we'll have a more permanent home for you soon. In the meantime, make yourself comfortable."

Lorkin woke with a jolt.

Looking around, he made out his "rescuers" and

fellow travel companions in the dim light of the carriage interior. All were asleep. He sighed in relief.

Since he had first joined them, the three Masters had pestered him for stories of his time among the Traitors. He'd refused to answer questions about even the most trivial details of Traitor life, saying that he dare not say anything until he had permission to from Ambassador Dannyl. Fortunately, their continuing attempts to worm something out of him were in a spirit of trying their luck. His silence on the subject was a challenge to them, but they did not want to risk the censure of those higher up in the Sachakan hierarchy—especially not the king.

The three men were determined to take Lorkin back to Arvice as quickly as possible. Lorkin hoped their motive was a desire to be credited with his rescue and safe return, rather than an expectation that the king would be eager to get hold of him and extract information. Master Akami had ordered the slaves to drive the carriage as fast as could be managed without ruining the horses, stopping off to change to fresh ones at estates along the way. The slaves took it in turns to drive, those who were resting binding themselves to the exterior seat at the back of the carriage so that they didn't fall off while they dozed or slept.

It had grown unpleasantly fragrant in the cabin, not helped by the pungent odour of the hunter's clothes Lorkin was wearing. They'd insisted he ditch the cape, but when they'd offered him typical Sachakan garb he'd declined, saying it was more appropriate that the next change of clothes he made was into Guild robes.

Looking out of the carriage window, he saw that everywhere was bathed in a pale light. It illuminated walls on either side of the road, and that could only mean one thing.

Arvice! We have reached the city! In just two days and nights.

It seemed incredible, considering how long it had taken him to get from the city to the mountains, but he and Tyvara had been on foot, not in carriages travelling at their fastest, with a change of horses whenever they tired.

"We're back," a voice said. Lorkin looked up to see that Master Akami was awake, stretching his arms and legs, and yawning simultaneously. The young Sachakan smiled at Lorkin, then tapped on the roof. "To the Palace," he said.

Lorkin felt a chill run down his spine.

"Straight to the Palace?" he asked.

Akami nodded. "We should get you delivered as soon as possible."

"But... I need to go to the Guild House first. It would be better if I had a bath and changed into robes before I presented myself to the king." Lorkin grimaced. "It's early, and if I were the king I wouldn't want to be woken up only to be greeted by a filthy Kyralian magician."

Akami frowned as he considered this.

"He's right."

Lorkin turned to see that Master Chatiko was awake, rubbing at his eyes. "The Palace will need to be told Lord Lorkin has returned, but they don't need him hanging about waiting for the king to emerge." Chatiko yawned. "And it's likely to be a waste of everyone's time, since Lord Lorkin is probably obliged to consult with the Ambassador before speaking to the king."

Akami looked thoughtful. He nudged Master Voriko

with a foot, and the young Sachakan roused himself reluctantly.

"What do you think, Vori? Take Lorkin to the Palace or the Guild House?"

Voriko had to be asked three times before he was awake enough to understand. He looked from Lorkin back to Akami, his eyebrows raised in an expression that suggested his friend was an idiot.

"Take him to the Guild House, of course. They won't even let him in the Palace, in that state. They mightn't even recognise him."

Akami shrugged, then nodded. He tapped on the roof again. "Take us to the Guild House."

As the carriage turned, Lorkin caught a glimpse of the crossroad they had been heading toward. The trees and flowers were familiar. It was the parade that led to the Palace.

That was close.

He hoped he didn't look too relieved.

A wait followed, in which all but Lorkin and Akami fell asleep again. When the carriage finally passed through the gate of the Guild House, Lorkin let out what he hoped was a silent sigh of relief.

"Here you are, Lord Lorkin," Akami said, opening the door with magic. The others woke and sat up. "Welcome back."

"Thank you," Lorkin said. "Thank you for bringing me home, too."

Akami smiled and patted Lorkin on the shoulder as he started down the carriage steps. "We'll let the Palace know you're back."

Lorkin turned and watched the carriage leave. The

Guild House slaves pushed gates closed behind it. He turned around to see two slaves lying face-down on the ground. One was the door slave, he remembered.

"Get up," he ordered.

The two slaves rose, keeping their eyes downcast. He felt a long-forgotten disgust and anger at their situation, followed by curiosity. Were either of these men Traitor spies?

"I am Lord Lorkin, Ambassador Dannyl's assistant," he said. "Take me to Ambassador Dannyl."

"Ambassador Dannyl is not here," the door slave said.

"Oh. Well. Take me inside. I'd like a wash and some clean robes."

The door slave beckoned and headed for the Guild House. Lorkin followed, feeling strangely powerful waves of sentimentality at the sight of the Master's Room and the rendered, curved walls.

I made it. I'm finally back where it all started.

The slave paused to whisper to a female slave. She nodded and hurried away. A less pleasant memory rose as the door slave led him into his old rooms: a memory of a dead woman, lying naked on his bed. That room was dark. The slave led him into a different bedroom in the suite, then prostrated himself. Lorkin told him to go.

Lorkin created a globe light, looked around and nodded. It had been very considerate of the slave to choose another room.

The female slave returned with a large bowl of water and some towels, then left. Another brought a set of robes. Lorkin warmed the water with magic, then stripped off the hunter's tunic and began to wash.

A sound drew his attention back to the doorway. He

expected another slave, but instead found himself staring at a woman in green robes. She was staring at him with equal astonishment, and a little hostility.

Then it occurred to him who she must be.

"You're my replacement," he exclaimed. *A woman assistant? Here in Sachaka?* He felt instant admiration at her courage in volunteering for the role.

She blinked, then understanding dawned. "Lord Lorkin! You're back!"

He nodded. "Yes. Where's Ambassador Dannyl?"

She rolled her eyes. "In Duna, having a nice time getting to know the locals. He left me all alone to deal with anything that turned up." Her gaze dropped to the hunter's trousers, then back to his face. "Like you."

Duna! It could take weeks before he gets back. What will I do if the king summons me before Dannyl returns?

"I'm Merria, by the way," she said. She smiled. "I'll let you finish. When you're ready, send one of the slaves to let me know. I'll be in the Master's Room. We had better work out what we're going to do. Do you need to get some sleep first?"

"No, but some food would be nice."

She nodded. "I'll arrange it."

Waking from a doze, Dannyl looked around the cabin. Soft snores were coming from Tayend's bed. The ship's pitching and rolling was still pronounced, but it had stopped shuddering and groaning for some time now. Dannyl had no idea how much time had passed. More than a few days, he suspected.

He heard a heavy footstep, then realised that this was what had woken him. The cabin door opened. Achati paused at the threshold, then let go of the door frame, staggered forward and grabbed the edge of his bed. He crawled onto it and collapsed, face down.

Dannyl got out of the chair and approached the Sachakan.

"Are you all right?" he asked.

Achati groaned, then sighed. "Yes. Just...tired." He rolled over onto his back with an effort. "Storm's passed. Go look, if you like."

Holding back a chuckle, Dannyl left through the open door, closing it behind him. He climbed the short, steep stair to the upper deck, pushing through the hatch into sunlight.

The few slaves still about stood with sagging shoulders, holding onto ropes or railing as if too weak to support themselves. The captain sat watching as another slave held the wheel, dark shadows under his eyes. As the man's eyes met Dannyl's, he nodded. Dannyl returned the gesture. A faint smile pulled at the captain's lips, then disappeared.

Glancing around the ship, Dannyl saw no sign of damage. Looking beyond, he saw that the skies to the south-east were dark with cloud. The edge of the storm, he guessed, moving away from them.

From the position of the sun, he reckoned it was mid-afternoon. The coast was visible to the right. A featureless land fringed by a short, eroding cliff. He considered the height of the latter thoughtfully. On the journey north he'd noted how the cliffs had grown steadily higher. If he could spot something now to indicate scale, he might be able to estimate how far from Arvice they were.

"Are we there yet?"

Surprised, Dannyl turned to see Tayend stepping through the hatch onto the deck. The Elyne looked tired and sick, but not as tired as Achati and not as sick as Tayend would have been if Dannyl hadn't been Healing away his seasickness since leaving Duna.

"I have no idea," Dannyl confessed.

"Achati's asleep." Tayend moved to stand beside Dannyl and looked around. "Storm's passed."

His observations didn't seem to need an answer, so Dannyl stayed silent. They stared out at the sea. *In comfortable, companionable silence*, Dannyl thought, but he found that the longer neither of them spoke, the more aware he was of Tayend's presence.

"How are you feeling?" he asked eventually.

"Not too bad." Tayend shrugged. "I'll probably take some more of that cure soon."

"You don't have to," Dannyl assured him.

"No, it's fine. I could do with the sleep."

Dannyl nodded. "So, did you enjoy the trip?"

Tayend didn't answer, and when Dannyl turned to look at him he saw the Elyne's lips were pursed in thought.

"Yes and no," Tayend replied. "I'm a bit disappointed I spent so much of it drugged. When we got to Duna it was better, though that ride up the canyon trail was rather unnerving. The tribes were interesting, but we only stayed a day and they only spoke to you."

Dannyl grimaced. "Sorry about that."

"Oh, don't apologise. It wasn't your decision."

They fell silent again. Tayend turned full circle, looking at the ship and checking out the coast. He stopped and faced Dannyl.

"And you?" he asked. "Come to any decisions?"

There was an accusing tone to his question. Dannyl turned to frown at Tayend. The Elyne's eyes were sharp and steady. Though Dannyl knew that Tayend was a lot smarter than his behaviour often suggested, he suddenly found that his former lover looked like an entirely different person. *An older person*, he thought. *A more mature person.*

"I *know*, Dannyl," Tayend said in a low voice. "You two are definitely more than…*friends*. Do you think I wouldn't be able to tell, after living with you for so long?"

Dannyl looked away, but not to avoid showing any guilt, he realised. To avoid glaring at Tayend in anger. He resisted the urge to glance back at the captain, or around at the slaves to see if any had heard, and created a barrier around them to contain sound.

"Nothing happened."

Tayend sniffed in disgust. "No?" he said. Dannyl met his gaze. Tayend's eyes narrowed, then he smiled thinly. "Oh, good. I managed to stop some part of your foolishness, then."

"You *were* keeping us apart!" Dannyl accused. "I thought you might be jealous, but this is—"

"This has nothing to do with jealousy," Tayend hissed. "He's a *Sachakan*. An *Ashaki*. A *black* magician."

"You think I haven't noticed this?"

"Yes," Tayend replied, his expression serious. "Because otherwise I'd have to consider that you're either going senile, are blind with love or are turning traitor. Out of those I have no proof of the first two, which leaves me in an awkward position as an Ambassador."

"I'm not turning into a traitor," Dannyl replied. "Last time I looked, having a foreign lover was not an act of treachery, otherwise I'd never have bedded you."

Tayend crossed his arms. "This is different. Our lands are allies. Sachaka is..."

Dannyl raised his eyebrows when Tayend didn't finish the sentence. "The enemy? It will always be our enemy, if we never stop treating it as one."

"It will never be our ally so long as Sachakans like Achati keep slaves and use black magic." Tayend's eyes narrowed. "Don't tell me your position is softening on that, as well."

Dannyl shook his head. "Of course not."

"Good. Because I'm watching you, Ambassador Dannyl. The moment you turn into a Sachakan, I'll know." Tayend turned away and moved back to the hatch, forcing Dannyl to quickly drop his sound-blocking shield. "Now I'm going to get some proper sleep."

As the hatch closed, Dannyl turned away to stare at the sea again.

Turn into a Sachakan. How ridiculous.

But as so often happened with Tayend, he felt a little seed of doubt take root. What if he was? Was Achati the cause? Or was it simply that he was growing too used to the Sachakan way of doing things?

If that's so, then there's nothing to worry about. Everything will return to normal once we get back to the Guild House.

CHAPTER 29

THE DECISION

*M*ost novices never get to see this room, Lilia thought as she followed Black Magician Sonea into Administrator Osen's office. *I've seen it more times than I'd ever want to.*

The Administrator was sitting behind his desk and Black Magician Kallen was reclining in one of the guest chairs, but they both stood up as she and Sonea arrived. A third magician, hidden behind the back of the chair he was sitting in, got to his feet. To her surprise, it was University Director Jerrik.

"Lilia," Osen said as he stepped around his desk and came forward to meet her. "How are you feeling?"

She blinked at him, feeling another twinge of surprise at such a conversational question.

"I'm well, Administrator Osen," she answered. *Tired of waiting to find out if I'm going to be locked up again*, she added silently.

"Good," he said. "As you know, we have been discussing what to do with you. I am happy to tell you that we have come to a decision, and it has been approved by the king." He smiled. "You may rejoin the Guild and complete your training."

She stared at him in disbelief, then felt a smile spring to her lips. "Thank you."

His expression became serious. "It is not offered without some conditions, however. You will be required to make the Novices' Vow again."

Lilia nodded to show she was willing to do so.

"You will not be allowed to leave the Guild grounds unless given permission by myself, High Lord Balkan, Black Magician Kallen or Black Magician Sonea," Osen continued. "You will not be allowed to use black magic unless, sometime in the future, the king approves you taking on the position of Black Magician. To identify you as one who knows black magic, your robes will feature a black band on the sleeves."

Nodding again, Lilia hoped her disappointment didn't show. Since meeting Anyi and hearing about the threat she and her father were facing from Skellin, Lilia had hoped to find a way to help her. If she was restricted to the Guild grounds, how could she do that?

"Because of the knowledge of black magic that you have, you will not be able to participate in lessons that require the linking of minds. In those situations, Black Magician Kallen or Black Magician Sonea will conduct the lesson."

She tried not to blanch at the thought of more mental contact with either magician. *But having my mind read was very different to the mind to mind lessons I had in the past. Still...I hope Sonea is the one who teaches me. Kallen is so stern and disapproving.*

"Kallen has offered to take on your guardianship. We think your having a guardian will reassure people that we have you well in hand." Osen's tone was lighter as he said this. "Since we anticipate a protest from parents if you stay in the Novices' Quarters, you will continue to stay in Black Magician Sonea's rooms."

Lilia suppressed a sigh of relief. For a moment she had been worried that she would have to stay with Kallen, but now that she considered it, she knew that it would be considered inappropriate for a young woman to stay in a single man's rooms, no matter the difference in their ages.

"Do you accept these conditions?" Osen asked.

"I do," she replied, nodding again.

"Then swear it."

She paused, realising that he expected her to remember the Novices' Vow. To her surprise the words came back to her easily.

"I swear that I will never harm another man or woman unless in defence of the Allied Lands," she said. "I will obey the rules of the Guild. I will obey the order of any magician of the Guild, unless those orders involve breaking a law. I will never use magic unless instructed by a Guild magician."

Osen smiled approvingly. He turned to nod at Director Jerrik. The man moved back to the chair he had been sitting in and picked something up. Returning, he held it out to Lilia.

It was a bundle of novice's robes. Gratitude washed over her like a physical wave of warmth. To her embarrassment, she felt tears tickle the corners of her eyes.

"Thank you," she croaked.

Osen placed a hand on her shoulder briefly. "Welcome back."

The other magicians murmured the same words. Overcome, Lilia could not speak. She felt Sonea touch her arm.

"That's it, I think." She looked at the others, who nodded. "Let's go back to your room so you can get changed."

Silently grateful, Lilia let the woman guide her out of the room, and back into a life as a Guild magician. *Though knowing black magic means I'll always be more restricted than most magicians*, she thought. *That's a lot better than being locked away. Or dead.*

And maybe, somehow, she could still find a way to help Anyi.

As the carriage pulled up outside the hospice side entrance, Sonea pushed aside a nagging reluctance and climbed out. She smiled and nodded at the Healers and helpers who greeted her, answering questions and asking them what she had missed since she'd last been there.

Their friendliness warmed her, and she was grateful all over again that she hadn't been given the task of executing Naki. She made her way to the treatment-room door, gathered her determination, and knocked.

The door swung inward. Dorrien smiled at her and beckoned. She moved through and sat down.

"Why the serious look?" he asked.

She drew a breath to answer, then her courage faltered. *We should chat a little before I deliver the bad news.*

"I was wondering how people would react, if I had been chosen to be Naki's executioner," she told him.

He gave her a reflective look. "Serious thoughts,

indeed." He looked away as he considered. "I don't think they would resent you for it."

"But they would not be able to help thinking about it, when they were around me. They would fear me even more."

"*Fear* you? They don't fear you," he told her.

She gave him a disbelieving look. He looked back at her, then shook his head.

"They're intimidated by you, Sonea. That's different. They're scared of black magic, but they're not scared of you. You've shown them that it doesn't make a person into a murderer."

"I've used it to kill," she pointed out.

He spread his hands. "That's different, too. It was in the defence of Kyralia. They'd do the same, in the same position."

She looked away. "I also used Healing to kill. That seems even worse to me." She looked around the room. "I'm a Healer. I'm supposed to mend people, not kill them. I think that, if I'd had to execute Naki, people would have found it difficult to reconcile the two."

Dorrien's jaw hardened. "She learned black magic deliberately, and killed with it for her own benefit."

Sonea shrugged. "Even so, I think it would have changed the way people thought of me. I never got a chance to choose a discipline. I would have chosen to be a Healer. I work as a Healer, but I can never wear the green robes. I am a Black Magician. While I would not hesitate to defend Kyralia again, that role is not the one I wanted."

He smiled wryly. "I prefer to think that Healing chose me."

She nodded. "And I suppose despite everything, it still claimed me, though you were a strong influence behind me wanting it to, too."

They regarded each other fondly. *Perhaps too fondly, in Dorrien's case.* She gathered courage and determination. *It's time I put an end to this.*

"Dorrien, I have been thinking a lot about... us."

"There is no 'us,' is there?" he said.

She looked at him in surprise. He gave her a wan smile.

"Father came to see me. Gave me the good news. Tylia will join the winter intake of novices. Kallen is probably going to be taking over the search for Skellin. 'Why don't you go back to your village?' he suggested."

Sonea stared at him. "*Kallen* is going to be taking over the search for *Skellin*?"

His eyebrows rose. "You didn't know? Father didn't say it was going to happen for certain."

"No." She resisted the urge to jump out of her seat and march straight back to Osen's office. *Unless... Rothen may have made this up in order to give Dorrien no excuse to stay in Imardin. But that seems a little extreme. Perhaps... I never told him about Dorrien's infatuation with me, but has he guessed?* She looked back at Dorrien.

He smiled crookedly. "He may be old, but it's still very difficult to hide secrets from him."

She shifted in her seat and pushed aside her annoyance. "I only asked him to see if Tylia could join the winter intake."

"Why?"

She forced herself to meet his eyes. "So you were free to go home, if working with me became unbearable after I told you that... well... there will be no 'us.'"

He winced. She could tell that he tried not to, but failed. "Why can't there be?"

"Because you are married. Because while the idea of 'us' appeals, it doesn't appeal enough that I would hurt Alina and your daughters. And because if you were to hurt them, then I would dislike you for it. And myself."

He looked down. "I see. Father said as much. He also pointed out that Alina and I didn't start getting along so badly until we came to Imardin." He sighed. "I was ready to try city life. She wasn't." He managed a guilty smile. "Would you believe me if I said I do care about her?"

Sonea felt a pang of affection for him. "I would."

He nodded. "I have to give it a try. That's only fair. We've disagreed before, but we always got past it." He shook his head. "It's a pity she was so jealous of you. She is usually so lovely to people."

Sonea shrugged. "I can't blame her though. Even without her being as perceptive as Rothen, there's all that black magic and reputation as a killer to get past."

Dorrien shook a finger at her. "Stop that. Remember, you are what you chose to be. Your robes may be black, but you've got the heart of a Healer."

Sonea looked down and shrugged. "Well, at least they make me look taller."

He chuckled, then stood up. "Well, I had best get home and start making plans for our return to the village."

Sonea rose and they swapped places. "When will you be leaving?"

"A few weeks after Tylia joins the University."

"Will she settle in all right, do you think?"

He nodded. "She has already made some friends here,

both starting at the same time as she will be now. Rothen will keep an eye on her."

"And we both know he'll do an excellent job of that."

He smiled. "He will. Goodnight, Sonea."

"Goodnight, Dorrien."

As the door closed behind him, Sonea looked down in the chair he'd vacated. That hadn't been as painful as she'd feared. For a moment she felt a pang of regret. *If Dorrien hadn't been married...*

She pushed that thought away, walked to the door and opened it, waving to a Healer to indicate she was ready to see patients.

Shrugging into his robes, Lorkin smoothed down the fine, richly dyed purple cloth and sighed with both appreciation and wistfulness. It was strangely comforting to be dressed in robes again. When he'd returned to his new bedroom to catch up on some sleep he'd even contemplated, though briefly, sleeping in them.

They were so much less itchy than the hunter's clothes, and yet the bulk of fabric felt overly indulgent and heavy after the plain, practical Traitor garb. He could not help enjoying the rich, dark colour, however. Though the dyes made in Sanctuary produced gentle hues, and he had come to see the aesthetic beauty in undyed fabric, there was something deeply satisfying about Alchemic purple.

And yet, I should not be wearing it. I should not be wearing robes at all. Not only because he was bound by his promise to return to Sanctuary and Tyvara, but because he had broken one of the Guild's most serious laws. *I learned black magic. Even if they saw fit to forgive that, they would probably insist I wear black robes now.*

How and when he would tell them, he hadn't yet decided.

Moving out into the central room of the suite, Lorkin saw Merria, who had been walking about the space, stop as she noticed him.

"Ah. Lorkin. You're awake. Good." She hurried over. "There's something I didn't think of until you were asleep. This."

She held out a ring. A blood-red stone glinted in the setting. He felt his heart leap, and reached out to take it.

"Mother's blood ring?"

"Yes. Ambassador Dannyl left it with me, since he took Administrator Osen's ring with him, so I could contact the Guild." She looked at him intently. "You'll want to tell her you're back, but I should probably still keep the ring. Is that all right?"

He smiled. "Of course. I won't be going anywhere until Dannyl gets back, anyway."

She looked relieved. "That's good to know." She looked at the ring, then at him, and smiled. "I'll leave you to it." She left the room.

Sitting down, Lorkin stared at the ring and gathered his thoughts. He slipped it on his finger.

—*Mother?*

—*Lorkin? Lorkin! Is everything all right? Are* you *all right?*

—*Yes. Everything's fine. Are you free to talk?*

—*Of course! Wait . . . I have a patient. I'll just . . .*

A long pause followed.

—*I am alone now. Where are you? Can you tell me?*

—*I'm at the Guild House in Arvice.*

—*Not at the Traitors' home?*

—No. Queen Zarala sent me here. She sent me on a mission of sorts.

—Queen Zarala?

—Of the Traitors.

—You're working for her now?

—Yes. But she knows I'd have never agreed to any task that would endanger the Allied Lands.

—That's considerate of her.

He detected a tinge of disapproval and resentment in his mother's tone. He smiled. He'd have been surprised if there hadn't been.

—How are you? he asked.

—Good. A few problems were resolved in the Guild over the last few days. We have another black magician, I'm afraid. Two novices managed to learn it from a book. One learned it deliberately and killed with it, and tricked the other into learning it so that she would be blamed for murder. The first has been caught and executed. The other…she proved herself honourable enough to be allowed back into the Guild and University, though with conditions.

Lorkin could not help feeling a trickle of hope at that. If the Guild had forgiven a novice for learning black magic because she proved herself honourable, would they forgive him for learning it in order to bring them stone-making magic?

They'll have to be more flexible toward black magic if they want to adopt stone-making magic, he reminded himself. *And if they don't, I'm going to return to Sanctuary anyway.*

—Sounds like you've had some exciting times lately, he said.

—You don't know the half of it. We also have foreign rogue magicians in the city, ruling most of the underworld. But I'll save that story for when you get here.

—I look forward to hearing it.

—So what is this mission the Traitor queen has sent you on?

—To negotiate an alliance between the Traitors and the Allied Lands.

Sonea did not respond for several heartbeats.

—I gather the rest of Sachaka isn't included in this.

—No.

—Exciting times ahead, I suspect.

—Yes.

—You want me to pass this on to Osen and Balkan?

—Yes. The queen sent me here because the route to the pass is not safe at this time of year. I suspect if I try to leave Arvice the Sachakans will try to stop me. I'm stuck here until Dannyl returns and officially orders me to return to Kyralia.

—I'll get right onto it. So, what prompted this willingness to seek an alliance? I had the impression the Traitors were too secretive to want connection to the outside world.

—They do and they don't. It's . . . complicated. It has to do with Father.

—Ah. Dannyl told me what you'd told him: that Akkarin promised them something in return for learning black magic, but he didn't deliver.

—He promised to teach them Healing, but he returned to the Guild because he wanted to warn everyone about the Ichani. Zarala gave me a blood ring of his—

—Oh! He said he'd made three blood rings, but he never said where the third one was.

—*She used it to communicate with him. She said that something always prevented him returning, and after her daughter died she stopped using the ring. A sickness had struck the Traitors and killed many, and he was blamed for it because they believed Healing would have saved them. That wasn't all there was to their bargain, however. Zarala promised Father that she would do something else, and she failed. She didn't tell me what it was, but it was so secret that she couldn't even tell her people. She said that sending me to negotiate an alliance had something to do with trying to achieve what she'd promised.*

Lorkin waited as his mother absorbed all this.

—*I'd really like to meet this woman*, she eventually said. Which was not what he was expecting. He had expected her to say something about his father keeping secrets from them all. *But then, he was a man of so many secrets, maybe it is no surprise that there were more.*

—*Hopefully I can arrange that. She is very old though. I don't know if she will be able to make it to a meeting.*

—*Old, you say? So she must have been a lot older than Akkarin when they met. Do you have any details on the proposed terms of the alliance?*

—*No. The spy network among the slaves is ready to pass on instructions. We are to let them know if and when the Guild is ready to meet with the Traitors, who will select a safe location. But I can tell you this: I learned how to make gemstones with magical properties while I was there.*

—*Dannyl learned of these gemstones while in Duna recently. He said the Traitors stole the knowledge from the Duna. He'll be excited to know they gave it to you. Well, so will all the Guild.*

—You've heard from him?
—He contacted Osen a few days ago.
—He was still in Duna?
—Yes.

Lorkin muttered a curse. It would take Dannyl many days to return.

—Could you tell Osen to let Dannyl know I'm here? And to hurry up and come back.

—Of course. Is there anything else that the Traitors have to offer us in an alliance?

—Well … stone-making is of no use if you have no source of gemstones, and may involve a risk the Guild is not willing to take. I believe the Traitors would consider trading stones for something. They have a rudimentary knowledge of Healing now, but they could benefit from the help of good teachers. They might also offer to help us if Sachaka ever attacked the Allied Lands again.

—Oh, the Guild is going to love this! Is there anything else? I should go tell them straightaway.

—I don't think so. If I think of anything, I'll put the ring on. And I'll check in with you in a few hours in case there's anything the Guild needs to ask or you need to tell me.

—Good idea. And Lorkin?
—Yes?
—I'm so happy that you're back. I love you and I'm very proud of you.

—I'm not back yet, Mother. But … thanks. I love you, too.

He removed the ring and slipped it into his pocket. He realised he was smiling, despite there being nobody to see it. *Exciting times ahead*, he thought. *Thankfully I have this ring and can work at negotiations via Mother, or all I'd have to do here while waiting for Dannyl to return is eat, sleep and talk to Merria.*

Judging from the unceasing chatter that had poured out of Dannyl's new assistant that morning, he suspected that the Healer, stuck in the Guild House with little work and no company, had been very bored and lonely since Dannyl had left. Though she had, at least, made some friends among the Sachakan women, she hadn't been able to leave the Guild House while Dannyl was absent.

He had to admit, though, it was nice to talk to other Guild magicians after all this time. It would be good to get more detailed news about the goings on in Imardin. And to find out how far Dannyl's research had progressed since Lorkin had left—especially on the subject of the storestone.

CHAPTER 30

THE CHOICE

Slumping in the chair, Lilia looked down at the pile of books and paper on the desk and sighed.

She'd met with University Director Jerrik that morning, before her first class since she'd learned black magic. He'd told her that he'd questioned her teachers, and gathered together a collection of exercises, practical assignments and essays that would bring her up to the same level as her fellow novices. Since she had missed the winter exams, she would have to study for those as well. It seemed like a lot of work for only a month or two of absence from the University, especially as she had to do not only that but also the work from her daily classes. The next few weeks were going to be very busy.

At least she could do the extra study in her room adjoining Sonea's guest room, where it was quiet and the antics of her fellow novices wouldn't distract her. After today's classes, she suspected she would be doubly grateful for that. The other novices had ignored her, when they weren't giving her dark, suspicious looks. Her old friends had made it clear they did not want anything to do with her now. Would they eventually forget what she had done, or would they continue to show their disapproval and fear, perhaps in other, nastier ways?

A muffled thump from the guest room made her jump. She got up, heart racing, and moved to the bedroom door. Putting her ear to it, she listened carefully.

And winced as someone knocked loudly on the door.

"Lilia? You there?"

At the familiar voice, Lilia's heart lifted. She opened the door.

"Anyi!"

The tall girl grinned down at her, then stepped back and turned around, arms held out at her sides. Lilia smiled as she recognised the long, black hide-skin coat she'd sent as a thank you gift. To her relief, it fitted perfectly. In fact, Anyi looked even more striking than before.

"I love it," Anyi said.

"It suits you," Lilia told her.

"I know," Anyi agreed, stroking the sleeves. Lilia laughed at the woman's gleeful vanity. "Cery says thanks for the knives."

"Sonea helped me choose them."

Anyi chuckled. "Yes, she'd know *exactly* what his tastes were." She looked at Lilia thoughtfully. "You know that Sonea and Cery were childhood friends, don't you?"

Lilia shook her head. "No. I knew she was from the old slums, and had worked with the Thieves during the invasion."

"Yes, Cery was her main contact among the Thieves. Akkarin recruited him to help hunt down Sachakan spies."

"So they kept in touch all these years?"

Anyi shrugged. "I guess they must have. When Cery told me how to get here I asked him why he went to all that trouble. He said that, until recently, Sonea was restricted to the Guild grounds—like you are now. The only other place she was allowed to go was the hospices."

"What do you mean by 'all that trouble'?"

Anyi shrugged out of the coat. "There's a bit of climbing, and apparently the tunnels are prone to collapsing these days. He'd do something about that if he wasn't hiding from Skellin." She tossed the coat over the back of a chair, then hesitated and looked close. "Curse it. The back got a bit scratched on the way up."

Lilia sat down on one of the guest room chairs, and Anyi dropped into the one beside it. "Sonea told me she goes into the bedroom when Cery leaves, so she doesn't see how he arrives, and that I should do the same thing when you go."

Anyi nodded. "He advised we do that."

"Sounds like you intend to visit on a regular basis."

"I do." Anyi smiled. "If you'd like me to."

Lilia nodded. "Very much. I've lost the friends I had here. The ones in my class won't talk to me. Naki is... gone. I don't think anyone else is going to want to be my friend," she lifted up her arms to show the black bands stitched around the sleeves of her robes, "now that I know black magic. Even if they wanted to, their parents would stop them. If they did want to, I'd have to worry what their real intentions were."

Anyi grimaced in sympathy. "That's going to be tough."

"It's not going to stop after I graduate, either."

"At least Sonea is willing to trust you." Anyi looked around the room. "She has friends, here and outside the Guild. Even if others don't take that as a good sign, you should. You should also know…" Anyi leaned over the arm of her chair and reached out to touch Lilia's cheek.

Surprised and unused to such contact, Lilia stilled. She met Anyi's gaze. The woman's expression was thoughtful and intense. Anyi slipped off her chair and knelt on the floor beside Lilia's in one graceful movement. Her hand did not move from Lilia's cheek, or her eyes from Lilia's.

"You should also know this," she said.

Leaning close, she kissed Lilia. It was a slow, lingering kiss. It was definitely not the kiss of mere friendship, and Lilia could not help responding in kind. It confirmed all that she had guessed about Anyi and all she had suspected of herself. *It was not just Naki*, she thought. *It's me—and it's Anyi. And it could be me* and *Anyi.*

Anyi pulled away a little, then smiled and folded herself back into her chair. She looked, Lilia mused, rather smug.

"I know it's too soon since Naki," she said. "But I thought you should know. In case you're interested."

Lilia put a hand to her heart. It was beating very fast. She felt elated and reckless. She laughed to herself, then looked at Anyi.

"I'm definitely interested—and it's not too soon since Naki."

Anyi's smile widened, but then she looked away and frowned. "Even so, I'd hate for Sonea to walk in on us…"

"She's at a meeting, and is going straight to the hospice afterwards. Night shift. Won't be back until morning."

"…or her servants," Anyi added. She tapped her

fingers on the edge of the chair, then stopped and smiled. "Tell me, how much do you know about the passages under the Guild?"

"I know of them, but I've never seen them. Nobody is allowed down there."

"Well, unless you're really serious about not breaking any rules any more, I could take you on a little tour."

Lilia looked at the scratches on the back of Anyi's jacket, then at her friend.

"I'll…I'll think about it."

Sonea sat down in the chair Osen had offered with silent satisfaction. The Administrator had arranged for more seating to be brought into his office and arranged it in a rough circle before his desk. He'd insisted that Kallen not stand by the wall any more, which meant that Sonea did not feel obliged to stand up as well.

Now she and Kallen sat on either side of Osen and Balkan. The rest of the Higher Magicians had arranged themselves in no particular order, Sonea noted. Usually the Heads of Disciplines clustered together. She expected they'd still be the most vocal in this meeting, however. Some things never changed.

Rothen looked up at her and smiled. She felt an answering smile spring to her lips. He had been overjoyed to hear of Lorkin's return, and since learning that Lorkin would be attempting to negotiate an alliance and would be bringing the Guild a new kind of magic he had been bursting with pride. At one point he'd sighed and looked sad, and when Sonea had asked what was wrong he'd looked at her apologetically. She winced as she remembered what he'd said.

"It is a pity his father never got to see this."

Which had made her heart ache for more than the obvious reasons. For Rothen to have said this of Akkarin indicated a level of forgiveness of the former High Lord that Sonea had not thought Rothen would ever reach.

For all that Lorkin had impressed others, Sonea was all too aware that he was not safe yet. What he was doing was risky. Even if the Sachakans did not know about it, they must still consider him a potential source of information about the Traitors. He would not be safe until he returned to Kyralia.

"The king has come to a decision," Osen told them. He turned to Balkan. "The High Lord met with him again this evening. What did he say?"

"He has gained the agreement of the other leaders of the Allied Lands," Balkan told them. Sonea felt an odd sensation somewhere between pride and regret. To consult with the rest of the Allied Lands so quickly would not have been possible twenty years ago. Now all Guild Ambassadors were given blood rings so they could communicate with the Administrator or High Lord whenever they needed to. "The meeting will take place and negotiations entered into. They have indicated their preferred terms. They have agreed that a Guild magician will represent the Allied Lands. The king has left the choice of representative to us."

"There is no small risk involved," Osen told them. "If King Amakira learns of the meeting he will try to prevent it. He may even see it as an act of war. We are, in effect, considering an alliance with the people he considers rebels and traitors."

"Whoever we send will be vulnerable. We could send

the entire Guild, and not be strong enough to counter an attack," Balkan said, then he smiled crookedly. "Amakira would hardly fail to notice if we send an army of magicians his way. For this reason, we have decided that only two magicians will go."

"However," Osen continued. "Two of us have the potential to be as strong as an army of us."

Sonea's breath caught in her throat. Surely they weren't going to send both her and Kallen? Who would be left to defend Kyralia? Lilia was far too inexperienced and untrained…

"We will send one black magician and an assistant," Balkan said. "The assistant must be willing to offer his or her magical strength, if required. Since there is a risk that, if attacked, the two magicians' minds will be read, the assistant cannot be a Higher Magician or know any more about the purpose of the trip than necessary. The black magician will wear Lord Leiden's mind-read-blocking ring."

Osen smiled thinly. "So, as you can see, our decision was reduced to one of two black magicians." He looked at Kallen, then at Sonea. "Are you both willing to take on this role?"

"Yes," Sonea replied. Kallen echoed her.

Osen looked around the rest of the circle. "Then the decision is left to the rest of us now. I will ask each of you in turn to speak your mind. Lady Vinara?"

Sonea felt frozen in place as the Higher Magicians discussed, often quite frankly, why they favoured her or Kallen as the representative. She was not surprised when Lord Garrel bluntly raised the issue of her trustworthiness, referring to her decision to learn black magic and her refusal to obey the Guild which had led to her exile. The others did not protest or agree, merely moved on to other matters as if what he'd said was not important. By the time the discussion wound to a close, she was unsure whether more of the Higher Magicians favoured her or Kallen.

"I think we have explored all the issues," Osen said. "Now we will put it to a vote. All in favour of Black Magician Sonea representing the Allied Lands in these negotiations, raise your hands."

Sonea counted. She noted that some who had argued for her had changed their minds, and vice versa. There was one less hand raised than lowered. Sonea felt her heart beat even faster with both excitement and anxiety. Osen turned to High Lord Balkan.

"Has your opinion changed?"

Balkan looked at Sonea and shook his head.

"My vote and the High Lord's go to Sonea," Osen stated. "Which tips our collective vote in her favour." He looked at her and smiled grimly. "Congratulations."

She nodded, too overwhelmed to speak. While she had hoped to be chosen, so that she could see and protect Lorkin as soon as possible, the weight of responsibility in representing not only the Guild and Kyralia, but all the Allied Lands, was daunting. So was the prospect of returning to Sachaka, though this time she would not be an exile, hunted by the Ichani.

After all I said to Dorrien about only wanting to be a Healer, I've gone and got myself a task that will involve using black magic. But not to kill. Those who give me power will do so willingly, and hopefully I won't have to use that power to kill, either.

"There are details to sort out and preparations to make," Osen told them all. He stood up. "Black Magician

Sonea will leave soon, but I expect it will not be for a few days at least. Perhaps not for a few weeks. Lorkin will need to relay our decision through the slave spy network to the Traitors and wait for a reply. There is the matter of choosing an assistant, but that will require further discussion and consultation. Thank you for your suggestions and advice. I need not remind you that this is all strictly secret. Goodnight."

As the magicians rose, Balkan stepped forward and touched Sonea on the shoulder.

"Stay," he murmured.

She nodded, unsurprised. When the last of the Higher Magicians had left the room except Osen and Balkan, she dropped back into the chair with a sigh.

"I'm not sure if I should congratulate you or not," Osen said to her as he returned to his seat.

Sonea smiled wryly. "It is reassuring, even flattering, that you are willing to entrust me with the task. Especially when I've failed at the last one you set me."

Osen frowned, then his eyebrows rose. "Finding Skellin?" He shrugged. "That is a trickier task than the one you have now."

"Who will be taking it over?"

"Black Magician Kallen, most likely," he told her. "Will your contacts consent to work with him?"

Sonea considered. "Yes, I think they will. They have little choice. Can I make a suggestion?"

He nodded. "Of course."

"Lilia befriended one of my contact's loyal friends and workers while she was looking for Naki. Since Kallen is also her guardian, it might be beneficial to everyone if Lilia was to be his assistant—or one of his assistants."

Osen looked thoughtful, and nodded. "I will consider it, and suggest it to Kallen. It won't be breaking the restrictions we set on her movements, if she is under Kallen's orders."

Sonea tried to imagine Cery meeting with Kallen, and failed. She tried not to wince.

Sorry Cery, but I can't be two places at once. Kallen is nothing if not thorough and dedicated. I'm sure he will find Skellin eventually. She wondered if there was anything else she could do to help him.

"Now, do you have anyone in mind to take as your assistant?"

Forcing her mind back to her new task, she considered the question, and nodded.

Everything was illuminated by lamplight. As the *Inava* drew level with the wharf, slaves on the deck tossed ropes to those waiting below. Staying out of the way, Dannyl looked out at the city. There wasn't much to see. Since the majority of the buildings in Arvice were single storey, the view was a rather boring stretch of similar rooftops.

"Ah, look," Achati said. "The Guild House carriage has arrived. I would have taken you home in mine."

Dannyl looked at the Sachakan and frowned in concern. "Perhaps it is better that you go straight home. You still look tired."

Achati smiled. "I am a little, but not from the overuse of power. Travel wears me more than it used to. As you know, I didn't sleep much last night."

A glint of amusement had entered his gaze. Dannyl smiled and looked away. The day the storm had passed, the ship had pulled in at an estate belonging to a friend of

Achati's. They had collapsed onto the offered beds and slept late into the next day, then decided to leave early the next morning to avoid sailing at night. Even so, unfavourable winds meant they had arrived at Arvice late.

The estate had been luxurious. Dannyl wasn't surprised when, Tayend having picked up on the possibility that their host might have goods to trade with Elyne, insisted Achati help him with all discussions on the matter, which went late into the night.

"Looks like we will be going our separate ways from here," Tayend said as he emerged from the hatch and took in his surroundings. He turned to Achati and smiled. "Thank you, Ashaki Achati, for arranging and guiding us on this adventure."

Achati inclined his head in the Kyralian way. "A pleasure and an honour," he said.

"Will we see you at the Guild House soon?"

"I hope so," Achati replied. "I will report to my king and deal with any matters that have accumulated in my absence first, of course. Unless one of those matters concerns one or both of you, I will be sure to make a social visit as soon as I am free to."

The captain approached to tell them the ship was secure and safe for them to depart. They went through more formalities as their trunks were carried off, then they followed their luggage to their respective vehicles.

Once inside the Guild House carriage, Tayend was uncharacteristically quiet. Dannyl considered striking up a conversation as the vehicle rolled through the streets, but the Elyne looked lost in thought. They both watched the walls of Arvice pass by in silence.

When they finally turned through the Guild House

gates, Tayend drew in a deep breath and sighed. He looked at Dannyl and smiled.

"Well, that was certainly an interesting adventure. I can say I've visited six lands now, though I suppose Duna isn't technically a country in its own right."

Dannyl shook his head. "No, but I suspect it may as well be. I can't see the Ashaki ever truly controlling it— or even wanting to, if they are sensible."

Pushing open the door, Tayend climbed out. Dannyl followed, noting the slaves lying prone on the ground.

"Stand up," he ordered wearily. "Go back to your duties."

The door slave hurried to the entrance and led them inside. They emerged from the end of the entry corridor into the Master's Room. Healer Merria was waiting for them...and another magician. Dannyl looked at the Alchemist and gaped in astonishment.

"Lorkin!"

The young magician smiled. "Ambassador. You have no idea how relieved I am to see you. How was your journey?"

Dannyl walked forward and grasped Lorkin's arm in greeting. "Nothing compared to yours, I'm sure. You have no idea how relieved *I* am to see *you*."

Lorkin grinned. "Oh, I'm pretty sure I can guess. Would you like to wash and eat before I give you the news?"

Moving to one of the stools, Dannyl sat down. Lorkin chuckled.

"I gather that's a 'no.'"

"If you don't mind," Tayend said. "I'd like to wash and eat. I'm sure you can fill me in later."

"Of course," Dannyl said. "Tell the slaves to prepare something for us both."

The Elyne hurried down the corridor to his room. As Lorkin and Merria sat down, Dannyl noted that both wore worried expressions.

"So is this good news or bad?"

Lorkin smiled wryly. "Both. The bad is this..."

He handed Dannyl a letter. Noting the Sachakan king's seal, already broken, Dannyl opened the letter and read. He felt a chill run down his spine.

"So," he said. "He forbids you to leave and informs you that he will summon you to meet with him once I have returned. It makes sense. You've spent months with the rebels so the king obviously wants to know everything you've learned."

"You don't expect me to tell him, do you?"

"Not unless the Guild—no, *our* king—orders you to."

Lorkin looked worried. "Can he stop me leaving? Do I have to meet with him?"

"That depends how much he's willing to test the peace between our lands." Dannyl frowned. "The fact that you left to live with the rebels probably tested that peace quite a bit already. If we ignore this and send you home, it will be an even greater insult."

"So what do we do?"

"You cooperate. You stay here. You meet him. You tell him nothing, respectfully and politely. We—myself, the Guild and king, and anyone else we can persuade to help us—work at persuading him to let you go."

"It might take a long time."

Dannyl nodded. "That's very likely."

Lorkin looked even more anxious now. He glanced

at Merria, then at the door Tayend had disappeared through.

"There is...something else. I gather, since you were surprised to see me here, that you haven't been in contact with Osen?"

Another chill ran down Dannyl's spine. "No. There was a storm and...I've been too preoccupied to put on the ring." He cursed silently. The blood rings were so useful and yet so limited. If only he'd been allowed to make a blood ring and leave it with the Administrator. Then Osen could have contacted him directly.

Lorkin met Dannyl's eyes, his expression serious. He suddenly looked much older than he was—or than Dannyl was used to regarding him.

"I can't discuss anything aloud in case we're overheard. You need to contact Osen," Lorkin said. "Now."

EPILOGUE

A noise down the passage alerted Cery before he saw
the light. Relieved, he stood up and waited for Anyi
to reach him. As she neared him he saw her smile and he
sighed with relief.

It was good to see her so happy. Good that she had a
friend. Being cooped up in the hideout did not suit her,
and no matter how many practice sessions he and Gol put
her through they wouldn't be able to curb her restless
nature.

*The only real danger in these visits to Lilia is the sta-
bility of the passages under the Guild.* No Thief has dared
to occupy them. The Slig, the slum children who had built
themselves homes in parts of the Thieves' Road, were
said to instinctively know and avoid unstable areas. Anyi
had taken Lilia down into the tunnels and they'd both
started to make repairs. He hoped they knew what they
were doing.

"You don't have to wait for me," Anyi said, and not for
the first time.

Cery shrugged. "I don't mind."

"I was gone for hours."

He looked at Gol. "We kept ourselves occupied."

She sighed and walked past him. "Where to now?"

"Home," he said.

As they travelled, slipping out of the Thieves' Road as soon as they reached a safe place, he thought about Sonea's message. He couldn't blame her for seizing the opportunity to meet Lorkin. He'd have done the same thing.

But he didn't trust Kallen in the same way he trusted her. *Not just because I don't know him like I know Sonea, or that he's not from the lower end of Imardin society, and not even because of Kallen's liking for roet. The man is too...* He searched for a word, and eventually settled on "rigid." Cery didn't doubt the man's promise to never give up in his search for Skellin, but it came first from a dedication to law and what was right, rather than a desire to protect others. He doubted that Kallen would ever bend the law or his idea of rightness, and that could lead to people getting hurt. *The people most likely to be hurt are Anyi, Gol and me.*

At last they reached the entrance to the hideout. It had been cold outside, and the chill clung to them. They were all keen to get inside and warm up, but forced themselves to go through all the precautions, and their numb fingers to work all the safeguards. Once inside, Anyi set about starting a fire while Gol checked for indications that the escape routes had been compromised.

Cery sat down. A bottle of wine and three glasses had been set on the table. He sighed. Right now all he wanted was a warmed glass of bol.

"Is there something to celebrate?" he asked, looking at Anyi and Gol.

They turned to regard him, their expressions puzzled.

Cery gestured to the bottle. "Your idea?"

The pair shook their heads.

He turned to stare at the bottle. His heart lurched. A rushing sound filled his ears. A tag hung from a loop of string about the bottle's neck. On it were scrawled three words. He looked closer.

For your daughter.

He staggered to his feet.

"Out," he gasped. "Someone's been here. We have to get out."

GLOSSARY

ANIMALS

aga moths—pests that eat
  clothing

anyi—sea mammals with
  short spines

ceryni—small rodent

enka—horned domestic
  animal, bred for meat

cyoma—sea leeches

faren—general term for
  arachnids

gorin—large domestic animal
  used for food and to haul
  boats and wagons

harrel—small domestic
  animal bred for meat

inava—insect believed to
  bestow good luck

limek—wild predatory
  dog

mullook—wild nocturnal
  bird

quannea—rare shells

rassook—domestic bird used
  for meat and feathers

ravi—rodent, larger than
  ceryni

reber—domestic animal, bred
  for wool and meat

sapfly—woodland insect

sevli—poisonous lizard

squimp—squirrel-like
  creature that steals
  food

yeel—small domesticated
  breed of limek used for
  tracking

zill—small, intelligent
  mammal sometimes kept
  as a pet

PLANTS/FOOD

anivope vine—plant sensitive to mental projection

bellspice—spice grown in Sachaka

bol—(also means "river scum") strong liquor made from tugors

brasi—green leafy vegetable with small buds

briskbark—bark with decongestant properties

cabbas—hollow, bell-shaped vegetable

chebol sauce—rich meat sauce made from bol

cone cakes—bite-sized cakes

creamflower—flower used as a soporific

crots—large, purple beans

curem—smooth, nutty spice

curren—coarse grain with robust flavour

dall—long fruit with tart orange, seedy flesh

dunda—root chewed as a stimulating drug

gan-gan—flowering bush from Lan

husroot—herb used for cleansing wounds

iker—stimulating drug, reputed to have aphrodisiac properties

jerras—long yellow beans

kreppa—foul-smelling medicinal herb

marin—red citrus fruit

monyo—bulb

myk—mind-affecting drug

nalar—pungent root

nemmin—sleep-inducing drug

nightwood—hardwood timber

pachi—crisp, sweet fruit

papea—pepper-like spice

piorres—small, bell-shaped fruit

raka/suka—stimulating drink made from roasted beans, originally from Sachaka

roet—plant from which a soporific drug and a perfume are derived

rot—slang term for the drug roet

shem—edible reed-like plant

sumi—bitter drink

sweetdrops—candies

telk—seed from which an oil is extracted

tenn—grain that can be cooked as is, broken into small pieces, or ground to make a flour tiro—edible nuts

tugor—parsnip-like root

ukkas—carnivorous plants

vare—berries from which most wine is produced

whitewater—pure spirits made from tugors

yellowseed—crop grown in Sachaka

CLOTHING AND WEAPONRY

incal—square symbol, not unlike a family shield, sewn onto sleeve or cuff

kebin—iron bar with hook for catching attacker's knife, carried by guards

longcoat—ankle-length coat

quan—tiny disc-shaped beads made of shell

undershift—Kyralian women's undergarment

vyer—stringed instrument from Elyne

PUBLIC HOUSES

bathhouse—establishment selling bathing facilities and other grooming services

bolhouse—establishment selling bol and short term accommodation

brewhouse—bol manufacturer

hole—building constructed from scavenged materials

stayhouse—rented building, a family to a room

COUNTRIES/PEOPLES IN THE REGION

Duna—tribes who live in volcanic desert north of Sachaka

Elyne—neighbour to Kyralia and Sachaka and once ruled by Sachaka

Kyralia—neighbour to Elyne and Sachaka and once ruled by Sachaka

Lan—a mountainous land peopled by warrior tribes

Lonmar—a desert land home to the strict Mahga religion

Sachaka—home of the once great Sachakan Empire, where all but the most powerful are slaves

Vin—an island nation known for their seamanship

TITLES/POSITIONS

Administrator—magician who sees to the running of the Guild

Ashaki—Sachakan landowner

Black Magician—one of two magicians allowed to know black magic

Directors—magicians in charge of managing novices within and outside of the University

Heads of Disciplines—in charge of magicians of the three disciplines of Healing, Warrior and Alchemy

Heads of Studies—in charge of teaching the three disciplines of Healing, Warrior and Alchemy

High Lord—the official leader of the Magicians' Guild of Kyralia

Ichani—Sachakan free man or woman who has been declared outcast

King's Advisors—magicians who advise, Heal and protect the Kyralian king

Lord/Lady—any magician of the Magician's Guild without a greater title

Master—free Sachakan

OTHER TERMS

the approach—main corridor to the master's room in Sachakan houses

blood gem—artificial gemstone that allows maker to hear the thoughts of wearer

earthblood—term the Duna tribes use for lava

lowie—slang term used in the Guild for novices from middle and lower class origins

master's room—main room in Sachakan houses for greeting guests

obin—separate house joined to the main house of a Naguh Valley house

snootie—slang term used in the Guild for novices and magicians from the Houses

slavehouse—part of Sachakan homes where the slaves live and work

slavespot—sexually transmitted disease

storestone—gemstone that can store magic

The Slig—a hidden people who live in the passages underneath Imardin

LORD DANNYL'S GUIDE
TO SLUM SLANG

blood money—payment for assassination

boot—refuse/refusal (don't boot us)

capper—man who frequents brothels

clicked—occurred

client—person who has an obligation or agreement with a Thief

counter—whore

done—murdered

dull—persuade to keep silent

dunghead—fool

dwells—term used to describe slum dwellers

eye—keep watch

fired—angry (got fired about it)

fish—propose/ask/look for (also someone fleeing the Guard)

gauntlet—guard who is bribeable or in the control of a Thief

goldmine—man who prefers boys

good go—a reasonable try

got—caught

grandmother—pimp

gutter—dealer in stolen goods

hai—a call for attention or expression of surprise or inquiry

heavies—important people

kin—a Thief's closest and most trusted

knife—assassin/hired killer

messenger—thug who delivers or carries out a threat

mind—hide (minds his business/I'll mind that for you)

mug—mouth (as in vessel for bol)

out for—looking for

pick—recognise/understand

punt—smuggler

right-sided—trustworthy/ heart in the right place

rope—freedom

rub—trouble (got into some rub over it)

shine—attraction (got a shine for him)

show—introduce

space—allowances/permission

squimp—someone who double-crosses the Thieves

style—manner of performing business

tag—recognise (also means a spy, usually undercover)

thief—leader of a criminal group

watcher—posted to observe something or someone

wild—difficult

visitor—burglar

ACKNOWLEDGEMENTS

As always, this book would have been a much poorer thing had it not been for the generosity and work of my feedback readers. This time around I received some opposing views on the stories and characters, which allowed me to decide what *I* wanted to do with them. I would like to thank Paul Ewins, Fran Bryson, Liz Kemp, Foz Meadows, Nicole Murphy, Donna Hanson and Jennifer Fallon for their insight, opinions, suggestions and error-spotting.

Thanks again to Fran and Liz and all the wonderful agents around the world. Thanks, too, to the wonderful Orbit publishing teams and publishers of foreign editions, working hard to send my stories out to readers everywhere, in beautiful print, accessible e-book and enchanting audio manifestations.

Lastly, a big thank you to all the readers. While I could still write books without feedback, it would be nowhere near as much fun, but I could never have been able to dedicate so much of my time and energy to it without people spending their hard-earned income on these little stories of mine. Thanks so much for your enthusiasm and support.

extras

orbit

meet the author

Trudi Canavan published her first story in 1999 and it received an *Aurealis* Award for Best Fantasy Short Story. Her debut series, The Black Magician Trilogy, made her an international success and her last five novels have been *Sunday Times* bestsellers in the UK. Trudi Canavan lives with her partner in Melbourne, Australia, and spends her time knitting, painting and writing. You can visit her website at www.trudicanavan.com.

introducing

If you enjoyed
THE ROGUE,
look out for

THE MAGICIAN'S APPRENTICE

by Trudi Canavan

In the remote village of Mandryn, Tessia serves as assistant to her father, the village Healer—much to the frustration of her mother, who would rather she found a husband. Despite knowing that women aren't readily accepted by the Guild of Healers, Tessia is determined to follow in her father's footsteps. But her life is about to take a very unexpected turn.

When treating a patient at the residence of the local magician, Lord Dakon, Tessia is forced to fight off the advances of a visiting Sachakan mage—and *instinctively uses magic. She now finds herself facing an entirely different future as Lord Dakon's apprentice.*

Although there are long hours of study and self-discipline, Tessia's new life also offers more opportunities than she had ever hoped for, and an exciting new world opens up to her. There are fine clothes and servants—and, she is delighted to learn—regular trips to the great city of Imardin.

But along with the excitement and privilege, Tessia is about to discover that her magical gifts bring with them a great deal of responsibility. Events are brewing that will lead nations into war, rival magicians into conflict, and spark an act of sorcery so brutal that its effects will be felt for centuries...

There was no fast and painless way to perform an amputation, Tessia knew. Not if you did it properly. A neat amputation required a flap of skin to be cut to cover the stump, and that took time.

As her father deftly began to slice into the skin around the boy's finger, Tessia noted the expressions of the people in the room. The boy's father stood with his arms crossed and his back straight. His scowl did not quite hide signs of worry, though whether it was sympathy for his son or anxiety about whether he'd get the harvest finished in time without his son's help, she could not tell. Probably a bit of both.

The mother held her son's other hand tightly while staring into his eyes. The boy's face was flushed and beaded with sweat. His jaw was clenched and, despite her father's warning, he watched the work being done intently.

He had remained still so far, not moving his wounded hand or squirming. No sound had escaped him. Such control impressed Tessia, especially in one so young. Landworkers were said to be a tough lot, but in her experience that was not always true. She wondered if the child would be able to keep it up. Worse was to come, after all.

Her father's face was creased with concentration. He had carefully peeled the skin of the boy's finger back past the joint of the knuckle. At a glance from him she took the small jointer knife from the burner and handed it to him, then took the number five peeler from him, washed it and carefully set the blade over the burner so it would be seared clean.

When she looked up, the boy's face was a mass of wrinkles, screwed up tight. Tessia's father had begun to cut through the joint. Looking up, she noted that the boy's father was now a pasty grey. The mother was white.

"Don't watch," Tessia advised in a murmur. The woman's head turned abruptly away.

The blade met the surgery board with a clunk of finality. Taking the small jointer from her father, Tessia handed him a curved needle, already threaded with fine gutstring. The needle glided easily through the boy's skin and Tessia felt a little glow of pride; she had sharpened it carefully in readiness for this operation, and the gutstring was the finest she had ever fashioned.

She looked at the amputated finger lying at the end of the surgery board. At one end it was a blackened, oozing mess, but there was reassuringly healthy flesh all through the cut end. It had been badly crushed in an accident during harvest some days before, but like most of the villagers and landworkers her father serviced, neither boy nor father had sought help until the wound had festered. It took time, and extreme pain, before a person could accept, let alone seek, removal of a part of their body.

If left too long, such a festering could poison the blood, causing fevers and even death. That a small wound could prove fatal fascinated Tessia. It also scared her. She had seen a man driven to insanity and self-mutilation by a mere rotten tooth, otherwise robust women bleed to death after giving birth, healthy babies that stopped breathing for no apparent reason and fevers that spread through the village, taking one or two lives but causing no more than discomfort for the rest.

Through working with her father, she had seen more wounds, illness and death in her sixteen years than most women did in their lifetimes. But she had also seen maladies remedied, chronic illness relieved and lives saved. She knew every man, woman and child in the village and the ley, and some beyond. She had knowledge of matters that few were privy to. Unlike most of the locals she could read and write, reason and—

Her father looked up and handed her the needle, then cut off the remaining thread. Neat stitches held the flap of skin closed over the stump of the boy's finger. Knowing what came next, Tessia took some wadding and bandages from his healer's bag and handed them to him.

"Take these," he told the mother.

Letting the boy's other hand go, the woman passively let Tessia's father lay the bandage across one palm, then arrange wadding on top. He placed the boy's hand over her palm so the stump of the finger rested in the centre of the wadding, then took hold of the pulse binder on the boy's arm.

"When I loosen this the blood in his arm will regain its rhythm," he told her. "His finger will begin to bleed. You must wrap the wadding around the finger and hold it firmly until the blood finds a new pulse path."

The woman bit her lip and nodded. As Tessia's father loosened the binder the boy's arm and hand slowly regained a healthy pinkness. Blood welled around the stitches and the mother quickly wrapped her hand around the stump. The boy grimaced. She smoothed his hair affectionately.

Tessia suppressed a smile. Her father had taught her that it was wise to allow a family to take part in the healing process in some small way. It gave them a sense of control, and they were less likely to be suspicious or dismissive of the methods he used if they took part in them.

After a little wait, her father checked the stump then bound it up firmly, giving the family instructions on how often to replace the bandages, how to keep them clean and dry if the boy resumed work (he knew better than to tell them to keep the boy at home), when they could be discarded, and what signs of festering they should watch for.

As he listed off the medicines and extra bandages they would need, Tessia removed them from his bag and set them on the cleanest patch of the table that she could find. The amputated finger she wrapped up and set aside. Patients and their families preferred to bury or burn such things, perhaps worrying what might be done with them if they didn't dispose of them themselves. No doubt they had heard the disturbing and ridiculous stories that went around from time to time of healers in Kyralia secretly experimenting on amputated limbs, grinding bones up into unnatural potions or somehow reanimating them.

Cleaning and then searing the needle over the burner, she packed it and the other tools away. The surgery board would have to be treated later, at home. She extinguished the burner and waited as the family began to offer their thanks.

This was also a well-practised part of their routine. Her father hated being trapped while patients poured out their gratitude. It embarrassed him. After all, he was not offering his services for free. Lord Dakon provided him and his family with a house and income in exchange for looking after the people of his ley.

But her father knew that accepting thanks with humility and patience kept him well placed in the local people's opinions. He never accepted gifts, however. Everyone under Lord Dakon's rule paid a tithe to their master, and so in effect had already paid Tessia's father for his services.

Her role was to wait for the right moment to interrupt and remind her father that they had other work to do. The family would apologise. Her father would apologise. Then they would be ushered out.

But as the right moment neared the sound of hoofbeats drummed outside the house. All paused to listen. The hoofbeats stopped and were replaced by footsteps, then a pounding at the door.

"Healer Veran? Is Healer Veran there?"

The farmer and Tessia's father started forward at the same time, then her father stopped, allowing the man to answer his own door. A well-dressed middle-aged man stood outside, his brow slick with sweat. Tessia recognised him as Lord Dakon's house master, Keron.

"He's here," the farmer told him.

Keron squinted into the dimness of the farmer's house. "Your services are required at the Residence, Healer Veran. With some urgency." Tessia's father frowned, then turned to beckon to her. Grabbing his bag and the burner, she hurried after him into the daylight. One of the farmer's older sons was waiting by the horse and cart provided by Lord Dakon for her father to use when visiting patients outside the village, and he quickly rose and removed a feedbag from the old mare's head.

Tessia's father nodded his thanks then took his bag from Tessia and stowed it in the back of the cart.

As they climbed up onto the seat, Keron galloped past them back towards the village. Her father took up the reins and flicked them. The mare snorted and shook her head, then started forward.

Tessia glanced at her father. "Do you think…?" she began, then stopped as she realised the pointlessness of her question.

Do you think it might have something to do with the Sachakan? she had wanted to ask, but such questions were a waste of breath. They would find out when they got there.

It was hard not to imagine the worst. The villagers hadn't stopped muttering about the foreign magician visiting Lord Dakon's house since he had arrived, and it was hard not to be infected by their fear and awe. Though Lord Dakon was a magician, he was familiar, respected and Kyralian. If he was feared it was only because of the magic he could wield and the control over their lives he held; he was not the sort of landowner who misused either power. Sachakan magicians on the other hand had, scant centuries ago, ruled and enslaved Kyralia and by all reports liked to remind people, whenever the chance came, what things had been like before Kyralia was granted its independence.

Think like a healer, she told herself as the cart bounced down the road. *Consider the information you have. Trust reason over emotion.*

Neither the Sachakan nor Lord Dakon could be ill. Both were magicians and resistant to all but a few rare maladies. They weren't immune to plagues, but rarely succumbed to them. Lord Dakon would have called on her father for help long before any disease needed urgent attention, though it was possible the Sachakan wouldn't have mentioned being ill if he didn't want to be tended by a Kyralian healer.

Magicians could die of wounds, she knew. Lord Dakon could have injured himself. Then an even more frightening possibility occurred to her. Had Lord Dakon and the Sachakan fought each other?

If they had, the lord's house—and perhaps the village, too—would be ruined and smoking, she told herself, *if the tales of what magical battles are like are true.* The road descending from the farmer's home gave a clear view of the houses below, lining either side of the main road this side of the river. All was as peaceful and undisturbed as it had been when they had left.

Perhaps the patient or patients they were hurrying to treat were servants in the lord's house. Aside from Keron, six other house and stable servants kept Lord Dakon's home in order. She and her father had treated them many times before. Landworkers living outside the village sometimes travelled to the Residence when they were sick or injured, though usually they went directly to her father.

Who else is there? Ah, of course. There's Jayan, Lord Dakon's apprentice, she remembered. *But as far as I know he has all the same physical protections against illness as a higher magician. Perhaps he picked a fight with the Sachakan. To the Sachakan, Jayan would be the closest thing to a slave, and—*

"Tessia."

She looked at her father expectantly. Had he anticipated who needed his services?

"I . . . Your mother wants you to stop assisting me."

Anticipation shrivelled into exasperation. "I know." She grimaced. "She wants me to find a nice husband and start having babies."

He didn't smile, as he had in the past when the subject came up. "Is that so bad? You can't become a healer, Tessia."

Hearing the serious tone in his voice, she stared at him in surprise and disappointment. While her mother had expressed this opinion many times before, her father had never agreed with it. She felt something inside her turn to stone and fall down into her gut, where it lay cold and hard and uncomfortable. Which was impossible, of course. Human organs did not turn to stone and certainly could not shift into the stomach.

"The villagers won't accept you," he continued.

"You can't know that," she protested. "Not until I've tried and failed. What reason could they have to distrust me?"

"None. They like you well enough, but it is as hard for them to believe that a woman can heal as that a reber could sprout wings and fly. It's not in a woman's nature to have a steady head, they think."

"But the birthmothers... they trust them. Why is there any difference between that and healing?"

"Because what we... what the birthmothers do is specialised and limited. Remember, they call for my help when their knowledge is insufficient. A healer has learning and experience behind him that no birthmother has access to. Most birthmothers can't even read."

"And yet the villagers trust them. Sometimes they trust them more than you."

"Birthing is an entirely female activity," he said wryly. "Healing isn't."

Tessia could not speak. Annoyance and frustration rose inside her but she knew angry outbursts would not help her cause. She had to be persuasive, and her father was no simple peasant who might be easily swayed. He was probably the smartest man in the village.

As the cart reached the main road she cursed silently. She had not realised how firmly he'd come to agree with her mother. *I need to change his mind back again, and I need to do it carefully*, she realised. *He doesn't like to go against Mother's wishes. So I need to weaken her confidence in her arguments as much as reduce Father's doubts about continuing to teach me.* She needed to consider all the arguments for and against her becoming a healer, and how to use them to her benefit. And she needed to know every detail of her parents' plans.